STARTING OVER

Maggie and Spence had tucked the girls in bed a while ago. Grace and Allison were asleep, safe and secure. A pipe rattled between floors. Spence was taking a shower.

She knew this house like the back of her hand, every sound, every nook and cranny. She strode to the window. The back light was on, the tree swing snow-covered and motionless. No matter what the season, she'd always thought of the backyard as her haven. How many nights had she stood, barefoot on the dew-dampened grass, looking up at the sky? It had always been so clear, the stars so bright. Everything in her world had made sense.

Nothing made sense anymore.

She wanted that life back. But she couldn't go back. Did she dare go forward?

She turned out the lights and made her way up the stairs. Spence was coming out of their bedroom as she was going in. They met in the doorway.

"Maggie."

"I'm sad," she blurted. "I'm ███ ███ █████"

"I know."

She lowered █ ███ ███ ███ ███ hate you, but I can't.'

"I love you, Ma██ ███ ███ ███ ███ tion. He was afraid to re███ ███ ███ ███ Maggie wasn't backing aw██ ███ ███ yearning in her eyes it nearly buckled his knees. He raised a hand, placing it on her slender cheek. Her eyes closed and she tipped her head slightly, resting her cheek in his hand, as if she was as lonely for his touch as he was for hers . . .

Books by Sandra Steffen

THE COTTAGE

DAY BY DAY

Published by Kensington Publishing Corporation

DAY BY DAY

SANDRA STEFFEN

ZEBRA BOOKS
KENSINGTON PUBLISHING CORP.

http://www.kensingtonbooks.com

ZEBRA BOOKS are published by

Kensington Publishing Corp.
850 Third Avenue
New York, NY 10022

All Kensington titles, imprints and distributed lines are available at special quantity discounts for bulk purchases for sales promotion, premiums, fund-raising, educational or institutional use.

Special book excerpts or customized printings can also be created to fit specific needs. For details, write or phone the office of the Kensington Special Sales Manager: Kensington Publishing Corp., 850 Third Avenue, New York, NY 10022. Attn. Special Sales Department. Phone: 1-800-221-2647.

First Printing: July 2002
10 9 8 7 6 5 4 3 2 1

Printed in the United States of America

Acknowledgments

Doing research for my books is one of the most enjoyable and difficult aspects of this thing I do. Research allows me to grow through the strangers I meet, the places I travel, the settings I experience. Throughout the course of this process I call writing, there are special people who help me. To my mom and dad, who are but a phone call away, and somehow always have the answer to even my silliest questions. . . . To my sons, who are so willing to ponder the perfect name when I say, "There's this character in my book who . . ." And to my sisters and sisters-in-law who so graciously stop what they're doing when the "perfect" word is on the tip of my mind, but refuses to travel to the tips of my fingers . . . To my friends, who offer insight into occupations and situations my characters find themselves in . . . To my husband, who puts up with what is left after the days, weeks, and months spent writing have drained me. To all of you, thank you, thank you, thank you. And especially, thanks to Beth Hinze, for sharing the painful and poignant details of the hours, days, and weeks her son spent in a coma when he was a little boy.

CHAPTER ONE

Spencer McKenzie parked on a side street around the corner from Harbor Avenue. Reaching for the dark suit jacket he'd folded over the seat an hour ago, he closed his door and hurried toward Gaylord and Yvonne Wilson's home a block away. The breeze was uncommonly warm for an evening in late April. It was the first truly warm weather they'd had in this part of Michigan this year. Shirtsleeve weather, he and his brothers used to call it. He would have preferred to roll up his sleeves and remove his tie. Instead, he slipped into his jacket, smoothed a hand along the length of his lapel, and started up the steps leading to the estate situated at the top of a steep hill overlooking Lake Michigan.

Party balloons bobbed atop the gold-colored strings mooring them to the polished brass railing that meandered upward through well-lit, immaculately tended grounds. Three-fourths of the way to the top, Spence paused, taking a moment to appreciate the view behind him. Trilliums were just starting to bloom on the sand dunes. Earlier that day, colorful sailboats had tacked back and forth near the shore. Farther out, yachts and tugs and tankers had skimmed across the horizon. Tonight, darkness was fast obliterating the line where water met sky. Already, lights dotted the shoreline. In the distance, the beacon of the Grand Haven Lighthouse flashed at the end of the pier. The tourist season was nearly upon them. Local businesses thrived on it. Spence tolerated it, preferring the slower pace of the off-season, when Grand Haven belonged to its local residents.

Several of those local residents were standing in small groups when Spence reached the patio on the first level of the Wilson estate. The breeze billowed through imported suits, designer dresses, and some pretty impressive stuffed shirts. It ruffled a toupee or two, but it didn't hinder the guests who had gathered for Gaylord's seventieth birthday celebration. Just as Spence had expected, anybody who was anybody was here. A rising star in the field of architecture, he was considered one of those anybodies, but he was here because his wife, Maggie, was here. Somewhere.

"There you are!" Gaylord's wife, Yvonne, placed an elegantly manicured and garishly bejeweled hand on his arm. "You're late."

Spence leaned down to brush his lips across the perfectly made-up, lined cheek. Yvonne made a clicking sound with her tongue. "All right, all right. I forgive you. The question is, will Maggie?"

He glanced around the courtyard for his wife. "Maggie knew I was going to be late. If she's upset, I'll have to think of some way to make it up to her."

Yvonne's eyes, slightly watery and faded, held warmth and humor. "If I were ten years younger." Looking him up and down, her expression became wry. "Better make that twenty."

"It's a good thing you're not," Spence said, indulging

the older woman with one of his rare smiles. "Because that, Maggie wouldn't forgive."

"I'm pleased Maggie doesn't have to worry about that," Yvonne insisted.

For all her social graces, Yvonne Wilson had a voice like a foghorn. Even her whispers could penetrate steel. Therefore, it wasn't surprising that several of her guests turned to look at them. Abigail Porter, whose husband was a known philanderer, strolled closer. Abigail and Yvonne had been friends for years, but not even Yvonne knew exactly how old her friend was. There wasn't a telling line on Abigail's face. In fact, her latest facelift had raised her eyebrows so far she wore a constant look of dismay.

"Every woman has to worry, darling," she said sadly. "It's the nature of the beast."

Not this beast, Spence thought, casting another practiced eye around the courtyard for a glimpse of his wife. Since he didn't see Maggie on this level, he excused himself, accepted a glass of wine from a passing waiter, then made his way toward the steps leading to the patio on the next level.

Fifteen years ago, a noted architect from Chicago had designed the Wilson house and the surrounding tiered gardens and patios. Personally, Spence would have used less glass, chrome, and cement, and more stone, iron, and other products that lent themselves to warmth and dimension, and blended with the rocky hills, sandy beaches, and jagged shoreline of Lake Michigan.

He wasn't here to critique the architecture. He was here because Maggie had asked him to attend. Although he didn't find her on the second level, either, he knew she was here because nearly everyone he came into contact with spoke of her. He shook hands with Gaylord's attorney, said hello to an accountant, spoke to a real estate tycoon who made it a point to attend all the right parties. Many of these men and women had been born to families who had made their fortunes in the shipping, mining, or railroad industries. Spence's association with the architectural firm of Hastings and Wiley might have been the reason the McKenzies had initially been invited to parties such as this one, but it was Maggie's warmth, charm, and poise that had won their hearts. She was their Cinderella, Grand Haven's princess.

It wasn't only the elite who sought her out. Maggie McKenzie was a joiner, a doer, a woman with a dozen causes and a hundred friends. Everyone loved her. And she loved everyone. But she loved Spence most of all. And he loved her. She was the reason he got up every morning and came home every night. She and their two young daughters made his life about as perfect as a man's life could be. It wasn't that other men didn't have what he had. It was just that few men appreciated it the way he did.

It took Spence half an hour to reach the other end of the wide patio. He said hello to the men and women he met along the way, discussing everything from politics and global warming to local building trends. Placing his empty wineglass on another passing waiter's tray, he finally reached the stairs leading to the highest courtyard surrounding the house. This patio, with all its curving walkways, black and white tables and chairs, and a host of abstract garden ornaments, was the most ornate, and the most crowded.

He spotted Maggie immediately, just as he always did. It was more than her blond hair that made her stand out in a crowd. She was talking to four of her friends from the Ladies Historic Society, who, along with Yvonne's help, had planned tonight's surprise birthday party for Gaylord. It required effort to suppress Spence's grimace at the sight of one of those so-called friends.

Jessica Michaels had been married to a friend of Spence's. She'd latched on to Maggie, and then had proceeded to make a play for him behind Maggie's back. He'd turned her down cold, of course.

Spence wouldn't have had to tell Maggie. She'd already known. It was no use wondering how she'd guessed. Months later he'd asked her why she continued to be civil to the backstabber. She'd said, "Jessica isn't best friend material, but she can't hurt me, Spence. Only someone you truly love can do that."

He thought about that as he watched Maggie from a distance. The flicker of candlelight and the glow of dozens of Chinese lanterns threaded her hair with gold. Her only jewelry was a narrow watch and the tiny diamond earrings he'd given her for their second wedding anniversary when they'd been struggling beneath the weight of student loans and their first mortgage. She hadn't spoken to him for three days, but she'd worn the earrings every day ever since.

Her dress was a pale shade of blue, and loose enough to allow for plenty of movement. It had a rounded neckline in the front and a row of pewter-colored buttons down the back. Spence liked that dress, liked the fit and the feel. She claimed it hid the ten pounds she'd battled since Allison had been born six years ago. Spence happened to like where she'd put those ten pounds.

There wasn't a man at the party who could take his eyes off her for an extended period of time. She appeared oblivious to everyone except the people she was talking to at that moment. It wasn't an act. Maggie McKenzie was the most genuine woman he'd ever known.

He was so intent upon watching his wife on the other side of the courtyard that he didn't notice Edgar Millerton's advance until the old codger had stopped directly in front of him, planted his feet, and said, "Spencer, my boy."

And then it was too late. Spence was cornered.

Chewing morosely on a dead cigar, Edgar launched into his favorite topic, his fascination with groundwater, sediment, pollutants, microorganisms, and their effect on all of mankind.

It promised to be a long night.

Maggie McKenzie hugged her arms close against a sudden chill. She'd been having a relatively innocent, innocuous conversation with Melissa Bradley and Hannah Lewis before Jessica Hendricks and MaryAnn Petigrue had joined them. Within seconds, the conversation had turned into a he-said-she-said gossip session, interspersed with a large dose of male bashing.

"Come on, Maggie!" Jessica declared. "Give us something low-down and dirty on Spence."

Maggie pulled a face. "I hate to disappoint you, but I'm drawing a blank."

"Are you telling me Spence doesn't do anything that annoys the hell out of you?"

Maggie ran a quick check through her mind. The truth was, she didn't have many issues with men. Spence wasn't perfect, but she didn't expect him to be. He'd grown up with three brothers, and the toilet seat had been a problem at first. She'd taken a few midnight splashes early in their marriage, but these days they both knew how to work the lid. He had a serious connection with the remote control, and he loved a clean garage but never seemed to notice when the house was a mess.

For lack of anything more serious, she shrugged and said, "Well, he's late for a lot of things."

"Not Peter," Hannah exclaimed. "He's on time for everything, and when I'm running late, he has this look, not to be confused with *a* look or *that* look. I'm talking about *the* look."

"Uh," Melissa Bradley exclaimed. "I know exactly what you're talking about. Aaron does that, too. Ever notice that when you and your husband are getting along, you like most everything about him?"

"And when you're not," MaryAnn Petigrue interrupted, "you don't even like the way he breathes."

Even Maggie smiled at that one.

The surprise party had been a success in every sense of the word. She, Yvonne, and several members of the Ladies Historic Society had planned it down to the tiniest detail, and yet Gaylord had surprised *them* with his announcement that he was making a six-figure donation to the society. It would be all over the papers tomorrow. Tonight, Maggie just wanted the party to wind down so she could go home, kick her shoes off, slip out of her dress, and unwind with Spence.

She'd been feeling strange all day. She wasn't prone to bad moods, and although she'd read about people who had premonitions, she rarely experienced them herself. Her parents, who were doing missionary work in Africa, would have blamed it on atmospheric pressure and a change in the weather pattern. Neither Joseph nor Adelle Fletcher believed in premonitions. Perhaps premonition was too strong a word. It was more like trepidation. Maggie felt antsy, uneasy. For the life of her, she couldn't say why.

She wondered where Spence was. He said he'd be here tonight, and Spencer McKenzie kept his word. She didn't know many women who'd been married nearly thirteen years and still missed their husbands simply because they hadn't seen each other all day. Sometimes, she worried that she loved him too much. How could she love him too much, when he loved her just as fiercely? She was almost thirty-four years old, and incred-

ibly, undeniably happy. No one could ever accuse her
of being weak. She didn't cling, and she certainly didn't
define herself by her husband's success. It was just that
she felt more alive when they were together.

The goose bumps that had been skittering up and
down her arms trailed away. More relaxed now, she
glanced at the guests scattered throughout the courtyard. Her gaze flitted over dozens of people, but it
settled on one man.

Spence.

Their eyes met, held. Something unspoken and powerful passed between them. Just over six feet tall, he
stood in the shadows with Edgar Millerton, looking
more like a shipbuilder of bygone days than a modern-
day architect.

No wonder she was no longer cold. He'd been watching her. All the years of marriage hadn't dulled or dimin-
ished the passion that had taken on a life all its own
the first time they'd met, but time had honed their
response to it.

She cast him a small smile, and watched the effect it
had on his features. His lips parted, as if he'd suddenly
taken a quick, sharp breath. The breeze lifted his dark
hair off his forehead and ruffled his tie. She couldn't
see the color of his eyes from here, but she knew they
were a deep shade of blue, as vivid and changeable as
the great lake they'd both come to love.

Spence could have lived anywhere from Alaska to
Timbuktu, but Maggie, the daughter of a career Army
man, had known this was where she'd wanted to grow
old the first time she'd visited the area some fifteen
years ago. She'd lived in twenty-two towns before she'd
graduated from high school, but she'd lived right here
in this one small city for the past thirteen. She and
Spence belonged here, the way she'd always longed to
belong as a child.

Spence nodded his head at the staunch old codger he'd been talking to, but Maggie noticed he didn't take his eyes off her. Almost of its own volition, her hand went to her hair. She twirled a lock around one finger. Nobody watching could have known that the simple mannerism was her way of telling Spence that her thoughts had taken a slow, luxurious stroll to the bedroom. But he knew.

He had an angular face and, when he chose to use it, a devastatingly attractive smile. Bidding Edgar farewell, he proved it, smiling as he strode closer. He kissed Maggie on the cheek, an old-fashioned, gentlemanly gesture few men bothered with anymore, then said hello to Melissa, Jessica, Hannah, and MaryAnn.

The other four women moved, en masse, to the buffet table. Maggie shifted slightly closer to Spence, so that her shoulder rested lightly against his arm. "How was the meeting?"

"All things considered, I'd say it went well. I'll tell you about it later. It looks like your party was a success, too, although everyone's more interested in talking about the surprise Gaylord had for all of you."

Maggie nodded. "Even Edgar Millerton?"

Spence ran the tips of three fingers up her arm, as if he'd waited as long as he could to touch her. Goosebumps of a different nature followed the path his fingertips took.

"You know Edgar," he said quietly.

Oh, dear. Maggie knew Edgar, all right. The man moved slowly, and spoke the same way. He took twenty minutes to order a sandwich. For excitement, he watched paint dry. Maggie herself had been known to go on and on about history, but even she had a difficult time staying focused when Edgar launched into conversation about sediment and water seepage. As tight-fisted as Gaylord was generous, Edgar idolized Jay someone or other, the United States' first Ph.D. to study ground-water. Once, Edgar had invited all the members of the Ladies Historic Society to his home, where he'd shown slides of how water drained through sand, gravel, and rock.

"Fascinating stuff, groundwater," Spence said close to Maggie's ear.

"You don't say."

"Did you know that it travels through pores in rocks one-seventieth of the speed of snails?"

Oh, dear. Maggie loved these social functions. She was perhaps the only person present who knew that they bored Spence silly. He made the best of them for her sake. It was one of the things she loved about him. There were plenty of other things.

"Biological reclamation is going well."

"Spence?"

"Evidently, it works by activating natural bacteria. It seems this natural bacteria eats most of the pollutants like degreasers and solvents and septic tank cleaners we humans have been dumping into the ground since they were invented."

She leaned lightly into him. "He must have had you cornered for a long time."

"It's hard to gauge minutes when time is standing still."

She shook her head. "You were bored to death."

"I'm a big boy."

He was a big man.

"I'm surprised to see Jessica Michaels here," he said tersely. "Last I knew, she was living in the Caribbean."

Maggie shrugged. "It's Jessica Hendricks again. She took back her maiden name."

Spence gave a derisive snort. "She took John for everything he had. I'm surprised she didn't want to keep his name, too."

Maggie whispered, "I don't think I could ever do that."

"What? Keep my name?"

"No. Waste so much energy hurting someone I loved."

Sometimes, when Spence looked at her the way he was looking at her right now, she got lost in his eyes.

"I'd be a fool to give you a reason."

She smiled, because Spence was no fool.

With the barest movement of his head, he gestured toward the back steps. That was all it took, one look, and she knew he was asking how much longer she wanted to stay.

Earlier, the courtyards had been bursting at the seams. There were still some forty guests milling about on this level, but the party was winding down. "We should be able to make our escape in half an hour or so. What did you have in mind?"

The sound Spence made deep in his throat was half moan, all male. Taking her hand, he led the way to a small dance floor nearby, where two other couples were dancing to music provided by a three-piece orchestra. Fitting her body close to his, he proceeded to give her a detailed outline of what he had in mind.

His words conjured up dreamy images that worked over Maggie like moonlight. Despite the heat emanating from him, she shivered again.

"Cold?" he whispered, close to her hair.

"Hmm. I don't know why, but I've been shivering all night." She closed her eyes, and for a moment, she felt as if she were looking at her life from outside herself, and something precious was about to slip away. A sense of dread washed over her. She kept her eyes wide open after that.

It didn't make sense. Her sister, Jackie, was home with the girls. Jackie loved Grace and Allison almost as much as she and Spence did. Jackie knew their favorite games, favorite foods, their latest secrets and oldest fears. She also knew the Wilsons' phone number by heart. Grace and Allison both knew how to dial 911. There had been no sirens, no weather rumblings or threats of disasters. Even the sky was clear. Why, then, did Maggie have to force herself not to hold on to Spence too tight?

"About that getaway," she whispered.

"I'm listening."

"Think anybody would notice if we crept away right now?" she asked.

Several guests turned at the sound of the little yelp she made when he followed his smooth turn in one direction with a surprise dip.

"Nice going," she chided once she was back on her feet. "Now everybody will notice."

"I aim to please."

Yes, she thought, he did. She was overtired, that was all. Everything was fine. Perfect. Feeling more like her old self, she finished the dance in Spence's arms. Then, hand in hand, they mingled with the other guests, enjoying being together, anticipating being alone.

They did manage to slip away half an hour later. Since they'd driven to the party separately, he walked her to the family van, then held her door. "I'm parked just off Harbor Avenue," he whispered. "I'll meet you at home."

Maggie smiled. Home, with Spence and their girls, was exactly where she wanted to be right now. And then, because it suddenly seemed of life-and-death importance, she called, "Drive safely."

He glanced over his shoulder and cast her another of his devastating male smiles. "You, too."

Maggie was shivering again as she started the van.

CHAPTER TWO

The ride from Yvonne and Gaylord's house took less than five minutes. As Maggie pulled into her own driveway, she saw Jackie's car parked near the house. A lamp was on in the bay window. In the window directly above it, Allison's night-light glowed a pale yellow. It was easy to picture Grace and Allie asleep in their rooms at the top of the stairs. Grace's hair would be smooth on her pillow; Allie's would most likely be in her eyes, her covers tangled around her ankles. It was a comforting image.

Maggie was in the process of unlocking the door between the garage and the back hall when she heard the other garage door begin to rise. By the time Spence joined her in the kitchen, her apprehension was slowly but surely draining away. She was home, surrounded by everything that was ordinary and everyday, the people she loved the most tucked safely in their beds upstairs. Ah, yes, everything was as it should be.

This house was a haven, but it was the expression on Spence's face when he entered the kitchen that had her pulse quickening and her breathing deepening.

Maggie held perfectly still, because she knew that look. She reacted to that look. God, she loved that look.

Hooking his jacket on one finger over his shoulder, he took a deliberate step in her direction. He'd already unbuttoned both cuffs and was starting with the top button on his shirt. Giving her a thorough once-over, he strolled around the table.

"At this rate," she said, her voice sultry and deep, "you're going to be out of that shirt before we get upstairs."

The second button slipped open an instant before he brushed his lips across hers. "I was thinking more along the lines of getting you out of that dress, and have been for the better part of the past two hours."

"Here?" Maggie knew how provocative that sounded. She'd become an audacious flirt these past thirteen years, but only with him. They'd been virgins, both of them, when they'd first met, but not for long. The attraction had been instantaneous, their desire stronger than either of them from the beginning. There had been no question of right or wrong, no worries that they were making a mistake, no doubt that before them was the one person in all the world they would spend the rest of their lives with. The wedding had come later, but the marriage had begun the first time they'd made love.

Spence strode closer, and closer. "You're feeling adventurous. I'll let you in on a little secret. I like that." He quirked one eyebrow, because that had never been a secret. "Unless you have your heart set on conducting an experiment down here, what I have in mind is best suited to a bed. Besides, I know you want to check on the girls, and so do I."

That was another thing she loved about him. He cared about their daughters every bit as much as she did. She knew men who were jealous of the attention their wives paid to their own children. She and Spence were too sure of one another for that. They had an idyllic life. They always had.

Another shiver worked over her.

"Cold?" he asked.

"No. Yes. I don't know."

"As long as you're sure."

She glanced up at him, only to ease into a slow, thoughtful smile in spite of herself. She didn't know what was wrong with her today, but there was nothing wrong between the two of them.

As she often did when she baby-sat for them at night, Jackie had turned off all the lights except the dim light over the stove; the kitchen was dark. Maggie and Spence had designed all the renovations together, but this was Maggie's favorite room in the house. Until five years ago, they'd lived in a cute little bungalow a few blocks away, little being the operative word. It had a small kitchen, two tiny bedrooms, a cozy living room, and a postage stamp yard. It had been adequate, and they'd all been happy there. Still, Maggie had always been fascinated with this place. Honestly, she couldn't remember ever having said it out loud. The house had been built in the forties. It had no great historic value, and yet something about the overgrown yard and wide front porch had drawn her.

She remembered the day she'd seen the For Sale sign go up in the front yard. That night at dinner, she'd mentioned it offhandedly. Just as offhandedly, Spence had said there was a sale pending. She'd been too surprised to mask her disappointment. If she'd been able to see Spence's face, she would have known he was up to something, but he'd been lifting Allie out of her high chair, his face hidden from her view. When he'd suggested taking the girls for a walk, she'd been completely unsuspecting of his motives. They'd ended up in front of this house. He'd waited for her to sigh, and then he'd held out the key, lovingly wrapping her fingers around it.

He'd known. There was no sense wondering how.

They'd moved in as soon as the renovations had been completed, seven months later. It had been home ever since. Maggie couldn't imagine living anyplace else.

Spence was on his way to the kitchen counter when he stumbled over the bicycle helmet Allison had dumped, and then forgotten, next to the table. Bending down, he picked up the bright pink helmet and two Biker Barbie tennis shoes. The rest of the kitchen was tidy. Jackie had stacked the mail near the phone and the dishes in the drainer. Grace had left a goodnight note, along with a blank permission slip for a field trip. Spence and Maggie read the note together, their heads bent close, matching smiles tugging at their faces at the drama behind their elder daughter's words.

"What are you thinking?" he asked, following the course of her gaze across the room.

It had been a long day, and tomorrow promised to be more of the same. Mornings were always hectic. "Maybe I should fill this out tonight, and then fill the coffeemaker so it's ready to go in the morning."

He traced her upper lip with the tip of his finger. "Leave it. I can wait for coffee in the morning. I don't think I can wait for this."

He kissed the places he'd just touched, the corners of her mouth, the delicate little ridge at the center of her upper lip, luring a sigh out of hiding. She knew how much he needed that first cup of coffee in the morning, but he was right. The coffee could wait.

While Spence locked the doors, she turned out the lamp in the bay window. They took the stairs together, stopping automatically at Allison's door. Farther down the hall, the door to the spare room where Jackie often slept was closed. She was probably asleep, too.

Light from the hall spilled into Allison's room as they crept to opposite sides of their younger daughter's bed. Allison Rose McKenzie had two settings: full speed ahead, and fast asleep. Maggie had felt her baby's kick long before the textbooks claimed it was possible. Allie had been born squirming, and had started walking at nine months. She moved, even in her sleep, half cyclone, half angel.

Maggie drew the sheet up to that adorable little chin, when she and Spence both knew she'd only fling it off again sometime during the night. Smoothing wisps of baby-fine hair away from Allison's eyes, Maggie kissed her daughter's cheek, then crept out of the room and on into the one across the hall.

Maggie and Jackie were a lot alike, but Gracie and Allie were complete opposites. Six-year-old Allison generally slept through anything, while ten-year-old Grace stirred at the slightest noise. As if on cue, her eyes fluttered open the moment Spence brushed his lips across her forehead.

"Hmmm. Daddy."

"Hey, Lady Grace," he whispered.

She hummed something neither of them could make out then murmured, "Empire . . . named after a schooner . . . got stuck in the ice in the harbor in eighteen sixty-three."

"You don't say," Spence said.

She looked at him as if he were the one who was mumbling, then turned to her mother. "Or maybe it was in eighteen sixty-two. Was it, Mama?"

"I believe it was in 'sixty-three, honey."

"That's what I thought. Did you sign my permission slip?"

"I'll sign it in the morning," Maggie whispered.

" 'Kay. Night."

Maggie and Spence shook their heads and shared another smile. Out in the hall again, Spence whispered, "She gets more like you every day. As you can see, the girls are okay, so unless you're planning to check on your sister, too, I have a few places that could use your attention."

They were halfway to their bedroom at the far end of the hall when the soft laughter that had risen up inside Maggie trailed away, leaving behind the traces of a smile on her mouth and a telling glint in her eyes. "Not so fast," she whispered.

He paused, because she had.

Resting a hand on his chest for balance, she rose up on tiptoe, and kissed him. The breath rushed out of him, even as his arms wrapped around her, one hand flattened along the small of her back, the other hand spread wide between her shoulder blades. The kiss went on and on, a mating of open mouths and tongues, their bodies straining for a closeness that could be achieved only without clothes.

His hands moved down her back; hers glided through his hair. She held his face still for her kiss; he held her hips still and pressed his into her, closer, closer. Still, it wasn't close enough.

"Uh-hum."

They turned their heads at the same time. Jackie was standing near the stairs. Fully dressed, right down to her navy spring jacket, she looked slightly sheepish and paler than Maggie would have liked.

Maggie drew away slightly from Spence, her hands trailing from his hair, down his back, to her sides. "I thought you were sleeping here tonight."

Jackie rolled her shoulders in a dismissive shrug. "I'm going home. I've slept so much these past six months

I should be able to stay awake for a month, straight. I didn't mean to interrupt."

"Nonsense," Maggie insisted. "Would you like a cup of tea?"

Maggie might not have been aware of the momentary change in Spence's expression, but Jackie was. "Don't worry," she told him with a wink. "I'm not staying."

"Spence and I just finished checking on the girls, didn't we, Spence?"

Spence didn't bestow his smile on many people, but he slanted it at Jackie. "You know you're always welcome here."

The resemblance between the Fletcher sisters had always been unmistakable. Both were blond, blue-eyed, pretty. There were differences, too. Jackie was two years younger and two inches taller. She'd always insisted that had made them equal. She'd been the more outspoken of the two when they were younger. She'd grown quiet this past year. Even though she'd tried to mask her sadness at the breakup of her marriage, Maggie was worried. "Stay," she insisted.

"I love you guys, but there are just some things sisters don't need to hear, or imagine, for that matter, especially soon-to-be divorced sisters who haven't had sex since, well, you know what I mean."

"You're the second person I've talked to tonight who's made a comment like that," Spence said.

Jackie and Maggie both looked at him in surprise. "Who else?" Maggie asked.

With a playful lift of his eyebrows, he said, "Edgar."

"Edgar Millerton?" Jackie asked.

"I thought you said he talked about groundwater and sediment," Maggie said at the same time.

"That, too." Spence turned to Jackie. "I could probably fix you up."

Jackie and Maggie wore identical expressions of distaste, but Jackie spoke first. "If I'm ever that desperate, please, someone, shoot me."

"You're not desperate at all," Maggie said on a rush. "David's affair has left your ego battered, that's all. It's his flaw, not yours. You're beautiful, and you know it. Tell her, Spence."

There was a trace of the old Jackie in the woman holding up her right hand in a halting gesture. "No offense, but compliments from brothers-in-law are about as inspiring as kisses from great-grandpas. At ease, you two." Turning, she started toward the stairs. "I'll let myself out. By the way, the girls were great."

"Good. Are you sure you won't stay?"

"I'm sure."

"I'll call you tomorrow," Maggie called.

"Okay."

Maggie waited to move until she'd heard the back door click shut. "I'd like to give my soon-to-be ex-brother-in-law a piece of my mind." She slipped out of her shoes, then bent at the waist. Hooking them on a finger on each hand, she padded barefoot toward the master bedroom, whispering as she went, "He wouldn't know a good woman if one bit him in the kneecap."

Arms folded, Spence leaned in the doorway, watching as she dropped the shoes near the closet then reached behind her and unbuttoned the top button on her dress. He'd wanted to do that.

"How could he just throw Jackie away like that?"

For a man his size, Spence had a light step and lightning-quick reflexes. Without making a sound, he was suddenly directly behind Maggie, nudging her fingers aside. He unfastened the second pewter button, and then the third. When Maggie's head fell forward, he couldn't resist pressing his lips to the pale skin at her nape. If there was one sound in the world he would hate to live without, it was the one she made right then, throaty, sensuous, stimulating.

"Jackie has so much to offer. Why couldn't he see that?" she asked on a shuddering sigh.

"It's his loss." Spence unfastened the last button, then stepped back far enough to allow the garment to glide down Maggie's arms. Cupping her bare shoulders, he drew her against him. She was still talking, but he could tell she was winding down.

"She's so lonely. A lot of people think she's lucky there are . . . mmmm . . . no children involved, but I think it would be easier for her if she and David had been able to have a child."

He and Maggie knew how it felt to yearn for a child. They'd tried for two years before she'd become pregnant the second time. Jackie had wanted a baby, desperately. She and David had tried almost from the beginning. Sadly, it had never happened. Although she'd gone, David had refused to visit a fertility specialist. It was a crying shame, because Jackie would be a wonderful mother.

"She's amazing with Grace and Allison. Hmmmmm. Maybe things could have worked out if David had agreed to see a marriage counselor."

"David and Jackie were never soul mates, Maggie."

"She's hurting. When we were kids, and one of us was hurting, the other always knew what to do. Ah. That feels nice. I don't know how to help her through this."

"She's strong. She'll get over him."

Her bra came off. Naked from the waist up, she shivered, this time neither from trepidation nor from the cold. His hand inched around her ribs, his fingers stretching, straining, kneading the outer swells of her breasts. She moved the tiniest bit, giving him better access. "I'd never get over you," she whispered.

"You'll never have to."

"I thank God for you, Spence."

He moved against her. "Is there anything else you want to discuss? Or would you like to stop talking now?"

Spence knew she was smiling before she turned around. Just as he knew how her touch would feel before she covered the fly of his trousers with her hand.

"You're too much man for me sometimes."

Dragging in a ragged breath, he let her have her way. "You're wrong, Maggie. We're a perfect match."

Her gaze held his as her fingers deftly worked his belt buckle free. For a moment, the only sound in the room was the rasp of his zipper, and his deep, shuddering breath. And then it was his turn to sigh, and moan and close his eyes, thanking God for this moment, this life, with this woman.

"Tell me a secret," she whispered. "And I'll tell you mine."

"A secret, hmm?" It was an old game to them. "Let's see." Their remaining clothes came off, one item at a time, falling wherever they landed. "I love you with nothing on."

She smiled. "That isn't a secret."

She moaned softly when he touched her here, and there, and everywhere in between. "Ah, Spence, I love that."

"That isn't a secret, either."

It was just a game. After all, they knew each other's secrets, each other's fantasies, and innermost desires. They'd learned them one by one over the years.

They found the bed together, and lay down, arms and legs tangled, the lamplight casting a golden glow that faded into the shadows across the room. Finally, they kissed. It was just a brush of air at first, slowly growing more intimate, enhanced by her smooth arch toward him, his slight tilt and turn, until their mouths were fully joined.

Their pleasure was potent, awe-inspiring, mind-boggling, wiping out all thoughts, all worries, everything except this moment. The mattress shifted beneath their weight, the house silent except for the wind outside and their sighs inside this room. She wasn't a noisy lover, wasn't prone to loud cries and sudden outbursts. She got her message across loud and clear in her own, quiet way. Their lovemaking brought more than a rush of blood and a fluttering of hearts. It brought a sense of burgeoning joy and peace, as if in this joining, everything they were made of was held safely in this room, this bed, this union. They were home. And it was heaven, just as it always was.

Later, lying on her side close to Spence, she whispered, "Are you awake?"

He made a sound that meant barely. And she smiled as she placed a kiss on his shoulder.

"Why?"

Snuggling even closer, she said, "I was just thinking."

"Not me. You wiped out my ability to think." After a moment's silence, he whispered, "What were you thinking?"

She smoothed her hand over his shoulder. "If I were running the world, I would give every good and kind person a life as full as ours."

He made another agreeable sound. Moments later, they both drifted off to sleep.

The last drops of coffee gurgled noisily through the coffeemaker as Maggie put the finishing touches on the girls' lunches. The power had gone out sometime after she and Spence had finally gone to sleep last night. They'd awakened half an hour late this morning, and had hit the floor running. Normally, everything ran like clockwork, but their schedules were completely off-kilter today.

It was going to take a miracle to get everyone out of the house on time, especially since Allison hadn't wanted to wear anything in her closet and Grace was more interested in the book she was reading than in the breakfast she was supposed to be eating.

"Mom, do you know why the Indians called Mackinac Island Michilimackinac?"

It was Maggie who had told the girls the story years ago, but she played along. "Why?"

"Because Michilimackinac means Great Turtle, and to the Indians living along the shore, the island looked like a huge, monster turtle. I bet they were scared to paddle out there in their canoes and find out."

Maggie imagined that they'd been greatly relieved to discover an island instead.

"Think they had a party when they got back?" Grace asked.

"I wouldn't be surprised. Now eat." Maggie couldn't help smiling. If she, Spence, Grace, and Allie had lived back then, there was no doubt in her mind that Spence and Allison would have been in that canoe—no wonder she worried sometimes—and she and Grace would have been planning the party back on shore.

Keeping an eye on the time and an ear tuned to the radio, Maggie was busily washing grapes at the sink when Allie's giggles carried into the kitchen. Maggie and Grace looked up as Spence barreled into the room, a bedraggled-looking six-year-old on his back. Shirt out, shoes untied, a baseball cap covering her uncombed hair, Allison, looking much more cheerful now, called good morning as her father crouched low so she could slide to the floor.

Grace, her spoon poised in midair at the bar, rolled her eyes and said, "Al, you're such a daddy's girl."

Maggie saw the quick wink Spence cast their youngest. And then he swooped close to Grace, rubbing his clean-shaven face on her prim and proper little cheek before kissing it with a loud smack. "I have three best girls, and you know it."

Grace grinned, rubbed at her cheek, then promptly kissed him back. Once again, the sibling rivalry inherent in every child with brothers or sisters had been tamed for the time being. Dropping a container of grapes into the lunch sacks, Maggie thought how lucky Grace and Allison were to have a father like Spence. Neither she nor Spence had a favorite, but Grace had more in common with Maggie, while Allison loved the things Spence loved. The two of them were invigorated by wind in their faces and weren't afraid of high speeds. Skinned knees barely slowed them down. Secretly, Maggie had always been glad that one of the girls liked what Spence liked. Although he never complained, she knew he'd always wanted a son.

Reaching for the hairbrush and purple ribbon lying on the counter, Maggie whisked Allison's baseball cap from her head and went to work on the tangles in her pale blond tresses. "Coffee's ready," she said around the clips she placed between her teeth.

Spence reached for a mug with one hand and the pot with the other. "Ah," he said after his first sip. "You know the way to my heart."

Their gazes met over the top of Allison's head, because, actually, Maggie knew of more than one way to his heart, and had proven it, again, last night. In their prechildren days, the look they were sharing would have landed them back in bed. He shrugged, and she nodded, both their gazes turning to their girls. These days sex was confined to late at night or early in the morning. It was a small price to pay for their little piece of heaven, and they both knew it.

Keeping an ear tuned to the radio just in case the DJ announced that school was delayed, she finished tying the ribbon in Allison's hair. Grace's field trip form was signed and tucked inside her backpack, the bright pink bicycle helmet Allison had decided to take for show-and-tell sitting on top of hers.

"It's foggy this morning," Maggie said as Spence helped himself to a piece of toast.

"I hope school isn't called off," Grace declared.

"I hope it is!" Allison said just as vehemently. "Then we could stay home with Mama."

Memories washed over Maggie, reminding her of days gone by, when all four of them used to huddle under the covers together on days off, happy and content and safe. Reminding herself that they were already content and safe, and on the verge of being late, she poured milk over Allison's cereal. While Allie ate, Maggie tied the girl's shoes, then ran through a mental checklist. Allie had a horseback-riding lesson immediately after school, and Grace had a flute lesson at four. Later that morning, Maggie wanted to check on a neighbor who'd had surgery. She had a Ladies Historic Society meeting at noon, and planned to get groceries immediately after. Spence had said he should be home in plenty of time for supper. They could discuss their plans for the weekend then. Now, the lunches were packed, and as long as the girls kept moving, they would be ready in time to catch their ride to school.

Spence ate his toast standing at the counter. With no time to finish his coffee, he made do with another sip before hurrying into the study. Moments later, he returned to the kitchen, a drafting tube under one arm, his suit coat folded neatly over it, his briefcase held loosely in one hand. "If I leave right now, I can make it up to Muskegon ahead of the Stewarts."

Maggie followed him to the door and out of hearing range of the girls. "I thought you were working at your office in town today."

Something in the tone of Maggie's voice made him glance over his shoulder. Maggie's brow was furrowed, a worried look in her eyes. "I'm meeting with the clients, the developer, and someone from the annexation committee. Why? What's wrong?"

"I don't know, but I've been having funny feelings."

She was even wringing her hands. His mother used to do that when she had what she'd called a blind foreboding. Spence and his three brothers had given her plenty of reasons to worry. A season had rarely gone by without one of them needing stitches or a cast. The poor woman had been on a first-name basis with the emergency room doctors in the small town in the middle of the state where he'd grown up. She used to tell them to be careful more than she told them hello. Spence and his brothers hadn't paid much attention to her premonitions. And then, one day when Spence had been seventeen, the small airplane his parents had boarded had crashed. He'd always wondered if she'd been nervous that day. He hoped she'd been oblivious to impending doom. He liked to think his parents had died happy.

Now that he was an adult, he didn't take premonitions lightly. "Define funny."

Maggie shrugged. "I don't know. I can't shake the feeling that something bad is going to happen."

He could hear the girls talking in the kitchen, but he glanced out the window. "To Grace or Allie?"

"No. To us."

"You mean to our marriage?" He said the words tentatively, as if testing the idea. "We're rock solid, Maggie."

She looked out the window, too. Spence was right. Nobody had a stronger marriage than they did. She was probably being silly. Muskegon was only a fifteen-minute drive away, on good roads along the Lake Michigan shoreline. "Look. The fog's lifting. I don't know what's wrong with me. Just promise me you'll drive carefully."

"I promise."

"And call me as soon as you get there."

"I'll call as soon as I get there. Crystal Douglas is driving the carpool, right?"

Maggie nodded. If it were anyone else, she'd do it herself. But Crystal was an excellent driver. On a scale of one to ten, Maggie and Crystal were neck and neck at ten and a half.

Now she had Spence worried. That hadn't been her intention. "Ignore me," she said. "I'm just being paranoid."

"Better safe than sorry, I always say." And then he kissed her. When the kiss ended, they both smiled, but it was Spence who said, "I wouldn't mind staying home today."

She swatted the hand that had slid from her waist to the back of her thigh, stopping in a strategic place or two along the way. Spence walked out the door, taking the sound of her sultry laughter with him out into the eerie white haze of a Grand Haven morning.

Crystal's full-sized van pulled into the driveway as Spence pulled out. "Girls," Maggie called from the back entryway. "Crystal's here."

Crystal rolled her window down. "Morning! Have you had a chance to look at the morning paper, Maggie?"

Maggie shook her head and strolled closer. "The power outage messed with our clock radio, and since we'd borrowed the backup battery for Grace's science project and never replaced it, we woke up late. It's been a madhouse around here."

Crystal nodded sympathetically. "Gaylord and Yvonne

are featured in the society section. Guess who's in the picture?"

"Not me."

Crystal chuckled. "The one and only."

Glancing over her shoulder toward the door Allison had just let slam, Maggie said, "I was hoping school would be delayed this morning."

"Visibility isn't bad at all."

Maggie was thoughtful for a moment. "Do you ever have premonitions, Crystal?"

Allison darted past Maggie, her cap in one hand, her backpack in the other. "Bye, Mama," she called.

"Wait a minute! You forgot something."

Allison, one of those children who would forget their heads if they weren't attached, grinned beguilingly, and accepted the kiss from her mother.

"Have a good day, sweetie. I love you."

"Love you, too, Mama." With a blithe hop and a skip, the little girl bundled into the van and moved to the back to sit with Crystal's two boys.

"I've had my share of premonitions," Crystal said. "I knew both of these guys were going to be boys. And I can always tell when my mother is going to call. I'm not getting anything today. Hold on. I'll make sure." She closed her eyes, concentrating. "Nope. Nothing. Why, are you getting something?"

Maggie nodded.

"It's probably this wonderful, unusual week of warm weather. But I'll be extra careful. I'd just die if anything happened to any one of these kids."

Maggie knew the feeling. "Allison, do you have your lunch?" she called through the open window.

Holding up two lunches, Grace practically floated toward her mother, her movements so suited to her name that it never ceased to amaze Maggie. "I have Allie's, too."

"You're a good big sister."

Bestowing a smile that was nearly identical to Spence's, Grace climbed into the seat next to Crystal.

"Seatbelts, everyone?" Crystal called.

When everyone was buckled in, Crystal backed out of the driveway. Watching until they drove out of sight, Maggie decided that the shivers working over her again must have had some other cause.

She scooped the newspaper off the front step. Opening to the society page, she began to read as she meandered inside.

She poured herself a cup of coffee and had taken the first sip when a bright pink splotch of color caught her attention. She lowered the paper, and picked up the bicycle helmet Allison had intended to take to school for show-and-tell.

That was it? Her premonition had to do with a forgotten object? Feeling immensely relieved, she finished the article, and had a second cup of coffee. Taking her purse and Allison's bright pink helmet, she got in the family van, and drove toward the girls' school.

It was a beautiful April morning, scented of freshly cut grass, moist spring air, and the little white flowers called trilliums that grew wild in this area. Easing to a stop at the traffic light, Maggie strummed her fingers on the steering wheel and hummed along with the song on the radio. The light turned green, and the car ahead of her started through the intersection. Maggie followed.

She caught a movement on her right. She jerked her head around. Her eyes went wide at the sight of the pickup truck heading straight for her.

"Oh no!" Her breath solidified as she looked all around her.

Oh, God. Traffic had stopped. She had no place to go.

The truck was going to hit her.

Stop!

It came closer, barreling toward her, so close now she could see the driver. Frantic, she laid on her horn.

Fear lodged sideways in her throat. Oh, no. God, no. Stop. Please.

She opened her mouth to scream. The sound was swallowed by a deafening roar. Horns blared. Tires squealed. Metal crunched. Glass exploded, shattered. Allison's bicycle helmet bounced off the dash.

And then there was only silence.

CHAPTER THREE

Sirens wailed through the ribbons of fog in the distance, the sounds inharmonious, like out-of-tune instruments, making it impossible to distinguish the police sirens from those of the ambulances. School children, their noses pressed to the windows, called, "I see them!" moments before the flashing red and blue and yellow lights sped by.

Teachers counted heads and offered up a silent prayer that, whatever it was, wasn't as bad as it sounded.

It sounded bad. Very bad. Worse than bad.

The shopkeepers and clerks who were unlocking their stores along the peaceful, tree-lined streets in downtown Grand Haven craned their heads for a glimpse of something, anything, that might tell them who, and what, and where. Jackie Fletcher paused in the doorway of Fiona's, her vintage clothing store, an old skeleton key in her outstretched hand. The sirens sounded mournful, like a death song. The thought made her shudder.

"I hope that isn't Gardner," Treva Montgomery called from the doorway of her art gallery next door.

Gardner? This was the first Jackie had heard anything

about a man by that name. Okay, she couldn't help asking, "What happened to Raoul?"

Lifting a graceful hand, Treva patted perfectly coifed platinum-colored hair that had been red last week, and smiled affectionately. "As far as I know, nothing. I spoke to him just last night. He's wining and dining an art dealer in Spain. I can hardly wait to see him."

Raoul was a work of art unto himself—tall, dark, and brooding. Jackie could well imagine that a man named Gardner was, too. Raising her voice in order to be heard over the sirens, she said, "Do Gardner and Raoul know about each other?"

"If they don't already, I imagine they will. I never promise any of them an exclusive relationship."

Tango, the stray tabby cat that had adopted Jackie a month ago, purred, wending around her ankles the moment she opened the door. "I must be doing something wrong," she muttered to the cat. She couldn't even hold one man's interest, while Treva, who was at least twenty years older and did nothing to disguise the fact, was juggling relationships with two younger men.

"It must be a bad one," Treva said, shivering beneath her boldly colored caftan. "Either that, or somebody just walked across my grave."

Jackie shivered, too.

It was difficult to judge distance in the fog, but it sounded as if the sirens had moved away from the downtown district and now hovered somewhere between here and the center of town where Spence and Maggie lived. Sliding the key into the pocket of her ankle-length skirt, Jackie followed Tango into her store.

The cat looked up at her and meowed, as if he thought she could turn off the annoying sirens. That was what she loved about Tango: his unfailing belief that she could do anything.

Lowering herself until she was balancing on the balls

of her feet, she smoothed her hand along his sleek, tan and butterscotch colored coat, and thought about the choices people made. Treva had never married, preferring the freedom of the single life. Jackie respected that, but she'd taken her vows seriously. She might have been able to forgive David for having an affair. It wouldn't have been easy, but she would never know, because he'd taken it a step farther, claiming he'd fallen in love with a massage therapist he'd struck up a conversation with during a flight from France. He hadn't wanted her forgiveness. He'd wanted bridgett, who spelled her name with a small *b* and had breasts that were anything but small. Jackie had been devastated. She still was. Now, she had to decide what to do with her life as a single woman. More difficult, she had to figure out what to do about this horrible tossing and turning, this restless yearning to have a child.

Tango leaped onto her lap, stretching higher and pushing his head beneath her chin. "I know," she said, scooping him into her arms and rising to her feet. "I've got you, and the store. And I have Maggie and Spence and the girls. I love, and I'm loved, by wonderful people who give my life meaning. I should be counting my blessings, and thanking my lucky stars."

The sirens stopped abruptly. Jackie and the cat both turned to look out the window. Tango stopped purring; both held perfectly still.

Suddenly all was quiet, too quiet. The silence seemed final somehow, eerily so.

The robins building a nest in the lilac bush growing wild near the back door of Spence and Maggie's house didn't so much as pause when the phone started to ring on the other side of the screen. It rang on the stand where the clock radio displayed the wrong time, next to the bed where Maggie and Spence had last slept. One of the extensions rang on the counter in the kitchen, next to the hairbrush Maggie had used to tame Allison's hair, near the book Grace had been reading at breakfast, not far from the newspaper, open to Maggie's photograph, beside Spence's coffee, cold now. It rang, and rang. And then it stopped. And the house, cold, too, was silent again.

Spence cut the power to his cellular phone, but he didn't immediately put it away. Maggie hadn't answered. She said she was going to be home this morning. He wondered where she was.

"Something wrong?" Tom Garvey asked from the other side of his cluttered desk.

Spence pushed the recall button. Seeing his own phone number displayed, he shrugged. "I told Maggie I'd call her as soon as I arrived."

He tried again. Again, it rang and rang.

He'd planned to chide her for worrying, and could easily imagine the sultry sound of her voice, breathless from dashing through the house to get the phone. He'd promised her he would drive carefully, and he had. The trip from Grand Haven to Muskegon had been uneventful.

The area was becoming more populated every year. Property that had once been deemed useless by anyone who wasn't an orchard grower or farmer had caught on like wildfire. Real estate was the new frontier. Resorts had sprung up from Chicago to Mackinaw City. Movie stars, businessmen, some of the wealthiest of the wealthy now owned property on the shores of the Great Lakes. Who could resist mile after mile of huge sand dunes that glistened white in the sun, and houses set high above the shore of a freshwater ocean?

Spence's client, a developer who'd moved up here from Georgia, had put a fortune behind the belief that no one could. At least no one with money.

Spence pressed the off button and slid the phone into his briefcase.

"No answer?" Tom asked.

Spence shook his head.

Tom looked him in the eye and, in a deadpan voice, said, "She's probably busy entertaining her Latin lover. It's what Judy tells me she does while I'm gone."

The idea was so ludicrous Spence smiled. Tom's hearty laugh hadn't changed since he and Spence had gone to college together. They were both thirty-six, but Tom's stocky build and head of graying hair made him look ten years older.

A buzzer sounded. He picked up the phone, listened for a moment, then said, "Send them in."

Seconds later, Felix Fitzgerald strode into the office as if he owned the place, members of the city planning committee and the annexation committee close behind. Handshakes were exchanged, and the meeting got under way.

Originally, Felix had been insistent upon developing a subdivision that boasted houses similar to Gaylord and Yvonne Wilson's house in Grand Haven. The idea Spence had pitched had included a sketch of houses more rustic and European in style, with stone fronts, pebbled walkways, and pathways through both elaborate and wildflower gardens. Felix had balked in the beginning. It wasn't until Spence had invited him to dinner, and Maggie had begun to spin her tales of places in Michigan riddled with history, that Felix began to soften. He'd been intrigued by the story of how, in 1833, Rix Robinson had built a trading post in what was now Grand Haven. When she'd mentioned Picketts Corners, a tiny establishment that had centered around an inn that had once been run by a man named Selah Pickett, who'd kept a tavern on the Kalamazoo-Niles Stage Line, Spence could tell Felix was more than intrigued.

Spence had altered his vision to include picket fences, stone walls, potting sheds that resembled tiny taverns, and streets named after stage lines. The rest had been a piece of cake. The city planners were as taken with the project as Felix. There were still hurdles to overcome, such as zoning issues, soil conservation, drain requirements, power supplies, but it was only a matter of time before construction on the new Picketts Corners began.

It wasn't the first time Maggie's ability to paint such nostalgic pictures of days gone by had captured a developer's imagination. Spence's mind wandered. He wondered why she hadn't answered the phone.

Where could she have gone?

Deciding he would dial up his home phone number again just as soon as Tom wrapped up today's session, he forced himself to concentrate on the project at hand. By the time the meeting was over, Felix was grinning. The others were envisioning homes on safe cul-de-sacs where kids like theirs could ride their bikes, where yards were separated by painted fences, where dogs snoozed and cats lazed in patches of late afternoon sun. That was what they said out loud. Secretly, nobody was opposed to the fact that the project would pad an ever-growing tax base, either.

A knock sounded on Tom's office door. All eyes turned as his middle-aged assistant entered. Chloe Gentry swallowed nervously, pointing to the phone. "It's for you, Spence."

"Is it my wife?"

The way she shook her head sent a whoosh of blood flooding into his brain. "Perhaps you should take it in my office."

Spence's nerve endings were standing on end now. With a decisive shake of his head, he reached over the plans on Tom's desk and raised the phone to his ear. "This is Spence McKenzie."

He didn't recognize the voice on the other end. "This is Officer Seth Gregory. Is your wife Margaret Mae McKenzie?"

Spence nodded, and he must have said, "Yes," because the policeman started talking again. The connection was clear, but the words were difficult to grasp. An accident. A van with a license plate registered in his name had been hit broadside. The purse in the vehicle contained several pieces of identification belonging to a Margaret Mae McKenzie . . .

Maggie.

"Is she . . ." Spence's voice shook. He couldn't think the word, let alone say it out loud. Dread, unlike anything he'd ever known, rose up inside him, gagging him, choking him, freezing him in place.

"She's alive," Officer Gregory said.

Those words changed everything. Maggie was alive. Alive, alive, alive . . .

Spence pulled himself together, his voice gaining strength as he asked questions, and listened intently to the answers. It was bad. The officer didn't beat around the bush about that.

All eyes were on him when he handed the phone to Tom. "Maggie's been in a car accident. She's being airlifted to Bentworth Hospital in Grand Rapids."

He was out the door before anyone had the presence of mind to put two words together, either to ask a question, or offer their support. Tom Garvey was the first to recover. "Spence, wait!"

Tom rushed after him. "You shouldn't be alone at a time like this. Hold on. I'll drive you."

"It's okay, Tom." He couldn't wait. Being alone

didn't matter—Maggie was alive. Spence unlocked his car door, put the key in the ignition, and turned it. She was alive. He had to get to her, to ensure she stayed that way.

She's alive. She's alive. She's alive.

He said the words in his mind, over and over and over. She was being airlifted. That meant her injuries were so severe she couldn't wait for ground transportation. He clenched his teeth and whipped in and out of traffic.

She was alive, the policeman had said.

Please God, let her still be alive when he got there.

Spence parked in the first space he found, then raced headlong through the first door he came to. Sweat trickled down his face, and yet he'd never felt so cold. He didn't know where he was. He didn't even know if he was in the right wing. Suddenly, he didn't know which way to go, where to turn.

He was panicking. He'd never panicked in his life. He ran his hand over his face. Seeing how much his fingers shook, he forced himself to regain his control. Maggie, his Maggie, was alive. She was here in this building. All he had to do was find her.

Spying a nurse who was obviously in a hurry, he ran to her. "Excuse me." He grasped her lower arm. "My wife."

He could tell she read the terror on his face, because she said, "May I help you?" even though her arm had to hurt like hell where he squeezed it.

"My wife, Maggie McKenzie, was brought here by helicopter from Grand Haven."

"When?"

His thoughts swam. He had no concept of time. Had it been an hour ago? Or minutes?

"I don't know. This morning sometime. I just got the call."

She pried his fingers loose. Rubbing her arm, she told him to follow her. She spoke to someone sitting behind a desk. Promptly the clerk picked up a telephone and spoke to someone else.

"This way," the nurse said interminable moments later.

She led him through a labyrinth of hallways, double doors, and corridors. Finally, they emerged into a room bustling with noise and activity. She strode directly to a stockily built clerk who seemed to be literally up to his elbows in papers and charts and ringing telephones. People shouted, children cried, gurneys creaked and rattled, equipment beeped, the sounds discordant and loud in Spence's oversensitized ears.

He saw Maggie's name on the list, and clasped on to it like a lifeline. A name on a clipboard wasn't much, but at least it was tangible evidence that she was indeed here. Right then, it was all he had.

Someone else dressed in white appeared. "If you'll follow me, Mr. McKenzie."

Spence followed a large man with ebony-colored skin and line-backer shoulders through another set of double doors, into a quieter area. "Le'me see what I can find out about your wife's condition." The man disappeared into a glassed room.

Spence lifted a hand and tried to speak. Wait! He choked on his desperation to call the man back, to beg him not to leave him alone with this fear and dread that was swallowing him whole.

Within seconds, a young woman with a kind voice and a gentle handshake joined Spence. "I'm Celia Winters." She stated her position at Bentworth. Spence heard, "Blah, blah, blah—"

"What about my wife?" he cut in more severely than he'd intended.

"Do you call her Margaret or Meg?"

What? Oh. "She goes by Maggie. How is she? Where is she? When can I see her? I have to see her . . ."

For the first time, Spence noticed the forms in the woman's hands. She glanced at them, reading unintelligible notes. "She's in surgery, Mr. McKenzie."

"For what?"

"Your wife was in a car accident."

He knew that much, dammit.

"She has a broken arm, several deep lacerations, but her most serious injury was the trauma to her head. There was cranial bleeding. Dr. Mohan is performing surgery to relieve the pressure."

"Is Dr. Mohan good?"

The woman nodded. "He's one of the best neurosurgeons in the world. Your wife is in good hands."

Spence noticed she didn't smile. "How much longer?"

"It's hard to say. Someone will bring you news of your wife's condition as soon as we have it. Could I get you a cup of coffee or a soda?"

Spence answered by rote. "Coffee. Black."

She returned sometime later, a cup of steaming black coffee in her hand. Handing it to him, she said, "I know this is a difficult time, and the waiting is hard, but I need you to sign a few forms."

Spence signed on the dotted lines. He would have signed away his house right then. For all he knew, he had.

Seemingly satisfied that all the paperwork was in order, the woman with the kind voice asked, "Is there anyone you'd like to call to wait with you?"

His mind was blank. He knew there were people he

could have called, people he should have called. He couldn't think, so he shook his head.

As if in slow motion, he settled his frame into a vinyl sofa that was every bit as uncomfortable as it looked. At some point, he realized that he was alone in the room and the coffee had grown cold. He placed the full cup on a low table, then leaned ahead, knees apart, elbows resting on his thighs, hands clasped as if in prayer. But no prayers would come. No words would form. Time stood still and everything in his world stood still with it.

"Mr. McKenzie?"

"Yes." Spence looked up at a man with a round, deeply lined face and a full head of thick, black hair.

"I'm Dr. Ramas Mohan."

Spence rose slowly to his feet, afraid to proceed, afraid not to. "How's Maggie?" He cleared his throat. "How's my wife?"

"Your wife is in recovery. I've been standing in surgery for hours. Let's be seated."

Spence had been sitting too long; he needed to stand. But this man who had held a scalpel to his precious Maggie's brain was calling the shots. He lowered to a chair adjacent to the one Dr. Mohan had taken.

"How is she, Doctor? I have to know."

"She is very ill. Head injuries are never taken lightly, and hers is more serious than most."

Spence closed his eyes, but only for a moment, because Dr. Mohan was talking, his accent making what he said more difficult to understand. It wouldn't have mattered if he'd spoken in plain English. What he said was difficult to grasp. Maggie was clinging to life by a thread. She was on life support, and had been given medication that would keep her in a deep coma, thereby allowing her brain to rest in order for it to heal. She'd sustained a closed head injury and facial lacerations. Her broken arm would be cast later, providing . . .

"How long?" Spence asked, his voice so tight he didn't recognize it as his own.

Dr. Mohan studied him, as if uncertain what Spence was asking.

Spence wanted to spring to his feet, sprint around the room, shed his own skin. "How long will she be in this medically induced coma?"

"The next forty-eight hours will be very telling."

Which didn't tell Spence a damn thing. He refused to read more into that than he had to. "She's going to make it, Doctor."

Dr. Mohan made no reply.

She was going to make it, dammit. "I want to see her."

"She will soon be moved to a room in Intensive Care." The tired doctor went on to describe what Spence would find when he saw her. Her head would be bandaged, her face swollen and bruised, tubes in her nose and mouth, machines beeping, IVs in her arm.

Spence's stomach pitched. "I don't care what she looks like. I want to see her." He had to see her.

"I'll send someone to get you as soon as she is settled in a room."

The doctor rose then. And Spence noticed the man's hands, and imagined them covered with Maggie's blood. His stomach pitched again, so violently this time that his head swam.

"Doctor?"

Mohan turned in the doorway.

"Thank you."

The other man nodded. Spence would have sold his soul for the hint of an encouraging smile. The doctor turned on his heel, and slowly left the waiting room.

* * *

Time. It very well could have been passing or standing still. Spence had no way to gauge it. He sat. He paced. He found a rest room. He waited.

It was strange, time. Until he'd taken that phone call in Tom's office, there had never seemed to be enough time. Seconds had raced by as obliquely as electrons and neutrons in an atom. He believed they were there because he'd been told they were there, but they were invisible, their presence based on faith, not hard evidence. Now seconds ticked by slowly, marking time that seemed distorted somehow, unrecognizable as time at all.

He hadn't been in a hospital in years. The last time was when Allison had been born. Spence had thought the waiting was awful then. His quiet, subdued Maggie had yelled like a banshee, clinging to Spence's hand while she called the doctor a liar because he'd said second labors were generally shorter and less intense than first ones. Her second labor had lasted thirty-two hours. God, she was such a fighter. Was it any wonder Grace and Allison were both so incredible?

God. Grace and Allison.

He looked at his watch. It was one-thirty. Time wasn't standing still, after all. The girls were still in school. Maggie always picked them up. Other arrangements would have to be made. Who could he call? His mind was blank. He couldn't think.

Jackie.

Yes, Jackie would help. Christ, he should have called her in the first place.

He looked around him, trying to remember where he'd left his cell phone. His suit coat and tie were nowhere to be found, either.

"Mr. McKenzie?" The same orderly who'd led him to this waiting area stood a few feet away.

Spence sprang to his feet.

"If you'll follow me, I'll take you to see your wife, man."

He didn't need to be asked twice.

They squeezed into a crowded elevator, and rode it up several floors. "This way."

The statement was unnecessary. Spence would have followed the man anywhere.

"By the way, my name's Tyrone." They started down a wide hallway. "You got any kids, Mr. McKenzie?"

Spence noticed that Tyrone's shoes squeaked, the left one louder than the right. "Two."

"That's nice." Squeak. *Squeak.* "Girls or boys?"

Spence looked straight ahead. "Girls."

"The wife and me got us a baby girl, too."

Squeak. *Squeak.* Squeak. *Squeak.*

Tyrone was obviously accustomed to filling awkward silences. He forged on as if Spence were participating in the conversation. "Before I had my own, I could take kids or leave 'em. Nothin' quite like kids, is there?"

"How much farther?"

Squeak. *Squeak.* Squeak. *Squeak.* "We're almost there. Anybody tell you what to expect?"

Spence nodded. "I don't care how she looks. It doesn't matter. She's going to make it. She's a fighter, my Maggie. She'll make it. You'll see. She'll show us all. You'll see."

The squeaking stopped. "Here's your wife's room. I can stay with you if you'd like."

Spence shook his head.

"I'll be seein' you around, Mr. McKenzie. Good luck."

"Yeah. I mean thanks."

The squeaking started up again, slowly fading in the

distance. Spence froze. He wondered if he should have taken Tyrone up on his offer to stay.

It was too late. Tyrone was halfway to the double doors leading out of this wing.

There was a window in the door, just above the doorknob he was squeezing so tight he threatened its integral structure. He stared through the glass at the machines that blipped like radar and the metal racks and the white sheet covering a slight woman's still form.

A sob came out of nowhere, lodging in his throat. Oh, Maggie.

A nurse was writing something on a chart, checking wires and tubes like a fussy housewife. Biting the inside of his cheek until he tasted blood, he turned the knob and entered the hospital room.

"Spence, wait!" The cry was wrenched from a place deep inside Jackie's chest, too faint for anybody to hear.

A man with squeaky shoes nodded at her as he passed. Other people were in the corridor. Walking faster and faster, Jackie fixated on Spence's dark head.

When he opened a door and disappeared, she broke into a run. Her beloved Maggie was beyond that door. Jackie's steps slowed, along with her thoughts, when she was a dozen feet away. A nurse opened the door, and left Maggie's room.

Jackie's mind cleared for the first time since she'd looked up at the sound of the bell jangling over the front door in her store and saw the expression on Treva Montgomery's face and heard her say, "Those sirens, Jackie? I just heard who they were for. It's Maggie, dear. It's bad."

Everything between that moment and this one had been a blur, as if her headlong rush to the scene of the accident hadn't been real, the voices piecing together explanations as jagged as the glass scattered on the street. She'd nearly retched when she'd seen the blood. Maggie's blood.

She'd pulled herself together. It had seemed to take forever to locate Spence. Only when she'd discovered that he'd been notified and was on his way to the hospital in Grand Rapids had she raced here, as well.

Her hand clasped the doorknob Spence had just clasped, her gaze on the scene he was living. In the midst of blipping machines and tubes coming out of everywhere, he bent over Maggie's still form, as if shielding her. Jackie had turned the knob when she noticed Spence's shoulders were shaking, his entire body wracking with a sob he was doing everything in his power to contain.

She closed her eyes for a moment, a sob rising precariously close to her own throat. She'd never seen Spence cry before, not once in all the years he'd been her brother-in-law.

She turned around, awarding him some privacy, her hand pressed over her quavering lips. He was Maggie's husband, the love of her only sister's life.

Jackie gave him another moment alone with Maggie. She used that moment to gather her wits, and her strength. She was going to need it. They all were. No matter what, she wasn't going to lose her sister. And that was final. Jackie would do whatever it took. She would pray, beg, barter, and steal. Maggie was going to live. If by Jackie's sheer will alone, she was going to come back to them, whole.

Taking a deep breath, Jackie lowered her hand to the doorknob. Time was up.

Ready or not, she opened the door and went in.

CHAPTER FOUR

Jackie didn't speak when she entered the hospital room. She couldn't. She let the click of the door as it closed and the quiet tap of her heels on the floor alert Spence to her presence. Eyes on her sister, fingertips over her mouth, she strode to the bed.

Maggie lay utterly still. Her head was bandaged. There were several superficial cuts on her face. A jagged line stretching from her earlobe to her temple had been carefully stitched. Nasty-looking bruises had formed along her cheek and jaw. A tube was in her nose; another larger one was taped to her mouth. There were wires leading to her chest, in her neck and arm. Machines blipped, hissed, and hummed, breathing for her, monitoring her heartbeat, her blood pressure, her temperature, and God only knew what else.

One eye was blackened; the portion of her head not covered in bandages was shaved. Her skin, normally the color of ripened peaches, was a dull shade of gray.

She looked . . .

Jackie banished the thought. "Can she hear us?"

She caught the slight shake of Spence's head. "The nurse didn't think so, but no one knows for sure."

Jackie eased closer. "Hey, Mags, it's me," she whispered, placing a hand on her sister's shoulder.

"Be careful." Spence's voice was sharp. As if realizing it, he softened it, and continued. "That arm is broken. It probably hurts."

Jackie's hand hovered an inch above the sheet. "Why isn't it in a cast?"

He shook his head, leaving Jackie to wonder if the doctors hadn't gotten to it yet, or if they were waiting to see if it would be necessary. Treva had said it was bad. Jackie hadn't been able to fathom how bad. Until now. Machines blipped. Maggie's chest rose. And fell. And rose again. Jackie broke out in a cold sweat. "God, I hate hospitals."

Spence looked at her for the first time. "That's right, you do. I'd forgotten that." He took a deep breath, his gaze returning to Maggie's face, as if he didn't dare look away for long.

They stood, unmoving, one on either side of Maggie's bed. Twice, Jackie realized that she'd matched her breathing to Maggie's respirator. She cringed in the face of the fact that Maggie needed a respirator. "Oh, Spence."

"She was in surgery when I got here." His voice was deep now, controlled.

Jackie pulled herself together, too. "What did the surgeon say?"

"Something about a closed head injury, cranial bleeding, a shunt and surgery to relieve the pressure, and a medically induced coma."

"What's his name?"

"Dr. Ramas Mohan."

"He's good?"

"The nurse said he's the best neurosurgeon in the

state, and possibly in the entire country." And then, on a shuddering breath, he whispered, "They said she lost a lot of blood."

Jackie closed her eyes, thinking about the blood she'd seen at the scene of the accident and the van that looked like a crushed aluminum can. "Anybody tell you what happened?"

"Just that she was in a car accident."

"A fifty-eight-year-old man driving an SUV ran a red light and hit her broadside on the passenger side of the van. The jolt employed her airbag, but the force of the accident slammed her sideways into another vehicle waiting for the light. It all happened fast, but it was probably the second collision that injured her the most. If the first man had been coming from the other direction, it would be even worse, and they would *both* be dead."

Until that moment, Spence had had a hard time imagining anything worse than this. His reaction time was about a tenth its normal rate. By the time the implication finally soaked through far enough to register, Jackie had been looking at him for several seconds. "The man driving the SUV died?"

She nodded.

"Anybody we know?"

She shook her head. "He was from Battle Creek. The paramedics think he had a heart attack and was gone before the collision. You wouldn't have believed the sirens."

Spence could picture it in his head, the explosion of metal and glass, and the family van being propelled sideways into another vehicle, his Maggie trapped helplessly inside. The sirens would have come later.

He ran a hand across his forehead, over his eyes, and slowly down his entire face. "She had a bad feeling this morning, like something was going to happen. She was worried about *me.* I told her I'd call as soon as I arrived in Muskegon. The phone rang and rang. Why didn't she wait for me to call?"

"The accident happened three blocks from the girls' school. My guess is she was on her way there."

"The girls." Spence looked at his watch. "They're at school. Maggie always picks them up. Someone else will have to . . . I can't leave her, Jackie. I . . ."

For a moment, Jackie's head swam. Of course Spence couldn't leave Maggie. She didn't want to leave her, either.

"I don't know who else to ask."

Clasping her shaking hands together, she said, "It's all right, Spence. I'll see to Grace and Allie."

She took a shaky breath, said goodbye to Maggie, then wrenched herself away from her sister's side. At the door, she said, "Do you want to tell those doctors to get their butts in gear and set Maggie's arm, or shall I?"

Then and there, a glimmer of hope and determination came out of nowhere. Like a living being, it marched over to Spence and smacked him on the side of the head the way one of his brothers might have if they'd been there. It hurt to smile, but it was a damned sight better than how he'd felt a minute ago. "I will. In fact, I'm looking forward to it."

"Good," she said. And then, in a softer voice, "What do you want me to tell the girls?"

"Tell them the truth. Tell them their mom was in a car accident. Tell them she has the best doctors and nurses and is in the best hospital for head traumas in Michigan. Tell them she's sleeping, and that I'll bring them to see her when she's better."

Slowly, she opened the heavy door. "When should I tell them you'll be home?"

He closed his eyes. "I don't know, Jackie. The surgeon

said we should know more after forty-eight hours. Will
you stay with them tonight?''

"You know I will." She propped the door open with
her foot. "Don't let them forget about Maggie's broken
arm." Casting one last look over her shoulder, she left
the room in the ICU.

The door closed slowly. Alone with the monotonous
racket of the machines that were keeping his beloved
Maggie alive, Spence thought there was something reas-
suring in Jackie's bossiness. Maybe in a hundred years,
he would figure out what it was.

He pulled a chair closer to the bed. The vigil had
begun.

"Jackie? What's going on? I've been trying to call for
two hours."

"Spence." Jackie squeezed the telephone with all her
might. "Your phone hasn't stopped ringing. How is
she?"

"Not much has changed. Her temperature started to
creep up a little. Turns out her bed doubles as a cooling
device. They have a contraption for everything. They're
keeping her cold."

"I hope she can't feel that. You know how Maggie
hates to be cold."

Shivering, Jackie realized that she was standing in
front of the open refrigerator in Maggie's kitchen. After
making room for yet another casserole dish, she closed
the door and said, "Word is out. Food is pouring in.
You're going to need a bigger refrigerator. Has the
doctor been in to see her?"

"Yes. He said about the same thing, almost word for
word that he said before. It's going to take time. Are
Grace and Allie in bed?"

His voice sounded deep, tired. There were no blips

or beeps in the background. Jackie wondered where he'd gone to make the call. "I tucked them both in an hour ago. Want me to get them up?"

"No. No. How are they?"

"They both cried when I told them. But then I took them with me to feed Tango, talk to Treva, and lock up the store. After that, I kept them busy helping me wrap up the food and answer your phone and door."

She'd made Maggie's and Spence's bed, cleaned up the crumbs from their breakfasts, dumped their cold coffee, reset every electric clock in the house. Grace and Allie had followed after her, quieter than Jackie had ever seen them.

"Grace wants to come up and wait with you, Spence."

There was silence on his end of the line.

"Spence?"

"I don't want her to see Maggie like this."

Jackie didn't know if that was a good idea, or not. Maggie would know what to do. God, how many times had she wondered if she was doing the right thing today? How many times had she wished Maggie were here to ask?

"Grace has a field trip tomorrow," Jackie said. "That'll help the time pass for her."

Spence and Jackie were both quiet, trying to figure out what to say to fill the silence, trying not to allow any negative thoughts to slip past the barriers they'd erected in their minds. Jackie eyed the cheese platter and dessert tray on the counter in front of her. "You wouldn't believe all the people who've offered to help."

"I'm not surprised. Maggie's the princess of Grand Haven. Everyone loves her."

The two people who loved her the most stood forty miles apart, clutching the telephone like a lifeline. Spence was in the hospital cafeteria, Jackie in his house in Grand Haven. Both were scared beyond belief, but refused to so much as whisper it out loud.

"What kind of help?" Spence asked.

It took Jackie a few seconds to understand the question. Oh. "Yvonne and Gaylord Wilson want to fly some world-renowned neurologist in from Switzerland. I told them to talk to you about that before they booked his flight. And there's already enough food here to feed an army. We're all going to weigh three hundred pounds by the end of the week. Melissa Bradley has organized a continuous prayer service at the Episcopal Church for the next forty-eight hours. Hannah Lewis is organizing one at the First Church of God for the next forty-nine hours. Maggie always says those two could make paint drying into a competition, but I figure the prayers won't hurt, right?"

Jackie hadn't been able to pray, though. She'd tried, but couldn't seem to get past, "Dear God, please . . ."

Spence hadn't been able to get that far. Maggie had always been the one in charge of praying. "I'll have to remember to thank them after Maggie wakes up. Who else has called?"

"Let's see. Crystal Douglas said she'll drive the girls to and from school until further notice. And Abigail Porter called to . . ."

She talked on, her voice a quiet murmur, a gentle cadence that ebbed and flowed in the quiet of another woman's house.

Upstairs, ten-year-old Grace McKenzie sat cross-legged on her four-poster bed, her pen with the pink ink, her favorite color, poised over her journal. She'd heard the soft thud of footsteps on the stairs a few seconds ago. Catching a movement out of the corner of her eye, she looked up as her little sister crept into view. Hair tangled, the hem of her pajamas uneven because one sleeve had slipped almost all the way off her shoulder, Allison stopped in Grace's doorway.

"You're supposed to be in bed."

Allie pushed her hair out of her eyes. "Hear that?" she whispered.

Grace listened intently. All she heard was Aunt Jackie talking on the phone.

"I woke up. I thought I heard Mama downstairs."

"It's Aunt Jackie."

"I know." Allison's lips quivered. "I want Mama."

Grace wanted her mother, too. She needed her mother. She already missed her so much she couldn't stand it. And she was scared. People wouldn't be calling and bringing food over if it wasn't bad. She'd decided to write down everything that happened so when her mom woke up, she could read it to her. Grace stared at her last few words, but she couldn't remember what she'd been going to write. Why did Allie always have to interrupt?

"Is Mama gonna die, Grace?"

Grace jerked her head up and around. "Don't say that. Don't even think it." She pointed out the door. "Now go back to bed."

Allison's eyes were rimmed with tears as she backed from Grace's room. Turning quietly, she darted across the hall. Grace tried to write. In the next room, Allison sniffled.

Feeling sadder and worse now, Grace put the pen and paper down, climbed out of bed, and marched across the hall. Aunt Jackie's voice floated through the house. She really did sound like their mother.

Grace climbed onto Allie's bed, and traced the star pattern on her comforter. Allison watched her sister somberly, her eyes big in her ragamuffin face. "I wish Daddy would come home," the little girl whispered.

"Daddy's staying with Mom at the hospital. You know how he can fix anything?"

Allie nodded.

"Well, he'll stay there and make sure everybody does what they're supposed to so she gets better."

Allie hiccuped. "Think he's yelled at anybody yet?"

"Maybe."

The girls shared a smile, and both felt better.

"Wanna sleep in my room tonight?" Allison asked shyly.

Grace shook her head. "I have a bigger bed. You can sleep with me."

Allison hiccuped again. Scooting out from under the covers, she padded, more noisily this time, behind her older sister, then promptly climbed into the big double bed. She snuggled under the covers, wriggling this way and that. Comfortable at last, she whispered, "I love you, Gracie."

"I love you, too, Al. Now you've gotta be quiet, so I can think about what to write so it'll be ready when Mom comes home."

Grace concentrated, and wrote, and concentrated some more. The next time she looked, Allison was fast asleep.

Jackie cinched the belt of Maggie's robe around her waist and rummaged through the drawer for a hairbrush. Locating it, she gave her hair a good brushing in front of the mirror in the downstairs bathroom. She hadn't thought to bring any of her own things. A day that had started out normal in every way had taken such a sudden and sharp curve it was difficult to think, period.

Normally, Jackie slept in one of two long, satin nightgowns, one beige, one black. The cotton chemise she'd taken out of Maggie's drawer felt strange. They'd shared clothes all the time when they were growing up. As adults, Maggie wore pastels and sweaters with dainty collars, and Jackie wore the quirky clothes from her vintage clothing store downtown. She'd lost weight after she'd learned of David's affair, and Maggie's nightgown hung loose on her thin frame.

It made her feel small.

She was already scared, and sick with dread, and probably with hunger, too. But she hadn't been able to eat. Staring at her reflection, she knew exactly what Maggie would say. "You have to take care of yourself, Jacks. You need to be strong, until I am again."

Hungry or not, Jackie marched out to the kitchen where she heated a portion of chicken casserole Maggie's neighbor had brought over. Her stomach protested a little, but the food stayed put. She rinsed her plate and placed it in the dishwasher along with the dishes the girls had used earlier.

The phone had finally stopped ringing. Needing to keep busy, she went upstairs to check on Grace and Allie. She wasn't really surprised to find both girls curled up in Grace's bed. It was what she and Maggie would have done if they'd been the children in this situation.

Moving quietly around to the far side of the bed, Jackie pulled the sheet up around Allison's shoulders.

"She'll just kick it off again."

Jackie glanced at Grace, who was huddled under the covers on the other side of the bed. "I thought you were sleeping."

Grace yawned. Just then, Allison turned over, dragging all the covers with her. Grace sighed.

Jackie had a sudden flashback of Maggie laughing about how active her second daughter was, even before she was born. Jackie would have given anything to hear Maggie laugh like that again. Instantly, she amended the thought. It was going to be wonderful *when* she heard Maggie laugh like that again.

"Come on, short stuff," she said, hauling Allison into her arms. Staggering beneath the child's weight, she wondered when Allie had become all arms and legs. She tucked her younger niece into her own bed, turned off all lights except for the pale yellow night-light shaped like a star, then returned to Grace's room. Bringing the satin edge of the blanket up to Grace's chin, Jackie whispered, "You're a good big sister."

Grace was quiet for a moment. In a small voice, she said, "Allie asked me if Mom was going to die. I yelled at her for it."

"Your sister doesn't hold grudges."

There was another moment of silence, and then Grace whispered, "Is she, Aunt Jackie?"

Jackie lowered herself to the edge of Grace's bed. Smoothing a hand over Grace's silky hair, so much like her mother's, she said, "I saw your mom. She's very much alive, just like I said. But she's in a deep, deep sleep. The doctors want her brain to rest completely, so all her energy can go to healing. Your dad's going to stay with her for a few days, to make sure the doctors do everything right, and I'm going to stay here with you and Allison."

"I'm glad you're here, Aunt Jackie."

Tears burned the backs of Jackie's eyes. "Where else would I be?"

Jackie sat with Grace until the child drifted off to sleep. After that, she prowled the floors, wandering through her sister's home. She'd been here a thousand times. Half of those times, she'd watched the girls when Maggie and Spence went out. Then, she'd always known Maggie would come walking through the door any minute, any hour. It felt strange, knowing that wasn't going to happen tonight.

She tried watching television, tried leafing through a magazine. Finally, she gave up and went to bed. She stared at the ceiling in the spare room where she'd slept often these past five years. Lonely, her thoughts turned to David, who was probably sleeping with his massage therapist right now. Or not sleeping. The thought hurt.

She'd missed him these past six months, no matter how hard she tried not to. Lonely or not, she was almost relieved he wasn't here right now. He wouldn't have understood what she was going through. She knew that for a fact. He'd always been jealous of the bond she and Maggie shared. Which was crazy. Spence wasn't jealous.

In her head, she could hear the blip and hiss of the machines attached to Maggie, could picture in her mind the utter stillness on that beautiful, kind, bruised face. Jackie had heard of people who willed themselves well. Maggie couldn't do that from her medically induced comatose state. So Jackie would do it for her. Focusing on the moon outside the window, she concentrated all her energies on imagining her sister well.

It was a long time before her eyes finally closed.

Spence was tired, so tired. A nurse named Rebecca had brought him a blanket and a pillow. He didn't want to sleep, but he leaned back in the vinyl chair and closed his eyes for a few minutes.

The machines hummed and beeped. Beyond those sounds, he thought he heard someone call his name. Sometime later, someone was kissing his chin, his cheek, and finally his mouth.

"Maggie?"

Who else, silly?

He heard her, but he couldn't see her. "Maggie, where are you?"

Suddenly, she appeared. No, not appeared. She'd

been there all along, hadn't she? She was propped up on one elbow, smiling down at him, twirling her hair around one finger in that way she had. He didn't know where he'd gotten the idea that her hair was gone, but he felt himself starting to return her smile, enjoying waking this way.

He wasn't sure where they were. In their bed, perhaps? She leaned over him and kissed him, and it didn't matter where they were. She was with him, boldly covering him with the flat of her hand. He tried to move, to give her better access, and to touch her in return, but couldn't.

She whispered something in his ear. What? She wanted to have her way with him? Who was he to deny her?

"Close your eyes."

He did as she commanded, then waited.

"What now, Maggie?"

Silence.

Maggie? He rolled over, or tried to, but his knee bumped into something unmovable, and he couldn't complete the maneuver. He reached for her. Her side of the bed was empty. Panic started low in his belly, coiling tighter as he got up. He looked for her in the chair in the corner where she sometimes fell asleep reading. He checked in the bathroom, in the girls' rooms, on the stairs, in the kitchen. He was running, his heart beating hard, as he searched everywhere. He thought he heard her voice far away, but he couldn't find her, couldn't reach her.

Unnatural, discordant sounds intruded. Beep. Beep. Beep. Hum.

Spence opened his eyes, and saw her, his Maggie, unmoving and bruised, in a hospital bed that was cold to the touch, in a room filled with machines and wires and tubes.

He'd been dreaming.

Maggie hadn't been kissing him, twirling her hair, having her way with him. She was in a deep coma, in a place where he couldn't reach her.

The waves of panic rose as far as his chest before he was able to force them back down to a more manageable level. Maggie wasn't lost. She was right here.

He went to her bed and stood next to her, holding her hand. He didn't sleep any more that night.

Jackie and Spence were both present when Dr. Mohan made rounds the next morning. Jackie stared at the cast on her sister's arm while the doctor examined her. Next, he reviewed Maggie's chart carefully. Everything had been measured and monitored: the cc's of liquid that dripped through her IV, her heart rate, the tiniest fluctuation of her temperature. Replacing the chart to its hook on the back of her bed, Dr. Mohan finally said, "There is no change. We will give it another day or two. Give the brain time to rest, the swelling to go down. Give it time. In a couple of days, we will see if she responds to light, to voices, or to a pinprick. Hopefully, she will start to show signs of breathing on her own. In a couple more days, we will know more."

Spence didn't ask what would happen if she didn't respond to light or sound or touch in a few days, and neither did Jackie, but the strain showed on both their faces.

Time passed slowly. But it did pass. Maggie was carefully weaned from the drugs that had kept her in a coma. She'd been wheeled somewhere where her brain activity was charted. Dr. Mohan felt confident that the swelling was going down. Jackie noticed that he didn't offer any guarantees.

She waited with Spence part of each day while the girls were in school. She hated hospitals, the antiseptic smells, the cold metal racks and plastic tubes, even the squeak of the nurses' shoes on the floors. Mostly, she hated the fear. Hour after hour, they watched for some sign of waking, some movement, the flicker of Maggie's eyes, anything.

Monitors beeped. Machines hummed. She slept on.

Every day was the same. Every day, Jackie cried all the way back to Grand Haven.

Spence kept up the vigil, rarely eating, barely sleeping. He called and talked to the girls every night. He spoke with Jackie, too. She kept him apprised of what the girls were doing and all the people who wished them well. She still hadn't been able to reach her parents, who were spending a year as lay missionaries in Africa. Jackie mentioned friends and neighbors that brought food over, but it seemed that most people were running out of things to say.

At three o'clock in the afternoon on the fifth day after Maggie's accident, a brisk knock sounded on her hospital door. Spence looked up, so tired, it wasn't easy to focus. A tall, black woman with short hair didn't wait to be invited in.

"I hear you haven't left the hospital in five days." She sniffed the air. "Who needs smelling salts when we have you?"

Spence had showered at the hospital that very morning and was wearing the clean clothes Jackie had brought him—but damned if he didn't almost duck his head for a whiff of his armpit. The woman didn't even try to hide the fact that she knew it.

"Can I help you?" Spence asked, none too warmly.

The look in the woman's eyes softened, but her voice

remained clipped as she said, "I'm here to help *you*, Mr. McKenzie. Let's take a walk."

He looked back at Maggie. Before he could do more than shake his head once, the other woman said, "Do you hold your breath when you drive through a tunnel, too, Mr. McKenzie?"

"You don't understand."

She waved his protest away with one hand. "I understand that you've been thrown face first into a situation no one can prepare for. I understand that you aren't eating or sleeping, and you almost never leave your wife's room. Come. Let's take that walk. Your wife will be here when you get back. You'll see. By the way, my name's Odelia Jacobs. I'm a counselor here at Bentworth."

Spence accepted the handshake by rote, then looked at Maggie again. Her chest moved up and down in a rhythm made constant by a machine.

Odelia strode as far as the door, then waited, her expression clearly that of a woman who didn't take no for an answer.

Spence thought she had a lot of nerve. Running a hand through his hair, he followed. *"You're* a counselor?"

"Boggles the mind, doesn't it? Did you know that the average counselor in a place like this burns out in five years? I've been at it for fifteen. Wanna know my secret?"

"You're a bully?"

He thought she was trying not to smile. "I think you and I are going to get along just fine."

She turned a corner, and he asked, "Where are we going?"

"I decided it might be a good idea to meet the neighbors." She pointed to the first room they passed. "His name's Scott. He's fourteen. He had surgery to remove a brain tumor last month. The good news is, it wasn't cancer. His family's still waiting for more good news."

Spence caught a glimpse of a man reading the newspaper, next to a bed where a teenage boy lay hooked up to machines similar to Maggie's. "Think they'll get their good news?"

"I hope so." They passed another room. The middle-aged man in the bed waved at Odelia. "That's Karl. He was in a car accident like your wife. Woke up after two weeks, asking for a steak, medium rare." Odelia pointed to the next room. "That patient is going home to her family tomorrow. There's a man farther down the hall that's been here for three months."

Spence knew what Odelia was doing. She was trying to show him that no two cases were the same. "You think Maggie could be here for a while."

She made no reply. They'd reached the end of the corridor, and were turning back when he noticed a little girl, younger than Grace and older than Allison, with no hair, being helped into a wheelchair by a man who was probably her father.

"Her name's Annie. She fell off her bike. It was one of those bizarre things that happen, like tripping over your own two feet. Dr. Mohan was her surgeon, too. When she first woke up, she couldn't walk or talk. She's relearning to do both."

Just then, Annie giggled at something her father said. The joy on her face, and on her father's, made Spence ache. "My girls have been crying at night. They need me, but I'm . . ." Did he dare say it? He swallowed, and blurted, "I'm afraid to leave Maggie."

Just then, the doors leading to the ICU opened. And there stood Spence's older brother.

Frank McKenzie was an inch taller than Spence and thirty pounds heavier. He'd scrubbed his hands clean of all but the last traces of grease he got on a daily basis in his auto mechanic shop in the middle of the state. "Hey, Spence."

"Frank. How did you know I was here?"

The brothers stared at each other. Frank shrugged. "I guess somebody up here squeezed the information out of Jackie. I'm not sure exactly who started the ball rolling, but some rich woman with a foghorn for a voice called me this afternoon."

Odelia backed away. "I believe the backup reinforcements have arrived. I'll be seeing you, Mr. McKenzie."

Spence glanced at the tall, dark woman about to disappear around a corner. He could well imagine who had gotten the ball Frank had mentioned rolling. After that, it must have been Yvonne Wilson who made the call.

They started toward Maggie's room. "God, Frank."

"I know, buddy."

But he didn't. Nobody, except maybe Jackie, knew how deep Spence's fear cut, how complete his dread.

"I called Brian and Tim. They're on standby. Pattie can handle things at home for a few days. She wants to know what she can send. What do you need, Spence?"

They entered Maggie's hospital room.

What did Spence need? He needed Maggie to wake up, to get better. He needed to turn back time, to prevent the accident from ever happening. He needed some sleep. He needed one promising sign. His throat closed up, making it difficult to speak. "I need to go home to see the girls. I guess the one thing we don't need is food."

"I'll tell her. Go home, Spence. I'll take over here for tonight. Go see your kids. And get some sleep."

"Thanks, Frankie."

"You can thank me later. After I box your ears for not calling me right away."

Spence hadn't heard that expression since he and his brothers were kids. The words were comforting, somehow. Leaning over Maggie's bed, he kissed her goodbye. "I'm going home to check on Grace and Allie. Frank's going to stay with you, Maggie. I'll be back. I promise."

"I'll call you if there's any change. Tell the girls hello from me, okay?" Frank walked Spence as far as the door.

Spence didn't remember answering. He strode through a labyrinth of hallways, and finally outside, into the sunshine of a cool, late April afternoon. He looked back once, wondering if he could figure out which window was Maggie's. He would work that out later. He had a lot to work out later. Now, he was going home.

CHAPTER FIVE

"And see this?" Allie pointed with one finger, keeping her other hand tucked firmly in Spence's. "It's s'posed to be the lighthouse at the end of the pier, but I broke my red crayon, so I made it blue."

"That was quick thinking." Spence smiled affectionately, studying the artwork stuck to the refrigerator door. Maggie once said Allie was going to grow up to be the kind of person that would make a cake if she broke an egg. Their younger daughter had always been a talker. Tonight, she'd hardly come up for air. She hadn't let go of his hand since supper, and she'd asked dozens of questions about her mother, wanting to know what she looked like, what she was wearing, if Spence thought she was dreaming, and if so, what was she dreaming of?

Emotions had welled up in his throat, making it difficult to reply. "She's probably dreaming about you and Grace."

Seemingly satisfied with his answer, Allie had continued to lead him around the house, pointing out all her things as if he'd been gone a month instead of five days. To a six-year-old, it probably felt that long.

He was thirty-six, and it felt longer.

"Okay, short stuff," he said upon reaching the kitchen table where they'd started. "Time for bed. You too, Grace."

He hiked Allie to his back, and reached for Grace's hand. She took it for a moment, then fell back, following them up the stairs from a distance.

"Are you gonna listen to my prayers, Daddy?" Allie asked.

It was something he and Maggie always did together. "Try and stop me."

Allison glided down to her knees beside her bed, folded her hands, and closed her eyes. "God bless Miss Johnson and Miss Bentley and Jessica and Ashland and Tyler and Billy and Amanda, even if she was a brat at recess. And God bless Aunt Jackie and Grace and Daddy and especially God bless Mama, so she'll wake up and come home soon. Amen." She started to get up. "Oh." She bowed her head again and, in a pose that was neither kneeling nor standing, said, "And God bless Tango." She opened one eye. "Is it okay to bless cats, Daddy?"

Spence felt a grin coming on. "I don't see why not."

She slipped between the sheets and snuggled into her pillow. He tucked the blanket under her little chin, inhaling the scent of children's shampoo and freshly laundered sheets and little girl.

He turned out the lamp, leaving the star-shaped night light to glow in the semidarkness. Next, he made his way to Grace's room across the hall. She was sitting cross-legged on her bed, her flowered cotton nightgown tucked around her knees, her pink pen poised over the journal she'd gotten for her birthday. He noticed her pen didn't move.

"You'd better get some sleep, too, Grace."

She looked up at him and then back at her journal. "Aunt Jackie lets me write in my journal until nine."

He could hear Jackie moving about downstairs, pushing in chairs, and putting things away before she went back to her house in Spring Lake. "In that case, you have about two more minutes."

Grace looked up at him quickly. Just as quickly, she looked away.

Spence took a seat at the chair next to her desk. "Aunt Jackie said you've been writing in your journal every night."

Her answer was a very small nod.

"Allie was full of chatter tonight. What about you? What did you do at school today?"

"Not much."

That from a girl who loved everything about school. "What are you learning in social studies?"

Her shrug was as small as her nod had been.

"What about in English?"

Again with the nod. At least this time, she answered. "We wrote poems." She spoke to her lap. "Mrs. Green said mine made her cry."

Spence added Mrs. Green to his list of people he needed to call. "We're going to get through this, Grace. I promise." When her eyes remained downcast, he reached a finger to her chin, drawing her face up. Tired to the bone, he would have given anything, done anything, to take the worry out of her watery blue eyes right then. "I wouldn't lie to you."

Sighing, she placed the journal and pen on her nightstand and slipped beneath the covers. He turned out her lamp, adjusted the sheet the way Maggie usually did, and kissed her forehead the way he always did. The weight of the world on his shoulders, he started for the door. "Night, Lady Grace. I'll see you in the morning."

"Dad?"

Dad? He turned slowly. Five days ago, she'd called him Daddy.

"Don't turn out the light yet. I know what I want to write." She picked up her pen again and, in her loopy handwriting, wrote, *Dad and Aunt Jackie are going to make sure everything turns out all right*. She dotted her *i*'s with hearts, replaced the cap on her pink pen, then slid under the covers. "Now you can turn out the light. Night, Dad. I'm glad you're home."

"Me, too." It hurt to smile.

Jackie was drying dishes when he returned to the kitchen. He didn't recognize the casserole bowl in her hand. For the first time all week, he took a long, hard look at her. She was pale, almost gaunt, and her hair, naturally wavy, hung limp and lifeless around her narrow face.

"What is it?" she asked.

"You look like hell."

She continued drying the dish, seemingly unaffected. "The kettle should look in the mirror before he calls the pot black."

He surprised himself by laughing.

"That's what I like about you, Jacks. Even when you're down, you aren't beaten."

They shared the kind of smile they'd been sharing for years. In some small way, it made him feel better.

A stack of mail lay on the counter. He opened the top letter. It was from the insurance company. The van was totaled. He would have to see to getting another one. Allison had tucked a picture she'd drawn under the second envelope. After pulling it out, Spence studied the artwork. She'd drawn a succession of pictures of a girl searching everywhere for her bicycle helmet. The real Allison hadn't been able to find her bicycle helmet, either. Thankfully, Jackie had offered to take care of buying her a new one.

He didn't know how he would have handled everything by himself. He looked at his sister-in-law. She seemed so alone. "Have you had any luck reaching your parents?"

Jackie shook her head. "There isn't much more I can do until they call us."

It had been this way all her life. Every year or so when she and Maggie were growing up, the Army had given the colonel a new assignment. Adelle Fletcher took care of the details of moving, and Maggie and Jackie took care of each other.

They'd always been close sisters; they were also best friends. They'd lamented over braces and boys, cheered, consoled, joked, and understood. They'd been maid or matron of honor at each other's wedding; Jackie was godmother to Grace and Allie. She'd encouraged Maggie when she'd had trouble getting pregnant the second time, and Maggie had shared Jackie's disappointment month after month when she'd been trying for a baby, too. Maggie was the first person Jackie had told about David's affair.

Some brothers-in-law would have resented the relationship Maggie had with her only sister. Spence not only tolerated it and accepted it, he seemed to welcome it. How many times over the years had Jackie and Spence stood on the sidelines at a social function while Maggie graciously accepted recognition for achieving results for some cause or other she believed in? Perhaps some sisters would have been jealous of their sibling's spotlight. Jackie was content in the shadows. But it was more than that. Spence and Jackie were Maggie's biggest fans.

Maggie McKenzie was a shining star, and she didn't even know it. That was part of her charm. She was a people person. In comparison, Jackie didn't need many people. She needed Maggie, though. And so did Spence.

Although it would have been nice to be able to confide

in her parents, Jackie had grown accustomed to things the way they were. She and Spence would get through this together.

Poor Spence. If Jackie was sick with worry, he was suffering more. It showed. His shirt was wrinkled, his pants hung loose at his waist. The lower half of his face was darkened by a five o'clock shadow, his eyes red-rimmed, as if he hadn't slept in a week.

He'd always been an incredibly, ruggedly handsome man. Maggie wouldn't have cared if he hadn't been. She loved his innate goodness, his honor and integrity. They were the same qualities that made him a great brother-in-law.

He'd outlined his plans over supper. Tonight, Jackie would go back to her place for more of her things. Tomorrow, they were going to be more organized. Spence was making arrangements for work, for the girls, especially for Maggie. He wanted someone to stay with her around the clock so she wouldn't open her eyes to the face of a stranger, or worse, an empty room.

Hanging the damp towel over the handle on the oven door the way Maggie always did, Jackie said, "How did Grace and Allie seem to you?"

"Allie was clinging, Grace is quiet."

They were both having a hard time with this. They showed it in different ways. Jackie planned to help in any way she could. With that in mind, she pushed a stack of books toward Spence.

"What are these?"

"Reading material that deals with comas. There's a lot we don't know. I thought it would be good to learn all we could. One of the books is about real patients, real families, real miracles. I checked all these titles out at the library this afternoon."

"You could have gotten the same information off the Internet."

She pushed her hair out of her face. "I like books better. You can feel them, touch and smell them. They're more like friends."

Opening the top volume, he said, "You're as old-fashioned as the clothes you stock in your store, do you know that?"

She shrugged much the way Grace had earlier.

And he said, "I know the past year's been rough for you. Maggie's been worried sick about you ever since . . ."

"You can say it out loud, Spence. Ever since David decided to bang Boobette."

"I thought her name was bridgett."

"If the shoe fits." She could have said, "If the bra fits," but she was too tired for more crassness. Besides, secretly she feared that David had found more lacking in her than the average size of her breasts.

She hadn't crumbled, turned to dust, and blown away on the Lake Michigan breeze. She'd wanted to, though. She'd given up so many of her dreams these past months: her marriage, the prospect of becoming a mother. Sales at the store were down even more than last year. One of these days, she was going to have to make a decision about her work, her life. Right now, Maggie needed her. Spence and Grace and Allison needed her. It looked as if the nervous breakdown she'd earned was going to have to wait.

"Everywhere I go, people ask about you." Jackie walked around Maggie's hospital room, watering the plants and flowers that had been pouring in these past two weeks. "Only you could be in a deep sleep, and still be a people person."

The sounds of nature played from Jackie's CD player in the background. Mood music full of birdsong and

woodwind instruments and thunder and rain flowed
through the room. It reminded her of spring.

Spring was Maggie's favorite season. And she was missing it. She was missing so much. Jackie wouldn't allow
herself to dwell on that. Instead, she'd become Maggie's
eyes and ears, telling her about everything that was happening in the life they were all waiting for her to wake
up to.

The books from the library cited many accounts in
which coma patients responded to conversation. So she
talked, about Grace and Allie and Tango and Treva and
her two lovers, Raoul and Gardner. She talked, and
sometimes she waited, willing her sister to answer.

Maggie slept on.

Jackie would sigh, and eventually continue. "Robins
built a nest in your pine tree again. And a pair of song
sparrows claimed the grapevine wreath on your front
door as their new home. They're making a mess of the
porch floor, but the babies have hatched. Oh, Maggie,
they're precious, and I just don't have the heart to
disrupt them. Grace put a note on the railing, directing
company to the back entrance."

Jackie reached for Maggie's limp hand, and in a whisper husky with tears, she said, "You have to wake soon.
I'm doing my best with Grace and Allie, and I don't
want you to worry about them, because for now, I think
they're okay, but they need you."

The heart monitor blipped, and Maggie's respirator
filled and emptied her lungs. Her hand remained limp,
her eyes closed.

"Suzanne Burchmeijer is getting married. The nose
job worked." The newspaper crinkled as Jackie folded
it to a new page. "And John and Kathy Flannigan are
getting divorced. No great surprise there. Still, who

needs the *Inquirer* when we have the *Haven Gazette*, right, Mags?"

Jackie turned the page again. "Oh, you're missing all the fun. The highway commission wants to widen Lake Shore Avenue. It would take several hundred-year-old oaks and ruin at least three historic properties. The Historic Society is up in arms. Yvonne and Gaylord Wilson have hired the best crackerjack attorneys in the Midwest. It's all anyone's talking about these days."

That wasn't entirely true. People were still asking about Maggie, but with less enthusiasm and optimism. In fact, on two separate occasions, Jackie had overheard people talking about living wills, and wondering if Maggie and Spence still had one.

Jackie had pretended she hadn't heard. She hadn't told Spence what people were saying. It would only hurt him. Besides, it didn't matter that they had living wills. No matter what the gossips of Grand Haven said, Maggie was going to come out of her coma any day now.

It was just a matter of time.

"You'll never believe who showed up on your doorstep, Maggie." Jackie was taping the get-well cards that had arrived that morning to the wall next to the window. "I opened the door, and there stood Edgar Millerton, chewing morosely as ever on a dead cigar, a pan of brownies in his hands. Homemade. Can you believe that? None of us could eat them because they smelled like cigar ashes. We didn't have the heart to tell him, though."

Other than Edgar's contribution, and those of a few die-hard neighbors, food had stopped trickling in. The girls' last day of school was this week. The robins in Maggie's backyard had flown away. A few days ago Allie and Jackie had watched the mother and father sparrows coax their offspring from the nest they'd built in the wreath on the front porch. Now, they were gone, too.

They were entering the fifth week of Maggie's coma. Jackie, who'd always hated hospitals, adjusted a flexible tube and some wires. Which just went to show that it was amazing what a person could become accustomed to. Jackie sighed, her mind wandering.

Spence had been quiet lately, too. He made certain he was present each day when Dr. Mohan made rounds. Yesterday, Jackie had been here, too. They'd held their breath, waiting, wishing, wanting, hoping. Dr. Mohan shone a light in Maggie's eyes, poked her in the foot with a pin.

Jackie and Spence had flinched. Maggie hadn't reacted to anything, not voices, not light, not even pain. Seeing the disappointment in Spence's eyes, Jackie had wondered if he was having as much trouble as she was holding the doubts and worries at bay.

"I see you've been reading to Maggie again."

Jackie started. Discovering Odelia Jacobs standing at the foot of Maggie's bed, she held up the newspaper. "The society pages."

The counselor made a sound Jackie hadn't been able to replicate. It started near the back of her throat, half hum, half harumph, endearing and annoying at the same time. "That's a lot better than the sports page Spence was reading to her yesterday."

Stifling a yawn, Jackie stretched a kink from between her shoulder blades and slowly found her feet. "Maggie hates sports."

"I told Spence I'd stay in a coma, too."

Jackie smiled.

"How are you, Jacqueline?"

Not even Jackie's mother called her Jacqueline. "We're doing all right. Spence and the girls are—"

"I'm not asking how Spence and Grace and Allison

are." The sharp edges in Odelia's voice drew Jackie's gaze. Odelia's size nine shoes were planted firmly on the floor, her hands on her hips, eyes on Jackie. "I know how Spence is, the thick-headed mule. He's spent so much time here he knows the doctors and nurses on every shift on this floor by name. He even knows the names of their kids and pets. I'm the one who put the bandages on his elbows. I told him he was going to wear the skin raw from all the time he spends leaning on Maggie's bed. That man doesn't listen."

Jackie had been at his house last night when he'd arrived home. He'd told her how Odelia had marched into Maggie's room, slapped some salve and Band-Aids on his elbows, none too gently, sputtering all the while that only patients had a right to bleed in her hospital. He'd thanked her. In a huff, she'd told him to hold his thanks until after he saw how much the hospital charged him for those two little Band-Aids.

". . . and I saw the girls the other day when he brought them to see their mother. My goodness, if they aren't the spitting image of you and your sister." Odelia was still talking. It was obvious she wasn't accustomed to being ignored. "I want to know how you are."

The question had Jackie blinking back tears. "I'm a survivor."

"And?"

She glanced at Maggie. "It's been over a month. And the doctors don't know why she hasn't come out of the coma. Sometimes I run low on patience. And sometimes, I get . . . ticked."

"Is ticked the word you want to use?"

What difference did that make? Jackie held her tongue and studied the outspoken counselor. In her early forties, Odelia never wore the typical hospital scrubs. She didn't wear blazers or pumps, either. Today, her outfit was neon lime green. If her eyes weren't so stinking knowing, she would have been like a breath of fresh air. But her brown eyes were knowing, and Jackie found herself spouting, "Would you feel better if I said I'm pissed?"

"At Maggie?"

Jackie took a moment to marvel at the way counselors picked and chose the questions they answered. "Yes, at Maggie. Which is crazy because she can't help being in this coma. Then I get . . ."

Odelia's eyebrows rose a good inch.

Jackie noticed the wrinkles in Maggie's sheet. The physical therapist came to her room every day, massaging her muscles, keeping her joints limber. You'd think she could cover her up properly.

Smoothing the sheet like a fussy housewife, Jackie said, "Let's just say that after I finish throwing a little internal hissy fit at Maggie, I pitch one at myself."

Odelia watched Jackie closely. "You've made a start in putting a few honest emotions into honest words. Feel better?"

"Honestly? No."

Odelia continued to stare unblinkingly at Jackie. Jackie knew she could have asked her what was on her mind. She was pretty sure she already knew, but unlike Odelia, Jackie wasn't ready to hear honest emotions put into honest words.

Jackie reached up on tiptoe, running her feather duster around a display of vintage hats. Ever since Tango had adopted Fiona's as his new home, she'd had to put anything containing feathers up where he couldn't jump or climb. He'd eaten most of one of her best old hats before she'd come to an important realization.

Cats liked feathers.

It just so happened that Grace and Allie liked cats.

They loved Tango. Now that the girls were out of school for the summer, she brought them with her to the store every morning. Tango had been miffed at first. Surprisingly, it had been Grace, and not Allie, who had succeeded in coaxing the big old tabby out of hiding.

Jackie wanted to believe that was a good sign. Spence had been taking the girls to see Maggie once a week. They'd both hoped the visits would lure Grace out of the quietude that had surrounded her since Maggie's accident. Allie had cried the first time, but since then, she'd chatted to her mother the way she always had. Jackie couldn't tell what Grace was feeling; she rarely let on these days.

The girl had always liked her privacy. Lately, she'd become a recluse, holing up in her bedroom, reading, or writing in her journal. She'd taken to locking the bathroom door, too. Yesterday, she'd turned down an invitation to attend a swimming party at a friend's house.

Spence and Jackie were both worried. If Maggie didn't wake up soon, Jackie was going to suggest they take Grace to a counselor or child psychologist.

"Aunt Jackie, look at me." Allison's voice carried from the back room.

Jackie pushed through the swinging door and into the room where the girls were playing dress-up. Allison had chosen a grown-up's dress from the fifties. The skirt dragged on the floor; the waist hung to her knees.

"How do I look, Aunt Jackie?"

"You look beautiful. I do believe red is your color."

Allison giggled adorably. "Gracie did my hair."

Jackie turned to Grace, who was sitting on the floor, still wearing her own clothes. "Don't tell me. You couldn't try on any dresses because you can't move with that big tan, tabby traitor sprawled on top of you."

Even Grace smiled. Tango opened one eye, closing

it again in obvious rapture beneath the gentle hand stroking his broad back.

"Tango can sleep on the chair while you try on dresses, Grace."

Allie twirled like a ballerina. "Grace doesn't wanna play dress-up on accounta she has boobies."

Allie froze in mid-twirl. Grace's hand stilled on Tango's coat. And the room, all at once, was quiet.

Jackie eyed both girls. "They're called breasts, Allison." Next, she turned to Grace. She was ten and a half. Was she starting to mature? Was that why she locked the bathroom door and turned down a chance to go swimming? "Are you, Grace?"

"I don't want them! They're gross. I hate them."

They weren't even visible through Grace's thin denim jumper.

"That's a shame," Jackie said. "Because they're part of who you are, like your hair and your hands and your smile and your brains. Grace Renee McKenzie, you're growing up."

"You mean like a teenager?" She jumped up, disrupting Tango, who fell with a thud the few inches to the floor.

The three of them watched him saunter away indignantly, his tail straight in the air. When he disappeared under the rack of vintage skirts, Jackie said, "We need to go shopping. Allison, let's get you out of that dress."

"But who will look after the store?" Grace asked, more like her old self than she'd been in weeks.

Allie shimmied out of the dress in two shakes. "Put the closed sign in the window, silly," the six-year-old said, bending down to tie her shoe. "Nobody shops here much anyway."

Jackie looked around her store. It had plenty of clothes and accessories. It just happened to be sorely lacking in customers. Allison Rose McKenzie wasn't one to mince words.

Tango sat in the window next to the closed sign, watching them set off down the street. The sun felt warm on their hair, the birds chirping in the trees lining the street. If Jackie had taken a moment to ponder it, she would have realized that she hadn't stopped to wonder how Maggie would have handled the situation.

"Hi sweetheart." Spence touched a finger to Maggie's cheek. "It's ninety-eight degrees out there today. You should see Grand Haven. Tourists are everywhere."

Spence paced to the window. The sun was so hot the parking lot had smelled of asphalt. It was nearing the end of June—deep summer, his mother had always called it. How could time pass and stand still at the same time? He moved around the room, agitated. "You know Annie, that little girl I've been telling you about? The one who fell off her bike? She went home, Maggie."

Already another patient had taken her room; another family was taking up a vigil. He ran his hand through his hair, over his eyes, down his face. It seemed that most people out there ran around like ants. They went to work, picked up their kids, and were busy every minute of every day. Their biggest complaint was the weather or taxes or the price of gasoline. Although Spence had always appreciated what he'd had, he'd been like that to a degree. Everyone was. Until tragedy struck.

Spence reached for Maggie's hand again then gently squeezed it, willing her to squeeze his in return. "Maggie." Her name came out on an anguished whisper. He stared at her face the way he had a million times. Lately, he'd caught himself trying to memorize it. And it scared the bejesus out of him. He'd been like this for the past two days. Ever since Scott, the fourteen-year-old patient down the hall, had contracted pneumonia and died.

His room hadn't been empty long, either.

It could have been Maggie. Spence closed his eyes.

The phone rang. He jumped. Swore. Heart racing, he grabbed it up. "Yes, this is Spence . . . Who? . . . Oh, hello, Jessica . . . I guess it has been a while."

He hung up a few minutes later. Although he hadn't grasped the entire conversation, the gist of it was that Jessica Michaels, or Jessica Hendricks now that her divorce was final, was in Grand Rapids visiting someone, and thought he might want to have a cup of coffee with an old friend. It occurred to Spence that he'd never considered Jessica a friend. Today, company, any company, was welcome, so he'd agreed to meet her in the cafeteria at seven.

Jessica was waiting for him just inside the cafeteria entrance when he arrived at a few minutes before seven. "Hello, Spence." She smiled warmly at him. She'd always been pretty, in a female-on-the-prowl sort of way. "I took the liberty of getting your coffee. I hope decaf is okay. And I got coffee cups, not Styrofoam."

She led the way to a quiet corner. Spence followed, thinking it was a good thing the room wasn't crowded. She could have put some unsuspecting diner's arm out with that walk.

He took a seat opposite her, and tasted his coffee.

Stirring cream into hers, she said, "How's Maggie, Spence?"

"Her cuts have healed and her hair's growing back. It sticks up in inch-long tufts all around her head. Jackie says she looks like a punk rocker from the eighties."

"How are the girls?"

"Growing like weeds. Allison lost another tooth and

Jackie helped Grace choose her first training bra. Are they still called that?''

Jessica chuckled. "I don't know. I developed so quickly I bypassed them completely."

Spence's gaze strayed below Jessica's shoulders before he could stop it. Suddenly, it felt awkward to be talking about bras, training or otherwise, with someone other than Maggie or Jackie. To cover his discomfort, he talked about the book about shipwrecks on the Great Lakes that Jackie was reading to Maggie. "Friends and family have been staying with her. People have been great. Some still call every day. Thank goodness Jackie's handling that."

"How about you?" Jessica asked. "How are you handling this? What are you doing for you?"

"What do you mean?"

She took another sip of her coffee, then licked her lips in a way that could only be trouble. "You must be lonely."

"I don't see what that has—"

Setting her coffee down, she raised her brown eyes to his. "Maggie once told me you have a strong . . ." She glanced down, and kept her eyes downcast. "Let's just say this must be terribly difficult for you."

"Well, sure, but—"

"She's been asleep for a long time. I'm alone, too. I understand about needs." She finally looked at him again. "I know how much you love Maggie. I just want you to know I'm here if you need . . . anything, anything at all. It would be our little secret."

He lowered his cup to the table and pushed back his chair. "Maggie isn't dead."

"Isn't she? She once told me that you both have living wills."

"She's going to come out of this." He'd spoken

louder than he'd intended. "She has to, because I'll never want anyone else."

Jessica stood. Combing her fingers through her short, dark hair, she said, "Never is a long time, Spence. Give me a call sometime. My offer stands." Without another word, she left.

Spence fumed all the way back to Maggie's room. His youngest brother, Brian, was waiting for him when he returned.

"What?" Brian asked, taking one look at his brother. "They serving rotten pickles in the cafeteria?"

Spence took a shuddering breath. "No, but I could have had a piece of Jessica Hendrick's on a silver platter if I'd wanted some."

"You don't say."

Spence made a disparaging sound.

"What did you tell her?"

"What do you mean what did I tell her? I told her no."

The youngest of Spence's brothers, Brian's hair was a little lighter than the others, but he was just as tall, his chin just as square, his face just as compelling. "Is she ugly? Never mind. Who cares in the dark? Did she give you her number? Before you wring my neck, let me just say that not all McKenzies are as discriminating as you."

"I'm not discriminating. I'm married. And this isn't funny."

Maybe not, but the conversation had the desired effect on Spence. He was calmer, his mind clearer when he kissed Maggie goodbye. Still, he would have sold his soul to have her kiss him in return.

A neighbor's dog was barking when Spence pulled into his driveway. He caught a whiff of someone's barbecue while he waited for his garage door to go up. His home had always been his haven, but these days his steps were heavy when he walked through the door.

Jackie was coming in from the backyard when he came through from the garage. She took one look at him and said, "What's wrong? What's happened?" She glanced behind her, out the patio door where Grace and Allie were playing. Lowering her voice, she said, "Is it Maggie?"

And Spence knew that the thought still turned her stomach, and made her as ill as it made him. "Maggie's the same."

"Thank God. I mean . . ."

"I know what you mean."

He came to stand beside Jackie in the breeze blowing through the patio door. Allie was trying with all her might to push Grace on the old-fashioned rope swing in the backyard. Maggie loved that swing. She used to spend hours pushing the girls on it. Sometimes, the child in her couldn't be contained, and she'd taken a turn. And he would push her, and she would soar through the air, and laugh, so full of sunshine and life.

"Brian's sitting with Maggie tonight, isn't he?" Jackie asked.

"Until around midnight. The nurses on the night shift get a little hostile if visitors stay much past twelve." And since Maggie's care was in their hands, Spence tried not to anger them. He thought about all the people who'd pitched in these past weeks. And he thought about the woman who'd had something else in mind. "Jessica Michaels-Hendricks-whatever-the-hell-her-name-is-now stopped in before Brian got there."

"Jessica? I'm surprised. What did she want?"

"This and that. She mentioned our living wills."

"Is this the first time anyone's brought it up?" At his

nod, she said, "I've been hearing people talk about it for a month now. At first I ignored it."

"And now?"

"Yesterday I told Melissa Bradley to mind her f'ing business."

"Did you say f'ing?"

"Yes, I did. What is it with everybody and my chosen word usage? Forget it. Why don't you go say hi to your daughters? I was just coming in to get the camera. I want to show Maggie a picture of this when she wakes up."

Spence slid the screen door open and walked into his backyard, wondering how Jackie could have known that that was exactly what he'd needed to hear.

A few hours later, the house was quiet. Jackie and the girls had gone to bed. Spence had had a conference call with Tom Garvey about the project at Picketts Corners. After they'd ironed out the few remaining glitches, he'd paid bills, something Maggie had taken care of before her accident. Before everything had changed.

He'd checked on the girls, lingering in their doorways, reluctant to turn in. When he couldn't put it off any longer, he went to his and Maggie's room. He opened the safe, and read through the document outlining Maggie's wishes. He already knew what it said. They'd prepared their living wills together. The two notarized forms read nearly word for word.

They'd both stated that they didn't want their lives extended in the event of irreversible brain damage. In essence, they'd agreed, in writing, that the quality of life must be evaluated, and steps taken to ensure that they would be set free of a mind and body that didn't function in any way on their own.

Spence stared at Maggie's signature so long it blurred

before his eyes. He remembered when they'd had the documents drawn up. It was the same day they'd bought the safe. They'd made a pact. And then they'd made love.

He looked at their bed, wishing . . .

He dropped his face into his hands, crinkling the document more. It was getting harder and harder to know what to wish for. Raising his head, he dragged his free hand over his eyes, his cheeks, and jaw. Hands shaking, he put the document away. He was tired. That was all. He wasn't giving up hope. He was exhausted, and when he was exhausted, it was more difficult to hold the nagging doubts at bay.

No wonder he was tired. He'd arranged his schedule around everyone else's needs. Maggie, the girls, work, home, groceries, laundry, Maggie, the girls . . .

Although he usually slept at least part of every night, he hadn't dreamed since that first night after the accident. He woke up groggy and muddle-headed. It was better than waking up aroused and panicked, reaching for Maggie, and grasping only thin air.

He took his shower and fell into bed, reminding himself that things were the same today as they had been yesterday. Jackie was taking pictures to show Maggie when she awoke. One of these days she would wake up. And everything would be perfect, the way it used to be.

Spence?

"Maggie?"

The room was quiet. He could hear Maggie, but he couldn't seem to open his eyes. Maggie, where are you?

"I'm here, silly." She kissed him on his mouth. Now that she had his undivided attention, she moved down to his chin, and then his chest, laughing, playful.

He couldn't seem to get a hold of her, but she certainly knew her way around him. "Oh, Maggie, I've missed you."

"I know. But I'm here, right here." She covered him with her hand, moving along his body, touching him, heating him, loving him.

"I love you, Maggie."

Silence.

"Maggie?"

Nothing.

"Maggie, where are you? Maggie!"

He woke up in a panic, clutching her pillow, the sheet tangled around his ankles. Moonlight spilled through the window, illuminating the foot of the bed and half of the mattress. Maggie's side was empty, as it had been for more than two months.

He straightened the covers, adjusted his pillows, and lay down. He stared at the ceiling, and cursed Jessica Michaels until the sun came up.

"Look at our sand castle, Daddy!"

Spence lowered himself to his knees a few feet from the castle the girls were building. It looked as if it was going to have a moat and a tower.

The sun was hot overhead. Luckily Jackie had reminded him to pack the sunscreen before she'd left for her store. He'd slathered a generous portion on Grace's and Allison's pale skin half an hour ago. It was the middle of July. Grand Haven was a zoo. Spence tried to stay away from the lakeshore this time of year, preferring his quiet residential street and their own backyard. He simply hadn't been able to come up with any good reason not to take the girls to the beach when they'd asked. Yvonne and Gaylord Wilson were sitting with Maggie. And there was nothing more to do on the Picketts Corners project until the county gave its final approval, which they were expecting any day.

Lake Michigan was relatively calm today. It was eighty miles wide. He forgot how long. Maggie would have known.

He sat in the hot sand, listening to the girls discuss design plans for their castle, careful not to close his eyes for more than a minute, lest he fall asleep. He didn't enjoy sleeping anymore. Invariably, when he awoke, fear, stark and real, lodged like a brick in his chest.

"Daddy?" Allie called.

He turned his head, putting to memory the picture the girls made as they patted wet sand into a hill that was supposed to resemble a castle. Allison looked adorable in her purple suit with its ruffles. Grace's was pink, and slightly more grown-up-looking than her last swimsuit had been. They were growing up. Maggie was missing so much.

"Yes, short stuff?" he asked.

"What's a vegetable?"

Grace stopped working on her turret to look at her father. "You know what vegetables are, Al," she said. "Broccoli, green beans, and corn."

Allison's chin jutted out in a way that indicated that she wasn't stupid. "Amanda said Mama's a vegetable."

Grace looked to Spence, tears in her eyes.

Easy, Spence thought. Take it easy.

"Humans are not vegetables," he said. "Humans *eat* vegetables." He made a play for both girls. Giggling, they darted out of his reach. He caught them both, eventually, and hauled them with him to the water's edge. They waded and splashed and swam. By the time they gathered up their beach towels and pails, Grace and Allie seemed to have forgotten Allison's difficult question. Spence couldn't forget, and nothing could

chase away the dread that had taken up residence inside
him.

The dawn of a new day brought no relief from
Spence's dread or fear. Dr. Mohan had called earlier
and, in his slightly broken English, had requested a
meeting with Spence. Neither he nor Jackie had spoken
during the ride to Grand Rapids. Nothing they could
have said would have kept the fear and dread he was
fighting from eating a hole through his composure.

Now that they'd arrived, Spence was doing everything
in his power to manage his nerves, talking to Maggie
about the first house to be built in Picketts Corners.
Usually, Dr. Mohan was late making rounds. Today, he
and the nurse entered the room at nine o'clock sharp.
There was something unnerving about his promptness.
Even more unnerving, a second doctor followed them
inside, and quietly closed the door.

CHAPTER SIX

"Good morning." Dr. Mohan paused opposite Spence. A heavyset woman who had short graying hair and big glasses that gave her an owlish quality stopped next to him. "This is Dr. Maxine Abraham. She's a fellow neurologist on staff here at Bentworth."

"I've heard a lot about you two," the woman said kindly.

Spence nodded perfunctorily before turning his attention to Dr. Mohan once again. "Has something happened to cause Maggie to suddenly need two neurologists?"

"I'm here as a consulting physician only."

Spence looked deep into the woman's eyes. If that was meant to make him feel better, it didn't work.

"Shall we get started?" she asked.

Spence and Jackie stood back, giving the doctors and nurse room to perform their examination. It went exactly as every other examination had gone, except this time, Dr. Abraham watched Dr. Mohan's every move, carefully monitoring every test. Maggie's chart was carefully scrutinized, her vitals taken. The thin scar along the side of her face was examined, as was the arm that had been broken and was now healed. Dr. Mohan shone a light in her eyes, and poked her feet, hands, shoulders.

She remained motionless.

When they were finished, Dr. Mohan looked at his colleague. If the lift of his brows was a silent question, Dr. Abraham's small nod was her answer. Spence could have chewed glass. If they had something to say, he wished to hell they would say it.

Or did he? He clamped his mouth shut, hating what his hope had been reduced to.

Jackie finally broke the silence. "What's going on?"

Dr. Mohan said, "There is a room down the hall. Let us go there to talk."

Just in case that didn't give Spence a full-blown case of panic, the nurse rounded it out with a glance dripping with pity. A lesser man might have given in to the heaviness rooting his feet to the floor. Spence sucked it in and followed Jackie and the others from the room.

Odelia Jacobs was waiting for them inside the small conference room around the corner. Spence swore under his breath, his battle against impending doom getting uglier by the second.

"Hello, Spence, Jacqueline."

"Odelia," Jackie said, "why do I feel like I'm about to be offered a blindfold and a cigarette?"

Again, it was Dr. Mohan who spoke first. "We here at Bentworth work closely with the patient's family, counselors, physical therapists and nursing staff, and finally, the insurance provider. You and your sister-in-law's dedication to Maggie have been nothing short of exemplary. All of us here had hoped . . ."

Two and a half months ago, Spence would have kissed this doctor's feet, walked on burning coals if he'd asked, aided him in any way he could. At that moment, Spence wanted to hit him for using the past tense. And Spence hadn't hit anyone since he was a kid.

"You'd hoped for what?" Jackie asked.

The staff members exchanged subtle looks. "We'd hoped," Dr. Mohan said, "that your sister would show some small sign of improvement."

"We'd hoped," Dr. Abraham said, "that she would give some indication, no matter how minute, that she was coming out of the coma. We here at Bentworth have been waiting for a sign that she could hear us, or feel, or was in some small way aware of her surroundings."

"I was hoping," Odelia said, louder than the others, "that Maggie would wake up, jump out of bed, and dance around the room. I still am."

Spence's throat convulsed on a swallow. A lone tear squeezed out of Jackie's eye and trailed down her cheek.

"Unfortunately, that hasn't been the case." Dr. Mohan indicated that he wanted everyone to be seated.

Spence and Jackie sat down in adjacent chairs. Dr. Mohan opened a folder lying on the glass table. He handed Spence and Jackie a brochure outlining the hospital's policy and procedures for dealing with coma patients. Next, he handed them a copy of Spence's insurance provider's rider. Spence recognized the letter attached to it. He'd received an exact replica a few weeks ago.

Jackie skimmed hers. "Are you kicking Maggie out?"

"It isn't like that, Miss Fletcher."

"Why don't you tell me how it is then?" She glared, first at Dr. Abraham, and then at Dr. Mohan.

Odelia intervened. "The hospital must continually evaluate a patient's treatment and care. Spence's signature is on the statement outlining the hospital's intent. There's been no change in Maggie's condition. You know that, Jacqueline." She spoke calmly, with no lighting of her eyes, her expression one of grave seriousness.

Jackie clasped her hands together, the sourness in the pit of her stomach threatening to eat a hole through to the outside. "What do you want us to do, pull the plug?"

An ominous silence settled over the room. The two doctors exchanged glances, but Odelia's gaze remained fixed on Jackie. "We're suggesting nothing of the kind. That would be for you and Spence to decide."

Spence jerked to his feet like a wire that had been stretched so tight it finally sprang. "If the insurance company doesn't want to pay anymore, I'll refinance my house."

"I can sell my store."

"We'll get the money." Spence heard the desperation in his own voice. Everyone in the room had. Awkwardly, he cleared his throat. He didn't know what else to say.

Odelia rose to her feet, too. It occurred to him that she was wearing low-healed pumps and a navy blazer today. Serious clothes. Obviously, she'd dressed for the occasion.

"We're not suggesting you give up hope," she said quietly.

"There are other facilities, less expensive places than hospitals," Dr. Mohan said. The man was in his early forties. He was of average height, had olive skin and compassionate brown eyes. This didn't appear to be easy for him. "Places that offer extended care for people like Maggie."

People like Maggie.

People who weren't going to get well. That was what he meant.

Spence glanced at Jackie just as another tear trailed down her cheek. "What kind of places?" she asked.

Odelia handed her a box of tissues. While Jackie was

regaining her composure, the neurologists exchanged a few words then left the room. Spence paced to the windows lining the far wall. He could see down the hall from here. John Belligan was waiting outside his wife's room. She'd taken a turn for the worse yesterday. The day before she'd been fine, or at least as fine as a woman in a coma and on life support could be. Somehow, she'd picked up a virus. They were losing her, and there was nothing anyone could do. A couple doors down, Tyrone—Spence realized he'd never gotten the man's last name—was escorting a woman to the newest patient on the floor. Tyrone nodded as he walked past. Spence wondered if his shoes still squeaked.

Had it really been nine weeks since he'd been the one being escorted to his beloved Maggie? Out of the blue, another thought came, unbidden. Who would take Maggie's room?

"They can't kick her out," Jackie said quietly. "We'll sue."

Behind him, Odelia said, "On what grounds? Even if you had a case, which you don't, is that how you want to spend the next year or two or ten? In court? Is that what Maggie would want?"

The final question took the wind from Jackie's sails. She yanked several tissues from the box and blew her nose again.

"You're overwrought," Odelia said. "Overtired. You've both been taking care of everything and everyone except yourselves."

Jackie wanted to protest that she was fine, that this wasn't about her or Spence. But Odelia led them both to a large gilt-edged mirror hanging on the wall above an artificial plant. Standing back a pace, she said, "Take a good look at yourselves. What do you see?"

Jackie saw that they both had dark circles beneath their eyes. Spence needed a haircut. Jackie needed a lot more than that. Beige and brown had always been her favorite colors. Her slacks and top looked awful. She looked haggard, and so did Spence.

"You have to take care of yourselves. Grace and Allison need you. How are the girls, anyway? I haven't seen them up here lately."

Spence turned away from his reflection. He hated to tell Odelia that they didn't want to come to the hospital anymore. Allie had run out of things to say to a mother that didn't talk back. And Grace said she felt closer to her mom at home.

It was as if Odelia already knew. She smiled, albeit sadly. "You're both exhausted. The past nine weeks have taken a toll of you. I'm not asking you to make any immediate decisions. I'm only suggesting that you take a good look at yourselves, at what you have, and at what you need, at what Grace and Allison need, and what Maggie needs."

"When?" Spence asked.

It was uncanny, the way she knew what he was asking. "If there's still no improvement in Maggie's condition in the next few days, you'll have to make other arrangements shortly thereafter."

She handed Spence two brochures depicting facilities for people who needed care such as Maggie's. One was here in Grand Rapids, the other across the state in a suburb of Detroit.

"Well." She sounded tired. She strode to the door. Opening it, she said, "I'll leave you two alone. I'll be here much of the next few days if you have any questions, or need to talk. If I'm not here, have me paged."

Spence and Jackie watched Odelia leave the room, staring after her until she'd disappeared around a corner at the far end of the hall. Jackie took a shuddering breath. "What are we going to do?"

Spence shook his head.

And Jackie said, "I hate hospitals." Something told her she was going to hate those other facilities a lot more. "For the record, I think Odelia looks better in neon green."

Neither of them could muster up the energy to smile.

Spence pulled into a parking lot behind a large, stone-fronted building. "What do you think?"

Jackie swallowed. "It doesn't look as much like a funeral home as the last one." In essence, that's what it had been. The people inside just weren't dead yet, that's all.

Although today's trip had been a relatively straight shot along I-96, Jackie couldn't imagine Maggie living so far away. Everything about the ride had been dreary. The highway was gray, the storm clouds churning on the horizon nearly an identical shade, a befitting color on such an unpromising day.

Staring straight ahead, Spence finally said, "Let's get this over with."

They walked through a wrought-iron gate and into a clean, brightly lit lobby. A woman dressed in a flowered skirt and blouse that was probably meant to look cheerful smiled at them from the front desk. Spence and Jackie introduced themselves. And the woman said, "You're right on time."

She led them on the grand tour, chatting the place up. Spence and Jackie asked few questions. What they saw and heard was enough. The place was clean, functional, the staff friendly enough. But the patients, or residents, as their guide called them . . . It was enough to turn Spence's stomach.

One of the patients made grunting noises when they passed her room. Spence didn't dare look at Jackie.

"Yes, Loretta," the woman in the flowered skirt said loudly. "That's right. We have company."

Loretta continued to make noises, none of which sounded human.

All the residents were confined to beds. Most drooled. Some were utterly still, like Maggie. A few, like Loretta, were able to make guttural sounds. There was no reading material about, no newspapers. Televisions droned. As far as Spence could tell, nobody watched them.

Maggie would hate this place as much as the last one they'd looked at. Or would she even know?

He closed his eyes. The view didn't change when he opened them. He'd seen enough. Too much.

By unspoken agreement, Jackie and Spence rushed out the door and into the rain. Without a word, they got in the car and drove away. Half an hour into the ride, Jackie said, "God help us."

Hours later, Spence pulled into the driveway of the house he'd so lovingly surprised Maggie with five years ago, and sat there, staring. The rain had followed them west. It pattered on the top of the car. "How can I put her in a place like that? How?"

From the corner of his eye, he saw her wipe away her tears. Neither looked directly at the other. It was as if they knew that if they did, they would both crumble.

"Remember when the phone rang the other day?" she asked. "And it was Dr. Mohan asking us to come to the hospital?"

"I remember."

"Was your first thought that it was good news? Or bad?"

He took his time answering. "Bad." The word came out, jagged and painful.

"Mine, too." She blew her nose. "Stinking tears. You'd think they would run out."

And they both knew: *They would be shedding a lot more tears before this was over.*

Jackie and Spence weren't the only ones who were shedding tears. In fact, Jackie thought as she checked on Allison late that night, crying had been the most prevalent mode of expression all evening.

She and Spence hadn't mentioned what they had to do. Grace and Allison must have sensed that something was gravely wrong. Allie, who Maggie used to say didn't cry unless a bone was broken, cried when she stubbed her toe and spilled her milk and broke a new crayon. Grace had held up slightly better, right up until Spence had asked her if she wouldn't like to go to the hospital with him the next day to see her mom. She'd sobbed all the way up the stairs. It was the middle of summer. It should have been Grace and Allison's favorite time of the year.

Odelia had been right. The girls were basket cases. They needed their father home more and a normal routine. They needed the adults who were caring for them to be strong.

Jackie sank to the bed, tears coursing down her face. How could she be strong? Maggie had always been the strong one.

This was Maggie's house. Maggie had decorated this room in white and powder blue. Those were Maggie's girls down the hall. Maggie's husband in the den. She was Maggie's sister, Maggie's best friend.

Jackie stared at her reflection in the antique mirror on the bureau Maggie had found at an auction sale the summer before last. Without Maggie, who was she?

She barely recognized the woman staring back at her. Those dark circles under her eyes, the limp hair, and the clothes that hung loose on her body. She'd lost more than weight. She'd lost a part of herself. And she just didn't know how she was going to bear to lose Maggie, this time forever.

She lay down, fully clothed. All these weeks, she'd been trying to pray, but couldn't. Suddenly, words formed. "Dear, God," she whispered, tears squeezing out of her eyes, wetting her hair. "Give me strength."

Jackie opened her eyes. She lay there, listening to the sound of her heartbeat in her own ears. It was after midnight. She must have fallen asleep. She wondered what had awakened her.

As she sat up, and swung her feet over the side of the bed, an anguished cry reached her ears. Spence.

Poor Spence.

A short time later, she heard heavy footsteps go past her door. Spence had gone downstairs. She waited awhile, and then she padded down the stairs, too. She heard Maggie's voice, and it filled her with so much joy it bubbled up inside her. Realization dawned, and with it, a deep, welling sadness.

She paused in the doorway of the den where Spence was watching home videos. He was sitting on one end of the sofa, his feet propped on the coffee table, one hand on the remote.

She took a seat on the far cushion, and despite everything, she smiled at the sight of Maggie on the television screen. Spence glanced at Jackie, and then away. He looked ravaged, his eyes little more than dark holes in deep sockets. He knew what he had to do. They both knew. Tomorrow, they had to take Maggie's living will to the hospital. They had to show it to Odelia, who would then take it before the board or whatever committee that ultimately made these kinds of decisions. And then, Maggie would be taken off life support. And her chest would stop rising and falling and her heart would stop beating and her body would die.

How could they do it? How could they not?

Jackie wished it were her.

There, on the television screen, Maggie laughed and talked, the sound musical, the words lyrical. She smiled her beautiful smile, her voice mellow. Oh, how they'd missed it these past nine, nearly ten weeks.

They were going to miss it forever.

Spence watched Maggie, putting her face, her smile and gestures and laughter, to memory. Tomorrow, he would take the first step in letting her go.

He'd already lost her. He just hadn't known. Or he hadn't accepted it. He'd kept a vigil, and he'd kept hope. It was time to face reality. He'd lost her that day in late April. And now, almost ten weeks later, he was going to lose her all over again. This time forever.

Forever without Maggie was an eternity he couldn't fathom.

Spence stared, dry-eyed, at the screen. He'd put in another tape. Jackie had drifted off to sleep. He didn't want to wake her. She needed her rest; they both did. They were going to need their strength to get through the next several days. He didn't know how he was going to get through the rest of his life.

He leaned his head back, watching the video. It was Grace's sixth birthday, shortly after they'd moved to this house. The girls were both so little. They'd changed so much.

Maggie was looking at the camera, Allison on her hip, seven little six-year-old girls giggling and playing in the background. "You're supposed to be taping the party," she said, her smile artful and serene.

"I was. The party's almost over." It was Spence's voice, laced with laughter.

Maggie's smile changed subtly. The light in her eyes deepened as she reached a finger to her hair, and twirled a long strand.

The screen went blank.

Spence remembered turning the camera off that day. He remembered how he and Maggie had held their desire to a slow simmer while the birthday party wound down and Grace's friends went home. Later, they'd hurried to put the girls in bed. And then, he and Maggie were alone in their room, in the house that was their haven, in each other's arms in their idyllic life.

A permanent sorrow seemed to weigh Spence down. He closed his eyes for a minute. Suddenly, he was back there, in that room with his beautiful wife. He could smell her shampoo, taste her kisses, feel her touch, and revel in touching her in return. Her skin was so supple, her breasts lush. Her hair was long. Which was confusing at first. Suddenly, his parents were at the door, battered luggage in their hands. That was confusing, too. But then they left, and he and Maggie were alone again, and the horrible, welling sadness inside him eased.

"I thought I'd lost you, Maggie. Sweet Maggie."

She sighed, and he could breathe again. He put his hand on her shoulder, and instead of thin air, he felt warm skin covered by soft fabric. He whispered her name. This time, she didn't disappear. She felt so real. Surely, she was real.

Was he sleeping?

No.

Maybe. He tried to wake, but couldn't. Nor could he let go. "Oh, Maggie, Maggie, Maggie . . ."

* * *

At first, Jackie didn't know where she was. She'd been falling through a sky so thick with fog she couldn't see, couldn't hear. She wanted to cry, but her sense of loss was beyond tears.

Gradually, she realized that she could see after all. The whiteness wasn't fog, but sadness. She'd heard once that depression was black. Sadness had a color, too. It was a milky white vapor that muffled every sound, obscured every sight, leaving her blind and shivering and alone. All alone.

Or was she?

A voice filtered through the whiteness, a whisper, and a plea. A hand, large and masculine, skimmed across her cold skin, warming her from shoulder to thigh. She tried to move toward the warmth, tried to see past the whiteness.

From far away, she heard a low, tortured sob. Not hers. Then whose?

She awoke in layers, and on every level, she became more and more aware that she wasn't completely alone. Someone else was lost with her in the milky white stillness. Someone else knew her anguish.

Someone was calling Maggie's name. Oh, Maggie.

A sob rose up in her throat, her grief so real she could taste it. For a moment, she felt as light as the vapors in her dream, and nearly as transparent. Any second now, she was going to disappear.

Groggy with sleep, paralyzed in a dreamlike state, she finally managed to open her eyes. It wasn't a dream that was paralyzing her after all. It was Spence, holding her, kissing her, calling Maggie's name. It was Spence, fully aroused.

Spence.

The milky whiteness lifted.

He opened his eyes, and went momentarily still. He looked as dazed as she was, and just as sad. "We've lost her, Jacks. We've lost Maggie."

The white fog was coming back, obliterating him, and her. "I know, Spence. I know."

"I wish it was me."

But it wasn't. He was alive, and so was Jackie. Neither of them was truly alone. As if needing proof, he raised a hand to her face. She covered it with her own. And it was as if everything they'd done to survive these past horrible weeks, all the hours they'd prayed, pleaded, worked, and organized to hold them, the girls, Maggie, together, were like the fog in Jackie's dream. Those days were gone, and they hadn't really been alone. They weren't alone now. Suddenly, it was as if they weren't floating at all. They were drowning, pulled under a cold, dark sea, gasping for air, grasping a lifeline. That lifeline was each other.

There was no thought of right or wrong, no thought of anything. They wrapped their arms around one another and held on for dear life.

The thinking set in the instant it was over.

Spence scrambled off the couch. His first thought was of Maggie. His second was guilt. A tidal wave of self-loathing and an even greater sadness followed. Good God, what had he done?

Jackie was already on her feet, straightening her clothes. Neither knew where to look.

"Spence, I . . ."

"Not you. Me. I didn't mean . . . I never . . ."

"I know. I didn't, wouldn't, ever, either . . ."

They'd both been out of their minds.

Jackie took a shuddering breath, trying to make sense

of it all. How could she? Nothing made sense, and hadn't in weeks.

The television screen was blue, the sky outside the window not quite pitch black. Her mind was still hazy. She looked at her watch. It was a little after four. She'd come downstairs shortly after one. She and Spence had watched home videos. They must have fallen asleep. But then they'd awakened.

Realization had dawned. Their hope was gone, and Maggie was gone with it. They'd clung to one another. And they'd . . .

It had been over as quickly as it had begun. But it had still happened. She closed her eyes. God. They'd been consumed with grief, a paltry excuse. What was it her father used to say? Excuses are the lifeboats of losers.

Spence stopped tucking in his shirt. "It . . . I . . . We . . ." He gave up trying to find the right words.

And Jackie said, "Neither of us intended . . . It didn't mean . . ." Tears swam in her eyes. Oh, for crying out loud, if she gave in to tears now, she'd never be able to stop. "Spence," she said. "If we've learned one thing from this tragedy and all the weeks that have followed, it's that we can't change what's done. What is, is."

"You're saying we should try to forget this ever happened."

Their gazes met, then shied away. Grief and despair tore at them. Maybe they could forget it, eventually. They still had to get through the next several days. And then they had to get through the rest of their lives without Maggie.

A tear trailed down Jackie's cheek. She started for the stairs. Suddenly, she didn't know if she should stay here. Not now. Not anymore. She glanced over her shoulder. Spence ran a hand through his hair, looking as wretched as she felt.

"It's almost morning," he said.

They were both silent as they thought about what they would do in a matter of hours. Jackie needed time to compose herself, time to think, away from Maggie's home, Maggie's husband, and Maggie's children. Finally, she said, "I'm going to get a few of my things and go back to my house."

She was halfway up the stairs when the phone rang. She froze. No one called this time of the morning. No one. Unless . . .

The phone rang again. For a moment, Spence couldn't move. He could see the caller ID from here. "It's Bentworth Memorial."

"Oh, God, Spence. No."

His hand shook as he reached for the phone and placed it to his ear. "What? Yes, this is Spence."

Jackie covered her quivering lips with both hands. She must have descended the stairs, because she found herself standing just inside the room.

"Yeah, Brian."

Jackie wondered what Brian was doing at the hospital this time of the morning. Spence had talked to him last night. He must have gone to tell Maggie goodbye.

"I'm here," Spence said.

"Is she . . ." Jackie choked on the question.

"You're with Maggie?" Spence asked. "Is she—" His vocal chords seized up. The phone shook in his hand. "Is she gone, Brian?"

All Jackie could do was wait, and whimper, and die a little inside . . .

CHAPTER SEVEN

"What did you say?" Spence asked. "Brian. Slow down. She moved her toe?"

Jackie rushed closer. "Who moved her toe? Maggie moved her toe?"

Spence nodded. He asked his brother more questions, listened intently to the answers. "All right, Brian. I'll be there as soon as I can." He hung up the phone.

Jackie stared at him, afraid she was trapped in another dream, and it would pop like a balloon and blow up in her face. "She's better, Spence, not worse?"

Spence's grin lit up the room. "She's better, Jacks. Maggie's coming out of the coma."

Jackie laughed. "Maggie's coming out of her coma."

Never had six little words sounded so lyrical. Basking in that initial moment of pure joy, nine weeks of worry and dread evaporated into thin air.

She and Spence started toward each other the way they had a hundred times before, only to stop suddenly, far apart. Spence gave an anxious cough. Both stepped back, awkward.

Jackie swallowed tightly, uncertain how to navigate

the wall of tension between them. "Maggie's coming out of her coma," she said again. Despite the fact that she'd had to clear her throat first, there was wonder in her voice. "What did Brian say? When did this happen? What was he doing there, anyway?"

Spence laughed, too. Rusty or not, it was the first honest-to-goodness laughter she'd heard out of him in months. He rubbed his eyes with both hands, then pushed his fingers straight up through his hair. He stood that way, holding on to his head, amazed and shaken and hopeful again. "Brian said he couldn't sleep, so he decided to pay Maggie a little visit. He always could talk to her, remember?"

Jackie remembered. Everyone could talk to Maggie. She always said she had one of those faces. Jackie believed it was more than that. Maggie had a presence that wrapped around a person like gentle arms and a warm smile. Jackie had missed it so much these past months.

"Anyway," Spence said, his hands falling to his sides. "Brian said he was having one hell of a one-sided conversation with her, and out of the blue, he decided to tickle her foot."

"He tickled her?" Jackie knew she sounded like a parrot, but she didn't care. "She hates that." And then, as an afterthought, she added, "Is he sure he wasn't imagining the movement?"

This time, Spence's laughter sounded less like a rusty engine trying to turn over and more like it used to. "He's sure. It happened more than once. The nurse saw it, too. Leave it to Maggie to handle all those pinpricks without flinching, then wiggle her toe when Brian tickled her."

Leave it to Maggie. "God, Spence, I wish I would have been there."

For a long moment, Spence looked at Jackie. He

wished the same thing, for more than one reason. He would have loved to witness that first movement. And if he'd been there, he wouldn't have been here, in this room . . .

He closed his eyes. When he opened them again, he saw that Jackie's fingers shook slightly as she pushed her hair out of her face. She started picking up things, as if she had to keep moving. He noticed she stayed on the far side of the room.

Spence remembered when Maggie had announced that the den was his space, his domain, the one masculine room in a house full of ribbons, flowers, and pastels. They'd picked out the big, leather furniture together. He liked the room with the plaid throw and pictures of tall ships, big tankers, and an antique map of the Great Lakes that hung on the wall. It turned out the girls weren't the least put off by the masculine furnishings. Their things had a way of filtering into the room no matter whose domain it was.

He was so lucky.

Until a few minutes ago, his life had seemed bleak, little more than an endless string of long, lonely months that led to a future he dreaded. Never had so many emotions assailed him at once. Fear, despair, grief, sadness, disbelief, sorrow. Guilt. One moment, he'd been beyond coping. One phone call had changed everything.

"Okay," Jackie said, forging ahead. "Maggie moved her toe. What did Brian do then?" She paused when she reached the television in the corner, her hands full of hair ribbons and stuffed animals, Allie's purple shirt and Grace's sunglasses and the book she'd been reading yesterday.

"He's Brian," Spence said. "What do you think he did then?"

"He tickled her again."

Their gazes met, and for a moment, it was the way it used to be. They both smiled. And then they started to laugh, loud and bawdy and maybe even a little hysterically.

"What's going on?" Grace called from the stairs. She stood on a middle step, squinting, looking regal and haughty even at this early hour.

Their laughter had awakened the girls. Well, Grace anyway. Allison sat at Grace's feet, still half-asleep.

Jackie said, "Your mom moved her toe."

Grace's eyes went round and her mouth dropped open. "You mean she's waking up?"

"Who's waking up?" Allison asked groggily, looking small in her baby-doll pajamas.

"Mom."

"Mama's waking up?" Allison sat up a little straighter.

"Your Uncle Brian tickled her foot," Jackie said. "And she wiggled her toe."

Suddenly both girls were scampering down the stairs, shrieking with excitement. "She wiggled her toe?" Allie asked, reaching for Grace and Jackie's hands.

Jackie nodded, and the three of them danced around one side of the room, Grace exclaiming, "She wiggled her toe. She wiggled her toe. I can't believe it. She wiggled her toe."

The moment they came to a stop, Allison ran over to her father. Hands on her hips, she looked up at him and said, "It took her long enough."

Spence swooped down and picked her up. "Yes it did, but that wasn't her fault."

Brian had said that Maggie's movements were stronger the second time he'd tickled her. He'd run to get a nurse. By the time he'd called Spence, Maggie had moved her foot three times. Spence had a feeling that if she could have, she would have kicked him. He danced Allison around a wing chair, picturing it.

On the other side of the room, Grace and Jackie danced, too. And he thought everything was going to be all right. Maggie was alive, and suddenly, the house felt alive again, too.

"Well?" Brian McKenzie sidestepped his two nieces, who were taking turns pushing each other in a wheelchair just outside their mother's hospital room. It was only ten o'clock, but already the entire floor was buzzing with the McKenzies' good news. Eyeing all the people crowded around Maggie's bed, Brian said, "What have we here?" He counted on his fingers. "The husband, the sister, three nurses, two orderlies, and a"—he paused long enough to read a name badge—"physical therapist. Where's the partridge in a pear tree?"

The orderlies and one of the nurses took the hint and left the room. Sidling closer to the bed, Brian said, "I touched your wife last night. And she responded. If you ever need pointers in the future, I'm your man."

Spence shook his head. Brian had always been cocky, a little outspoken and, at times, crass. He'd never been lacking in ego, either. Now, there would be no living with him.

"You aren't even going to try to put me in my place?" he asked.

"I owe you, big time."

"Sheee-it. As soon as this wears off, you'll put my balls in a sling if I ever so much as think about touching her again."

The remaining hospital personnel sputtered in disgust then left in a huff. Brian assumed the spot one of them had vacated. Under his breath, he said, "You can thank me for clearing the room later. Hey, Jackie. Some night, huh?"

Spence noticed that she kept her expression carefully

schooled and her eyes on Brian as she nodded. It had been some night, all right. The worst night of his life.

He never wanted to think about it again.

"What in the hell is keeping the doctor?" Brian ran a hand through his hair.

"Dr. Mohan was here, Brian."

Brian's double take was comical. "I went downstairs to get a lousy donut and cup of coffee, and I missed the doctor's visit? What did he say?"

Out in the hall, the girls started to bicker over whose turn it was to ride in the wheelchair. Watching to see how far the argument would go, Spence said, "Dr. Mohan deemed it nothing short of a miracle. Maggie's responding to stimuli, to light and sound and touch. She's waking up."

"I knew it," Brian said.

Spence had watched Dr. Mohan perform his examination, hopeful and terrified at the same time. What if Maggie's movement was a fluke?

It wasn't a fluke.

Maggie was showing every sign that she was coming out of the coma. Dr. Mohan couldn't explain it. The swelling had gone down weeks ago. And yet the coma had persisted. It was as if a switch had been flipped, and some huge, cosmic electrical current had jump-started Maggie's brain.

The bickering over the wheelchair was heating up out in the hall. The girls had kissed their mother, tickled a foot, and giggled when she moved it. Satisfied that she was indeed waking up, they'd soon grown bored. Already tired from being awakened so early, they were getting cranky, too. And really, a hospital was no place for children.

Brian must have thought so, too. He made noises about seeing what he could do about the skirmish then headed for the hall.

"Hey, Brian?"

Brian turned around a few paces from the door. "If you thank me again, I'll flatten your nose."

Growing up, the McKenzie brothers had demonstrated their affection for one another by pouncing around corners and wrestling on the floor like bear cubs. A lot of things like vases and lamps had gotten broken in the process, but noses weren't among them. After they were older, they'd resorted to headlocks and arm punching and telling off-color jokes. Then and there, Spence had a strong urge to hug Brian. Since Brian would have been more comfortable with a headlock, Spence squelched the impulse and said, "You're just looking for a reason to rearrange my face so you'll be the best looking."

"Assuming I'm not already."

Spence felt a grin coming on. "Think I could get you to do me another favor?"

"Name it."

"Would you take Grace and Allison home?"

A look of surprise crossed Brian's face. He glanced at Jackie, as if he'd expected Spence to automatically ask her. "Sure."

With a smile that put Spence in mind of their father, his youngest brother strolled on out the door. Within seconds he was hunkered down, talking to Grace and Allie.

Spence glanced at Jackie, and found her looking at him.

"I could have taken them back to Grand Haven, Spence."

"I know. I mean, I appreciate it." He let out a long, audible breath. "I appreciate everything, all your help with them. It was unfair of me to assume, all these weeks . . ."

Jackie knew that Spence was trying to shoulder all

the blame and guilt. It felt wrong to let him, but what could she say? Things were stilted between them. How could they not be, after . . . ?

"This entire situation has been crazy from the start," she said. "The accident, Maggie's coma, the waiting, the fear, the worry. Maybe those few minutes last night were the craziest of all. The world didn't end because of it."

"I know. It's just that . . ."

His voice trailed away. Spence McKenzie wasn't accustomed to making mistakes. The few times he had, he'd fixed them. He didn't know how to fix this.

She gazed lovingly at Maggie. She was getting better. That was all that mattered. It was going to take time; that was all. One day, everything was going to be the way it had always been.

It was evening, the sky outside the window in Maggie's hospital room already streaked with pink and lavender and gray. According to the radio, it was still hotter than blazes outside, but here in Maggie's room, the temperature was a steady seventy, a damn monotonous temperature as far as Spence was concerned.

His older brother, Frank, and his wife, Pattie, had been only too happy to keep the girls for the remainder of the week. Jackie had gone home a few hours ago to help them pack. He'd thought about what she'd said, and she was right. The world hadn't ended because they'd made a mistake, no matter how astronomical. Or if it had, it had started up again the moment Maggie had started to awaken. Her awakening was what he needed to concentrate on.

Dr. Mohan had returned shortly after everyone else had gone. Once again, Dr. Abraham had accompanied him. This time, it was with a smug feeling of satisfaction that Spence had watched them conduct their examination. Both doctors agreed that Maggie was indeed coming out of the coma.

There, he wanted to say, see? You should have kept the faith a little while longer. They all should have. He closed his eyes, hating himself, because he should have kept the faith most of all.

He called the girls to tell them good night. And then he waited, alone, as darkness crept through the room. Finally, he accepted a blanket from a night nurse he hadn't met. Leaving only a dim light on in the corner, he leaned back in a vinyl chair, within touching distance of the bed, as he had countless other nights.

Monitors blipped. The respirator that was still helping Maggie breathe hummed.

He closed his eyes.

Sometime later, a strange sound stirred him from a dreamless sleep. He opened his eyes, blinking, trying to place the irregular, unusual noise. For a moment, he didn't know where it was coming from or what it meant. He looked around, and saw uneven lines on the heart monitor.

He was on his feet and next to the bed before the blanket hit the floor. A nurse came running as he leaned over Maggie.

For the first time in more than nine weeks, he looked into his wife's eyes. He was filled with wonder and awe, for Maggie was looking back at him. Her eyes had always been a startling blue, as blue as the sky, he'd always said. Tonight, the pupils were dilated in the near darkness, so that only a narrow circle of blue surrounded them. He searched them for recognition, and had to clear his throat in order to speak. "Well, hello. Look who's awake."

Her eyes grew larger. She seemed to be trying to move. The monitor went wild. She was panicking.

"It's all right, Maggie. I'm here. Don't worry, I'm here."

The nurse started checking her vitals, reading monitor printouts, adjusting wires and tubes. "Keep talking to her," she whispered. "She's soothed by your voice."

Talk? he thought. There was so much he wanted to tell her, so many lonely days to make up for. He didn't know where to begin, but he began quietly. And as he talked, he touched her face, her cheek, her chin. The panic in her gaze abated, and the monitor quieted. Later, he wouldn't remember what he said; but he would never forget the way Maggie had stared deep into his eyes. She was there. He knew it as surely as he knew his own name.

Just when he was beginning to relax, her eyes closed, just slid shut like a steel door slamming to the ground. It was his turn to panic. "Maggie! Don't go. Wait."

"It's okay," the nurse said. "Look at the monitor. Her heart is strong."

Spence took a deep breath, let it all out, then unclenched his fingers one at a time from the fists he'd made at his sides. It was a good thing he wasn't hooked up to the monitor, because he was pretty sure someone had blown a hole through his left ventricle.

Three hours later, Maggie opened her eyes a second time. Spence was waiting for her. Sidling closer, he eased into a grin. "Hey, sleepy head. Remember me?"

The expression in her eyes went from disorientation, to affection. There was no question that she recognized him. Her lips quivered. And she smiled.

A sob lodged sideways in his throat. All the fear, all the dread, all the worry he'd been tamping down, blew like the cap on an overheated radiator.

He laid his head on her chest. "Oh, Maggie, Maggie. My Maggie. You're back."

The nurse tiptoed out of the room, tears in her own eyes.

Later that night, Dr. Mohan started the process of weaning Maggie from the respirator, explaining that, like the rest of her muscles, her lungs had to be strengthened again before she would be able to breathe completely on her own.

Less than two days after she'd first wiggled her toe, the respirator was removed. Spence and Jackie held their breath as they waited to see what she would do. Her chest rose and fell on its own. Jackie laughed. Spence grinned. Even the serious Dr. Mohan nodded approvingly.

Although she'd received physical therapy every day to keep her joints limber and her muscles from becoming atrophic, no one knew if she would be able to move or speak. The fact that she recognized Spence was a positive sign. Not even the pessimists who whispered about brain damage could dispute that fact.

Odelia was with them in Maggie's room later that day when Maggie awoke again. This time Jackie was standing the closest to her. "Hey, Mags," Jackie said.

There was an instant's softening around Maggie's eyes and mouth. Her lips moved. After agonizing minutes, she whispered, "What . . ."

Spence, Jackie, and Odelia crowded closer to the bed.

It seemed to require incredible concentration to hammer out another word. "H-h-ha-a-appened . . ."

Spence bent over her, his hand going to the side of her face. "You were in a car accident. But you're better now and everything's going to be all right."

Her eyes moved, looking from Spence to Jackie. "To
. . . you two. What happened . . . to you . . . two?"

Odelia made a clicking sound on the roof of her
mouth. She pushed her way in, until she was in Maggie's
line of vision. "I've been telling them they look like
death. They've been worried about you. Don't be too
hard on them. Not everyone's had the luxury of a nine-
week beauty sleep like you have. Hello. I'm Odelia
Jacobs. I've been looking forward to meeting you."

After interminable seconds, Maggie said, "Nine . . .
weeks?"

Odelia chuckled.

Spence grinned, too. Not only was Maggie awake, she
was talking. And she'd comprehended what Odelia had
said. No easy feat for someone who *hadn't* suffered a
severe head trauma let alone for someone who had.

"Grace?" Maggie said. She turned her head. Another
good sign. "And Allie?"

"They're fine, Maggie. They've missed you. We all
have." Spence squeezed her right hand. For the first
time in months, her fingers moved in his.

He remembered when Gaylord Wilson had called her
the princess of Grand Haven. Now, she was more like
Sleeping Beauty. He didn't need a fairy-tale ending. She
was coming back to him. If this was as much as he ever
got, it was enough. As long as she was in his life, able
to think and comprehend, speak and smile, he would
never ask for more.

CHAPTER EIGHT

Maggie leaned her head against the back of the chair and closed her eyes. Jackie was fixing her hair, or at least what was left of it.

She'd never worn her hair short in her life. She felt naked without it. People were always asking her how she was feeling. Not about her hair. About other things. She told them when she was hungry or tired or cold. Sometimes she felt shy. Most of the time she was scared. She didn't tell them either of those things, though. Her memories of her life were hazy around the edges, and yet she had a recurring image about how she used to be. And she hadn't been shy or scared. She wanted to get well. She got panicky when she couldn't do things. Whenever it got really bad, she tried to think about something good. Usually, she thought about Spence and Grace and Allie. Oh, and Jackie.

From the moment she'd been able to hold her eyes open for more than a few minutes, she'd pushed herself to improve. Within a few days she'd been sitting up and feeding herself broth and pudding and terrible-tasting Jell-O. She didn't know why the doctors and nurses were so excited about that, because it wasn't always pretty. Sometimes it was downright embarrassing. Everyone else seemed to think she was some kind of miracle. If she moved too fast, she got dizzy. The same held true if she tried to think too fast or if someone spoke too quickly. How could that be a miracle?

She'd been wheeled to a different room. She forgot when. The trip had exhausted her, and she'd slept for a long time after. This floor was a lot noisier than the ICU.

She wanted to go home.

"The girls," she said, trying to speak louder than the blow-dryer Jackie was using on her hair. "Grace and Allison . . . are coming to see me."

"They sure are."

Maggie heard Jackie turn off the hair dryer. Ah, the silence was blessed. She felt so warm, so relaxed. "When?" she whispered.

"Open your eyes, Maggie." That voice reminded her that someone else was in the room. A woman with curly brown hair was sitting in the corner. Whenever Maggie closed her eyes, the woman told her to open them.

Maggie tried, but it wasn't easy. Everything seemed so clear when her eyes were shut. She didn't get dizzy, and it was easier to identify sounds that way. Right now she could hear Jackie shaking a bottle of some sort of hair stuff. The woman sitting on a stool in the corner started scribbling something in her notebook; her pen scratched across the paper. Maggie tried to remember what the woman was doing here.

Observing. That's right.

"Open your eyes, Maggie," she called again.

Maggie forced her eyes open.

Donna Burns, that was the woman's name, said, "Your husband called half an hour ago. He and your daughters are on their way. Jackie already told you that, remember?''

Maggie looked up at her sister. Jackie's eyes were steady as she looked back at her.

That's right, she thought. Spence and the girls were on their way. Jackie had told her that more than once. She remembered. She'd just forgotten that she remembered.

Donna started writing in her notebook again. Jackie had said the therapist was an idiot. Maggie thought the therapist thought *she* was the idiot. It made her feel sad. She didn't want anyone to think she was an idiot.

She understood what people said, but couldn't always remember it later. At first, it had been hard to talk at all. It was getting better, but she still bobbled the words sometimes. It used to be so easy. She missed that. She missed the girls. She missed Spence, too. But he was coming. Jackie said he was coming. And Jackie never lied.

Maggie took a deep breath and tried to concentrate with her eyes open. She'd been in a coma for nine weeks. Nine weeks. She wasn't positive, but she thought that was a very long time. She didn't know how long she'd been awake. The days blended, hours blurring together. It was all so confusing.

"There," Jackie said quietly, stepping back. "All done. And a darn fine job if I do say so myself."

Maggie loved the way Jackie talked. Her voice was soft. Often there was laughter around the edges. She never got dizzy when Jackie talked. "How do . . . I look?"

Jackie blinked tears out of her eyes.

Maggie tried to smile. "That bad?"

"No, silly. I'm just so proud of you. And for your information, not many women could pull off that hairstyle. You look beautiful." She handed Maggie a mirror. "See for yourself."

Maggie concentrated on holding the mirror steady. Her hair was an inch and a half long. Jackie had tamed the tufts that had been sticking out in odd directions. Although not what Maggie would call pretty, it covered most of the scar on the left side of her head. It was much too short to cover the one snaking down the left side of her face in front of her ear. Carefully, she brought her hand to the edge of her cheek. Her fingers shook as she traced the red line.

"It'll fade," Jackie said. "If you want to, we can ask Abigail Porter for the name of her plastic surgeon."

"It doesn't . . . matter." She placed a fingertip to her earlobe. "Where are my . . . earrings?"

"I'll bring them, Mags. The next time I come." Jackie felt weepy. That sister of hers had always had her head on straight when it came to vanity. Scarred or not, Maggie looked beautiful. It wasn't her hair or her skin or the sky blue dressing gown Jackie had brought from Maggie's closet that very morning. It was her inner strength that made her truly lovely.

Good old Donna scribbled something in her notebook. It was all Jackie could do to keep from turning on the woman and yelling, "Now what?"

"Hey, beautiful."

Jackie and Maggie looked up at Spence, who had paused in the doorway, his eyes on Maggie. Jackie couldn't help smiling. He was a lot happier these days. Maggie was, too. Why didn't Donna write that?

He strolled on into the room. Jackie stepped back discreetly while he kissed Maggie's cheek. Maggie smiled, seeming to glow now that Spence was here. "Where are . . . Grace and Allison?"

"Pattie's helping them choose a gift for you down in the gift shop. It's going to be a surprise."

"Who's Pattie, Maggie?" the therapist asked.

Spence straightened. "She's my—"

Donna cut him off. "I'd like Maggie to answer the question, Mr. McKenzie. In fact, why don't you and your sister-in-law wait for the girls out in the hall."

Jackie really hated it when people pretended something was a question when it was really an order. She cast the therapist a long look that let her know it, then turned her attention to Spence. She knew he wanted to argue. She didn't blame him. Donna's bedside manner needed work. But Jackie didn't want to upset Maggie just before the girls arrived, so she motioned to him and spoke to her sister. "We'll be right outside in the hall, Mags."

"But . . ." Maggie said.

"Do you know who Pattie is, Maggie?" Donna repeated loudly.

Out in the hall, Spence paced. "That woman is the kind of woman men hate."

Jackie snorted. "She's the kind of woman everybody hates." She held up the fingers on her right hand and, in an exaggerated, nasally voice, said, "How many fingers am I holding up? As if Maggie was three years old." She spun around, paced to the wall and back again. "And what's with the loud voice? Maggie was in a coma. She's not deaf. What's your full name, Maggie? How old are you, Maggie? Where do you live, Maggie? Do you have children, Maggie?" Jackie stuck her hands on her hips and shook her head. "How does she stand it? If I were her, I'd flip the nanny goat off and say, 'Hey, Donna. How many fingers am I holding up now?' "

Spence chuckled. "Nanny goat?"

Jackie paused, thoughtful. The expression harked back to her formative years when she would have gotten her mouth washed out with soap if she'd used anything harsher. Jackie knew the taste of soap well. She smiled, albeit grudgingly, thanks to Donna. At least things were better between her and Spence. Not the way they had always been, maybe, but less strained than they'd been several days ago.

Spence looked less haggard, but no more rested. His navy chinos were clean, the white shirt slightly wrinkled, the sleeves rolled up haphazardly. His skin was naturally olive toned. Normally, he got darker in the summer. This hadn't been a normal year.

As if by unspoken agreement, neither mentioned what had happened, and never would again. They'd fallen into a routine of sorts, dividing their time between the hospital and the girls, and their respective jobs. These days Spence called on his brothers to help more, too. That left Jackie with more time to spend at her store. Now that Maggie was on the road to recovery, Jackie was going to have to take a hard look at her ledgers and balance sheets.

Just then, Allie came bounding down the hall. Grace followed more slowly, a foil gift bag in her hand. Spence's sister-in-law waved from the double doors at the end of the hall.

"Where's your Aunt Pattie going?" Spence asked, meeting the girls halfway.

"To have a cup of coffee," Allison said importantly. "On account'a only the 'mmediate family can get in to see Mama." She spied her mother. "Mama!" She shook off her father's hand and darted into Maggie's room. "You are up!"

By the time Spence, Grace, and Jackie had entered the room, Allison was climbing onto her mother's lap, seemingly unconcerned that Maggie wasn't strong enough to help her. "Your hair looks like my doll's. Remember? The one I cut with my school scissors?"

Maggie lifted her hand to Allie's flyaway golden hair. "I look that good . . . do I?"

"I think you look pretty." All eyes turned to Grace, who hung back shyly near the door.

"Thank you, Grace." Maggie smiled. "Come here."

Grace came forward slowly, contemplatively.

"How are you?" her mother asked.

"Okay."

"Just . . . okay?"

Allison squirmed on Maggie's lap. "Gracie wears bras now."

The room, all at once, was quiet. Everyone seemed to be waiting for Maggie to say something. Finally, Jackie broke the silence. "Allison Rose McKenzie."

"What?"

"We don't talk about underwear in public."

"This isn't public. It's Mama's hospital room."

All this conversation and activity was making Maggie dizzy. Donna was writing, fast and furious, in her notebook. Maggie knew something was going on, but she couldn't quite grasp what. Fixing her gaze on her younger daughter, she said, "Where are your teeth?"

Allison beamed. "They fell out when I was eating a dill pickle. Daddy says nobody loses two teeth at once, but I did. The tooth fairy brought me a dollar for each."

Maggie knew she should know what that was, but the meaning escaped her. Although her thoughts were jumbled, she had a sudden flashback of days gone by when her hair had been shoulder length, her voice lilting. She could see herself talking and laughing and reading to the girls. She remembered holding her babies, and later, fixing their hair, tying their shoes, buttoning their sweaters. She'd gone to college. She couldn't remember what she'd studied. Jackie had told her. What had she said?

"Mama, are you sleeping?"

"No, Allison. I'm just . . . resting my eyes." She forced them open.

"We brought you a present." Grace held a pretty little bag toward her.

"Why don't . . . you open it . . . for me . . ."

Grace drew some tissue paper from the bag. And Allison reached inside, drawing out a little crystal on a string. "Aunt Pattie called this a . . . What did she call it, Gracie?"

"A prism. If you hang it in the window, you have a rainbow every time the sun shines."

Maggie nodded. "It's beautiful. You're both so big. I've missed . . . so much."

"It's okay, Mom," Grace said. "I wrote in my journal every night since your accident. I'll bring it next time."

Maggie didn't remember any accident. Spence said it was the middle of July. The last she knew, it had been April. She was so confused.

Grace had moved backward, her arm going around Spence's waist. It occurred to Maggie that her older daughter was hanging back. There was something strange about that. She didn't know what. Allison was talking to Jackie. And talking and talking. Maggie felt as if she were floating, far away.

She could hear the activity going on all around her. She felt Allison climb off her lap, heard her say, "Mama, are you sleeping?"

Spence answered. "Mama's tired."

She smiled when her daughters kissed her goodbye. Then, Donna was telling Spence she wanted to talk to him. And Spence was kissing her goodbye, too. And then, everything in the room was quiet.

History. That was it. She'd studied history in college.

"Maggie?"

Oh. Jackie was still here.

"Do you want me to call a nurse to help you get back in bed?"

"In a minute." Sitting in that chair, unable to walk, too tired to move, too weak to hold her eyes open, Maggie realized just how long nine weeks was. It was

long enough for Allison to lose two teeth and for Grace
to no longer be a little girl. Nine weeks was a long time
to be asleep. How was she ever going to catch up?

"Jackie?"

"Yes, sis?"

"What's the . . . tooth fairy?"

"Do you have any questions, Mr. McKenzie?"

Spence's gaze was direct as he looked around the
glass table at the four assorted hospital personnel wearing white coats and the one woman wearing orange and
magenta. He had a boatload of questions, but he shook
his head.

"Then you heard and understand everything we've
said."

Spence gave a curt nod.

Papers were shuffled, eyeglasses adjusted. It was clear
they expected him to bow to the wisdom of their knowledge and experience. Spence wasn't in a frame of mind
to do any more bowing.

"I heard what you said. Now do me the same courtesy,
and hear what I say."

Five sets of eyes showed surprise.

"Maggie wants to go home."

"She isn't ready to go home," Donna said.

Donna's insistence was getting on Spence's nerves.
The only indication he gave that he was irritated was
the dark, layered look he gave her. He didn't like her.
She'd ambushed him with her little request to talk to
him. He'd entered a room expecting to have a few
words with her, only to discover several other hospital
personnel present.

It was one against five. Or maybe two against four, if
Odelia was on his side. Either way, it wasn't going to be
a fair fight. Why not? Couldn't they see that Maggie was

breathing on her own, eating, drinking, talking? All the tubes were gone, the wires disconnected. He'd been a hairsbreadth from losing her. Now, every moment he spent with her was a gift. She wanted to come home. And he was going to give her what she wanted, dammit.

"I gave Maggie my word."

"Then you'll have to talk to her again," Donna insisted.

"I can take care of her."

"She needs to go into rehab so she can relearn to take care of herself," a man with a goatee and glasses said.

Spence didn't back down. "She's my wife."

"Is that how you want her back?" the psychologist asked levelly.

Spence felt the first pin pricks of uncertainty. "What do you mean?"

"Do you want Maggie home as your wife? Or as a child?"

"What kind of question is that?"

"An important one."

It wasn't easy to hold the psychologist's gaze. "Maggie's made incredible progress."

"Yes, she has, Mr. McKenzie." Great, Donna was talking again. "But she doesn't understand a lot of what goes on around her. Her sister thinks Maggie's being humble. I don't think Jackie knows how humble Maggie is. Just this morning she—"

Spence cut Donna off. "Maggie understands a great deal. Earlier, I told her that her parents finally called. Know what she said? How's the colonel like Africa? She remembers more every day."

"Yes, she does."

Spence focused on the hairs growing on Donna's chin. She wasn't an attractive woman. Neither was his Aunt Edna. He would have given his aunt a kidney if she needed one. For all he cared, Donna could take a flying leap off a short pier.

"She remembers how she was," she said. "But she isn't there yet. It's in my report. Your wife can feel her legs, but she can't walk. You were the first person she saw when she opened her eyes. She's fixated on you, and is dependent on you. It's very common in coma patients. Right now she's very much like a child. Your older daughter saw it."

A slap wouldn't have stung more.

"I know you want what's best for Maggie." Odelia, at least, seemed to be on Spence's side. He looked at her, but he didn't relax his guard.

"She needs the help of professionals." The psychologist made it sound so cut and dry.

After a long moment of silence, during which Spence fought for self-control, he said, "You call the therapy she's been getting helpful? How many fingers am I holding up? What color is the sun? How many days in the week? She isn't an imbecile."

"No one said she was. She does, however, have to be reminded to keep her eyes open," Donna said.

"She's weak and tired."

"Brain damage is often accompanied by weakness, Mr. McKenzie."

The entire room seemed to take a collective gasp. Spence pushed his chair back very, very slowly. The blood rushing through his head was so loud he wondered if anyone else heard. He could feel the anger glittering in his eyes as he slowly stood, could hear it in his voice as he said, "Who's in charge of Maggie's case?"

The lab coat in the middle said, "We work as a team here, but I suppose I am."

"Then suppose you write this down in big black letters. Donna here isn't to go near my wife again. Is that understood?"

"Mr. McKenzie—"

"Is that understood?"

"Brain damage isn't a dirty word," Donna said in her defense. "I didn't mean to imply . . ."

He continued looking at her supervisor, his decision made.

Donna looked around. When it became clear that her peers weren't going to come to her rescue, she clamped her mouth shut, then left the room without saying a word.

No one seemed to know what to say, how to proceed. Spence figured that if any of them hadn't known what they were dealing with before, they knew now.

Odelia broke the ensuing silence. "Would the rest of you excuse Mr. McKenzie and me, please?"

The remaining three professionals rose quietly and followed the course Donna had taken from the room. Once the door had been firmly closed, Odelia turned to him. "You know," she said huffily, "people like you are the reason someone coined the phrase 'It's the quiet ones ya gotta watch.' "

"I'm just looking out for Maggie's best interests."

"No, you're not."

He jerked around.

"You're emotionally involved. Shoot, Spence, you can't see the forest for the trees."

Spence had always hated that saying. He especially hated hearing it now. He didn't speak in riddles, and he didn't appreciate others doing it, either.

"Donna's right." Odelia held up her bony, dark hand. "It rankles, believe me. Off the record, I can't stand the woman, either. But Maggie's not ready to go home."

"She's only been awake for a week. She's doing damned good under the circumstances."

"That's wonderful. It doesn't mean she's ready to go

home." She silenced him again with a wave of her hand. "Hear me out. It isn't only what she relearns that's important. It's how she relearns it. There are certain steps the brain takes in the process of learning. What Maggie is exposed to and what is expected of her in the next few weeks will have a lasting and profound effect on what she regains and what she doesn't."

Spence stared at Odelia. Above the orange and magenta stripes in her garish shirt, her lips were set firmly, attitude written all over her face. One eyebrow was cocked, daring him to make something of it. But her eyes themselves held concern. That concern was his undoing.

"If it were your husband, or your sister, or your daughter, would you—"

"I'd have her butt in the rehab hospital by nightfall." She rattled off the names of two facilities. One was there in Grand Rapids, and another, smaller center was located in Muskegon.

Spence sank into a chair.

"Don't let the term 'brain damage' scare you. Maggie's problems aren't as severe as a lot of people's. No one can wake up from a nine-week coma without some adverse side effects. I believe, with the right treatment, most of Maggie's can be overcome."

The knife in the pit of Spence's stomach stopped turning, but the pain didn't go away.

"That sigh sounded as if it came from the vicinity of your knees."

His hand went to the knot at the back of his neck. "Which rehab center is better?"

"Both have excellent staffs. St. Ann's is closer to your home. She could start out as a resident, then continue therapy on an outpatient basis."

Reality sank in. Maggie wasn't going to get well overnight. He rose slowly, and started toward the door.

"Good luck, Spence. I'm going to miss you around here."

"No, you aren't."

"Fine. Have it your way. Why on earth would I miss a thick-skulled, bull-headed mule like yourself, anyway?"

If he could have, he would have smiled.

The others were standing in a group in the hall when Spence opened the door and walked through. Odelia and the speech therapist watched him go. "Think it's possible to love somebody too much?" the younger woman asked.

"Hard telling," Odelia said quietly. "One thing's for sure. He's going to try to coddle her, catch her before she can fall. Make a note in her chart. Whoever is in charge of her case over at St. Ann's is going to have his work cut out for him when it comes to dealing with Spence McKenzie."

"Your room is nice, Maggie. It's yellow. Your favorite color."

Maggie didn't reply. She wouldn't even look at him.

"St. Ann's. Remember when we thought about naming Allie that? Not the saint part. Just Ann?" He eased to the edge of her bed.

She turned the other way, presenting him with her version of the cold shoulder. Her arms were crossed, her mouth set, her eyes downcast but open. She was sulking. She was mad at him. That was it in a nutshell.

He'd gone back on his word.

What choice did he have? Couldn't she see that he didn't want to leave her here? The truth was, Odelia had been right. Maggie would never be content to be less than she'd been. In order to achieve that, she needed physical therapy, occupational therapy, speech therapy.

He was doing the right thing.

He felt like something he'd stepped in.

The lights flickered, the signal that it was time for all visitors to leave. "I have to go, Maggie." He would have felt better if he could have stayed with her, the way he had at the hospital. That wasn't allowed here. "I'll call you tomorrow. And I'll be back after lunch."

He leaned closer to kiss her.

For the first time in her life, Maggie averted her face. Spence didn't know what else to say. He got up quietly and started toward the door. He looked back when he reached it. "Good night, Maggie."

She made no reply.

He left quietly, his steps heavy, his shoulders stooped.

Maggie's gaze darted around the room as soon as Spence's footsteps faded down the hall. It made her dizzy. She moved suddenly, panicking. She tried to get up. Her legs wouldn't work. The muscles spasmed. "Spence, wait!"

It was too late. He couldn't hear. He was already gone.

He was going home without her.

She looked around her at the yellow walls and the yellow ruffled curtains and the yellow bedspread. She hadn't known yellow was her favorite color. Tears stung her eyes. She wouldn't give in to them.

Voices sounded out in the hall as strangers called goodbye to other strangers. She was afraid. Of the dark. Of those voices. Of sounds she didn't recognize and things she should know but didn't.

She turned onto her side, curling away from the view through her door. She imagined the girls at home, and pictured them playing in the backyard. Allison would be swinging high on the swing, Grace pushing her with one hand, a book opened in the other. Inside would be cooler, the rooms shadowy and inviting. Soon it would be bedtime. She wondered if Spence would get home in time to tuck them in.

She wanted to do that. Yearning rose up inside her like an ache. She missed them, her girls, her house, and her yard. Her life. She wanted to go home.

Why had Spence left her here?

A hot tear ran down her face. She swiped it away. She was being a baby. She never used to cry so easily. She wouldn't cry now, either.

A sound in the hall made her jump. What if there was a fire? What if there were bad people here? She was too weak to defend herself. What if . . .

What if Spence didn't come back?

She told herself not to think about those things. Spence would come back. She tried to think about happy things. She took a deep breath. And shuddered. She was tired. So tired. "Good night, Spence," she whispered into her pillow. "Good night Gracie, and Allie."

A second tear squeezed out of the corner of her eye. Try as she might, she couldn't hold back the rest. Lost and alone, she lay, motionless in the strange bed in the strange room in the strange facility. And wept.

"It says here you've been lethargic. Weepy. Not yourself at all." Ivan Decker studied his newest patient. Margaret McKenzie didn't even shrug.

She was sitting up straight in her wheelchair in the main physical therapy room. Her skin was pale and, except for the red scar, flawless. The few times he'd seen her eyes, they'd been the color of the sky on a blustery day. Her hair was light blond, her brows and lashes slightly darker. She possessed an ethereal, Virgin Mary sort of beauty. Right now, she was pissed. Her husband had insisted that his wife have the best therapist on staff at St. Ann's. Ivan had been handed the case.

He'd met the husband yesterday. Spencer McKenzie was a tall, dark-haired man who looked like he'd been pulled through a knothole backward. He'd squared off opposite Ivan, his eyes steady and assessing. "They call you the kid."

It hadn't been a question, so Ivan didn't answer.

"They also told me you're the best therapist at St. Ann's. That true?"

"I have a high success rate."

Spence McKenzie had nodded. Finally, he extended his hand. He had a strong grip, a steady gaze. With a nod, he'd left quietly.

Ivan got the feeling that the other man had learned as much about Ivan during the brief exchange as Ivan had about him. Spencer McKenzie didn't care about looks or age any more than Ivan did. It almost made Ivan feel mature. He was twenty-seven. Christ, if he wasn't careful, one of these days he was going to grow up.

He'd spent the last fifteen minutes rereading Maggie McKenzie's chart. She'd sustained a closed head injury as the result of a car accident and had been in a coma for more than nine weeks. They'd been about to pull the plug. And then, voilà. She woke up. In a matter of days, she'd been breathing on her own and feeding herself and talking. Pretty impressive, all things considered.

He held out his hand, practically shoving it under her nose where she couldn't ignore it. "I'm Ivan Decker, your physical therapist." At least she looked at him, even if she didn't shake his hand. "What do you like to be called?"

She cast an arched look at the file he'd just been studying. As far as actions went, hers was extremely telling.

"Okay," he said. "I already know your friends and

family call you Maggie. Fine, Maggie. What do you want to do today?''

Even though, according to her chart, sudden eye movements made her dizzy, she made a careful perusal of the room where a handful of other therapists and their patients were participating in various types of physical therapy. Finally, she said, ''I want to go home.''

''Big deal.'' Her eyes showed her surprise. At least he had her attention. ''I want to play professional hockey.'' He pointed to his feet. ''Do these look like hockey skates to you?''

She glanced at his size twelve Nikes and then back at his face. Under her breath, she muttered, ''Ivan the Terrible.''

It was his turn to be surprised. ''I've been called a lot worse. Young punk, arrogant jerk, selfish, egotistical, good for nothing. After that, the names stop being nice.''

He couldn't be certain she caught the humor, wry though it might be, but she was no dummy. She raised her chin defiantly, as if she didn't care what he thought.

''You want to go home? I want you to go home, too. First, we both have work to do.'' He put a tennis ball into her hand. ''Here's the deal. I need to know what muscles are strong and which ones aren't so I know what we have to work on. Go ahead. Toss the ball.''

The ball rolled out of her hand and bounced feebly to the floor next to her wheelchair. He glanced at the ball, then quietly turned to go.

''Wait! You can't leave me here.''

The panic in her voice stopped him in his tracks. Ivan knew damn well that how he reacted to it and what he did in the next minute or two was going to decide whether he failed this patient or helped her.

He faced her, hands on his hips, his feet firmly planted. ''I figured you wanted to sit there and feel sorry for yourself for another week or two. Me, I got things to do." He drew a folded sky-boarding magazine from his back pocket, then plucked the ball from the floor and put it back in her hand. "Let me know when you're ready to get to work."

He'd taken two steps when the tennis ball plopped to the floor a couple of feet ahead of him. The toss had been too weak to get much bounce, but it was still a lot more than he'd expected. He scooped the ball off the floor again.

His patient was looking at him, as haughty as a half-starved alley cat, and just as untrusting. "Were you aiming at anything in particular?"

She swallowed. Her chin quivered and her lips shook as she said, "Your head." That said, she held out her hand expectantly, palm side up.

Ivan reached her in three long strides. "You think I'm dumb enough to give you the ball at this close range?"

She moved her hand again in silent demand.

He lowered himself stiffly to his haunches. He was accustomed to being the cocky one. Balancing on the balls of his feet, he looked at her, one eyebrow arched recklessly. "Go easy on me, okay?"

He placed the ball in her hand, then used the parallel bars to propel himself backward. The ball missed its target a second time. Still it had been close enough for him to catch. He scoffed. "You'll never be a relief pitcher at this rate."

"I hate . . . baseball."

He wasn't fond of the sport himself. It was too tame. There was almost never any blood involved. He'd always told people he'd become a physical therapist because it was as grueling as hockey. After only six years, he'd been thinking about giving it up. As he placed the ball in Maggie McKenzie's hand, curling her fingers around it, he was glad he'd waited.

She squeezed the ball while her hand was still in his. It was as if he could feel her will to get stronger. "Stand back," she said.

"You're awfully bossy."

The ball bounced feebly off his forehead from three feet away. She didn't laugh. She didn't apologize, either.

Ivan reached for the ball again. He had work to do. In the meantime, he and Maggie McKenzie were going to get along just fine.

CHAPTER NINE

"Do you . . . have the time?" Maggie looked over her shoulder at the nurse pushing her wheelchair. A week ago she probably wouldn't have known what to make of the way the nurse, a middle-aged, matronly woman named Camille, shook her head discreetly at the perky young occupational therapist they passed in the hall. Today, it reminded Maggie that she'd learned—make that relearned—to tell time, one of many skills she'd regained since coming to St. Ann's.

Some things still confused her, and at times, she forgot what she remembered. That made perfect sense to her but apparently not to everyone else. She studied her watch. "It's five, ten . . . fifteen minutes to four. We have to hurry!"

Camille lifted her hand to within an inch of the button that would open the double doors that led to the main physical therapy room. "You sure you don't want to take a leisurely stroll around the grounds?"

"Only if you want . . . to explain why we're late . . . to Ivan."

Camille feigned a shudder. "And face his wrath?" She

punched the button, and the automatic doors opened. They entered the large physical therapy room where Maggie had spent much of her waking hours these past three weeks.

Ivan appeared via another door, meeting them halfway. Camille stepped aside. Relinquishing her position behind Maggie's chair, she leaned over slightly, and with a wink, she said, "If this was any other place, I'd tell you to break a leg."

Although it took a few seconds, Maggie smiled in understanding. She was so much better. Everyone said so. It had been a grueling three weeks, mentally, physically, emotionally. Evidently the time frame itself was something of a miracle in itself, although three weeks seemed like a long time to her. She'd received daily muscle massages that were at times painful. The exercises were worse. Painful or not, she stretched, rolled, pushed, pulled, lifted, pressed. Again. And again and again.

Her progress had been remarkable. She could tell just by looking around every day that not everyone at St. Ann's was that lucky.

Her right side was weaker than her left. She was right-handed, so her handwriting was atrocious. Still, her finger dexterity was improving, and her mind was sharper. She could read, but she didn't always comprehend every word. Humor no longer escaped her. Neither did sarcasm. She supposed she had Ivan to thank for that.

As soon as he positioned the wheelchair in front of the parallel bars, Maggie set the brake. Her hands were sweaty. She smoothed them down her knit skirt then turned them over to study the calluses that were forming where her blisters had been. She'd taken extra care with her appearance, donning the skirt and top Jackie had brought that very morning. She'd even applied mascara, although it had taken both hands to apply it, and even then she'd had to wash away a few smudges. Camille had said that Maggie's concern for her appearance was a sure sign that she was improving. Signs were okay, but Maggie was going to show Spence and the girls. She had it all planned.

She almost asked Ivan for the time. At the last second, she remembered to check her own watch. It was twelve minutes before four. "Hurry," she said. "I want to be standing . . . when they arrive." She wrapped her hands around the bars, getting a feel for the wooden rails.

"Hold on." With a slight grimace, Ivan dropped down to his knees in front of her. "Let's do some stretches first. Unless you want a repeat of that charley horse you had yesterday."

"Did you find out . . . why it's called that?"

Ivan moved her skirt aside and started massaging her right calf. The muscles were tight. The massage probably hurt. Rather than complain, she asked questions. Asking questions was her MO.

He didn't know what she'd been like before, but she was damned inquisitive now. Hell, everyone had experienced the pain and stiffness that resulted from muscle strain of the quadriceps. Did anyone else ever wonder why the muscle spasm was called a charley horse?

He'd looked it up yesterday. While he was at it, he'd looked up Ivan the Terrible. It seemed the first czar of Russia had been cruel and crafty. Not a bad likeness, all things considered, although Ivan had never been cruel anyplace other than on the ice.

"The term 'charley horse' was derived from the British," he said, moving to her left calf. "Charley is slang for fool. So I guess a charley horse is a pain that happens to people who are too foolish to stretch out before they overdo."

"Do you think I'm . . . foolish?"

He never knew what she was going to ask. It kept him on his toes. He continued kneading the muscles in her lower leg, considering his answer. Foolish? "A royal pain in the butt sometimes, but not foolish."

An expression of satisfaction spread across her face. "I'm ready . . . Help me up."

"You are one bossy woman."

"Now you sound . . . like Jackie."

Ivan didn't bother replying. Usually, he nailed the group dynamics in families after a few encounters. He'd known this one for three weeks, and he hadn't figured them out. Maggie's sister's name slipped into her conversations almost as much as the husband's and children's did. Jackie visited almost every day. Sometimes she brought the girls to St. Ann's. Sometimes Spence did. To hear Maggie talk, they were all one big happy family.

Jackie Fletcher looked a lot like her sister, only her hair was a little darker and a lot longer. On anyone else, the clothes she wore would have looked eccentric. Long and fluid and gracefully subdued, they suited Jackie. Maggie had said her sister was coming out of a bad marriage. That might have explained the shadows in her eyes. She razzed Maggie, but it was quite obvious that she would do anything her sister needed.

He pulled Maggie's chair a little closer, then reset the brake. Twisting around, he made certain nothing was in her way.

"Camille said you were wearing . . . your new shirt."

Ivan wasn't surprised she'd noticed. The shirt probably cost all of five bucks and wouldn't survive its first washing. It fit him like a glove, molding to his chest and shoulders. The staff had presented it to him at lunch. IVAN was spelled out across the front, THE TERRIBLE across the back. Somehow, Maggie's nickname for him had caught on. He'd probably never live it down.

Maggie took her feet from the footrests on the wheel-chair and reached for the bars. He'd never known a patient who pushed herself harder. Except maybe himself.

She'd been able to support her own weight for only two days, and yet she insisted she was ready for this. Ivan believed she was. Still, she was his patient, which meant he was in charge of her care. And he didn't want her to get overly tired. "Hold on. What if Spence is late?"

"He won't be late."

The husband was another enigma. He was obviously completely committed to his wife. Attentive to a fault where Maggie was concerned, he was demanding of the staff. He wanted, make that mandated, that he be apprised of every step, every detail and facet of Maggie's treatment, care, and progress. And yet he was always courteous, and didn't ask anything of anyone that was out of line. He came across as a decent, honorable guy. Ivan usually liked decent, honorable people.

"Okay," he said. "Steady as she goes."

With the help of the arm Ivan wrapped around her waist, Maggie rose to her feet. The muscles in her arms trembled, her knuckles turned white, but her feet stayed underneath her. Three weeks of work, three weeks of sweat and pain and tears, of pushing herself, of learning to crawl and roll and lift and pull, of working muscles that had to be reprogrammed, melted away beneath her feet. She was doing it. She was standing. Laughter bubbled up inside her, spilling over.

She didn't know what made her look up. Once she had, she never wanted to look away. The four people she loved most in the world stood near the door.

Every time she saw her daughters, she was in awe of their utter perfection. They were beautiful in their blue jean skirts and tennis shoes. Surely there were no smarter girls in the world. And they were hers and Spence's.

Balancing shakily, Maggie smiled. "I knew you'd . . . be early."

Allison clapped. Grace smiled. Jackie stood slightly behind the others, smiling, too. Maggie's gaze was inexplicably drawn to Spence. He'd always been attractive, but the summer had chiseled away at his features. He was leaner, his cheekbones more defined, his eyes a vivid blue she could see all the way from here. She knew how she looked. Her skirt hung loose on her thin frame, her hair was in tumbled disarray, her eyes huge in her pale, narrow face. She looked like a waif, and yet the way he looked at her made her feel beautiful, just as it always had.

"What do you think? No, wait. Don't . . . answer yet." She bit her lower lip, so rapt was her concentration as she took a tentative step. Slowly but surely, she took another. And another.

"Mom! You're walking."

She didn't nod until she had reached the end of the bars. "I wanted . . . to surprise you."

Spence was glad he didn't have to try to talk around the lump that had formed in his throat. In some far corner of his mind, he was aware that Jackie had taken Grace and Allie's hands and was easing them closer. He couldn't take his eyes off Maggie. She stood, unbelievably frail, undeniably proud. He wouldn't have been more in awe if she'd just walked on the moon.

He swallowed with difficulty, moving separate from the others, propelled forward by something unspoken and powerful. Stopping directly in front of her, he reached a hand to her face, taking the touch he needed. "You're amazing."

"I'm still a little shaky . . . on the turns."

"You're amazing."

Maggie smiled, humble and glowing at the same time. "Ivan says that . . . as soon as I master walking with a walker . . . I can come home."

Spence was vaguely aware that her therapist was hovering nearby, but his remaining senses were filled with Maggie. He was so proud of her, so incredibly lucky. His hands went automatically to her waist, drawing her closer. "I can hardly wait."

Continuing to grip the bars, she leaned into him. "Oh, Spence, what did I ever do to deserve you?"

He squeezed his eyes shut and wrapped his arms around her, hugging her tight. When he opened his eyes, he saw Jackie turn away, the pain on her face mirroring his.

Ivan turned a page in his extreme sports magazine, the paper crinkling as he folded the publication in half and brought it closer to his face. The article featured an old friend of his who liked to jump off mountains. The guy either had balls or a death wish, but he made interesting reading. Interesting reading was what Ivan was looking for.

Interesting reading and a little peace and quiet.

He'd tried the main lounge first. It had been crammed with therapists and nurses, every one of them in the mood to talk. It was Maggie McKenzie this and Maggie McKenzie that.

She was going home today.

He'd taken himself and his magazine to another lounge off the beaten path. Finding it empty, he'd stolen in, settled his lanky frame on the sofa, propped his feet on a low table, and opened his magazine to a great article.

The story filtered in a little of his friend's background, where he grew up, the chances he'd taken as a kid, that sort of thing. Ivan was just getting to the good part about the mountain diving when the door opened. He looked up long enough to nod at the two orderlies and the speech therapist that entered. Now. Where was he?

While the others took a seat at the table, he started over at the top of the page. Somebody put something in the microwave. One of the orderlies poured himself a cup of coffee. A soda can top popped. Ivan read the paragraph a third time.

"Maggie McKenzie's going home today."

"The place won't be the same without her."

"I know I'm sure gonna miss hearing her laugh."

Make that a fourth time.

"She's one of those patients that comes along maybe once a year."

"Isn't that right, Ivan?"

He ignored the eyes that were drilling holes into him and simply shrugged.

They seemed to take that as an indication to continue. "We never know when they first come in if they're going to get their happy ending. I sure am glad Maggie McKenzie's getting hers."

"Half the staff's already stopped by her room to say goodbye."

"You wish her well yet, Ivan?"

Ivan answered without lowering the magazine. "She'll be back as an outpatient three days a week."

"But she won't be staying here."

He lowered the magazine far enough so he could see over it. "That's the idea. We bully them into regaining what they can, then we send them home."

Accustomed to Ivan's clipped replies, the three friends took their beverages and left the room. Ivan studied the photograph of his old frat buddy diving off a mountain. The picture was out of focus. Ivan was having a hard time focusing, too.

Maggie was going home today. A lot of patients went home. He was happy for her. If anybody deserved a happy ending, she did. He hoped she got it. He did.

Why wouldn't she? She had a family who loved her, friends, neighbors. Some rich, old couple had made a generous donation to St. Ann's in honor of the care she'd been given. He saw an article about it in the paper a few days ago. The Princess of Grand Haven, that's what they called her. From the looks of things, she had an idyllic life to go back to.

Why wouldn't she be happy?

Ivan wouldn't have questioned it if he hadn't seen the look on the husband's face that day. It was the look of pain. The sister had seen it. She'd had to turn away. There was a deeper significance to the visual exchange. What? Did the sister have a thing for the husband? Ivan didn't think so. What then? Whatever it was, the atmosphere surrounding them had been thick enough to slice.

He found himself standing at the window overlooking the wide driveway in front of the hospital. Several cars were parked at the curb down below. A green sedan pulled out, and a gray minivan took its place. Spence McKenzie got out, then disappeared under the awning.

Ivan felt agitated. He needed to do something a little more strenuous than reading. He pictured himself cramming a hockey puck through a three-inch gap in a goalie's defenses. There were a few problems with the fantasy. It was eighty degrees outside. And he couldn't skate anymore since he'd blown out his knee. He was damned lucky he could walk. Walking wasn't going to cut this agitation.

He could think of another activity that would suffice. It required a dark room and a willing woman. The little redhead who'd moved into the apartment next door had expressed an interest. Maybe he'd snag a bottle of

wine and go over and say hello later. There was always
Chloe, the speech therapist working the pediatric floor.
He'd heard she'd described him as that dreamy, brood-
ing Casanova with hair four shades of brown.

Hair four shades of brown? That was a new one.

Spence McKenzie lifted Maggie into the passenger
seat. Someone else stashed a walker and other parapher-
nalia in the back. In no time at all, the minivan pulled
away from the curb, following the curving drive to the
exit sign.

"Hey, Ivan?"

He jumped.

One of his colleagues had poked his head in the
door. "Didn't you hear them page you, man? Your next
patient is here."

He looked at his watch. Break time had been over
ten minutes ago.

The minivan stopped at the end of the driveway, then
pulled out into the traffic on the street. Ivan folded his
magazine in half, tucked it in his back pocket, and said,
"I'll be right there."

One day shy of a month after she'd entered St. Ann's,
Maggie was going home. She'd been anxious and
excited and nervous for days, weeks. And now, here she
was, in the van, heading south along winding roads that
lent occasional glimpses of Lake Michigan. The water
was a deep, dark blue today, the sky dotted with clouds.
The hot, humid air streaming through her open window
smelled like deep summer and felt like heaven.

The moment they reached the city limit, tears
streamed down her face. Grand Haven was breathtak-
ing. It was all so familiar, the street signs, the houses, the
lampposts, the bustle of activity and the signs directing

tourists to the beaches. Maggie was certain her chest
was going to burst with emotion.

When Spence had first pulled into traffic, she'd felt
as if a fist had closed around her throat. It was the first
time she'd been in an automobile since the accident.
It brought back shards of memory and flashes of panic.
Without saying a word, he'd reached for her hand, and
slowed the new van to a crawl. "We'll follow the back
roads. We're going to take this nice and slow."

She'd looked at him, putting his new, chiseled profile
to memory. Little by little, her panic had subsided.

Everywhere, people looked up, waving as she and
Spence drove by. She'd been worried when she'd
learned that half the town was going to turn out as they
drove by. Feeling ill-equipped to handle so many faces,
she gripped Spence's hand with one hand, and waved
with the other. With him at her side, she doubted there
was anything she couldn't handle.

They drove through dappled shade, past kids on bicy-
cles and a little boy manning a lemonade stand. Finally,
they turned onto Fifth Street, and there was their house
with pale yellow siding and its sloping lawn, the sweeping
front porch and the bay window she and Spence had
chosen together years ago. Fresh tears coursed down her
cheeks. Someone had hung a WELCOME HOME MAGGIE
banner over the porch steps. Grace and Allison stood
on either side of Jackie underneath it, the girls in gauzy
summer dresses Maggie didn't recognize. The top of
Grace's head was even with Jackie's shoulder. Even Allison seemed taller.

Maggie's sense of loss was acute. It was the middle of
August. The best part of spring and most of the summer
had passed while she'd been gone. The girls had grown,
changed, blossomed.

"You're home again," Spence said, his voice mellow
and deep and emotion filled.

Yes, she thought, she was, home again, surrounded by everything ordinary and wonderful. That was what mattered most.

"We have an audience." Spence indicated the Stevensons with a slight movement of his head. The neighbors on either side were in their yards, those across the street at their windows. "How do you want to do this?"

Maggie wet her lips and swallowed the nerves that had a way of interfering with her thought process these days. Raising her chin a notch at a time, she said, "I want . . . to walk in."

"Atta girl."

He parked the van, got her walker from the back, then opened her door. "Okay," he said as soon as she was on her feet. "Here we go."

Jackie and the girls had rushed over. "Hi, Mom."

"Hi, Mama."

"Welcome home, Mags."

They made quite a procession, Maggie first, Spence at her side, Grace, Allie, and Jackie following close behind. She wouldn't win any races, but she didn't falter. Spence and Jackie helped her navigate the three steps leading to the tiny side porch. From there it was a short walk into the house. She stopped suddenly inside her kitchen, her eyes taking in the gleaming hardwood floors, the maple cabinets, the sunny yellow walls.

"You okay?" Spence asked.

She closed her eyes, opened them again, and nodded. She was far better than okay. She was home.

There was a decorated cake on the table. Balloons tied to colorful ribbons were moored to every chair. "Grace?" she asked, moving slowly about the room. "Did you . . . pick those wildflowers . . . for me?"

Grace nodded, and Allison dashed to the refrigerator, where she'd fastened her latest artwork. "Aunt Jackie got the cake, Gracie picked the black-eyed Susans and put 'em in water, and I drew you a picture. See?'' The paper fluttered in her hand. "It's all of us. Here. Home."

At only six years old, Allison already possessed an artistic flair. In this picture, she'd drawn two yellow-haired women, two yellow-haired girls, and one dark-haired man. They all wore Charlie Brown smiles. The woman with the short, spiky hair had one eye open and the other eye closed.

"It's lovely, Allie . . . But why am I . . . winking?"

"You're not. You're better, but not quite as better as you were."

Maggie glanced around in time to see Grace roll her eyes at her little sister. Spence and Jackie wore similar expressions of bewilderment. Only Allison appeared unaffected. Looking into the beguiling face of her younger daughter, Maggie said, "Well put."

She was home. And even though she wasn't quite as better as she used to be, there was no place in the world she would rather be.

"Good night, Mom."

"Yeah, night, Mama."

"Good night, Grace. Good night, Allison."

From a chair in the family room, Maggie watched the girls flit up the stairs with their father. She sighed. Tucking them in had always been one of the best parts of her day.

She'd been so confident in her regained abilities at St. Ann's. She'd been home only half a day, but already she'd come face to face with a dozen simple things she couldn't do.

With the help of her walker, she got to her feet, and focused on the things she could do. She made her way to the bathroom, washed her face, and brushed her teeth. Although it took longer than she ever would have imagined before the accident, she got out of her clothes and into the nightgown Spence had laid out for her.

Next, she made her way back to the family room and climbed somewhat clumsily into bed. Lying on top of the covers, she listened to the patter of feet overhead, and looked around her at the photographs lining a shelf. Her collection of pewter was in the hutch; the cozy throw she'd received from her parents last Christmas was draped over the back of an easy chair. The only thing out of place in the room was the bed. She'd asked Spence why he'd set it up in here. He'd told her his brothers had helped him carry it downstairs because he didn't think she'd want to deal with stairs just yet. That made sense, and yet it didn't fully answer her question. Although, by then, she couldn't put her finger on exactly what the question had been.

Her first day home had been memorable and exhausting. Jackie had gone home a few hours ago, shortly after they'd had birthday cake. Maggie hadn't realized she'd slept through her birthday until Jackie had placed the cake in front of her on the patio table, and Allison had asked her how old she was. Spence had answered while Maggie was still trying to remember. She was thirty-four. Grace had told her to make a wish. Closing her eyes, she'd thought that, at least, was easy. "If I could have one wish," she'd whispered, "it would be to resume . . . the life I left behind three . . . and a half months ago."

A pipe rattled upstairs. Lying in the drowsy warmth of her own bed after so many weeks away, she identified the patter of Allison's feet on the rug in the upstairs hall, the heavier thud of Spence's. A drawer scraped open. That would be Grace. Maggie slid deeper into the pillows.

Sometime later, she heard footsteps at the bottom of

the stairs. When she opened her eyes, she found Spence in the doorway, feet bare, his shirt untucked. He moved with an easy, masculine grace, and had finished unbuttoning his shirt before he realized she was watching. He paused, giving her the most heartrending smile.

"I thought you were asleep."

"I've been waiting for you. Are . . . the girls okay?"

He nodded.

And she sighed. "I disappointed Grace today."

"Grace is going through a phase."

"Honestly . . . I'd forgotten I wasn't supposed . . . to say my birthday wish . . . out loud . . . lest it not come true."

He moved closer, his eyes delving into hers. "I told Grace the same thing I'm going to tell you. I believe you are the exception to that rule."

Something shifted in her chest, spreading outward like waves on a quiet shore. "Talking about Grace . . . isn't the only reason . . . I waited up for you."

His gaze roamed over her. His breathing hitched. That was all it took for her to know the effect she'd had on him. He'd always been like this. She wouldn't have it any other way.

"Why don't you . . . come closer?"

"I can wait, Maggie. Maybe we should, if you're too tired, or weak, or sore. We have the rest of our lives."

Soft-touched thoughts shaped her smile. Drawing in a deep breath, she felt a lingering vibration, like emotions tugging at her heartstrings. "There are a lot of things I can't do. That isn't . . . one of them. Besides . . . I want the rest of . . . our lives to start right now."

Spence's gaze strayed over the Mona Lisa smile on Maggie's lips and along the entire length of her body. Her nightgown was sleeveless, the neckline scooped, the fabric soft-looking, covering her to her knees. The lamp was on in the corner, the house silent except for the sigh of the wind in the maple tree outside the window and the night insects chirping from their hiding places in the grass. The sun had set half an hour ago. Despite the early hour, he'd been prepared to crawl into bed without waking her. He would have been content with that, at peace simply to fall asleep next to her.

"Unless you're not . . . up to it."

The scamp grinned. If Spence lived to be a hundred, he would never stop thanking his lucky stars for this woman, and a life with her in it. Up to it? "I'll show you up to it."

"I think you . . . should put your money . . . where your mouth is."

"I have a better place in mind to put my mouth." His shirt landed on the floor.

She gasped at the first brush of his lips on her breasts, then arched her back for more. And more is what he gave her. Their remaining clothing came off in stages. They whispered, and sighed, the mattress shifting beneath their bodies. Her movements weren't as agile as they'd once been. He didn't seem to mind. He kissed her, and stroked her, and she him. He kissed the scar where her feeding tube had been, the places on her wrists where IVs had been attached. It was reverent, almost. And then he covered her mouth with his.

He caressed her until she whispered her need. His was just as strong. He loved her gently, completely, and when it was over, he gathered her close. She fell asleep almost instantly. Drawing the summer-weight blanket over her shoulders, he thought that although she was the one who'd blown out the candles and made a wish today, he was the one whose wishes had come true.

CHAPTER TEN

Spence's side of the bed was empty when Maggie woke up the next morning. A radio was playing somewhere. And she smelled freshly brewed coffee. It was after eight o'clock. It looked as if the day had started without her.

Her nightgown was lying at the foot of the bed. She stretched languidly, remembering how it had gotten there. There had been too many times to count throughout their marriage when Spence had made the earth move. He'd been ardent last night, but infinitely gentle.

Thunder and lightning had awakened them in the wee hours of the morning. They'd lain listening to it, safe and secure in each other's arms. It was wonderful to be home. She had known it would be.

She threaded her hands through the sleeves of her lightweight robe. Easing her legs over the side of the bed, she reached for her walker.

She freshened up in the bathroom, and was maneuvering down the hall leading to the kitchen when Spence spoke behind her. "I wondered where you'd gone."

She turned slightly and gave him a sweeping glance from head to toe. He was freshly showered, and was casually dressed in a burnt orange polo shirt and black chinos. They shared one of their morning-after smiles.

He looked rested, content. Happy. "Sleep well?" she asked.

He shrugged one shoulder, his eyes lighting from the inside. Another step brought him close enough to touch her. His arms came around her from behind, and his lips brushed her cheek, all in one motion. She leaned against him, fitting her backside to the juncture of his thighs. He was hard instantly.

"Good morning . . . to you, too."

"Allie's upstairs getting dressed and Grace is in the kitchen. She wanted to fix you breakfast in bed." He lowered his voice to a husky whisper. "If we were alone, I'd want you back in bed for another reason."

The idea of sampling a breakfast Grace had lovingly prepared was appealing. So was what Spence had in mind. "We don't have . . . the house to ourselves." She smiled at the breath of frustration he released. "Let's all have breakfast . . . at the table . . . together."

"Whatever you say."

Grace was getting bowls out of the cupboard when Maggie entered the kitchen. "You're up."

Maggie smiled. "I smelled coffee . . . I thought it would be . . . nice if we all ate together."

Allison skulked into the room looking bedraggled and a little grumpy. Her face lit up the instant she saw her mother. "I wasn't dreaming."

Her bad mood forgotten, she flitted to the drawer for the spoons. Spence entered the room a minute or two later. He was in charge of the milk and cereal and toast. Maggie would have liked to help, but wound up getting in the way, so she retreated to her chair at the table.

The others took their seats. Spence poured everyone's juice, and the milk over Allison's cereal. Spoons and dishes clattered. Maggie tried to think of something to say.

"Have you girls been . . . up this early all . . . summer vacation?"

Allison pulled a face that let Maggie know exactly what she thought of being up so early. "When Aunt Jackie stayed with us, we got to sleep in. Then she took us with her to the store. Lots of times when Daddy stayed with us, he took us to somebody's house so he could come see you."

Maggie didn't think she would ever stop feeling staggered at what everyone had gone through because of her accident. She wasn't the only one who'd missed out.

"We have swimming lessons at ten," Grace said matter-of-factly. "I have flute lessons on Wednesday mornings. Al has her riding lessons on Mondays."

Maggie had known about the riding and flute lessons, but she hadn't known they were taking swimming lessons. She should have remembered. They lived within blocks of a huge body of water. They went swimming and sailing often; therefore, they needed to be strong swimmers. The girls took swimming lessons every summer. Of course Spence would have done everything in his power to keep their lives normal, in balance.

He outlined their agendas over breakfast. Every day for the past two weeks he'd dropped the girls at Kaitlyn and Breanna Patterson's house, where they spent the remainder of the morning until Mrs. Patterson drove them all to swimming lessons. Today was the last day of formal lessons, and tomorrow was free swim. School was set to start in less than two weeks. Jackie had already taken them shopping for clothes and supplies. Spence had hired a cleaning service to help with the deep cleaning. He'd been working from home as much as possible.

From now on, on those days when he had to go to the office, he'd arranged for either Jackie or Crystal or Mrs. Stevenson next door to come over and sit with Maggie and the girls. He'd seen to so many details. Maggie tried to take it all in.

When breakfast was over, Allison slid from her chair. Grace reached for their bowls. Allison gathered the silverware. Spence picked up everything else. They were an efficient team. Maggie felt like royalty, or worse, company. She'd known her routine at St. Ann's. Breakfast, a shower, physical therapy, lunch, then more therapy. Now that she was home, she didn't quite know what to do with herself.

Spence went upstairs with Allie to help her locate her missing swimsuit. Maggie sat at the table watching Grace traipse about the kitchen.

"Have you been helping . . . like this all summer?"

Her daughter stopped loading the dishwasher and looked across the kitchen at her. Grace was mature for her age. Ten going on twenty, she and Spence used to say. Pointing to the book lying open on the island, Maggie asked, "What are you reading?"

"Aunt Jackie signed me'n Al—Allie and I, or is it me? Anyway, she signed us up for the summer reading program at the library." Shyly, she held up the book. "It's called *Khardomah*. It's an Indian word. I forget what it means. You read it to me last summer." The round blue eyes Grace turned toward her mother were brimming with hope and excitement. "It's about an Indian woman who saves fur traders when they get lost in a blizzard. What was her name again?"

Maggie floundered. "I remember the . . . story, Grace." Vaguely. "But not the Indian woman's name."

Grace's face fell. "Oh."

"I'm sorry, honey."

"It's all right."

It wasn't all right. She'd slipped another notch in Grace's eyes.

A lump rose to Maggie's throat. Grace had returned to her chores. Spence was helping Allison. It seemed everyone had a purpose except her.

She thought about that as she made her way to the family room, where the dresser containing her clothes was now. She was home. But everything wasn't the same. Getting her life back wasn't going to be as easy as one, two, three, the world's biggest understatement.

The telephone rang while she was slipping a loose-fitting jumper over her head. Dressing still required intense concentration. It would be so much easier when she could stand without the aid of the walker. She brushed her hair and was putting on her shoes when Allie came bounding into the room.

"Daddy says to tell you he's on the pho . . . You look pretty, Mama."

Maggie looked up from the shoes she'd chosen. They were comfortable, had nonskid soles, and would be perfect for practicing her walking. There was one problem. "Allison? Would you run upstairs . . . and bring Mama her brown loafers?"

Allison stuck her hands on her hips. "What's wrong with those shoes?"

"They have laces."

"So?"

"I don't remember . . . how to tie them."

The child breezed forward as if she were riding a current of air. "It's simple. Watch." She crouched down so quickly her long hair fluttered around her face, her forehead scrunched in concentration. "First you do this and pull it tight. That's one. Now you make a loop. That's two. Now you twist it and pull it through. That's three. See?"

Maggie leaned down so that her head was touching Allison's. "Show me that again."

Allison went through the steps a second time. One. Two. Three. "Want me to tie the other one?"

"I'd like to try." Maggie followed her daughter's directions. She bobbled it the first time. Although a little sloppy and a lot looser than the other shoe, her second attempt at tying was a success. Allison did a cartwheel. Maggie laughed out loud, which brought Allison bounding back for a hug.

Maggie wrapped her arms around her child, marveling at the strength in her daughter's thin little arms. Allison had always been this way, so open and honest and accepting. Maggie would have liked to hold on a little longer, but Allison drew away with an impish smile that meant she had things to do and places to go.

A movement in the hall drew Maggie's gaze. Grace hung near the doorway, utterly quiet, the complete opposite of her little sister. Maggie's older daughter was a deep thinker, but she'd never been reticent. Something was wrong.

"Hey, Gracie," Allie said, scooting past her on her way out of the room. "Guess what? Mama just tied her own shoe."

Clutching a book close to her chest, Grace watched her little sister go. "She's not supposed to run in the house."

"I'll have to work on that . . . with her. Come on in."

She did as her mother said, but hugged the far side of the room. From the moment Maggie had first looked into Grace's eyes ten and a half years ago, she'd been completely enamored of this child. They'd had a connection from the beginning, a mother-daughter closeness she hadn't shared with her own mother. Maggie didn't know how to breach the gap now. "Grace?"

"What?"

There was anger in that voice. Why? "You're so quiet. What's wrong?"

"Nothing."

Which meant everything.

"Happy home," Grace said, a little defiantly.

"Pardon me?"

Grace turned watery blue eyes to her mother. "That's what Khardomah means. It was the name of an Indian chief. You used to know that. You used to know everything."

Grace's hair was shoulder length, the same color Maggie's had been at that age. She may have been wearing her first bra, and she may have believed she was grown up, but the child standing forlornly on the other side of the room was still very much a little girl. A little girl who needed her mother.

"You probably don't even remember the story of why the Indians called the great lake Michiguma."

Maggie nearly flinched from the accusation in her daughter's voice, but she didn't answer. She couldn't. She didn't know the answer.

"I waited all summer for you to come home. I was so good. I even let Allie sleep with me." Grace tossed the book onto the bed and dashed from the room. Seconds later, a door slammed upstairs.

Maggie sat for a full minute, feeling like a failure. Slowly, she got up. She was halfway to the bed when Spence entered the room. Glancing toward the staircase, he said, "What's wrong with Grace?"

Maggie didn't reply until she came to the bed where the book had landed. "She's . . . angry with me."

"Why?"

Painstakingly, she let go of the walker with one hand, and slowly reached for the book. She was doing it. She was balancing without using both hands. The accomplishment was overshadowed by Grace's outburst. The book wasn't a book at all. It was Grace's journal.

"Because I'm not the mother . . . she's accustomed to."

He started toward the stairs. "I'll talk to her."

"No." She'd spoken more sharply than she'd intended. Softening her next words, she said, "This is between Grace and me." Carefully, she lowered herself into the overstuffed chair. Sitting again, she said, "Who was on the phone?"

"Tom Garvey."

"What did he . . . want?"

Spence went to the window. Opening the blinds, he stood looking into the backyard. "Felix Fitzgerald is throwing another temper tantrum. Tom wants me to come in and talk to him."

She recognized Tom Garvey's name. Felix Fitzgerald's was only mildly familiar. "When are you going?"

"I'm not."

"Why not?"

The quiet emphasis in her voice drew him around. "I don't want to leave you alone on your second day home."

"I'm not a cripple."

The cryptic delivery caused him to take a closer look at his wife. He remembered saying something similar with just that amount of vehemence when Maggie had first awakened from the coma. "She's not an imbecile." He'd been right. And so was she.

Her short wispy hair was tousled this morning. From this distance, her loose-fitting knit dress looked yellow. Upon closer inspection, he saw that it was flecked with gray. It was feminine, pretty. Like her. There were twin spots of color on her cheeks. Her chin was set at a haughty angle, but the look in her eyes was as naked as pride.

"I really don't want to leave you on your second day home."

"If it would make you feel better . . . call Jackie . . . or Crystal . . . or Mrs. Stevenson, like you said."

There was absolutely no reason why his body should start to thrum, heating in all the usual places. It hadn't even been twelve hours. It was just that—what? He loved her. He was so damned proud of her.

"While you're out, would . . . you do me a favor?"

"Anything."

"I need some books . . . from the library."

"You want something to read?"

"I want . . . books about the Great Lakes . . . and the first settlers in Michigan. And shipwrecks. I need to find out what . . . the Indian word 'Michiguma' means."

"It means Big Water."

She slanted him a look he hadn't seen in a long time. "Now you've . . . spoiled the surprise."

Spence reached her in three strides. He sat down on his haunches directly in front of her and took both of her hands in his. "You were bright before. You're bright now."

He was pretty sure she wanted to ask him to say that again. But her pride wouldn't let her. Not only was she getting stronger, more coordinated every day, but she was also restaking her claim, her rightful place in Grace and Allison's lives. In all their lives.

"I love you, Maggie McKenzie."

"Good." She gave him that one word in a voice soft and warm enough to slip into. And then she drew her pale, thin hands from his and opened Grace's journal to the first page. When he failed to move, she spoke without looking up. "Did you want me to . . . call Jackie or Crystal?"

Spence felt a chuckle coming on. He couldn't help it. This bossy streak of hers was new. He liked it. A lot.

"I'll call. And I'll see how many books I can find at the library."

"Thank you."

It was then that Spence realized that not only was she regaining what she'd lost, but she was going to be even better, even more than she was before.

"Something wrong?" she asked. This time she looked at him.

He'd been staring. He couldn't help it. His chest brimming with emotion, he shook his head. "I'm going. I'm going."

He went out to the kitchen to make the phone calls. Jackie didn't answer. Crystal was busy. Mrs. Stevenson next door was on her way over.

Spence hollered for the girls, made sure Allie had her swimsuit and towel, then gathered up his briefcase and some of his sketches for Picketts Corners. After letting Mrs. Stevenson in, and kissing Maggie goodbye, he walked out of his house, whistling. He hadn't whistled in a long time. The sun was shining. Birds splashed in puddles left over from last night's rain. And Maggie, his Maggie, was home. Everything was right with his world.

"Is something wrong, dear?"

Treva Montgomery's question drew Jackie from her trance. She'd been looking out the back window of her store.

It was one of those rare August mornings when the humidity was low and the sky was clear, and everything looked clean and fresh. Everyone who came in to Fiona's had talked about the storm that had blown in overnight. There had been reports of hail the size of marbles and damaging wind. Branches were down, sails torn, shingles blown off. Some sections of the city had lost power. Jackie had slept through it all; she hadn't heard a thing.

"Wrong? No. Nothing's wrong."

"Are you sure?" Treva asked.

"I'm sure," she said, smiling kindly at her eccentric friend who owned the art gallery next door. "I'm a little groggy this morning, that's all."

It wasn't unnatural for Jackie to be a little groggy in the morning. Unlike Maggie, who woke up like a burst of sunshine, Jackie awoke in layers.

Treva's hand fluttered to the neckline of her silk tunic, down her arm, and over the hip hidden by the flowing lines of the brightly colored pantsuit. "I haven't slept well ever since that episode with Raoul and Gardner."

Jackie started toward Treva, only to stop suddenly, dizzy. Closing her eyes, she waited a moment for the spell to pass.

"See what I mean?" Treva asked. "You're ill."

"I think I'm fighting a flu bug."

"The flu this time of the year? I'll bet exhaustion has finally set in now that Maggie's home. How is that dear sister of yours, anyway?"

"She's getting better every day."

"That's nice."

Jackie couldn't agree more. Now that Maggie was home, everything seemed better, and at the same time, more normal. Things were looking brighter all the way around. Sales were up slightly here at Fiona's. Not enough to make her rich, but enough to pay the rent on the store, her utilities, and her quarterly taxes. Part of the rent on the summerhouse she'd leased after she and David had separated was still going to have to come out of her savings account, but at least her financial situation was improving. Now, if she could just get over whatever germ she'd picked up.

Tango rubbed against her leg the way he always did when Treva visited the store, which had been often since Raoul and Gardner had found out about each other and demanded that Treva choose, or else. Treva hadn't taken kindly to their ultimatum, and had told them both what they could do with their terms.

Running a hand through her hair, which showed her gray roots this morning, Treva said, "You're as pale as a ghost. Maybe you should see a doctor."

Jackie hated hospitals. Doctors' offices were almost as bad. "I've seen enough doctors and nurses these past three and a half months to last a lifetime."

"I suppose you're right." Treva meandered to the front of the store, and looked absently through a display of old hats. "Medical doctors couldn't do anything for what ails me."

"Heartsickness, you mean? I've been there, Treva. If it's any consolation, it'll pass, eventually."

The older woman sighed. "I miss him."

"Which one?"

Treva's silk tunic shimmered with the deep breath she drew. "That's just it. I miss both of them."

Tango looked up at Jackie, her cue to pick him up, which she did. The action made her woozy. She straightened in stages, then held perfectly still, waiting for the nausea to pass.

"You should go lie down," Treva said sternly, only to sigh yet again. She left the store soon after, not nearly the cyclone she'd been a few months ago.

Carrying Tango with her, Jackie strolled to the display case filled with old gloves and period stockings. "Treva's sad because she's in love with two men."

Tango looked at her with his big, round, unblinking eyes.

"I know. If anyone should be depressed, it's me. I mean, I'm the one who doesn't even have one man to love." Settling the big tabby more securely in her arms, she ran a hand along his broad back. He purred so loudly that she smiled.

"Not that every woman needs a man, or vice versa. Maybe we should get another cat."

Tango purred on. The rumble was cut short when she dumped him unceremoniously to the floor and went running for the bathroom.

The varsity football players were practicing when Jackie passed the high school, the sight at odds with the drone of a lawnmower in the lot next door and the children who were running through a sprinkler at the corner. It was that time of the year when every flyer advertised back-to-school sales, when half the residents of Grand Haven talked about the approach of autumn and the other half prepared to take their summer vacations.

Spence and Allison were shooting baskets when Jackie pulled into the driveway. Maggie and Grace sat in the shade on the porch steps. Except for Maggie's walker, it was a scene Jackie had witnessed countless times in the past.

"Look at me, Aunt Jackie!" Allie called the second Jackie got out of her car. "I can dunk it."

Spence swung Allie up and held her over his head while she put the basketball through the hoop. "Good one, Allison, but don't you people know it's hotter than blazes out here?"

Grace closed the book she'd been reading with her mother, and Maggie carefully rose to her feet. "You even *sound* like you're . . . feeling better."

Jackie met Maggie on the sidewalk. "Like night and day." It was true. The flu had finally passed. She'd slept another solid ten hours last night, and had awakened famished instead of woozy. She ate a hearty breakfast, then took a leisurely walk along the shore of Spring Lake. It was something she hadn't done all summer. She hadn't even known she'd missed it. It had felt heavenly. She felt heavenly.

Afterward, she'd showered, then slipped into an old-fashioned summery dress nearly the same shade of blue as the cornflowers growing beside the porch steps at Maggie's feet. "It looks like you're ready."

Maggie nodded. Spence had taken her to her physical therapy session on Friday. Because of her flu, Jackie hadn't seen Maggie since the afternoon she'd come home. Of course, they'd spoken on the phone every day. Watching her now, Jackie was certain she wasn't imagining that Maggie's walk was steadier, her steps more even.

It was Monday. Spence had a meeting with an important client this afternoon. Grace and Allison were going to spend the afternoon at the beach with Crystal Douglas and her kids. Jackie had offered to drive Maggie to St. Ann's for her physical therapy session. She'd hired a high school girl to work at the store in her absence. While she waited for Maggie, she planned to browse through her competition, a vintage clothing store in Muskegon called Wednesday's Whimsy.

Heat rose in waves off the cement driveway. Dressed in sandals, shorts, and a tie-dyed T-shirt, Allison hopped on the bicycle that had been leaning against the garage. While she rode to the end of the block, Grace meandered closer, until she was standing next to Maggie. Spence hurried to open Maggie's door. To Jackie, he said, "You'll drive carefully?"

With a roll of her eyes, Maggie said, "Don't be surprised . . . if he asks for that . . . in writing."

Spence was grinning when his gaze met Jackie's over the top of her car. "She says I'm slightly overprotective."

"Slightly?" Maggie asked.

"Who, you?" Jackie said at the same time.

All three of them grinned. For a moment, it felt the way it used to, all of it, the girls, Maggie, Spence, her.

"You're going to . . . be late. And Felix . . . will be angry."

Spence leaned down so that his face was level with Maggie's. "This from a woman who had to relearn to tell time." He planted a quick kiss on her lips. While he was down there, he planted another on Maggie's cheek.

Seat belts were fastened and doors firmly closed. Maggie waved at Spence and the girls. And they were on their way.

Jackie picked up a large cup containing a strawberry slush and pointed to the grape-flavored drink she'd bought for Maggie. After taking a long draw from the straw, Maggie said, "This reminds me . . . of when we were kids."

Jackie nodded. "No matter what new town we lived in, we could always find grape and strawberry slushes."

They spent the next ten minutes slurping slushes and trying to talk with frozen tongues and laughing about it. Maggie spoke about the book she and Grace were reading, and Grace's journal, which made Maggie cry each time she read another entry. Jackie mentioned the customer who'd seen two bald eagles soaring over the lake from Five Mile Hill.

"Five Mile Hill . . . They call it that . . . because from there you can see ships on . . . Lake Michigan five miles away."

Jackie's eyes brimmed with tears. "I'm impressed."

Shrugging sheepishly, Maggie said, "I just read that . . . in one of Grace's books."

They'd reached the Muskegon city limit. "It looks like things are better between you and Grace."

Maggie nodded. "Not a hundred percent. But . . . better, yes. I'll be glad when Spence is back . . . to one hundred percent."

Jackie couldn't bring herself to reply.

Maggie didn't seem to notice. "He's so considerate. Gentle. Careful." She pulled a face. "Bother the . . . man. He wasn't this . . . careful after the girls were born."

Coasting to a stop at a red light, Jackie reached for her icy drink. "Give him time, Mags."

"That's easy for you . . . to say. You don't know how good he . . ."

Jackie gripped the steering wheel with one hand and her drink with the other, praying that Maggie wouldn't finish the statement.

"What if there's something wrong . . . with me?"

"Wrong? What do you mean by wrong?"

Maggie didn't reply.

"You mean physically, mentally, emotionally? Uh-uh. Wrong. No way. None of the above, Mags. Did you see the way he looked at you fifteen minutes ago?"

Maggie sighed. "Maybe you're right."

Jackie started to relax.

"But he wasn't this . . . careful after the girls were born. Or before . . . for that matter. Remember how sick I was . . . with Allison?"

"Sick?" Jackie froze, and it had nothing to do with the cold beverage. She couldn't very well leave the paper cup suspended in midair two inches in front of her face. With blood rushing through her head, she brought the straw the rest of the way to her lips and took another drink.

"Remember, Jacks? We all . . . thought I had the flu."

Jackie's coughing spell lasted until the light turned green. The churning in the pit of her stomach lasted a lot longer.

Nerves, she told herself. A relapse of the flu. She wet her lips, willing the sweet drink to stay put in the pit of her stomach. Her throat and tongue felt stiff, making it difficult to swallow.

Oh, no.

St. Ann's was just around the corner. She pulled into the lot and parked close to the door. "We're here." Pasting a semblance of a smile on her face, she got out, retrieved Maggie's walker from the trunk of her car, then helped Maggie inside. Her stomach roiled with every step.

She kept up that normal pace until they reached the main therapy room. Once inside, Jackie forced herself to exchange pleasantries with Ivan and Camille. Finally, she left Maggie in their capable hands and headed back the way she'd come.

The instant she rounded the corner and was out of their sight, she clamped her hand over her mouth. And ran.

Oh, no, oh, no, no, no.

She made it to the rest room and into an empty stall just before her stomach turned itself inside out. She sank to her knees. Oh, no. God, no.

Her elbows resting on the rim of the commode, she held her head in both hands, and tried to remember how many times she'd found herself in this position these past four days. "Too many," she whispered after the toilet had flushed and she was able to stand.

She really hated hospitals.

She splashed her face with cool water, then stared at her reflection in the mirror. Her eyes were bloodshot, her skin pasty, her lips gray. She certainly looked sick enough to have the flu.

Please, God.

She pressed a hand to her forehead. Let it be the flu.

Or a tumor. Or exhaustion, like Treva had said. An embolism would work, or botulism, a virus, any virus, the black plague. Anything but what she was thinking at that very moment.

Anything but that.

CHAPTER ELEVEN

Jackie would not panic.

That had been her mantra for the past four—she looked at her watch—make that four-and-a-half, hours. She would not panic. She was probably overreacting anyway. What were the chances that she was ... She couldn't even think the word.

She'd left the rest room at St. Ann's as soon as her knees had stopped shaking. From there, she'd done what she'd planned, driving to the downtown shopping district in Muskegon. She'd parked on a side street, then browsed through a vintage clothing store she'd been hearing about. She'd spent an hour in Wednesday's Whimsy, but couldn't recall much about the store later. She only knew that when she left, she'd been carrying an old magenta velvet hat with a purple plume. She didn't know why she'd bought a hat. She never wore them, and she already had a large display of vintage hats in Fiona's. Hats didn't sell. It wasn't as if she'd been looking at the hats. She'd been browsing through the dresses on the sale rack when the clerk had asked, "May I help you?"

Perhaps if Jackie hadn't looked at the other woman, she would have been okay. But she had looked. And the woman, a petite brunette about Jackie's age, had a Madonna smile, and one hand resting gently on her stomach. Her very round, very pregnant stomach.

I will not panic. I will not panic. I will not panic. And she hadn't. Instead, she'd strolled to the hat display nearby. The rest, as they said, was history. She'd taken her purchase, and dazedly left the store.

It was hot outside, and yet she couldn't seem to stop shivering. She went into a small diner and ordered a glass of ice water and a bowl of soup. The nourishment helped. When she was fairly certain she was steady enough to drive, she'd paid for her meal and left.

She would not panic.

She'd made one other purchase before returning to St. Ann's. The first, she left in the back window in plain view. The second, she hid in a brown paper sack underneath her seat. Somehow, she'd found the strength to walk back into St. Ann's and face Maggie. Luckily, Maggie had done most of the talking during the drive back to Grand Haven. She'd been full of news about other patients at the hospital, chatting about the staff, and the progress she was making in her physical, speech, and occupational therapy.

Spence's car was in the garage when Jackie and Maggie returned. Jackie had a perfectly good reason not to accept Maggie's invitation to stay for supper. She had to get back to her store.

She didn't panic. Not while she paid Sarah, the high school girl who occasionally watched the store in her absence, not while she waited on a few straggling customers. Not when she put the closed sign in the window. Not while she drove the seven miles from Grand Haven to Spring Lake.

She took the kit from under her seat and carried it

into her house. Cool, calm, and collected, she read the
directions, twice, even though she had used these kits
before. She and David had tried for five years to have
a baby. Five years of thermometers and charts, of hoping
and praying, and of having sex regularly, had resulted
only in disappointment. The timing had been difficult
because David had traveled and she'd often had irregular periods. The doctors had blamed *that* on stress, and
the rest on the fact that she was trying too hard.

What had she been under these past several months
if not stress? What were the chances now? Slim to none.
That was why she wouldn't panic.

Okay, maybe she panicked a little, enough to make
her hands shake and enough to cause her to lock herself
in her own bathroom. She read the directions again.
And followed them to the letter. It was pretty straightfor-
ward. A positive sign would mean she was. A negative
sign would mean she wasn't.

She picked up the wand. And dropped it as if it were
on fire.

It landed on the tile floor, the positive symbol so vivid
it might as well have been a neon sign.

Positive.

It was positive.

Now she panicked. Her stomach roiled. It was difficult
to breathe. Impossible to think.

She sank to the edge of the bathtub. It couldn't be
right. She'd only . . .

Once . . .

And hardly even then. Just that one time. For those
few minutes . . . When she'd been drowning in sorrow
. . . When she and Spence both had been drowning in
sorrow . . .

Oh God. Spence.

She jumped to her feet and paced until she came to
the shower. Turning, she repeated the process in the

opposite direction. She was pregnant. And it was Spence's child. It would kill him. It would annihilate Maggie.

Both hands covered her mouth. Oh, God. Sweet Maggie.

What was Jackie going to do? What?

In her mind, she saw Maggie as she'd been when they were girls, starting at a new school yet again. Jackie had been what, eight? She'd hung back at the crosswalk in front of the school, scared to death. Ten-year-old Maggie had reached for Jackie's hand and whispered, "We'll do this together." Years later, when Maggie's date had stood her up, Jackie had canceled her plans, too. They'd spent the evening in their room, leafing through glossy teen magazines and listing all the boy's faults, giggling, because by the time they were finished with him, he was pathetic, indeed. When Jackie decided to open a vintage clothing store, Maggie had toasted to the venture. When Jackie had cried over the breakup of her marriage, Maggie had held her, whispering that she would do anything to help. Jackie felt the same way. She did. She would do anything for her only sister.

What had she done?

She came to a stop at the sink, her eyes on the reflection looking back at her. If she hadn't been alone, someone else might have heard her breaking apart inside, like a window cracking in the cold.

Each time the woman sitting next to Jackie moved, her vinyl chair creaked. Each time Jackie heard that creak, she had to force her eyes to remain fixed on the magazine she was pretending to read.

From the corner of her eye, she could see the rounded girth.

After letting out one particularly long-winded, long-suffering sigh, the woman finally said, "Sorry. My back is killing me, and this chair isn't helping. Last trimesters are hell."

Jackie couldn't help herself. She looked directly at that enormous belly, and then at the woman's face. "When is your baby due?"

The woman puffed up her cheeks. "Four days ago. The first two came early. This one's being stubborn about the whole thing. How about you? This your first?"

Jackie's eyes widened and her mouth dropped open, but she couldn't rally quickly enough to deny it. Finally, she croaked, "What makes you say that?"

The other woman smiled kindly, and cast a sweeping glance at the four other women, all in different stages of pregnancy seated throughout the room. Lowering her voice to a whisper, she said, "This *is* an obstetrician's office."

The heat climbing up Jackie's neck could only be a blush. For crying out loud, she was a mental case. She'd driven all the way to Grand Rapids to ensure that no one knew her. No one here did. Shrugging sheepishly, she said, "I'm here to find out for sure."

She'd done the home pregnancy test on Monday. Today was Friday. Every hour of every day in between she'd tried to decide what to do. In exasperation, she'd realized that she couldn't make a decision, any decision, until she knew for sure. What if those home pregnancy kits were wrong? She'd called Dr. Alice Green's office in Grand Rapids yesterday, and had been put on a cancellation list. This morning, an opening had occurred in the schedule.

She gave up pretending to read and simply waited for the nurse to call her name. When she did, Jackie followed the woman through a labyrinth of hallways. Her finger was poked, and she was handed a little cup and sent into a tiny rest room with instructions to fill it. Jackie really, really, really hated doctors' offices.

Next, she was given a hospital gown, a little privacy to undress, and instructions to wait for the doctor's knock on the door. She didn't have to wait long. Dr. Green wore her gray hair in a bun, and had round red glasses that slid halfway down her nose. She was kind, gentle, and efficient. After the examination, she helped Jackie to a sitting position. "Would you prefer to proceed wearing this gown or dressed in your clothes?"

Jackie took a deep breath. Smoothing a hand over the wrinkled paper gown, she said, "It's a little late for modesty, don't you think?"

The doctor smiled. "Okay. Here's the deal. You're thin, and slightly anemic, and pregnant. I'd say you're approximately six weeks along."

There was nothing approximate about it. Jackie knew the exact month, day, and time she'd gotten pregnant. She took another deep breath, and had to remind herself to release it.

Her hands flew to her face. She was pregnant.

She wasn't in shock. The shock had come four days ago. But hearing it out loud made it more real, somehow.

"I take it this wasn't planned."

Jackie shook her head.

"Is the father—"

Jackie cut her off with a sharp voice. "There is no father."

Dr. Green made no reply. Obviously, she'd been in this profession long enough to have heard it all. "What do you want to do?"

"I don't know."

The doctor started for the door. "Why don't you dress? I'll be back shortly."

Dazedly, Jackie did as the doctor suggested. When

Dr. Green returned, she handed Jackie a sample of prenatal vitamins to help with her anemia, and several pamphlets for her to read. Leafing through them, Jackie saw that they covered everything from prenatal care to labor, birthing coaches, and pain medications. The pamphlet titled "Alternative Choices" gave her pause.

Dr. Green noticed. "As your obstetrician, it isn't my place to offend or judge. The latter is particularly difficult for me because both my children are adopted. No matter what my personal feelings are, you do have options."

"I need time to think."

Dr. Green nodded. "Time is one thing you have. Depending on which option you choose, you have seven and a half months, to be exact."

Jackie left the office, her vitamins and pamphlets in her hand, the word "options" running through her head.

Spence entered his house the way he usually did, via the garage. The kitchen was quiet, but apparently hadn't been for long. There were cookie crumbs on plates and an inch of milk left in the bottom of two glasses. It was the end of August. School was starting tomorrow. Evidence was everywhere. Two new backpacks hung on the backs of chairs. Crisp notebooks and brightly colored folders and boxes of brand new crayons and sharpened pencils littered the island.

He dropped his jacket over a chair and followed the drone of the television to the living room. Mrs. Stevenson was engrossed in one of her soaps, but Maggie and the girls were nowhere in sight.

It was a little after three in the afternoon. He was home early. These days, he couldn't seem to stay away for even an entire day. The high twitter of Allie's laugh,

Grace's soft giggle, and the mellow, full-hearted sound of Maggie's voice drew him to the French doors leading to the backyard. And there were the reasons, all three of them, why he couldn't stay away.

Allison swayed on the tire swing, leaning all the way back so that her hair brushed the grass. Grace and Maggie were on their backs on a blanket nearby.

He strode closer for the plain and simple reason that he couldn't help himself. Maggie and the girls did this every summer. Seeing it this year was more poignant because they'd come so close to losing her. The scar on the side of Maggie's face was a constant reminder of just how close she'd been to death. Not that he needed a reminder. There was a place deep inside his chest that felt as if he'd been bludgeoned with a dull knife. Spence accepted the ache. It was a small price to pay for the second chance he'd been given to live in this private piece of heaven.

Maggie's hand made a graceful sweep through the air. Spence paused, listening. She was telling a story, her speech somewhat halting, the words themselves conjuring up images of a ship sailing the Great Lakes, and a captain whose two little girls had stolen on board.

Allison stopped pushing off with her foot, so rapt was her attention on her mother's tale. Grace's gaze never left Maggie's face.

"At twelve o'clock that day, a fierce . . . wind began to blow. And the two . . . little girls crept into their father's cabin, but it was empty . . ."

Maggie chose that moment to look up, her gaze meeting his. Perhaps she'd noticed the shadow that fell along the edge of the blanket. Or perhaps she'd felt him looking at her.

She smiled, and it was as if the wind in her story was the same wind that was knocked out of him. "Don't stop," he said, lowering himself to the blanket near

Grace. "I want to hear what happens to the two adventurous little girls."

Grace nodded and Allison smiled, and Maggie picked up the tale where she'd left off. Spence sat as motionless as the girls, certain he'd never seen so much emotion, so much tenderness, so much pleasure on any of their faces. Maggie's ankles were crossed, her white shorts were baggy and wrinkled, her sleeveless top a shade of blue somewhere between the color of her eyes and the sky. The breeze toyed with the short wisps of her hair. Her smile enticed, her eyes danced.

Heat thrummed through his body. He didn't allow what he was feeling to turn into desire. He was content simply to go on watching her with their girls. If he lived to be a hundred, he would never ask for more than this life, with this woman and these two children, in this haven they called home.

The low heels of Maggie's pumps clicked as she made her way across the kitchen floor. Jackie was due any minute, and the two of them were going to attend the annual Ladies Historic Society's September luncheon. Maggie was practicing walking in shoes that didn't have rubber soles. It was her first social outing since her accident, and she didn't want to trip over her own two feet.

She'd been looking forward to attending all week. Suddenly, nerves fluttered in her stomach. Spence must have noticed, because he said, "Are you sure you want to do this?"

She looked across the room where he stood in the doorway. His hair was slightly windblown and in need of a trim, his white shirt tucked into the waistband of low-slung dark pants. "Yes. No. Maybe."

"As long as you're sure." He started toward her. "You

don't have to attend yet. Not that you don't look beautiful in that dress." He followed the compliment up with a slow, steady smile that caused her to smile in return.

He'd come home for lunch. The girls were in school, which meant they had the house to themselves. If he'd suggested helping her out of her dress, she might have considered staying home with him. But he didn't. He just stood there, looking at her as if he couldn't get enough of doing just that. How in the world could a woman complain about that?

She pulled a face. "I'm going a matter of a few blocks . . . Not to the moon." It was true. She'd always been more interested in these social functions than he was. She enjoyed socializing, but the real reason she attended was because she loved history, loved using her mind, and putting her organizational skills to good use. That was why she was nervous. She knew how she looked, how she talked. She also knew that she wasn't different, not inside where it mattered. So she would attend. She would hold her head high, and let the members think what they wanted. No matter what they thought, some things hadn't changed. She and Jackie attended the luncheon every year. Maggie didn't want to miss it. Especially this year, when she'd already missed so much. Also, she hadn't seen much of Jackie lately, and she was looking forward to catching up.

"Don't worry," she said. "Jackie will be there if I need anything . . . anything at all."

"Like what? What do you need?"

A sound in the doorway drew their attention.

Jackie stood there, her gaze going from Maggie to Spence and back again. "Is something wrong?"

Maggie shook her head. "No, but would you please tell . . . Spence that you wouldn't let . . . anything bad happen to me . . . any more than he would?"

Jackie glanced at Spence, and then quickly away. Hoping she was too far away for Maggie to see how difficult it suddenly was to swallow, Jackie pasted a smile on her face and said, "I think he already knows, Mags."

With that, she turned away, and held the door.

The Braden House, a beautiful bed-and-breakfast inn with significant historic value, wasn't far from Spence and Maggie's. Most years, Maggie and Jackie walked. Next year, Maggie told herself after she'd made her way across the wide expanse of the inn's sprawling lawn, and took a seat at the first table she came to.

It was a perfect day for a luncheon. The sun wasn't too hot. The breeze wasn't too cool. The gardens were as beautiful as ever, the tables set with delicate china on lace tablecloths and fine linen napkins. Everybody made a fuss over Maggie. She lost track of how many people called her name.

"Maggie! Let me look at you!"

"Maggie. Welcome back."

"Maggie. It's good to see you."

She smiled each time someone spoke to her. Yvonne Wilson leaned down to plant an affectionate kiss on her cheek. "I'm so glad you came."

It was good to be here. Dizzying, but good.

Jessica Hendricks breezed over to her table with Hannah Lewis and MaryAnn Petigrue. "I can't believe you're really here!"

"You gave us all such a scare!"

"Why, you look great."

"Look at that hair!"

"Are these seats taken?"

By the time Jackie returned to the table with two dinner plates, Maggie's head was spinning again. It was with great relief that she turned her attention to eating.

Try as she might, Jackie couldn't muster up much

enthusiasm for the gossip Jessica was spreading. Jackie was more interested in the newborn baby in his mother's arms at the next table. He was unbelievably tiny. She could see the bones in his head, covered only with brown hair so fine it looked like downy peach fuzz. Something startled him, and he let out a little squawk.

Maggie said, "I didn't know Tricia Cohagan . . . had her baby."

Hannah Lewis said, "He was born eight weeks ago."

Now that the conversation was centered on the baby, Jackie had free license to look openly at him. She couldn't get over how perfectly shaped his little fingers were. His eyes were closed, his legs drawn up slightly. Every once in a while, his little bow lips moved as if he was suckling in his dreams.

Babies, babies, babies. Where had so many babies come from? She saw them everywhere, in Fiona's, on the street, in restaurants, in the grocery store, infants, crawlers, and toddlers. Babies in overalls and little blue caps, or lace booties and pants with ruffles on the seat and bonnets with delicate ribbons.

"He weighed over nine pounds when he was born," MaryAnn Petigrue said. "Tricia had so many stitches she couldn't sit down for a week."

"And stretch marks!" Jessica exclaimed. "She'll never wear a bikini in public again, that's for sure."

Jackie didn't think *not* wearing a bikini in public was too big a price to pay for the miracle sleeping peacefully in Tricia's arms. Before the tears that were so prevalent these days spilled over, she forced her attention to the food she was pushing around on her plate.

Somehow, the conversation had turned to swimsuits that had been spotted at the beach that summer, and what they did and did not cover. "What would instill a two-hundred-and-fifty-pound woman to wear a string bikini in public?" Jessica said.

Spoken, Jackie thought, spearing a chunk of fresh watermelon, by someone who spent her ex-husband's money on liposuction, collagen, and facial peels. Maggie nudged her with her foot, letting Jackie know she was thinking the same thing.

Unaware of the private joke, Hannah Lewis said, "Probably the same thing that makes a two-hundred-and-fifty-pound man think he looks good in a Speedo."

Even Jackie and Maggie laughed at that.

Jessica leaned ahead. Looking Maggie in the eye, she fervently said, "It's good to see you laughing. You had all of us worried. Spence, especially. The circles under his eyes were almost as gray as the tile floors at Bentworth."

"You visited me . . . at Bentworth?"

The garden, all at once, was quiet. Jessica rarely floundered, but she opened her mouth a few seconds before words formed. "I didn't actually visit you. I mean, I couldn't. It was family only."

"But you saw Spence?"

Jessica shifted in her chair and cast a practiced smile, first at Jackie and then at Maggie. "I was in the neighborhood, that's all."

"That was . . . thoughtful of you."

Jackie thought Maggie's bland expression deserved an award.

"It was nothing. I bought him a cup of coffee in the cafeteria. Oh, look. There's Abigail. Yoo-hoo. Abigail." She hurried away.

Eyes narrowed, Maggie watched her leave. Her speech may have been halting, but Jackie's only sister was very astute.

Maggie went back to buttering her roll, and Jackie went back to pushing her food around on her plate. What was she going to do? That question had been haunting Jackie for more than a week. She was so weary, she just wanted to lay her head down and sleep. At least when she was sleeping, questions didn't assail her.

The baby started to cry. His little arms flailed, his fingers curled into fists, his eyes squeezed tightly shut. His mother took a bottle from an oversized bag. The second the nipple touched his mouth, the crying stopped.

Fresh tears burned the back of Jackie's throat. She had options, but each one felt more horrible than the last.

What was she going to do? What?

CHAPTER TWELVE

Maggie hummed as she rinsed out Allison's glass and wiped up cookie crumbs from the girls' bedtime snack. There were no giggles, no voices, no footsteps pattering overhead. Grace and Allison must have fallen asleep quickly. It was the middle of their second week of school. Already, they were becoming accustomed to turning in early. The dark clouds that had formed a wall between Grand Haven and the setting sun had helped, making it seem later than nine-thirty.

The air streaming through the French doors was heavy with the musky scent of newly mown grass and something subtler and less tangible, like the atmospheric excitement of the storm brewing off the shore of Lake Michigan. According to the weatherman, those clouds wouldn't be going anywhere anytime soon. It was a good thing the Ladies Historic Society had held their luncheon today and not tomorrow.

Every day, her life felt a little more normal. Attending that luncheon had been wonderful. Being home when the girls returned from school was doubly so. Maggie looked forward to the day when she was back, one hundred percent. In the meantime, she took pleasure in the simplest of things. Listening to Grace and Allie's banter as they worked on their homework, watching Spence mow the grass, being able to rinse out a glass, and to be an active part of her own precious family.

The wind picked up, billowing through the curtains and clanking blinds against windowsills. She moved about her house with the help of her walker, closing windows on the first floor.

Some people were afraid of storms. As long as they weren't too violent, Maggie liked them, especially at night. It was like tossing a pinch of powder from an unmarked jar into a cauldron of bubbling magic potion. You never knew what was going to happen, but it was sure to be exciting.

The heavy thud of footsteps sounded behind her. She turned, and saw Spence sauntering toward her. He was light-footed when he chose to be, which meant that he'd wanted her to know he was back.

"Grace and Allison asleep?"

He nodded. His hair was still damp from his shower; his feet and chest were bare, his jeans zipped but not buttoned. Awareness had been in the air all evening, in his gaze, and just beneath the surface of his fleeting touch. For her, it had started when she'd watched him work in the yard, a bead of sweat trailing down his neck, dampening the sparse hairs on his chest.

Their simmering attraction had remained playful. After all, the girls and chores had required that it be so. The chores were done. And the girls were asleep. And the awareness between them rose up, roiling and swirling like waves of heavy steam.

This was another element of her life that was returning to normal. She twirled a lock of her short, crazy hair, then stood back and watched as he responded to the gesture. She moistened her lips, reeling him in. He didn't put up much of a fight.

She'd taken a shower, and had donned the only seductive nightgown she owned anymore. She doubted she would soon forget the expression on Spence's face when she'd asked him to bring it downstairs for her. She was more interested in the expression on his face right now.

She circled the bed in the family room, her anticipation mounting in direct proportion to the mounting storm. He closed the window, then took a moment to adjust the blinds to award them some privacy without completely closing out their view.

"If I'm not careful," he said, "you're going to say I'm easy."

Watching the play of muscles roll across his shoulders as he folded the bedspread back, she laughed, a deep throaty sound that bubbled up from deep inside, bringing her desire ever closer to the surface. "If you're not careful, I'll . . . say you're instant."

Spence sucked in a ragged breath, and slowly lowered his zipper. Again, her gaze followed his every move. He'd used every trick he knew to be gentle with her these past two weeks. The light in her eyes let him know she'd had enough of being careful.

"Why didn't you . . . tell me?"

She'd asked the question without taking her eyes from the part of him begging for her attention. It made thinking coherently difficult. "Tell you what?"

"About what happened."

Honestly, his mind was blank. He stopped a foot in front of her, and ran a hand up her arm. "What happened when?" Leaning down, he whispered a kiss along the side of her neck.

"When I was . . ." Her eyes closed, and her head lolled back, her face beautiful in the near darkness.

He threaded his fingers through the short, soft hair

above her ear, slowly letting his hand glide down her neck, over her shoulder, taking the narrow strap of her blush-colored nightgown with it.

"When I was in the . . . coma."

Spence's mind reeled. It was as if a fist had wrapped around his vocal chords, making it impossible to speak.

"Jessica Hendricks made you . . . another offer."

His throat convulsed. The grip on his windpipe loosened. "Nothing happened, Maggie." Not then.

"Don't worry. I know you . . . would never do such a thing."

The fist moved from his throat to his heart, where it stayed, a painful reminder that he didn't deserve her unfailing belief, her unquestioning faith in him. He didn't know if it was possible to make something like that up to her, but he was going to try, every day, every way, for the rest of his life.

He started with another kiss, trailing another, and another from her ear to the center of her chest. Her skin was smooth, the breast he'd uncovered white and supple. Her nipple was hard when he took it in his mouth, her moan of pleasure an echo of his. She teetered a little bit, from dizziness, or from letting go of her walker, he didn't know. He swung her into his arms, then pushed her walker aside. Slowly, he lowered her to the bed.

Except for the occasional lightning flickering in the distance, the room was dark. He eased onto the bed next to her, stretching out beside her. She turned onto her side, and covered him with her hand. His heart nearly exploded. His heart wasn't all. "Easy," he said.

"I don't . . . want it easy tonight."

Who was he to deny this incredible woman what she wanted? With a hand on her shoulder, he rolled her onto her back. He skimmed his fingers over her breasts, squeezing, pleasuring, circling, lower, and lower, until he found the slit in her nightgown, and gained access to her most private flesh. Just in case her shiver was from the cold, he drew the sheet up over them both, then glided his hands over her all over again.

The lightning was closer now, a psychedelic slide show that allowed him to see the pleasure on her face. He didn't know if the thunder he heard was outside, or inside his head. And he didn't care. All he cared about was the look of rapture on Maggie's face, and the sounds she made deep in her throat. He kissed her, long and deep. She answered his kiss on the most primal of levels, opening her mouth, kissing him in return.

She'd always been a quiet lover, not prone to loud cries or sudden outbursts. She didn't need to yell for him to know she responded to his every touch, his every caress. And oh, how she responded. It wasn't easy to take it slow, when he wanted to take it all, to stake his claim, again and again and again.

A whimper sounded from outside their haze of passion. "Mama. Daddy."

They both went momentarily still. The voice had come from upstairs.

"Allison?"

Footsteps sounded overhead just as a streak of lightning lit up the room. "Mama!" There was more terror in Allie's voice now. She must have gone into their room upstairs automatically. "Mama! Daddy."

"It's okay, Allie . . . we're down here."

Seconds later, their younger daughter bounded down the steps, into the room.

"Where are you?"

"Here." Just then, lightning flickered, and she saw them. With another whimper, she landed in bed between them. "My night-light went out."

Maggie wrapped her arms around her child and drew her close.

"And my star lamp won't come on."

"The power must be out." Spence swung his feet over the side of the bed and unobtrusively pulled on his jeans. "I'll be right back with a flashlight."

"And candles," Allie called bossily.

"And candles." Spence's voice was part frustration, part wry humor. Allie was getting as bossy as Grace. His brother had been telling Spence for years that he was going to be in for it when the girls were older. The only male in a house full of women, he was sure to be outwitted, outnumbered, outmaneuvered. Outhormoned.

Feeling his way to the kitchen, he rummaged through the junk drawer. Once he had located the flashlight, he went in search of candles and matches.

Maggie's nightgown was back in place and Allison was under the covers with her mother when he returned. She stayed in their bed as he sighed and lit three candles. Leaving them to take the edge off the blackness of the night, he took the flashlight with him to check on Grace.

The storm had awakened her, too. "Hey, Lady Grace."

"Hi, Dad." She spoke to him sleepily, then turned on her side and went back to sleep.

Allison's eyes were closed when he returned to the makeshift bedroom. Maggie placed a finger to her lips.

"Is she already asleep?" he whispered.

Maggie nodded. And something powerful passed between their gazes.

"I'll carry her back to her own bed."

A clap of thunder shook the ground and rattled the window. Allison whimpered, clinging to Maggie. Spence took a steadying breath, then crawled into bed to wait out the storm, alone on his side of the bed.

This was part of parenting, not the best part maybe, but Spence knew better than anybody that the good far outweighed the bad. And he wouldn't trade it, any of it, for all the gold in the world.

When the storm was over, he carried Allison back to her own bed. By then, Maggie was sound asleep, too. Mindful that she needed her rest, he crawled carefully into bed beside his wife.

He knew from experience these past months that it wasn't going to be easy to sleep in his condition. He lay on his back, staring at the ceiling, counting his blessings instead of sheep, listening to the rain, his Maggie a warm presence next to him, their children safe and sound, sleeping upstairs.

Maggie groaned softly, the sound the closest Ivan had ever heard her come to a complaint. "Does this hurt?"

"I'm okay."

He cast a quick glance at her face, and eased up a little on the pressure he was applying to muscles he was massaging in the back of her thigh. He didn't, however, stop. "Serves you right for overdoing."

Not that she would quit pushing herself.

It had been raining when he'd come to work. Ivan didn't mind subzero temperatures. Hell, he loved them, but he'd never had much use for dismal rain. His coworkers claimed it made him grouchy. Nothing wrong with that. After all, grouchiness helped him maintain an emotional distance. He needed all the help he could get, because it was damned difficult to stay ornery when Maggie McKenzie was around.

Ivan wasn't afraid to break most rules. He drove fast, double-parked when it suited him, disregarded the dress code and usually wore blue jeans and T-shirts to work. Truth be told, he enjoyed ruffling feathers and breaking rules. That was one of the things he'd liked about hockey—it was a sport built around breaking rules.

There were two rules, the Cardinal Rules of physical therapy, that he didn't so much as touch with a ten-foot pole, let alone break. He didn't get emotionally involved with his patients.

And he sure as hell didn't get turned on by them.

Maggie moaned. Ivan bent a knee, easing the fit of his jeans. For Christ sake, the woman was in pain, not in the throes of passion. Dammit to hell, those Cardinal Rules were easier to keep when his patients were big, burly men.

He took his hands off her and stepped back. "Okay," he said more gruffly than she deserved. "Let's get you back to the bars and work on your balance."

Ms. Independence sat up without taking the hand he offered, just as she always did. Gingerly, she slid her feet to the floor. With the use of her walker, she started toward the parallel bars.

"I need to learn how to climb . . . stairs so I can sleep upstairs with Spence."

They passed a middle-aged patient who was crying that she couldn't do what her physical therapist wanted her to do. Keeping his voice low so the others wouldn't hear, Ivan said, "You don't sleep with Spence?"

"Well, yes."

They'd come to the bars, but she didn't stop at them. It took a few of Ivan's longest strides to catch up with her. Where in the hell was she going? "Where do you sleep?"

He clamped his mouth shut and shook his head. It was none of his business where she and her husband slept.

"In the family room. Our bedroom's . . . upstairs. Allison was scared of the storm last night. She woke up . . . and couldn't find us. I want to . . . I have to . . . learn to climb stairs, so we're upstairs . . . if it happens again . . ."

"It's understandable that you want to learn to climb stairs so you'll be there for your kids, but . . ."

"And for privacy."

"You mean so you can . . ." Ivan clamped his mouth shut and ordered the image that flitted into his mind *out*.

Maggie smiled at the very idea that she was saying this to anybody other than Jackie. "I've been confiding in you . . . more and more lately." She was following the track around the outside of the room, and was concentrating on trying not to limp. "Guess that's because . . . Jackie hasn't been over much lately. I hope you don't mind."

"You and Jackie have a fight?"

For weeks, the speech therapist had been having Maggie work on organizing her thoughts so she would finish one topic before jumping to another. She was getting better at it, but it required intense concentration, something that was difficult to do when she was already concentrating on walking. It was frustrating.

"Argue with Jackie? Of course . . . not."

"What was I thinking? Who would argue with agreeable little you?"

Other than him, nobody. Maggie didn't allow herself to grin. "Exactly."

He made a sound that only another man could replicate. Now, she grinned.

She enjoyed the physical therapy more than the other sessions. Maybe that was because she was better at it. Or maybe it was because she could be herself with Ivan. He certainly didn't try to put on airs with her. Monday, he'd been wearing an IVAN THE KID T-shirt. Today he was wearing one that had the words I DON'T SUFFER FROM STRESS. I'M A CARRIER spelled out across his chest.

"I don't think you cause . . . stress."

"Would you do me a favor and tell my boss that next time you see her?"

Maggie picked up her right foot and eased it in front of her left one. "I'll tell her . . . you usually see reason . . . when it hits you on the head. Now, about climbing stairs . . ."

"Don't pick your leg up from your hip. Use the muscles in your thigh. That's better. It's too soon to think about navigating stairs."

"I can scoot down them. How do I get up them?"

"You can't."

"Not yet, but I will . . . Teach me how."

"You could fall."

"So could . . . the sky."

"You can't, Maggie."

"Watch me."

"Maggie. You can't climb stairs with a walker."

Maggie looked at him again. She was accustomed to the sheer size of him, the breadth of his shoulders and the stubborn set of his chin. He was young, twenty-six or -seven at the most, and had a slew of muscles, a devil-may-care attitude, and a stern expression that probably intimidated a lot of people, just not her. "I know that, silly."

She grinned, because it was pretty obvious from his expression that not many people called him silly. She let him seethe for a moment, then said, "That's why I need . . . to learn to walk without it."

He crossed his arms at his chest, and glanced at the patient riding the stationary bicycle a few feet away, and at the other patients and their therapists working throughout the room. "Look," he said. "Do you see anybody else telling their therapist what to do? We're the ones who push, who set parameters, limits, and goals. Of course you want to be able to climb stairs. And you will. But it's going to take time."

"Everything takes too damm much time."

He covered his ears with both hands.

And she said, "Ex—hockey players do not . . . have sensitive ears."

"We'll work on climbing stairs in a week or two."

"Today."

"Who in the hell is in charge here, anyway?"

She looked him in the eye. "I thought you . . . knew."

Ivan uncrossed his arms. Letting them fall limply to his sides, he simply stared.

"Now, what do . . . I have to do?"

"Climbing stairs requires balance and muscles you haven't used in a long time. We would have to start with small steps, a harness, heavy-duty railings, and work our way up to actual stairs."

"Where do we . . . find these small steps?"

Ivan started to point, but ended up shaking his head. She grinned at him, as if fully aware that she'd won.

He rocked back on his heels, wondering when he would learn that a mere man didn't tell Maggie McKenzie that she couldn't do something when she put her mind to it. Whoa. Since when had he become a mere man?

It was Saturday afternoon, laundry day at Maggie's house. The low drone of masculine voices carried to the kitchen where she and Jackie were folding towels and clothes. Jackie placed a basket of freshly dried towels in front of Maggie, then returned to the laundry room for the basket containing Grace and Allison's things.

Maggie had barely made a dent in the mountain of washcloths and towels when her sister pulled out a chair opposite her, and put another basket on it. They worked in companionable silence until a particularly loud clank shook the floor.

"Are you sure all Frank and Brian are doing is disassembling the bed and not building a rocket or something?"

Maggie smiled encouragingly. "There is . . . a lot of racket going on, isn't there?"

Jackie had started folding Allie's shirt with the butterflies on it. It awarded Maggie a moment to study her sister. Jackie looked okay, didn't she? It was hard to tell with her hair hanging in her face. She was dressed all in black, and black had never really been her color.

Jackie was quiet these days, and she'd never been a quiet person. She was helping with the family laundry, just as she did every Saturday afternoon while Spence, Grace, and Allison went to the grocery store. Maggie sorted and folded, and Jackie did the lifting and transferring and carrying.

Maggie thought about what Ivan had said about an argument. She and Jackie hadn't argued. That much she was sure of. She studied Jackie's face, feature by feature. She'd always been pretty, and always would be. Since childhood, she'd possessed an inner fire, a spunk that Maggie didn't see today. It wasn't just the fact that she was wearing black. Something was different. She couldn't quite put her finger on what it was. It was more than quietude, too. Jackie looked sad. Or worried. Or something.

She twisted slightly and reached around beside her for another garment, the action drawing her plain black shirt tight across her chest. It occurred to Maggie that Jackie had gained a little weight. She still looked terribly pale, though. And the smudges under her eyes were so dark they looked like bruises.

She remembered that Jackie had had the flu a few weeks ago. Now, she was worried. "Jackie? Is everything . . . all right?"

"What's the matter? Aren't I folding these clothes right?"

"Am I really . . . that bossy?"

Jackie looked up quickly, obviously surprised. "I was kidding. And yes." She smiled. "It's a Fletcher trait."

Maggie would have felt better if Jackie had held her gaze a little longer. It had been two weeks since Maggie had started learning to climb stairs. She was getting good at it if she did say so herself, good enough, in fact, to make it safely to the top. Although it was an arduous journey, now she could do it without a harness or help. She hadn't told Spence because she wanted to surprise him. While he and the girls were out, Frank and Brian were taking the bed apart, lugging it up to the master bedroom, where they would put it together again.

It was one of those gorgeous days in late September when the sky was clear, the air warm and fragrant. Summer humidity was a thing of the past. The leaves hadn't started to turn yet, but autumn was in the air. It was a perfect day for a picnic supper on the beach, something Maggie hadn't done all summer. She was going to surprise Spence and the girls with her plans. She had a different, more private surprise in mind for Spence later, in the privacy of their own room.

Jackie had been in on the scheme. She was the one who'd gotten the picnic basket up from the basement. Still, while she'd been helpful as always, something was different. Try as she might, Maggie still couldn't fathom what it might be.

Jackie felt Maggie's gaze on her. Busying herself with her task, she pretended she didn't notice. When the dryer buzzed, she hurried into the laundry room and away from her sister's assessing gaze. By herself in the small room, she took a calming breath.

She was rarely nauseated these days. That, at least, was a relief. She opened the dryer. The sheets were dry, and ready to be put back on the beds. If only figuring out what to do about her situation was a fraction as easy.

Every time she thought about terminating the pregnancy, she cried. She couldn't do it. That much she knew for sure. She was nearly two-and-a-half months along. No matter what they called the life that was growing inside her, the splitting of cells, a fetus, an embryo, she couldn't kill it. That left two options. She could have the baby and lie about its father for the rest of her life. Or she could go away until the baby was born, and an adoption could be arranged. How could she give her baby up?

How could she not? What if the baby looked like Spence? People here would see the resemblance. How would she explain that?

Maggie knew how desperately she'd always longed for a child. If Jackie ever found the strength to choose the second option, Maggie would never understand. Therefore, Jackie couldn't tell her. Keeping her secret from Maggie was the hardest thing she'd ever done. What else could she do?

Tears filled her eyes. Swiping them away, she took three deep breaths, then transferred another load of laundry from the washer to the dryer. By the time she'd carried the basket of clothes to the kitchen and placed them next to Maggie, she had her emotions back under control.

"Jacks?"

"Hm?"

"Aren't you sleeping . . . well these days?"

All she wanted to do was sleep. "I sleep fine. Would you stop worrying about me?"

"You've been so withdrawn . . . and there are dark circles under your eyes."

Jackie felt her throat closing up, and fresh tears burn in her eyes. It should have been the happiest time of her life. She should have been dancing for joy. She should have been able to share it all with her only sister.

"What is it? What's going on with you? What ... haven't you told me?"

Jackie knew a moment of pure panic. "What do you mean?"

"Are you sick? Do you have ... cancer? What?"

"No, no," she rushed to assure her. "I'm fine, really."

"Is it David?"

Grasping the subject like a lifeline, she said, "Mom asked the same thing when she called this morning."

"Mom called?"

Jackie shot Maggie a sardonic look. "As if you didn't put her up to it."

Maggie waited expectantly.

And Jackie sighed. "It's final."

"What's final?"

"My divorce."

"Already? I didn't know ... you'd even signed the final papers."

"I did that when you were at Bentworth."

"I hope you told David ... what you thought of him."

Jackie hadn't seen him; everything had been handled long-distance via their separate attorneys. "Telling him off wouldn't change anything, Mags."

Maggie swung her legs around and reached for her walker. She rose shakily to her feet. Once she was standing, it didn't take her long to make her way to the other side of the table where Jackie stood folding a light blue shirt. That didn't give Jackie long to take a quiet breath and get herself under control. Maggie placed a hand over Jackie's where it rested on the small shirt. Her touch was tender, strong enough to give comfort and unbelievably warm. Surely, she'd noticed that Jackie's hand was ice cold.

"Jackie?"

Jackie couldn't very well keep her eyes downcast. Willing her lips not to quiver and her chin not to shake, she met her sister's gaze.

"Your divorce has been final all this time, and you didn't . . . tell me?"

"You have so much going on in your life. You're getting better, and you're working so hard. You've already been through enough."

Maggie blinked back tears. Good job, Jackie thought. Now she'd gone and hurt Maggie's feelings.

"I'm still your sister. You can . . . always come to me, can always tell me anything."

Not this. She could never tell her this. "I don't want to upset you, Mags, but I've been thinking . . ." Her voice trailed away.

"What have you been . . . thinking about?"

Jackie looked Maggie in the eye and sighed. Her short hair gave her a waif-like look, her beige chinos and crisp, light green shirt a neat and tidy contrast. The scar along the side of her face was beginning to fade around the edges. Jackie sighed again. "Maybe this isn't the time to tell you this."

"Tell me what?"

"I've been thinking that maybe it's time for me to make a change."

"What sort of . . ."

"I'm thinking about moving."

"Back to Grand Haven?"

"No." She'd spoken more severely than she'd intended.

"Where then?"

Good question. "I'm not sure, but maybe to Traverse City."

"But Jackie, that's so far away. We've never . . . lived more than twenty miles apart."

"Actually, Mom suggested it."

"Mom suggested you move away?"

Jackie tried to smile, but it wasn't easy. "Not exactly. She told me I probably need a change of scenery. She invited me to Africa for a visit. I think she's right. Not about Africa, but about needing a new place, a new beginning." Traverse City was a beautiful city on Lake Michigan's Grand Traverse Bay. It was a hundred and seventy-five miles from Grand Haven, on curving roads and highways. Industry, tourism, and merchandising were all booming there. Jackie had visited several summers ago, and again in early spring, before Maggie's accident. The more she thought about it, the more sense the idea made. Who knows, she might even find peace there, at least until she decided what to do about the rest of her life.

"But why? What about . . . the store?"

"I'm going to close it."

"I thought sales were . . . better. If you need money . . . I'm sure Spence and I could loan you—"

"No!" She'd spoken sharply. Instantly remorseful, she said, "I guess I'm getting cranky in my old age. Actually, my attorney was very good. How did he word it? I'm fiscally sound."

"That's good, right?"

Maggie was looking at her, her blue eyes round and warm and soft enough to slip into. She'd always been this way, a port in a storm, waiting with open arms, a warm sweater, and a cup of steaming tea. She was the best, the kindest, the dearest person Jackie knew.

"Jacks? I want to help. Tell me . . . what I can do."

Jackie's face crumbled, tears squeezing out of her eyes.

Balancing by keeping one hand on the table, Maggie

wrapped her other arm around her sister. Jackie shuddered, and for a moment, it felt so good. She relaxed, inhaling the clean scent of laundry and shampoo. She hadn't been hugged in a long time. Sometimes she forgot how lonely she was.

She was about to draw away. Maggie beat her to it. This close, it was easy to see the innate intelligence in Maggie's eyes. Jackie feared she was putting it all together: the tears, the circles under her eyes, the increase in bra sizes, her sudden need for a new beginning.

She wished the phone would ring, or the girls would come rushing through the door, or either Frank or Brian would stick his head in the room to flirt a little and maybe ask Maggie a question. The refrigerator hummed. Farther away, the washer began its spin cycle. Maggie's gaze remained trained on Jackie's face.

"Jackie?"

Frozen like a deer trapped in the glare of headlights, all Jackie could do was wait for the question she dreaded.

CHAPTER THIRTEEN

"Jacqueline Fletcher. You're . . . pregnant."

It hadn't been a question after all. Denying it would only make matters worse. The moment of truth had arrived. More like the moment of lies.

The sisters were only two feet apart, their eyes nearly the same shade of blue and equally as wide. Both stood perfectly still, Maggie, because moving required careful planning, and Jackie, because all her energies were tied up in knots along with her emotions.

Jackie finally nodded, a hand on each cheek.

"How did this . . . happen?"

She had no idea how to reply.

With a roll of her eyes, Maggie said, "The usual way . . . I'm sure."

Jackie still couldn't answer, because it hadn't happened in the usual way. Her child hadn't been conceived out of love, or even in passion. This child had been conceived in sorrow.

She cried at the drop of a hat these days. Strangely, her eyes remained dry now. She was thankful for that.

"When?" Maggie asked.

Since the question could have referred to several things, Jackie chose her response carefully. "I'm two and a half months along."

"Then you've been to a . . . doctor?"

"A month ago."

"And you didn't tell me?" Maggie's eyes filled with tears.

Jackie didn't know what to say. She only knew what she couldn't say. She'd thought she could keep her condition a secret until she'd decided what to do. She hadn't made much progress in that department these last four weeks. The past was unsettling, the present vague. The future was bound to be painful no matter what choice she made. She'd run out of time, and was going to have to rely on instinct, and try to explain as best she could. "I didn't know at first, Mags. I thought I had the flu. But it came and went, and didn't feel like any flu I'd ever had. Finally, it dawned on me that I might be pregnant." Actually, it had dawned on her like a ton of bricks.

"Did you tell Mom . . . and the colonel?"

"What? No. I've been the bearer of a lot of bad news this past year. David's affair, our divorce, your accident. I don't know what they'll say about this." Until two minutes ago, she hadn't known if she would ever tell anyone.

"It isn't as if you're sixteen!"

Okay, now tears stung the back of Jackie's throat. Leave it to Maggie to defend her, even now. But then, Maggie didn't know. She could never know.

"A baby, Jackie."

There was no sense pretending that Jackie didn't hear the wonder in her sister's voice. For a moment, she felt the wonder, too. She was going to have a baby.

Reality rose up, swallowing the wonder whole, and her with it. Maggie had lived through a horrendous car accident, brain surgery, a nine-and-a-half-week coma, grueling physical, speech, and occupational therapy. Jackie didn't think she would survive the truth. To make matters worse, now that she knew about Jackie's pregnancy, all the lies in the world wouldn't be enough to explain why she would give her baby up. Now that Maggie knew there was going to be a baby, Jackie's decision had been made for her. Deep down, she'd never wanted to give her child to some nice couple, any nice couple. She loved this baby, and she wanted this child more than she'd ever wanted anything in her life. But at what cost?

"You're happy . . . aren't you?" Maggie's voice shook. "I mean, after all this time . . . you're going to be a mother. And Spence and I . . . are going to have a niece or maybe a nephew."

Jackie's throat closed up so tight she couldn't swallow or breathe. Somehow, Maggie managed to take that last step without falling. The next thing Jackie knew, she was crying and Maggie was patting her shoulder. "It's your hormones. Pregnancy turns them upside down . . . and inside out. Is it possible . . . that you and David might reconcile?"

Jackie sniffled. David?

Of course Maggie would assume the baby was David's. Jackie let her believe one lie instead of a hundred. One lie was all it took to darken a soul, wasn't it? She wondered what measure God used to gage a sinner's wrongs. Was a sin a sin? Did circumstances and good intentions make up for anything?

She could hear Spence's brothers half-dragging, half-carrying the box spring up the stairs. It reminded her to keep her voice low. "David doesn't want anything to do with me. He's in love with someone else. Our divorce is final, and will stay that way."

"But fathers have . . . responsibilities."

Jackie's guilt was so strong she could taste it. She smoothed her hands down the sides of her lightweight skirt. Inside, yearning to tell somebody the truth rose up. On its heels came the need to protect Maggie from that same truth. She pushed the yearning back down, into the deepest part of her, where it would stay, her secret, her baby.

Hers alone.

There was a loud, booming clunk, as if somebody had dropped something heavy in another part of the house. Spence's younger brother cursed, which prompted his older brother to tell him to watch his language. At least it gave Maggie some other place to look, and Jackie something else to say. "It sounds as if your bed is on its way back where it belongs."

"Not necessarily . . . in one piece."

It seemed that Maggie was getting everything back, even her sense of humor. Jackie slid the walker to her, then carefully stepped out of her sister's reach. "I didn't intend to unload my problems on you today, Mags."

"What are sisters . . . for?"

Jackie was glad Maggie was looking down, and not at her face. She didn't think she would be able to explain everything she was feeling, the guilt, the remorse, and the worry for her future, for all their futures.

"Jackie, I want to help."

She had to force herself to meet the sincerity in Maggie's eyes. Taking a shuddering breath, Jackie said, "I don't want you to worry about me. It sounds like the guys are almost finished. I'll take the sheets and blankets up and make up the bed."

"You've done so much for me. For all of us. And I've never thanked—"

Jackie couldn't let her finish. "I haven't told another living soul about, well, the baby." She tried to continue, but couldn't bring herself to ask Maggie for a favor, any favor.

Somehow, Maggie knew. "Your secret's safe with me ... I promise I won't tell a soul. Except Spence, of course."

Jackie reached the laundry room in the nick of time, sinking onto the narrow bench before her knees gave out from under her. That had been a close one.

Then and there, it occurred to her that this was all about timing: Maggie's accident, her coma, this baby's conception, Maggie's recovery and continued progress. Jackie was going to have a baby. And Spence was going to find out. It was just a matter of time.

Maggie sat in the middle of the old, faded quilt they always used for outings to the beach, the empty picnic basket near her feet, a book about lighthouses open on her lap. Other than a few power walkers and a flock of noisy seagulls, she, Spence, Grace, and Allison had this stretch of Lake Michigan nearly to themselves.

They'd munched on thick, roast beef sandwiches and potato salad and wedges of watermelon and store-bought cookies. It was a little too late in the year to swim. The breeze was strong and carried the faint scent of fall, the air a sunny seventy-five degrees. A man and a woman waved as they chugged past in a yacht. Farther out, a huge tanker disappeared over the horizon. Spence had always said he liked the off-season the best. It was amazing that it had taken waking from her coma to see what he meant. It was late September, but the world felt brand new.

Spence and the girls had gathered their used paper plates, then stashed them in a covered trash container nearby. Leaving half-empty cans of soda on the quilt for Maggie to guard, Grace and Allison had raced to the water's edge. Now, they were running through the sand, their kites soaring, seagulls swooping, Allison yelling, Grace and Spence grinning.

Some children were afraid of seagulls. Not Allison. She didn't like them, and made no bones about hiding that fact. Every time she saw several of them sitting idle on the sand, she ran at them, scattering them to the wind. They squawked and swooped at her kite, which only infuriated her more. It was comical. Maggie didn't know who was noisier, Allie or the birds.

Spence was between the girls, helping with Allie's kite, steadying Grace as she reeled hers in and let it out again. When Allison got too close to the water's edge, he grabbed her up, running backward mere inches ahead of the breaking waves. The instant he set her on her feet again, she raced away, her kite climbing higher and higher.

He stood watching the girls, hands on his hips. The wind billowed through his burgundy shirt, lifting his dark hair off his forehead and blowing it straight back. Maggie doubted she would ever tire of looking at him.

He chose that moment to glance her way, their gazes meeting over the tops of the girls' heads. He started toward her, his love so tangible she felt it, all of it. She was warmed, flushed with heat at his smile, excited by something as simple as a look.

With stern instructions to the girls not to go too far, he dropped down to his knees next to Maggie on the quilt.

"Having fun?" she asked.

He nodded. "Are you?"

"You know I am. Next year . . . I'm going to be out there with you . . . helping the girls fly their kites."

"I believe you."

His belief in her nudged her from the inside. While he watched the girls playing a hundred feet away, she studied him. The lines beside his eyes hadn't been there last spring, and his nose and cheekbones were chiseled as if by a divine hand.

"Here." She patted her lap. "Rest for a few minutes. I'll keep an eye . . . on the girls."

He stretched out on the quilt, his knees bent, his head nestled on her soft lap. His eyes closed at the first touch of her fingers combing through his hair. The breeze lulled, the waves lapped, and Spence made an agreeable sound deep in his throat.

He was exhausted. She often forgot how difficult these past months had been for him. Sometimes she took his quiet strength and unfailing belief in her for granted. Earlier, he'd carried her down to the beach, the quilt and cooler of drinks piled on her lap, Allison and Grace lugging the picnic basket between them, their colorful kites dangling from their other hands. How many men would do what he did without ever so much as complaining?

Grace still watched her closely at times, but day by day, Maggie was regaining her older daughter's belief in her abilities and capabilities as a competent mother. She thought Spence looked tired, although not as tired as he had two and a half months ago when she'd first awakened. He rarely talked about what it had been like for him all those weeks while she'd slept. Once, she'd asked about their living wills. He'd said that time in his life had been a nightmare, one that had ended the moment she woke up. He hadn't offered any details. Much of what she'd learned, she'd read in Grace's journal. It was difficult to read, for it made Maggie sad. Once, Grace had written, "Dad took us to see Mom. I hate it there. It smelled funny. And Mom looked dead." Most of the entries were short. One in particular left Maggie feeling hollow. "Dad cried tonight. I'm scared."

Jackie had answered a few of Maggie's questions

regarding that period, but she, too, hadn't wanted to dredge up the past. It had to have been awful to cause both of them to look so haggard and drawn. Now Maggie knew that Jackie was dealing with other issues, too. She didn't understand why her only sister would even consider moving at a time like this, but at least she knew why she looked so pale.

Keeping her eyes on Grace and Allie, who were hunkered down, looking at something in the sand, Maggie smoothed her hand over Spence's brow. "Want to know a secret?"

She interpreted the movement of his head as a nod. "I have big plans for you later."

"How big?"

She held her hands a good distance apart the way a fisherman might. Spence opened his eyes a slit, and chuckled. "I hope I don't disappoint you."

"You never have. You're too . . . much man for me sometimes . . . and you know it."

Desire started deep inside Spence, pulsing, radiating outward. He wasn't too much man for her; they were perfect for one another. He'd tried to take things slow, to be careful with her since she'd been home. Somehow, his intentions had a way of getting short-circuited between his brain and the rest of him.

He closed his eyes again, enjoying the feel of her fingers in his hair. The girls' voices blended with the wind and the waves in the distance. He felt so relaxed he never wanted to move.

"I finally figured out what's . . . bothering Jackie."

Maggie was a talker, one of those women who thought out loud. He would never again take the sound of her voice for granted. "I didn't know anything was bothering Jackie."

"That's because she's my sister, my confidante, not yours."

She was right. Maggie usually was.

"Daddy!" Allie called.

"Her kite's getting away from her, Spence."

Groaning, he sat up. Shading his eyes with one hand, he called, "Reel it in a little, Allison. If it goes too high, the wind might snap the line."

Allison started reeling hers in. When Grace had finished winding her own line around the spool, she tried to help Allie with hers. Allison informed Grace that she wasn't ready to reel hers all the way in. Grace left her own kite on the ground, then raced off in search of fossils and artifacts that might have washed ashore from shipwrecks of old. Next to Spence, Maggie said, "Aren't you going to ask what's going on with Jackie?"

"I'd rather hear about those big plans you have for me later."

She nudged him with one shoulder.

"All right. What's going on with Jackie?"

"You remember when she had the flu . . . when I first came home from St. Ann's."

"I guess."

"It wasn't the flu."

Seagulls swooped at Allie's kite, squawking noisily. Allie squawked right back. Shading his eyes with one hand, he kept a careful watch on her, lest she dart too close to the water again. "What was it then?"

"Nothing that a total of nine months won't cure."

The first pinpricks of trepidation stuck him in the back of his neck. "Nine months?"

"Jackie's pregnant, Spence."

The pinpricks turned into sledgehammers. He was stunned, literally.

Grace came bounding over, dumping an armload of sticks and stones she'd found along the water's edge. "Look," she said, kneeling in front of her mother. "I think this might be an arrowhead."

Allison traipsed over, too, kicking up sand, her kite dragging behind her. "Dumb birds."

"Are you girls . . . ready to go home?"

The blood rushing through Spence's ears sounded like a freight train. Strange, because he didn't feel as if there was any blood left in him. There was little air, either. And only one thought.

Jackie was pregnant?

As if from a great distance, he heard Maggie tell the girls to pick up their things. And then she was telling him about David, and how the low-down, dirty, no-good, no-account, poor excuse for a man wasn't going to have any part in Jackie's life.

David? Jackie was pregnant, but the baby was David's? An ounce of relief allowed him to take a deep breath.

"She wants to move . . . to Traverse City before the baby is born . . . She's only two and a half months along. There's still time . . . to talk her out of that."

Spence's mind reeled, and the bottom fell out of his stomach. Jackie was two and a half months along. Two and a half months ago, he thought Maggie was lost to them forever. The time frame had too great a significance to be a coincidence.

He didn't know how he managed to stand up and put one foot in front of the other, let alone to do it with Maggie in his arms and the girls talking a mile a minute as they carted their kites and the picnic basket with them back to the van. He drove them home, and they went inside. Maggie busied herself with taking care of the picnic items.

It was eight o'clock by the time they all sat down to watch the latest Olson twins movie Grace had been begging to see. The coming attractions had barely started when, out of the blue, Allison declared, "I want ice cream."

"You just . . . ate."

"I'm hungry."

"Me, too." Now, Grace was in on the scheme. Both girls turned to their father. They probably thought it was the flutter of their eyelashes that made him putty in their hands, when really, he was completely unable to offer up any resistance, completely unable to think, period.

Driving to the store for ice cream was preferable to staying in that house where Maggie might notice his dazed expression. At any given moment, she might ask him what was wrong. And he wouldn't be able to tell her, because telling her would mean the end of her trust, her faith in him. He would sooner be unmanned.

"What flavor?" he asked from the door.

"Surprise us," Grace instructed.

"Yeah," Allison agreed.

He didn't know if he could handle any more surprises that day.

It had never been easy for Spence to carry on a one-sided conversation with God. He believed. He'd just always left the actual praying to Maggie.

From the moment he got in his car in his own garage, until the moment he raised his fist and knocked on Jackie's door in Spring Lake, he prayed for a miracle. *Let it be David's. Let it be David's. Dear God in heaven, let it be David's.*

Jackie came to the door, opened it, then stood back so he could enter. "That was fast."

She'd been expecting him. Him. Not David. So much for his prayers being answered.

He and Jackie had always shared an easy camaraderie. Until two and a half months ago, that is. Tonight in particular, he didn't have any idea what to say.

"Maggie told you." She closed the door. As if needing

its support, she leaned against it. "You look like hell, Spence. See there? I cussed. Odelia would be pleased." She pulled a face, and seemed to be working to swallow the nerves that were congregating in the back of her throat.

He knew the feeling. "It's true?"

She brushed her hair behind her shoulders and lifted her chin. Finally, she said, "You know it's true, or you wouldn't be here. That night, when we were both drowning in our greatest, murkiest sorrow, I became pregnant."

He closed his eyes. He needed to sit down. He couldn't move. "I'm sorry, Jackie."

She pushed away from the door, took a step toward him, only to stop abruptly. "You think I don't know how sorry you are?" She spun around, pacing to the other side of the room. "You can be sorry all you want. I'm the one who has to deal with this."

It was the equivalent of being kicked while he was down. Maybe he deserved it, but he hadn't expected it. Not from Jackie. "I have to deal with this, too. My God. You know how much I love Grace and Allison, how much Maggie and I wanted another child. And now . . ."

"You're not having another child, Spence. I am. You can't think of this baby as yours."

Those words squeezed the rest of the air right out of him. "But . . ."

"But what?"

"I want to help."

"You can't. Don't you see? Anything you would try to do to help would only end up hurting all of us, Maggie most of all. She can't know. She can't even guess. Ever."

He knew that, dammit. "But what about you?"

He saw the tears in her eyes, and hated himself.

"What about me?"

"This isn't fair to you."

Her chin quivered, but she spoke anyway. "Haven't you heard? Life isn't fair."

"What are you going to do?"

"I'm going to move away, and have my baby, and pray it doesn't look like you."

Jackie had never been one to mince words. He found his gaze straying down to her stomach. She was wearing one of the dresses she sold in her store. This one was purple. He saw no signs of a pregnancy. That didn't mean he doubted her word.

"How will you live? There must be some way I can help with the support."

She, too, was having a difficult time standing. She closed her eyes and made fists at her side. "What will you do? Write a check every month? How would you hide that from Maggie? Better yet, how would you explain it?"

The words sliced him clear to the bone. She must have noticed. She took a shuddering breath, and softened her voice. "She's smart, Spence. You know that. I'm not destitute. David's affair cost him. My attorney made certain of that. I have enough money to live on, and enough left over to invest for college. In the meantime, I can work to help support myself and my child, because this baby can only be mine. Mine, alone."

He hung his head.

"Go home to your wife and children. It's where you belong."

He took a deep breath, straightened his spine, and squared his shoulders. Realizing that there was nothing more to be said, nothing else he could do, he did what she'd told him to do. He walked out of her house, got in his car, and drove back to Grand Haven.

* * *

Maggie and the girls were still watching the movie when he returned. Allison jumped up the moment she heard the door. "I thought you'd never get home!"

"Forty-five minutes to buy ice cream?" Grace asked.

What could he say? It hadn't taken forty-five minutes to buy ice cream. It had taken only two minutes to do that. He'd gotten all the way to their street before he'd even remembered the reason he'd gone out. The reason he'd given Maggie. He'd made a U-turn at the corner, and rushed back to the store.

"What kind did you bring?" Grace asked.

Spence had no idea. "I thought you wanted me to surprise you."

"Let's go find out." Maggie pushed the pause button, then reached for her walker. Turning on lights as she went, she led the way to the kitchen.

Grace plucked five half-gallon cartons from the paper sack Spence had placed on the counter. Maggie smiled. "I told the girls you . . . probably ran into somebody you knew."

He was reaching for the bowls, his back to Maggie. He froze, because he had no idea how to respond. If she asked, he was going to have to lie, when he'd never lied to her in his life. Luckily, she let it go.

The girls were thrilled with all their choices. He couldn't really take the credit. He'd been so dazed he hadn't realized he'd stacked so many different flavors in his basket until the bagger asked him if he wanted paper or plastic.

They all watched the rest of the movie together. Most of his sundae melted in the bottom of his bowl.

It was almost ten o'clock by the time Maggie told the girls it was time for bed. Spence hadn't been aware that Allison had fallen asleep next to him. He jostled her, then dazedly carried the dirty dishes out to the kitchen.

"I'll tuck the girls in," he said when he returned to the family room.

Allison peered up at him sleepily. "Mama said you're gonna do that together."

Spence looked at Maggie, who nodded. "It's part . . . of my surprise."

Of course. She'd told him that before. He'd forgotten.

For the first time since before her accident, she parked her walker next to the banister, and made her way up the stairs. She was painfully slow at it, but she reached the top all by herself. She beamed as she took the canes Grace and Allison handed to her, her eyes bright. The girls clapped, hugging her carefully. Spence got in on the hug, but he hoped she didn't feel the stiffness in his muscles, and wonder at the cause.

They tucked Allison in first. Grace was putting the cap on her pink pen and closing her journal when they entered her room. Sitting on the edge of the bed, Maggie took the journal from her, and placed it carefully on the bedside table.

Grace snuggled under the blankets. "This has been the best day. I love you, Mom."

"I love you, too, sweetie."

It was so damn touching. Spence was so damn lucky. And he knew that, for the second time in a matter of months, he could lose Maggie. The first time had been to death. The next time would be to something worse.

"Good night, Dad."

He pulled the sheet up to Grace's chin, then brushed a kiss on her forehead. "Night, Lady Grace."

He and Maggie left their older daughter's room, pulling the door shut behind them. Allison was already asleep in her room across the hall. Those two children were as different as night and day. He'd always wondered if a third child would have been like either of them . . .

"Spence?"

He'd thought he would never know. He'd accepted that.

"Spence?" Maggie had called his name, probably more than once. She stopped at the doorway in their bedroom, and was watching him closely. "Is something wrong?"

He'd never kept secrets from her. He wasn't good at it. He was even worse at lying. "I guess I'm more tired than I thought."

"Too tired?"

She reached the bed ahead of him. Sitting on the edge, she looked up at him. His body was already reacting to the sultry look in her eyes, the brash little pout on her lips. He *was* exhausted, physically, mentally, emotionally. His heart was heavy, his guilt strong. He doubted he deserved her, and yet he couldn't deny her.

He locked their door with one hand, unbuttoned his shirt with the other. Tugging it from the waistband of his jeans, he took a step toward her. "What did you have in mind?"

"Why don't you help me . . . out of my clothes, and I'll . . . show you."

Her shirt came off in his hands. In almost no time, her bra, jeans, and panties landed on the floor. His clothes came off, too, and suddenly, finally they were naked, skin to skin, chest to breast, thigh to thigh. Husband to wife.

The need to take her then and there was strong. He would have, if she hadn't stopped him. She crawled into bed wearing nothing but her smile and the diamond stud earrings he'd given her for their second wedding anniversary. She patted the bed. When he followed her, stretching out beside her, she glided her calf sinuously down his leg. Her touch was bold, sensual. It took the edge off his paralyzing sense of dread.

"Oh, my. Whatever will I do . . . with you?" She was a tease. Always had been. She liked to talk during love-making. He liked to let her do whatever she liked. "No. Wait. Don't tell . . . me. I'll have to figure it out . . . by myself."

"Figure away."

She laughed, a deep, throaty, sexy sound that went straight to his senses. "That's what I like about . . . you. What I've always liked about . . . you. You're always so willing to let me explore."

The mattress shifted as she moved a little farther down his body. His chest heaved at the feel of her moist lips on him. She was wanton, bold, shameless. Eventually, she worked her way back up his body, talking as she went. "What we have is so special . . ."

He groaned his agreement.

"One of the things that makes it so special is that neither of us has ever . . . been with anyone else."

His heart skipped a beat, then seemed to stop altogether. He closed his eyes, his thoughts a tumult.

He moved quickly, without conscious thought. He rolled her onto her back, and poised himself over her. With a thrust, he joined them.

Maggie gasped, rising toward him, accepting a little more of him, feeling full and yet still wanting more. She knew her movements weren't as fluid as they'd once been, but her body was just as responsive. She watched his face. His eyes were closed, his jaw clenched, his lips pressed into a straight line.

She placed a hand on his cheek, and felt the muscles beneath her palm relax. He started to move. Her eyes closed automatically. She whimpered as tremors over-took her, and then him. Moments before he came, he covered her mouth with his, as if he had to connect with her on every level. The kiss went on and on, catching her cry of release, and his. Afterward, he pulled her close, and wrapped his arms around her.

"Spence, I can't breathe."

He loosened his hold, but didn't let her go completely.

She lay there, listening as his breathing deepened. It was their first night in their own room since her accident. He didn't talk. It was unusual for him to forget to say good night. She wondered what he was thinking about.

She knew he was tired, and yet it took him a long time to fall asleep. She lay there, awake, long after he finally went to sleep.

CHAPTER
FOURTEEN

Maggie peeked inside the oven. The chicken casserole was bubbling, browned to perfection. The table was set; everything was ready. All she needed to complete the meal was her family.

She looked out the window over the sink. Just last week the maple tree had been a brilliant orange. Today, most of the leaves were on the ground. Spence was leaning on his rake, talking to Ben Lewis over the back fence. He distributed his weight from one foot to the other, fidgeting. Grace and Allison were raking leaves into a huge pile near the tire swing. Something told her that any minute Allison was going to jump into them. Some things never changed. And yet Maggie felt as if something was the slightest bit off-kilter. She hadn't quite figured out what it was.

After putting the recipe in its box, she made her way across the room. Until she advanced to using only one cane, she still preferred to use her walker in the kitchen. It rolled easily, and allowed her to keep one hand free to open a door or a cupboard, butter toast, or prepare a meal. She remembered when she'd known the recipes

for her family's favorite dishes by heart. Specific ingredi-
ents and amounts escaped her memory now. Following
written instructions was tedious, arduous. Consequently,
cooking took her three times longer than it used to,
but at least she could now manage everyday household
tasks she'd once taken for granted.

Maggie didn't take anything for granted anymore.

Even the simplest things felt like blessings. She could
prepare a meal for her family, and stay with the girls
by herself. She was getting out of the house more, too.
They'd all gone to church this morning. It had been
her first time back since before the accident. The girls
had sat between her and Spence. Allison had fidgeted.
There was nothing peculiar about that. Spence had
stared into space. He'd been doing that a lot lately. She
didn't know quite what to make of it. She hadn't made
much progress convincing Jackie not to move away,
either.

Maggie knew she had to be patient and scale one
hurdle at a time. With a flick of her wrist, she turned
the oven off, and went to the French doors to call her
family in for Sunday dinner.

"I'll be in touch." Jackie saw Nadine Valentine to the
door at Fiona's. Alone again, she made her way into
the back room, skimming the papers the other woman
had just delivered as she went. The bell over the door
jangled before she'd read the first page.

Tango meowed, miffed at yet another intrusion.
"You'd better get used to sharing me, buster." She slid
the papers into the top drawer in the desk tucked in
the tiny alcove she used as her office.

"Jackie? You back . . . there?"

"Maggie?" Jackie and Tango pushed through the
purple velvet curtain separating the back of the store

from the front. Purring loudly, Tango trotted directly to Maggie and did figure eights around her ankles.

"He remembers . . . me."

"He's a smart cat, all right."

Meandering closer, Jackie saw that Maggie's hair no longer stuck out in odd directions. It had been cut in layers, some almost five inches long, the edges trimmed, so that the tresses framed her slender face. Other than the canes, a stranger would never guess that she'd nearly died. She was dressed up in slacks and trendy boots with clunky heels. The collar of a plum-colored blouse was open at the neck beneath the V of her gray jacket.

"You look great. What are you doing here? How did you get here? You didn't walk all this way, did you?"

Maggie tilted her head slightly, thoughtful. "Thanks. I came . . . to see you. Yvonne dropped me off. And no."

Jackie shook her head. "Smart aleck."

Maggie continued forward, her canes thudding across the old hardwood floor. "Yvonne and I are going to attend the . . . Ladies Historic Society meeting."

"Where is Yvonne now?"

"She had an errand to run."

Jackie straightened a blouse on its hanger. "So you took advantage of the opportunity to work on me a little more, is that it?"

"Do I need a reason to visit . . . my only sister?"

Something in the tone of Maggie's voice drew Jackie around. Maggie was looking at her earnestly. It made Jackie feel like something she'd stepped in. "Of course you don't need a reason . . ."

"Good." Her eyes widened with affection and innocence. "Now, as long as I'm here." Maggie winked.

And Jackie knew the affection may have been real, but the innocence wasn't. They shared a grin, and for a moment, it felt the way it used to.

Jackie bent down to pick up Tango. Petting him softly, she said, "Did you notice a woman leaving when you arrived?"

"The redhead who dresses . . . like you?"

Leave it to Maggie to notice that. "Her name is Nadine Valentine."

"Is she . . . a new friend of yours?"

"No. Yes. Well. In a sense, we've become friends. She wants to buy the store."

"Buy Fiona's?"

"She delivered her written offer personally."

"Then you're . . . really going to sell?"

"I told you I was, sis."

Maggie ambled closer, her limp more pronounced because she was distraught. "That seems so . . ."

"Daring?" Jackie asked.

"Drastic."

Jackie tried not to be offended, angered, well, thoroughly ticked. It wasn't easy. Of course Maggie didn't understand why she needed to start over someplace else. Still, it was Jackie's life. She had every right to move to another town, another state, another country if she chose. As happened whenever she thought of Maggie in a negative way, remorse followed. None of this was Maggie's fault. Perhaps it wasn't anybody's fault. That didn't make it any less real, and it certainly wasn't going to make these problems disappear.

"It's not as if I'm moving to Mars, Mags."

Maggie didn't look very convinced.

Jackie tried again. "All my life, I've had dreams and hopes, desires that I was passionate about. I always thought I tried to make them come true."

"You did."

"Did I? I've been doing a lot of thinking lately. The other day, I remembered the time David and I visited the Grand Canyon. He wanted to take the mule ride down to the bottom. I had some excuse not to, but the truth was I was afraid to venture into that vast unknown. So I stood there, on the edge of life, looking down at that awe-inspiring natural wonder, too chicken to do more than look.''

"Not everyone cares to risk their lives . . . climbing down ravines with rattlesnakes and wild animals.''

"It isn't just climbing into ravines, Maggie. The same thing happens whenever I get to the edge of my heart's desire. I can visualize them, smell them, practically taste my dreams, but for some reason, I've never quite been able to take that final step to happiness.''

Maggie stared deep into Jackie's eyes. "Your heart's desire . . . is to move to Traverse City?''

Her heart's desire was to have this baby, and protect Maggie from the truth at the same time. She couldn't do that here. "I need to start over someplace brand new.''

Maggie sighed, and Tango purred, and Jackie took her first easy breath in a while.

"I'm going to miss you.''

"We have telephones and cars, Maggie.''

"I don't drive yet.''

"I do. And I'll be around.''

Maggie sighed again. "It won't be the same.''

She was right about that.

They all looked up when the bell over the door jangled and Yvonne Wilson bustled in. Looking like a million dollars as always, she strode directly to Maggie's side and, in her fog horn voice, asked, "Any luck, dear?''

Maggie shook her head forlornly.

Next, Yvonne turned to Jackie. "Your cat has put on a little weight, and so have you. It looks good on you.''

"Thanks. I think.''

Yvonne chuckled, her faded, watery eyes friendly and sincere. "It was a compliment. Now, if I could get Maggie to put on a little weight, I'd be thrilled." She bustled around Maggie to help with the door. "We'd better hurry, dear. We don't want to keep Abigail Porter and the board waiting."

Jackie watched them go, thinking that Yvonne really did love Maggie as if she were her own daughter. Jackie felt better leaving her sister in good hands.

She hoisted Tango more securely into her arms. "So, we're both getting fat, are we?" Tango looked up at her with unblinking green eyes. Jackie rubbed her chin on the top of his head. "They ain't seen nothin' yet."

One thing was certain. If Yvonne was noticing Jackie's weight gain, others would, too. Jackie needed to act quickly.

She returned to the desk and took the offer to purchase from the drawer. She'd worked in real estate once, one of several careers she'd tried over the years. She studied the offer, countered with a few stipulations of her own, then signed on the dotted line.

Spence stood at the window of his office in the hundred-year-old brick building that housed the architectural firm of Hastings & Wiley, LLC. He didn't flinch when the outer door slammed. Good riddance. He only hoped the solid old door hit that rich old bastard in the back of his thick skull on his way out.

He didn't know how many minutes passed before he heard a light rap on his door. He'd lost track of time. "Yes?"

The door opened on squeaky hinges. "Looks like a good day for an ass reaming."

Spence recognized that voice. "I didn't know there was a good day for that." He wondered what Tom Garvey was doing here.

"Do you have any lubricant lying around?"

The strange request almost made Spence forget his seething anger. It certainly made him turn around. "Lubricant?"

Tom ambled in with a shrug and a cocky wink. "For those hinges. It's too late to lube things up for that reaming."

Spence laughed in spite of himself.

Tom helped himself to the small tin can of oil Spence found in the bottom desk drawer, then oiled the squeaky hinges one by one. "Nice to see you're still capable of laughing. I was beginning to wonder."

"Felix Fitzgerald is a spoiled little man who has more temper tantrums than a two-year-old. He thinks having money makes him superior. He wouldn't have a dime if his father hadn't been rich before him."

"He gets his rocks off by throwing his weight around." Tom sank into a chair. "You knew that when you took on this project. People like him never used to get to you. What's going on?"

Spence ran a hand through his hair, but only shrugged.

"Hastings giving you trouble?"

"Nothing out of the ordinary."

"Maggie still doing okay?"

Spence relaxed a little. "Maggie's doing great. And before you ask, Grace and Allison are, too."

"Then what's wrong?"

Wrong? Spence sank into his office chair. Fingers steepled beneath his chin, he looked his old friend in the eye.

Back in college, Tom had always been the first to chug a beer, sniff out a party, cozy up to a girl in the library or cafeteria. Other than Spence's brothers, Tom had been one of the few people he went to with a problem.

Never had the need to confide in someone been so

great. Tom sat across from him, silent and patient. His shirt was open at the neck, his graying hair recently cut, the diet he and his wife had gone on, working. Spence knew better than to mention it, and Tom knew better than to rush Spence, just as he'd known better than to have Spence's bachelor party at a strip joint. To this day, he was the kind of man who would keep a secret. This was one secret Spence couldn't reveal. He couldn't, ever, say, "I have a problem, all right. I'm going to be a father again. Only guess what? It isn't with Maggie."

He felt stinking useless, helpless, guilty, angry, and a few emotions he couldn't label. He couldn't say that, either. So, he said, "It's been a long day, a long month, a long year. Now. What brings you to Grand Haven?"

Tom stared at Spence for interminable seconds. Spence could tell Tom didn't buy his paltry explanation, but he was a big enough man, and a good enough friend, not to probe any deeper. He pulled a set of blueprints out of his tattered leather briefcase. Spreading them on Spence's desk, he said, "You aren't the first person Felix has reamed today. It's amazing any of us can sit down." He pointed to a cul-de-sac on the plan. "He wants this changed."

The two old college roommates spent the rest of the afternoon with their heads bent over the prints. By the end of the day, they had a plan, and a solution. Spence wished there were a solution to his dilemma. One thing was certain. If Tom had noticed that he'd been acting strangely, Maggie would, too.

He was going to have to get better at covering up.

Allison looked from the picture in the book they'd checked out of the library, to the stack of items in front of her on the kitchen table. "Are you sure you don't wanna be a hippie for Halloween like me, Gracie?"

"I'm sure, Al." Grace bent over the table, painstakingly attaching feathers to a headband.

Maggie watched the expression on Allison's face. It seemed that "all" the girls in the first grade were going to be hippies this year, and she didn't want her big sister to be left out in three days when Halloween arrived.

"Mama's gonna braid my hair, and I'm gonna wear these love beads and bell bottoms."

Grace replied without looking up. "Mom's going to braid my hair, too." She looked at Maggie suddenly. "Do you know how to braid?"

Maggie held up her fingers. "I've been practicing at St. Ann's."

Grace smiled and Allison crossed her arms matter-of-factly. "Everybody's gonna think you're just a plain old Indian. Nobody's gonna know you're Khardomah, that great Indian chief who used to live around here."

Grace seemed to be considering her answer carefully. Finally, she said, "I'll know. And that's all that matters, right, Mom?"

Maggie melted inside, her chest filling with pride. "I couldn't have said it better myself."

The telephone rang twice, then stopped. Spence must have answered it in his makeshift office, where he'd been spending long hours. Leaving the girls to their costumes and conversation, Maggie made her way into the den in time to see Spence put the receiver down.

"Who was that?"

"Nobody." He sounded tired, as usual.

"A wrong number?"

"No."

"Another woman?"

He looked at her, his expression severe. "I hardly think that's funny, Maggie."

Obviously. He jumped from one end of the spectrum to the other. One minute he was ardent, the next edgy.

He never used to have a short fuse. What bothered her most were the times when he was withdrawn. "Is everything going all right at work?"

"Now you sound like Tom."

She waited patiently. When he made no move to reply, she did a little prodding. "Is everything all right at work?"

"I'm way behind, and have to go into the office tonight."

"Again? On a Monday?"

"Yes, again. I missed a lot of time, all right?"

His fuse got shorter every day. He wasn't the only one who could get ticked around here. If she hadn't needed the canes, she would have struck a pose, hands on hips, chin stuck in the air. As it was, the most she could do was square her shoulders and raise her chin defiantly. "When I was in the hospital, you mean."

"Yes."

"That must have been a terrible inconvenience for you. Not that I would know, because you never talk about it. Just how difficult did I make your life, Spence?"

His expression changed instantly to one of remorse. Two deep lines formed between his eyes. "That isn't what I . . . I didn't mean . . ."

She let all her breath out in a noisy huff. Tilting her head slightly, she took the remaining steps separating them. "I'm usually the one who can't put thoughts in order when I'm upset."

She balanced one cane against his desk, and raised her free hand to his face. The whisker stubble of his five-o'clock beard felt coarse, his skin, warm to the touch. He had masculine, appealing features. She'd always thought so. His eyes showed intelligence and heat that beckoned to her irresistibly.

She tilted her face up as he brought his down. Their

lips touched, little more than a brush of air at first. He made a sound in his throat. And then, as if he couldn't help himself, he wound his arms around her back, drawing her to the length of his body. He kissed her again, this time long, and soulful and deep.

Her hand found its way to his chest. Even after the kiss broke, his heartbeat was strong beneath her palm.

"That was some kiss." She smiled.

"I aim to please." His eyes glowed like summer lightning.

"In that case," she said, tongue in cheek, "you're forgiven."

He drew her to him quickly, but not before she saw his face close, as if guarding a secret. Maggie searched her mind for a plausible explanation. There simply wasn't one.

"Spence? Are you sure there's nothing wrong?"

He set her away from him gently. "Felix Fitzgerald wants you to cut the ribbon at the ceremony next week."

"He wants me?"

"Not as much as I do."

Swatting the hand that had strayed to nether regions, she recognized the gleam in his eyes. "Do you really have to go into the office?"

He nodded sadly.

"Then hold that thought until you get home."

He'd never been one to smile at the drop of a hat. Lately, his smiles had been even rarer. That made the one that stole across his face right then more poignant.

Without warning, he kissed her again.

Once her toes were curled and her breathing ragged, he set her away from him, gathered up his drawings, told the girls goodbye, then left. Maggie was left wondering, thinking, confused.

"Okay, Allison. Now we need the love beads."

Allison slapped the beaded necklace into Jackie's hand as if she were a nurse handing a doctor a surgical instrument.

"Do I look like a flower kid, Aunt Jackie?"

"Flower child," Grace said, watching her sister through the mirror.

Maggie reached the end of Grace's first braid. After securing it with a rubber band, she began dividing the thick tresses on the other side. All four of them were crowded into the downstairs bathroom. The quarters were cramped, excitement high.

Allison struck a pose, arms crossed, one foot in front of the other. "I still think I should'a stuffed one of Gracie's bras and put it on."

"Hippies didn't wear bras, Allie," Jackie insisted. "They burned them."

That got both girls' attention. Jackie pulled a face at Maggie in the mirror. She'd forgotten that Allison had developed a fascination with breasts, which she called boobs, ever since Grace had started to grow them. What had Jackie gotten herself into?

Maggie saved the day by diverting Allison's attention. "Did I hear Daddy's car?"

Allie rushed out to see. By the time she returned, disappointed because Spence wasn't home, she'd forgotten all about bra burning. Relieved on several levels, Jackie made certain no one else heard her release the breath she'd been holding.

Every year, she came over to help Maggie get the girls in their costumes on Halloween. She hadn't been able to come up with a good excuse not to this year. She needn't have worried. Spence wasn't home.

Maggie secured Grace's other braid. Ushering the

girls from the room, she said, "Let's go light the jack-o'-lanterns."

Jackie was the last one out of the bathroom. Grabbing her camera from the kitchen table where she'd left it, she followed the path the others had taken out to the front porch. The wind had picked up the way it always did near Lake Michigan this time of the year. It made lighting candles a challenge. Once the jack-o'-lanterns were glowing, the girls assumed their positions in front of the porch steps. Jackie snapped several pictures while Maggie dumped more candy into the huge bowl she would use to administer treats to the children in the neighborhood.

A car turned onto their street. Tires crunched. Allie called, "Daddy!"

Jackie snapped a picture of her own feet.

Maggie said, "You're as jumpy lately as Spence."

Attempting a nonchalance she didn't feel, Jackie shrugged. "It's Halloween. Who doesn't get spooked on Halloween? You girls have fun!" she called, partway down the sidewalk.

"You aren't staying?"

Turning around to face Maggie, Jackie could hear Spence's footsteps crunching in the leaves behind them. She hadn't seen much of him these past several weeks. As if by unspoken agreement, they'd steered clear of one another. It was easier this way. Better. "You told me you don't like people hovering over you. Besides, between packing up the items I'm not selling with the store, and everything at the house, I don't know if I'll ever get done."

Shivering against a sudden chill, Maggie pulled her sweater together in the front. "You're packing tonight?"

The wind tugged at the strands of Jackie's hair secured loosely in the clasp at her nape. "It has to be done sometime, Maggie."

"You're as touchy as Spence, too."

The girls had raced to the edge of the driveway. "Peace," Spence said to Allison.

The child giggled.

"How!" he said to Grace.

"Native Americans only said that in the movies." Grace bent down to tie her moccasin. "They got the shaft."

"Grace!" Maggie said. "Where did you hear that phrase?"

Grace glanced up at Jackie, but didn't reply. Jackie eased closer to her niece's side. "Keep giving away my secrets, kiddo, and your mom's going to be glad I'm moving."

There was an uncomfortable moment when Spence and Jackie found themselves face-to-face on the sidewalk. Spence recovered first. "Hello, Jackie."

"Hey, Spence."

Up and down the street, children wearing sheets, vampire teeth, even Elvis costumes traipsed from house to house.

"Hurry, Daddy!" Allie insisted. "Or all the good candy's gonna be gone."

Eyeing a football player, a ballerina, and a six-year-old prom queen, who, goodness gracious, did appear to have breasts, and large ones at that, heading toward her own front porch, Maggie said, "I'd better get to . . . my post. Have fun."

"We will. Bye, Mama. Bye, Aunt Jackie."

"Bye, sweetie."

"Drive carefully," Spence said.

Maggie heard Jackie say, "Thanks." And then, "I will."

There was something about that slight pause that caused Maggie to watch Jackie walk to her car and get in. Again, she felt as if something was the slightest bit off-kilter.

The little ballerina called, "Trick or treat!"

By the time Maggie had exclaimed over the children's costumes, Jackie had driven away and Spence and the girls were out of sight. But not out of mind.

"You're quiet today." Ivan worked a particularly stubborn kink from Maggie's left shoulder in a muscle she'd pulled during today's session. "You usually talk during your massage."

She was staring at a poster on the wall on the opposite side of the table. "I think there's something wrong with me."

"Like what?"

"I don't know."

"I've known enough women in my time to know that means you have a pretty good idea."

"You've known a lot of women, have you?"

Voices, some that Ivan recognized, some that he didn't, carried to his ears as patients and therapists traversed the corridor outside the massage area. Keeping his own voice low so that the others wouldn't hear, he said, "I thought we were talking about you."

She shrugged. "Spence works. A lot."

"A lot, huh?"

"Yes, and, er, well, of course he's tired. Stressed. Exhausted."

"Ah." Ivan moved down to the small of Maggie's back. Weeks ago, he'd added weight training to her regimen. She still looked slight enough to be blown away by a mild breeze, but she was strong. And she was getting stronger every day. One of these days she wasn't going to need therapy. He pretended he didn't dread the day, just as he pretended he didn't look forward to Mondays, Wednesdays, and Fridays.

"Spence is getting older, ya know? And old guys can't always . . ."

She made a huffing sound. "He's thirty-six, not a hundred and thirty-six. And he can." Her voice dropped in volume. "He does. We do. A lot."

A lot. Great. "Then what's the problem?"

"There isn't really a problem."

Sure there wasn't.

"It's just that things are, well, different."

Different, Ivan thought. It wasn't any of his business. And he wasn't talking about sex with Maggie. Nope. Uh-uh.

And that was final.

"Different, how?" He closed his eyes and gave himself a swift mental kick.

"It's hard to describe. He seems preoccupied."

Change the subject, Ivan told himself. "You mean while you're . . ."

"Not during. But before sometimes. And after. Maybe he's not the problem."

Ivan didn't see a problem. The guy was getting it, and getting it often. He made a face.

"He takes care of me, but . . ."

"But?"

She shook her head. "Never mind. I can't talk about this with you. I can't even talk about it with Jackie. I miss her. She moved recently. Did I tell you that? Even . . . when she visits, I miss her. It doesn't make sense. Are you finished with me, Ivan?"

"What?"

"My massage. Is it over?"

Ivan was still stuck on her reference to her sister moving. He motioned for her to sit up. Crossing his arms at his chest, he rocked back on his heels.

"What?" she asked.

She'd caught him staring at her. "I was just thinking. You're a good judge of character, and I was wondering. What do you see when you look at me?"

She studied him closely. "You're young and big and rugged. Right now, I'd say . . . you're annoyed. And most of the time you look impatient. Which only proves that sometimes looks are deceiving, because you're one of the most patient men I've ever met. You're pensive, too." She paused for a moment, introspective. "Spence has been pensive. It seems everyone I know . . . is pensive. Even Jackie. That could just be hormones."

"Hormones?"

She snapped her mouth shut. "Never mind." She reached for her cane.

Ivan dropped down to his haunches. "Before you get up, I want to work on this gastrocnemius." He began massaging the back of her right calf.

"You probably say that to all your patients."

Ivan paused, both hands wrapped around Maggie's calf. Was she flirting with him? He studied her face. No. She was just being herself, friendly, funny, charming. She was definitely not flirting with him. After all, her life was full and her heart was taken. "Spence is a lucky man."

"I used to think he thought so."

"And now?"

"Maybe Spence doesn't find a woman . . . who limps . . . exciting."

"That's probably it."

Her double-take was almost comical. Now that he had her attention, he said, "You're witty, smart, funny." He feigned a shudder. "And beautiful. Men hate that."

"I'm not beautiful."

"Fine. You're ugly. That face, those eyes, that body. Decrepit."

She laughed, a deep, throaty, sensuous sound that made Ivan's Cardinal Rules damned difficult to keep. It was impossible not to join in.

Spence walked into the room while Maggie and Ivan were still laughing. Now that it was November, there was a chill in the air outside. It didn't look too chilly in here.

Maggie chose that moment to glance his way. "Spence."

He would have had an easier time relaxing his fingers from the fists at his sides if her smile hadn't been left over from her earlier laughter. Imposing an iron will on himself, he greeted Ivan civilly, then took Maggie home.

Spence stood beneath the hot spray of the shower, letting the water pummel his head, neck, and shoulders. It was late. The girls and Maggie had been asleep when he'd come upstairs.

He'd put in another long day, but the plans for the complex east of town were under way, and the Picketts Corners project was almost complete. He would be glad when construction began. Then, if Felix Fitzerald wanted changes, he was going to have to pay for them through the nose.

Scrubbing his hands over his face, Spence imagined the water washing the kinks out of his muscles at the same time it washed his troubles down the drain. It had been a hell of a day. In retrospect, he knew he'd overreacted to the sight of Maggie laughing with Ivan Decker this afternoon.

Spence flipped off the shower, dried off with a big towel. He hung up his towel, turned out the light, and made his way into the master bedroom. By the time he had reached his side of the bed, his eyes had adjusted to the darkness, and he could make out Maggie's sleeping form in the moonlight. Much mellower now, he climbed in beside her.

She made a sound in her sleep, a deep, throaty, sensual sound that called to mind other moonlit nights when he'd awakened her with a kiss. He missed her. He loved her. God, what an understatement.

His body was heating, responding to the knowledge that she was but a hairsbreadth away. Easing closer, he stretched a leg toward her and placed his hand on her shoulder.

She hummed, and he imagined that she was smiling in her sleep. She was a tummy sleeper. He glided his hand along the supple curve of her arm, up to her shoulder, down her back to her waist.

He almost didn't hear her whisper, "Ivan."

He froze. Slowly, he lifted his hand from her skin, and rolled to his own side of the bed. He lay on his back, trying to get his thoughts and his breathing under control.

He was exhausted. He needed to sleep. He wanted to break something. Ivan Decker's nose came to mind.

He threw the covers back. Swinging his feet over the side, he sat up.

"What time is it?" Maggie whispered.

"It's late." He whispered, hoping it would disguise the anger he was feeling. "Go back to sleep."

"Where are you going?"

He didn't reply.

"Spence?"

"At least you know my name when you're awake."

She opened her eyes wider. "What?"

"Spence. That's *my* name."

She looked puzzled.

"Maybe you could keep that in mind, so the next time I touch you, you call out the right name."

"The right . . ." Wide awake now, she propped herself up on one elbow. "What did I call you?"

Maggie couldn't see Spence's face clearly, but she could read his body language. His shoulders were stiff, his movements jerky as he shoved his arms into his robe and belted it at his waist. He was angry. Spence didn't get angry without a reason.

"What did I call you, Spence?"

"Ivan."

Her hand covered her mouth. She'd called him Ivan? What could she say? It was just that lately, Ivan touched her more often than Spence did.

"I'm sorry. Where are you going?"

He was on his feet, heading for the door.

"You're not jealous. Not of Ivan."

She switched on the lamp. And he turned, his eyes glittering with anger, his jaw clenched. "I'm only human, Maggie."

"You have nothing to be jealous about. Ivan is my therapist. Nothing more."

"Sure. Whatever you say."

"What's that supposed to mean?"

"Any fool can see the guy's in love with you."

Maggie looked at Spence. He was serious. She reached a hand toward him. "You know I could no more be unfaithful to you, than . . . you could be unfaithful to me."

She'd expected him to take her hand and come back to bed. He didn't move.

"Spence, tell me what's really wrong?"

He heaved a sigh. "I know you and Ivan aren't . . . Christ, I can't even say it. Guess I'm as ornery as a bear with a sore paw lately. It's not your fault."

"Are you coming back to bed?"

He did seem to melt a little, then. "My mother used to say feed a cold, starve a fever. I'm not sure what the antidote is for an ornery bear with a sore paw."

"I know."

For the first time that she could remember, he didn't take her up on her offer. He smiled, though. Securing the belt on the waist of his flannel robe, he said, "I'm going to make myself a sandwich. Get some sleep, okay?"

Lovingly, he covered the shoulder he'd just touched, then turned out the lamp. She listened to his footsteps in the hall. They sounded heavy. She didn't understand, and it didn't have anything to do with her difficulty processing information. Something was bothering him. Why wouldn't he tell her what it was?

CHAPTER FIFTEEN

Maggie entered the therapy room from the outpatient doorway, as she had countless times these past three months. She'd been terrified the first time Spence had wheeled her here three months ago. Three months. That period in her life was hazy, but that memory was stark and vivid. She'd done what she'd had to then. In a sense, she was doing the same thing today.

Ivan was waiting for her in his usual place in the outpatient section of the large center. She moistened her lips and concentrated on keeping her gait even, her limp minimal. He sauntered toward her casually. She knew the exact moment he noticed that she wasn't dressed for physical therapy.

It had been two weeks since she'd called out his name when Spence had touched her. During those two weeks, she'd paid closer attention to Ivan during her therapy sessions. Spence was right. Oh, she couldn't say for certain that Ivan was in love with her, but his gaze *did* seem to linger on her, as soft as a caress, when they spoke. He didn't touch her in anything other than a professional manner, but she could sense what his will-power was costing him.

He came to a stop directly in front of her. "Somebody plan a dress-up day and forget to tell me?"

He had a cocky grin and a steady gaze. She was no longer fooled by either of those things. Still, she couldn't help smiling as she said, "For someone so young, you have a lot of attitude."

"I'm what, seven years younger than you? That would only be a big difference if we were dogs." He motioned to her clothes. "Did you bring something more comfortable to change into?"

She'd dressed for success in brown pleated trousers and a cream silk blouse. If her outfit was mundane and the complete opposite of sexy, all the better. "No, Ivan, I didn't."

Suddenly, he was very serious. "Are you sick?"

"Actually, I'm better." She took a moment to read his T-shirt. TELL ME WHAT YOU NEED AND I'LL TELL YOU HOW TO GET ALONG WITHOUT IT. Ironically, she was going to do just that. "Could we talk? Privately?"

He shrugged. "It so happens I just had a slot open up in my schedule." With his right hand, he indicated the door closest to them. "This way."

Her shoulder brushed his arm once as they walked down the corridor. Maggie made certain it didn't happen again. They talked about the weather and the approaching Thanksgiving holiday. As far as small talk went, it was pretty benign. "What's up?" he said the moment he closed the door in the small conference room at the end of the hall.

She didn't know why she was so nervous. She was doing the right thing. Still, as innocent as her feelings for him were, she was going to miss him.

"Maybe we should sit down. I know your knee hurts you sometimes."

Drawing a tattered magazine from his back pocket, he dropped casually into a plastic chair. She lowered herself shakily into a seat opposite him. "I just came from a meeting with my therapy coordinator."

Ivan sprawled out, the epitome of calm. "Oh, yeah? Nobody told me anything about any meeting."

"That's because I called for the meeting myself."

"But why . . ."

"I asked her to convey my appreciation to Emily and Rachel. I wanted . . . to thank you in person."

"Thank me for what?"

She looked at him steadily. "For all your help while I was here at St. Ann's."

"You going someplace?"

She nodded, and he sat ahead, forearms on his thighs, his hands clasped loosely between his knees. She knew him well enough to know that, no matter how casual he appeared, he was going to argue. So she said, "A friend is waiting to drive me home today. Winter is approaching, and this drive will get more difficult. I've made arrangements . . . to begin therapy right in Grand Haven."

He looked at her. She stared back in waiting silence.

She saw a glint of raw hurt in his eyes, but he kept it out of his voice as he said, "I see."

It occurred to her that he was more mature than she gave him credit for. Finding her feet, she slanted him a smile that brought out the yearning on his features. He rose to his feet, too, and said, "It looks as if The Kid can chalk up another success."

"You're no kid, Ivan. You're a man. A wonderful one, at that."

"You're not so bad yourself."

Grasping her cane, she said, "Thank you for everything. For all your work. For putting up with my stubbornness. For laughing at me when I needed it. And for badgering me when I needed that, too."

"No problem."

"Well. Goodbye."

"Yeah." Ivan kept his feet glued to the floor. Keeping his distance was the only way he knew to keep from touching Maggie. God help him, he wanted to touch her. All these weeks he'd been doing just that, touching a woman he could never have. Somehow, she'd known. And now she was setting him free.

She opened the door by herself, which proved that she was right. She probably didn't need him anymore. "It's going to be drab around here without you."

She glanced at him over her shoulder. "There are prettier women in the world. One of these days, you're going to meet the right one. The right woman . . . would be crazy not to realize what she'd be getting . . . with you."

Ivan couldn't bring himself to smile. Instead, he shrugged, his fingers automatically running along the edge of the magazine that had somehow gotten crunched in his hand. Watching Maggie leave, he thought, some woman, but not her.

On Thanksgiving, Maggie awoke to a sky gray with rain. Big, round drops pattered against the windows, running in rivulets down the roof, into down spouts, and along the ground to the drain in the street.

Maggie and Spence and the girls, and Jackie, of course, had been invited to Yvonne and Gaylord's house for dinner. Edgar Millerton was coming, too, as he had no family. Rainy or not, Maggie loved the holidays. This year in particular, they had so much to be thankful for.

On top of everything else, she could hardly wait to see Jackie.

By nine o'clock, the temperature had dropped to below freezing. By ten o'clock, Jackie called to say that there were reports of accidents all along the highway, and she wasn't going to venture out in this weather.

Maggie stood holding the phone, bereft.

She missed Jackie. For some reason, she missed her even more now that she'd started receiving her physical therapy at the small facility right here in Grand Haven. Maggie hadn't realized how important her friendship with Ivan had become to her, or how much of the closeness she'd once shared with Jackie she'd transferred to her friendship with Ivan. Until she'd started receiving her therapy here in Grand Haven, that is.

She hung up the phone. "Jackie isn't coming."

Spence came up behind where she stood looking out the window at the dismal sleet. "Maybe this isn't as bad as it looks." He squeezed her shoulders, drawing her against him.

"I don't know," she said, feeling better simply because she felt understood. "It looks pretty bad."

"The van is a four-wheel drive," he said. "I don't think I can get to Jackie's, but I might be able to get us to Yvonne and Gaylord's. I want to see how bad it is before I attempt a trip across town."

"You'd do that?"

"I wouldn't for just anybody." He was already reaching for his coat.

"Be careful."

They shared a long, searing look. "Don't worry. I already came this close to losing the most important element in my life. I have no intention of giving the fates a second chance."

She smiled, tears springing to her eyes. Turning up the collar on his coat and donning his leather gloves, he went outside.

She continued to watch out the window, thinking how

lucky she was to have a man like him, and wondering how Edgar was going to manage in this ice. She heard the garage door go up, and watched as Spence backed down the driveway. Actually, he slid down the driveway. Their gazes met through two separate windows, and thirty feet of air filled with sleet.

If he couldn't make it to the end of the driveway safely, they couldn't make it across town. After much maneuvering, he managed to get the van back into the garage. Stomping the ice from his shoes, he said, "It would be suicide to try to drive in this. It looks like it's just going to be us for Thanksgiving dinner."

"I don't have a turkey, or pumpkin pie."

"Turkey and pumpkin pie are overrated. We're all together. And it's still Thanksgiving."

She tilted her head a little, thinking. "I suppose we could improvise."

Spence squeezed her hand. "That sounds adventurous."

He could tell she was warming to the idea. For the first time since they'd been married, they had a nontraditional Thanksgiving. They cooked hot dogs in the fireplace, and made hobo pies out of bread and canned pie filling. They played board games and watched movies. It was just the four of them, a family, intact.

Later that night, when the day was almost over, darkness had long since fallen, and the girls were tucked safely in bed, Maggie and Spence sat close under the throw on the sofa, staring at the flames and embers in the dying fire. She felt warm and loved and happy. "It's been a good day."

"Yes, it has."

"I miss Jackie, though."

Spence kissed the top of Maggie's head, but made no reply. Secretly, he was relieved that Jackie hadn't been able to make it. He felt awkward when she was

around, and so did she. It was easier this way. For all
of them.

"Isn't this the best Christmas tree you ever saw?"
Allison exclaimed.

"You say that every year, Al."

Spence and Maggie shared a look, because Grace said
that every year, too.

"Set it right here, Daddy!" Allison pointed to the
exact spot where she was standing.

"Bossy, bossy, bossy." Spence heaved the tree through
the archway and generally tried to get it into position
on the other side of the room without doing permanent
damage to the house or the furniture in the process.

"Bossing is what girls do," Grace said matter-of-factly.
"We're planners. Mom says the world couldn't go
around without us."

Spence chuckled. He didn't know about the rest of
the world, but he knew his world wouldn't go around
without these three females, bossy or not.

The girls' cheeks were still red from traipsing around
the Christmas tree lot. They'd traipsed from one end
to the other. He must have held up fifty trees for their
inspection. Of course, in the end, they'd chosen the
second one they'd looked at in the very first row. It was
the tenth of December, and their eyes were bright with
excitement.

It was already dark outside on this Friday night as
Maggie put Christmas music on the stereo. Grace
handed Spence the lights while Maggie and Allison
poked through boxes. Once the lights were on, Grace
and Maggie started hanging ornaments on the prickly
branches, and Spence lifted Allie high so she could put
the star on top.

After every ornament had been placed just so, Grace,

who had drawn the longest straw, had the honor of plugging the lights in for the very first time. Allison stood back, her hands pressed together as if in prayer, the ribbon in her ponytail untied, a beatific expression on her face. "I love it."

"No," Grace said, backing up to get a better view. "We like it. We talked about this in school. Everybody says they love stuff. Mrs. Green says love's different than like."

Spence looked around the room at the three blondes standing amid the clutter of discarded boxes and wreathes and a strand of lights that didn't work. Allison was looking up at Grace, all the awe a little sister could feel for her big sister shining in her eyes. Grace held herself regally, and Maggie seemed to glow. "What would you say love is, Grace?" she asked.

"Love is what's in Dad's voice when he tells us good night."

"What else?" Maggie asked.

Allison took a turn. "It's how Mama tries to be so careful when she combs the tangles out of my hair. And it wasn't in that bratty Gina Greystone when she wouldn't let me play with her at recess today, that's for sure."

Maggie was laughing when she caught Spence's eye. Lately, she'd felt as if they were turning a corner, finding their way after being the slightest bit off course. He still gazed into space sometimes, but it happened less often, and his moods were less unpredictable. He was more like his old self. She was feeling more like her old self, too.

The newspaper was open on the coffee table. In it was a grainy photo of her cutting the ribbon at the Picketts Corners ribbon-cutting ceremony. The article mentioned Maggie's nine-week coma, calling her recovery a miracle. Actually, the only aspect of her life that wasn't what she'd hoped it would be was her relationship with Jackie. They spoke on the phone often, but Jackie rarely visited. She was working in a novelty gift shop up in Traverse City. And as Spence said, this was a busy time of year in the retail business.

"What do you think love is, Mama?"

Allison's question brought Maggie from her musings. Looking around the room, her heart felt full. Christmas was truly just around the corner. Last year could very well have been her last Christmas, her last anything. But it hadn't been. She was here, and she didn't want to miss a thing. "I want to hear more of your ideas."

Allison couldn't seem to think of anything else to say. She turned to Grace, who said, "Love is what's in the birthday candles before you make a wish. And it's what's in the room on Christmas, after all the presents are open and everyone's tired and quiet and happy."

Allie tucked one hand in Spence's, the other in Maggie's. "It's in the room right now, Gracie. Hear it?"

"I hear it, Al."

"Do you hear it, Daddy?"

Spence squeezed his daughter's hand. He heard it, all right, and saw it, and felt it. He'd almost lost this, all of it. But he hadn't lost it. He was still tied up in knots over what to do to help Jackie. He doubted he deserved this life, but he thanked God for the second chance he'd been given.

He didn't know how, but he thought that maybe, just maybe, everything was going to be all right.

"I guess that's it." Abigail Porter patted her perfectly styled hair. "Another lovely Christmas luncheon, compliments of Yvonne and Gaylord."

The Wilsons graciously accepted everyone's thanks. One by one, the dozen members of the Ladies Historic

Society, who had met for lunch at The Golden Goose, aptly named for the prices on the menu, pushed their chairs back and reached for their coats.

"It's so wonderful to see you, Maggie," Abigail exclaimed.

"It's wonderful to see you, too," Maggie said. And she meant it. It was wonderful to be back in the swing of things, even though her head was spinning with the effort to remember so many names of the people the society talked about, and the dates and their contributions to the history of the area. Had she really once known them all by heart?

She had a lot to relearn. Not even that dampened her spirits today. For Jackie was coming for a visit later this afternoon. And Maggie could hardly wait.

"Maggie, dear," Yvonne said while Gaylord was taking care of the check. "I'm going to pay a little visit to the ladies' room."

Just then, Maggie noticed the silhouette of a man who looked familiar. Trying not to be conspicuous, she peered around diners at the next table. "I believe I see someone I used to know."

"You go say hello. I'll only be a minute."

Maggie reached for her cane and rose to her feet, slowly making her way to the man sitting alone at a table in the corner. "Hello, David."

Her ex-brother-in-law looked up at her in surprise. "Maggie." He rose partway, and pushed out the adjacent chair.

Taking her seat, Maggie tried to remember how long it had been since she'd seen David. Several months before the accident, certainly. His hair was lighter than she remembered, his face tanner.

"Are you back in Grand Haven to stay?" she asked.

"Just visiting." He cleared his throat. "Actually, I'm mixing business with pleasure. You know, catching up with old friends and conducting a business call, all in one trip.''

Maggie couldn't remember what business he was in, and she didn't care. He'd never been exactly what she called an easy person to talk to. Running a fingernail along the edge of the fine linen tablecloth, she said, ''Have you talked to Jackie?''

''No.'' As if aware of the uncomfortable silence, he added, ''I noticed she sold Fiona's.''

Maggie relented a little. Maybe she was being too hard on him. Perhaps he'd tried to get in touch with Jackie, after all. Giving him the benefit of the doubt, she said, ''She moved to Traverse City.''

His eyes showed genuine surprise.

''I could give you her number if you'd like.''

He shifted uncomfortably in his chair. ''I don't think my wife would appreciate that.''

It was Maggie's turn to be surprised. ''You're married?''

''Two weeks ago.''

''But what about the baby?''

There was a moment of stilted silence. ''What baby?''

''Your baby.'' Noticing the people looking at them, Maggie lowered her voice. ''Yours and Jackie's.''

David was shaking his head. ''Wait just a minute.''

Maggie wanted to tell him to wait a minute, but he didn't give her the chance.

''I don't know what you're talking about. I don't know anything about a baby, but I do know that I've been in Europe for the past eight months. And this is my first visit home in all that time.''

That didn't make any sense to Maggie. She saw him looking at the scar on the side of her face. When he next met her gaze, she saw pity in his eyes. ''Somebody mentioned that you'd been in a terrible accident.''

She sat back, perplexed.

"You were in a coma."

"Yes." And then, "I'm fine now."

The tone of his voice had changed, the way some people's did when they spoke to children, or the mentally impaired. "Of course you are. I mean. I'm glad to hear it. Real glad."

He thought she was brain damaged. In her agitated state, all she could do was sit there and stammer, which undoubtedly added credence to his assumption.

"It was nice seeing you again, Maggie. Give my best to the rest of the family." He made a hasty retreat about the same time Yvonne returned.

She and Gaylord collected Maggie, and drove her home. Maggie fumed inwardly all the way. She'd never liked David Bower. Brain damaged, indeed. The man had had an affair with a French masseuse. And who knew how many other floozies. He was probably lying about how long he'd been in France. A man who turned to another woman wasn't exactly saint material.

She continued to fume long after she got home. In fact, she sputtered all the while she put out after-school snacks for the girls.

Spence heard her from his makeshift home office. "Something wrong?" he asked upon entering the kitchen.

"I'll say ... something's wrong." She plopped two juice boxes down on the counter. "I just ran into that no-good ... former ... brother-in-law of mine."

Spence's nerve endings went on red alert. "You saw David?"

"At The Golden Goose."

Tension wrapped itself around his windpipe. "You talk to him?" Of course she'd talked to him, he thought to himself. She wouldn't be this agitated otherwise.

"He thinks I'm brain damaged."

"Did he say that?"

"He didn't have to. What a jerk. I don't know what Jackie ever . . . saw in him."

Spence's breath solidified in his throat. Every fear he'd had since finding out about Jackie's pregnancy gathered in his chest, churning, roiling like a volcano waiting to erupt. "You're right," he said. "Jackie was always too good for him. Forget about David Bower."

He reached a hand toward her. She'd already moved so quickly, his fingers met with only thin air before his arm fell limply to his side.

"He says it isn't his baby." She was speaking into the refrigerator, the big enclosed space giving her voice a slight echo. "I mean, who else's baby could it be? Jackie doesn't sleep around. She may have changed . . . but she couldn't have changed that much. She stayed here with the girls when I was in that coma. You would have known if she was seeing someone." She bounced from one thought to another much the way she bounced around the kitchen. "Not that you've noticed the changes in her . . . I mean, the two of you haven't been in the same . . . room more than a handful of times . . ."

She paused, slowly turning to face Spence.

"Since . . . I came home."

She went perfectly still. Then swayed slightly. Steadying herself with both hands on the back of a chair, she looked at the snacks she'd laid out for the girls. Slowly, she looked at Spence.

Her knuckles turned white, her face ashen. "My God."

She swayed again. Spence rushed to her. The look in her eyes stopped him in his tracks.

Maggie felt as if she were moving in slow motion. She stared at Spence. She could see him clearly, even though everything around him was out of focus. She'd noticed the changes in him before: the lines between his eyes. The chiseled features. His Adam's apple wobbled. The color drained out of his face, the paleness in stark contrast to his dark blue eyes.

A lifetime passed as she stared into those eyes. When she couldn't stand it anymore, she closed hers, for she'd seen the truth from six feet away.

Jackie had to bite her lip to keep it from quivering as she pulled into Maggie's driveway. Spence's car was home. Rats.

They'd been avoiding each other. It was easier that way. It wasn't that seeing him was difficult. She didn't blame him for what happened any more than she blamed herself or the fates. The difficult part was pretending an easy, unaffected camaraderie with him while Maggie was around.

Pretending felt like lying. It left a bad taste in her mouth, and a bad feeling in the pit of her stomach.

It was with a sense of dread that Jackie threw the shifting lever into Park, cut the engine, and got out of her car. She'd never knocked on Maggie's door in her life. She couldn't very well start now. So, she pasted a smile on her face, swallowed the trepidation she always felt when she, Spence, and Maggie were going to be in the same room anymore, and opened the door, calling, "Yoo-hoo. Anybody ho—"

Her voice trailed away at the sight of Maggie and Spence, standing six feet apart. Other than their heads, which they'd turned when she'd entered, they seemed frozen.

"Hey, you two."

Still, neither of them spoke.

Jackie's fingers felt like icicles as she closed the door. It matched the ice water that began to inch through her veins. "What's wrong?"

Spence opened his mouth, but no words formed.

Maggie wasn't even trying to speak. Jackie hadn't bothered to button her coat. The wind had separated the lapels, and plastered her loose-fitting dress to her body. Maggie stared at the rounded outline of her stomach.

Her entire body shaking, she finally met Jackie's gaze. "How? Could? You?" Her gaze swung to Spence. Again she said, "How? Could? Either of you?"

As if unable to stand the sight of them, she closed her eyes.

"Mags."

A sob rose up from Maggie's throat, deep and mournful, as if she was in physical pain. "Get . . . out . . . of . . . my . . . house." Her face contorted with the effort to keep from crumbling at her feet. "Get out . . . of my house. And don't ever come back."

Turning stiffly, she limped from the room.

CHAPTER SIXTEEN

Spence saw that Jackie was shivering violently. She was staring past the archway where Maggie had disappeared. The last time he'd seen that expression on her face, they'd been in Maggie's hospital room the day of her accident, tubes and wires coming out of everywhere. That had been seven and a half months ago. He'd experienced some of the most terrorizing, horrifying, and humbling moments of his life during that time.

Jackie turned watery eyes to him. "You told her?"

"What?" Spence knew how it felt to be gut shot. "God. No."

"Then how—"

Tears spilled over Jackie's eyelashes. His eyes burned dryly. "She ran into David."

"Oh, no."

A lone sob carried on the still air from a room at the back of the house. Tears coursed freely down Jackie's face. Spence stood alone in the middle, sick and sorrowful, unable to go to either of them.

"What are you going to do?" Jackie asked.

He pressed both hands over his eyes. "I don't know yet." What could he do?

"I have to go, don't I?"

He nodded. That was it. There were no more words to be said.

She left. Sometime later, her car disappeared down the street.

Maggie was quiet now in the other room. Grace and Allison would be home soon. He had to pull himself together, too.

He walked aimlessly around the kitchen, then strode quietly into the family room. Maggie was huddled on one end of the sofa. It was a blustery day outside. The room was in shadow, so he couldn't see her face. Although she wouldn't look at him, he knew she'd heard his approach.

A raw and primitive grief overwhelmed him. His worst nightmare had come true. There were no words. No reasons. No excuses or explanations. There was only reality. And somehow, reality had to be dealt with.

He lowered himself to the leather ottoman opposite Maggie. He glanced at her face, and couldn't look away. He loved her so goddamn much. And he'd hurt her more than he'd ever thought he was capable of hurting anybody.

"The girls will be home soon," he said.

Maggie had never heard Spence's voice so deep. It hurt her ears. Everything hurt, listening, seeing, thinking. She shook with the effort it required to breathe. Spence. And Jackie. She couldn't believe it. But they hadn't denied it. The clues were everywhere. And the evidence couldn't be ignored.

She was tired, empty, and drained in a way she'd never felt before. "No wonder you've been distracted . . . and preoccupied."

She looked at him then. His eyes were sunken, his

lips gray. She wanted to shout that she couldn't help that he was in pain. "Do you love her?"

Maggie hated herself for giving in to the self-doubt that formed that question. She hated herself even more for being so weak that she'd allowed it to slip out. She wanted to hate him. Perhaps she would. Later.

"It wasn't like that."

"I don't think I can bear . . . to hear what it was like. While I lay, dying . . . you were . . ." She choked on the last words. "You were having an affair with my sister."

"Not an affair."

She couldn't meet his gaze. She just didn't have the strength.

"Once, Maggie. Only once."

Fixing her eyes on a blurry object in the distance, she said, "Yes, well, in case you . . . haven't heard . . . once is all it takes."

"Maggie, I'm so . . ."

She turned on him then. "My sister is pregnant . . . with your baby. Sorry is a little feeble . . . don't you think?"

The image of Spence, with Jackie, flooded her mind. She was quivering, shivering. She couldn't stop. For an instant, she wished she'd never come out of that coma.

The item she'd been staring at came into focus. It was a recent photograph of Grace and Allison. They were the reasons she'd awakened.

How was she going to protect them from this?

She looked at the Christmas tree they'd all decorated just days ago. They'd all been so happy that night. It had been an illusion.

She'd lost the illusion today. Not to death, but to betrayal. Jackie's betrayal cut to the bone. Spence's seeped into a place she couldn't name. The hurt went deeper than her heart, deeper than her soul.

Just then, the kitchen door opened, and the girls

burst into the house. She heard their backpacks drop, their voices raised happily.

"It's snowing!"

"And I'm starving."

Without looking at Spence, Maggie said, "I can't . . . face them yet."

"Maggie."

"Tell them I'm not feeling well, and . . ." She swallowed the sob threatening her fragile composure. "And I'm lying down."

"Maggie."

"Don't touch me." She realized she was shaking uncontrollably. He was trying to hand her the throw. Careful not to let her fingers brush his, she took it. "Just tell them."

His footsteps were heavy as he left the room.

She lay down on the sofa, drawing the blanket around her. Curling into a ball, she listened to the girls' voices, and tried not to listen to the deeper cadence of Spence's. She did what she could to keep her mind blank. In case the girls came to check on her, she wouldn't let herself cry.

She still hadn't given in to tears later, after the girls had indeed checked on her. She'd assured them that she was nursing a terrible headache and would be better soon. She'd lied. She wondered how many lies Spence and Jackie had told.

Spence and Jackie.

Maggie crept up the stairs and crawled into bed, shoes and all. Spence had made the bed this morning. She remembered now. He never fluffed the pillows like she did. She could see the indentation where his head had rested last night after they'd made love.

Love.

She turned her back on his side of the bed.

Love, Grace had said a few days ago, was what was in

the room on Christmas after all the presents were opened and the house was quiet, and they all listened. Maggie didn't know what was in the room with her right now. But it wasn't love.

Love didn't hurt like this.

A tear squeezed out of her eyes. The dam broke. Tears wet her pillow and huge sobs wracked her body.

Still, she shivered.

Maggie opened her eyes to the gentle brush of Allison's lips on her cheek. She must have slept.

"Feel better, Mama. See you in the morning."

"Good night, Allison. Night, Grace."

Spence was there, too. But he didn't speak. While he tucked the girls in bed, she went into the bathroom and washed her face, brushed her teeth, and donned her nightgown. She should have been more comfortable when she crawled back into bed. She felt no better.

At least she wasn't crying anymore when Spence entered the room sometime later. She kept her back to him as she said, "Christmas is in eleven days. I don't want . . . to spoil it for the girls. We have to pretend that nothing . . . has changed. At least until the holidays are over."

For the first time in their married life, they intentionally slept apart. Maggie heard Spence moving about throughout the house at all hours. She doubted he slept. But then, neither did she.

Days passed.

Spence was up before her every morning. He no longer worked from home. She assumed he spent most of the daylight hours at the office. He didn't look as if he was getting much sleep. She couldn't bring herself to comment, though.

The arrangement seemed to be working. As far as Maggie could tell, Grace and Allison were none the wiser. So far so good.

Since it wouldn't have been Christmas for the girls without the McKenzie family party, Maggie kept up the pretense while all of Spence's family gathered around the Christmas tree at their house the following weekend. Brian and Tim and Frank and especially Frank's wife, Pattie, watched her closely. Apparently, they weren't as easy to fool. Maybe that was because Maggie didn't try as hard. They weren't the ones she needed to protect.

Still, it was with great relief that she saw them to the door with Spence. It was the closest she'd been to her husband in a week. She remedied that as soon as the door closed.

Her heart was broken, her belief in Spence shattered. She'd thought he was above the average man's weaknesses. She might never have known if Jackie hadn't become pregnant. But she did know. Spence's child was growing in another woman. Not just any woman. It was growing in Jackie.

There were four days until Christmas. And another week before New Year's. After that, she had a decision to make.

Grace and Allison were still wired after their aunt and uncles and cousins had left that night. It was Saturday, and it was long past their bedtime. Spence carted Allison up the stairs on his back.

"I just love Uncle Brian," she said dramatically. "I'm gonna marry him when I'm big."

Grace admonished. "You can't marry your uncle."

"Why not?"

"Because it's against the law."

Any other year, any other month, Spence and Maggie would have shared a private smile at the way Allison accepted Grace's explanation, no questions asked. Spence glanced at Maggie. She kept her eyes downcast.

"Well," Allison said, sliding down her father's back until her feet touched the floor. "I can't marry Daddy because he's already married to Mama. Who am I gonna marry, then?"

Maggie was the one who answered. "Only time will tell."

It was four days before Christmas, Spence thought. And another week after that until the holidays were over. Grace and Allie could hardly wait until Christmas. Like a man on death row, he dreaded the passing of every day. The clock was ticking on his marriage. Eleven more days, and it would blow up in his face.

Grace meandered into her own room to write in her journal. Allison floated down to her knees to say her prayers.

Maggie went to bed soon after. Walking the floors much later, in the house that was once his haven, Spence thought about Allison's bedtime prayers. They came so easily to her. He didn't know what to pray for.

He remembered when his father used to say that it was easier to ask for permission than forgiveness. Spence didn't know how to ask for forgiveness for this. He only knew he couldn't simply let the clock run out without trying.

The cigarette smoke coming through the register from the efficiency apartment next door was enough to make Jackie gag. Clem, short for Clementine, a big bruiser of a woman who tended bar at a seedy establishment down the street, started smoking about ten o'clock every morning and didn't stop until she left for work around seven. It hadn't been so bad when Jackie had been working at that posh little gift store downtown. Then, the neighbors had been like two ships passing in the night. When Jackie was home, Clem wasn't, and vice versa. But Jackie had lost that job when she'd failed to show up for work four days in a row.

She didn't remember much about that day after she'd left Spence and Maggie's house. It was probably a miracle she'd arrived back in Traverse City in one piece. She'd been so haunted by the look of pain, disillusionment, and utter sadness on Maggie's face that she hadn't gone anywhere or done anything for nearly a week.

She'd called Spence at work to check on Maggie. His voice had been flat and lifeless. She could only imagine what it was like in that house. Jackie feared Maggie would never be the same. Would any of them?

Tango made a miffed sort of sound as he grumpily found his feet, stretched, then walked, stiff-legged, to a place three feet away. He didn't like the smelly, secondhand cigarette smoke any better than she did.

Jackie didn't see what else she could do. She'd tried cracking a window. This was a one-room apartment, and while the air was decidedly fresher, she and Tango nearly froze. She'd tried appealing to Clem's sense of decency when she'd knocked on the other woman's door two days ago. She'd calmly explained that she was five months pregnant, and therefore concerned about her unborn child being exposed to secondhand smoke. Clementine's response had been something to the effect of, "It's a free country," and "Don't believe everything you read." She'd proceeded to ask Jackie if she wanted a beer.

The house she was going to rent wouldn't be available

for another month. At this rate, it was going to be a long month.

Picking Tango up, Jackie stalked to the door and threw it open. The sky above the apartment house across the street was the same dull shade of gray it had been all week. At least the air was fresh. After taking several deep breaths, she said, "What do you say we get out of here?"

Tango jumped from her arms and trotted after her into the bathroom, his tail curved in a friendly half-circle. That was what she liked about Tango. He was always so open to possibilities.

Half an hour later, the tan and butterscotch colored cat had his nose pressed to the back window. "Hey," she said, eyeing him through the rearview mirror. "You're supposed to look where we're going, not where we've been."

She thought about that statement for the next ten minutes. She lost track of how many miles. Maybe she should take her own advice. There was one problem. She didn't know where she was going, figuratively, or literally. One day soon she needed to find a job, and a peaceful place to live. Right now she could have used a good map.

Inching her car into an intersection, she peered in every direction. "Does this road look familiar?" she asked Tango.

He jumped over the front seat and rubbed his head on her elbow. He was either completely unconcerned that they were lost, or he had complete faith in her ability to find her way again. She hated to be the one to break it to him.

Normally, she had a good sense of direction. A little sunshine would have helped. November was supposed to be the gray month in Michigan, rivaled only by March, a month of brown. Just her luck, the gray had waited until December this year. Still, driving around the countryside, even somewhat lost, was preferable to sitting in that bleak, stuffy, one-room apartment studying the change in her belly button, breathing poisonous smoke, and feeling sorry for herself.

She backed up, and turned left onto a snow-covered trail that might have passed for a road in nonindustrialized countries. It occurred to her that she still had her sense of humor, warped though it might be. She had her camera, too, and four-wheel drive, a warm coat, a nearly full tank of gas, a bottle of water, a cell phone, and the radio.

The cell phone wasn't much good in all these trees. She flipped the radio on, though, and punched through the stations until she found one playing hard rock. She cranked it up for the hell of it, and then she rolled down the window, even if it was cold and damp outside. Maybe she didn't know where she was going exactly, but by God, everybody and everything was going to hear her coming from a mile away.

Five minutes later, she wasn't quite ready to smile again, but she'd loosened her white-knuckled grip on the steering wheel. The way she saw it, she would either come to Lake Michigan, the Grand Traverse Bay, the Mackinaw Bridge, or Lake Huron on the other side of the state. Not that she planned to go that far. The next time she saw a house or a corner store, she would stop and ask for directions.

Feeling empowered for the simple reason that she had a plan, she drove on. When a Guns 'n Roses song came on the radio, she turned up the volume even more, and sang along. "Welcome to the jungle . . ."

She saw the smoke in the distance about the same time the next song started. She turned the volume down and looked around. The road dead-ended in a wooded area at the bottom of a hill. A narrow driveway that was actually two muddy ruts in the snow led through the scrub trees.

The scent of wood smoke in the air reminded her of the house she and her family had lived in one winter when she'd been small. It had a wood-burning fireplace. She and Maggie had been certain that Santa would get stuck in the tiny flue.

Closing her mind to thoughts of Maggie and the pain that went with them, Jackie concentrated on the matter at hand. Where there was smoke, there was fire. And where there was fire, there were bound to be people. All she had to do was find the cabin, knock on the door, and ask for directions back to Traverse City.

Rather than chance getting stuck in the lane, she parked her SUV at the side of the road. She rolled up her window, locked her doors. With the camera dangling from the cord around her neck, she started up the hill. Tango climbed onto her shoulder, and every now and then, she snapped a picture of an interesting tree or bird or little animal footprints in the snow.

Walking felt good, her coat warm, Tango a calming presence on her shoulder. She'd forgotten how much she enjoyed taking pictures. What other simple pleasures had she forgotten?

By the time she reached the top, she'd used up half a roll of film. Now, the small rustic cabin was in plain view. Gray smoke curled from a gray stone chimney. There was a path from the back door to what appeared to be a little shed. A pile of logs lay near the side door. She took a picture of those logs, that door, the path.

Twigs snapped. There was a rushing sound, like something charging through the brush. Before she could put her camera down, something wild and ferocious charged around the corner. It was a dog, big and black. Tango curled his claws into Jackie's neck. The dog lunged. Jackie screamed. And Tango scrambled up the tree at her back.

The dog's teeth were bared, his growl low and menacing. Jackie's heart was in her throat. She was going to die. Alone in the woods.

"Down, boy. Easy." The voice belonged to a man. Perhaps she wouldn't die alone after all. It was little consolation.

"Inch away from the tree. It's your cat he wants."

"He can't have Tango. He's all I have."

She had yet to take her eyes off the dog. Therefore, she had yet to look at the man. His voice had an exasperating quality as he said, "The cat's up the tree. My dog can't reach him. Do as I say, dammit. Easy, boy. Easy. Back up. Atta boy. A little more. Good dog."

The hair on the back of the dog's neck was still standing on end, but his teeth were no longer bared. He didn't seem quite as menacing now. "Good dog? He treed my poor cat, and would have eaten me for lunch in a heartbeat, and you call him a good dog?"

The man's silence drew her gaze. She got her first look at him. In his late thirties, he had brown eyes, a two- or three-day beard, and a mouth set in a straight line. "My dog isn't the one who's trespassing."

Jackie realized she was in no position to find fault. "Is it safe for me to move?"

At the man's brief nod, she eased around to one side of the tree and looked up. "Asking for directions didn't turn out to be such a good idea, did it, Tango? What do you say we get out of here and find our way back to Traverse City?"

Tango's tail was about four inches in diameter. He meowed. Roughly translated, it meant, *Not on your life, sister.*

She studied the situation, then glanced at the man. "If you would take your dog inside for a few minutes,

I might be able to coax my cat out of *your* tree so we can get off *your* property."

She could feel his eyes on her. He made a clicking sound with his tongue. Without a word, he and the dog walked away. Jackie began trying to lure Tango down as soon as she heard the door close. She tried talking to him. She tried being sweet, assertive, bossy, demanding. Tango didn't budge.

The cabin door opened again. The man returned, a ladder on his shoulder. With a word to his dog to sit a fair distance away, he placed the ladder against the tree, adjusted its footing, then started up. He didn't bother wasting small talk on Tango. He simply climbed up a rung at a time, grabbed the cat by the scruff of his neck, tucked the big lug rather roughly under one arm, and climbed back down, where he placed the cat gruffly into her waiting arms. "Hold on to him."

Jackie wasn't accustomed to such blunt treatment. "Yes, sir."

Other than the barest lift of one eyebrow, he showed no indication that he'd caught her sarcasm. Cat in hand, Jackie started back the way she'd come. She hadn't gone far when she realized she hadn't asked for directions.

She stopped in her tracks. Turning around, she saw that the stranger and his dog were ambling back toward the cabin. "Sir?"

Man and dog turned in unison. She couldn't see the color of either of their eyes from here, but she could feel the intensity of both their gazes. And she simply couldn't bring herself to ask anything else of either of them.

"Thank you for rescuing Tango. I hope you and your dog have a nice holiday." Again, she started down the trail.

"It's that way."

She glanced over her shoulder. "What's that way?"

He was pointing to the right. "Traverse City. It's fifteen miles that way."

She was surprised, and yet she wasn't. He was a man of few words, but he wasn't unkind. She studied him. He was of average height, average build. Most women probably considered him good looking. She wasn't interested in finding a man, any man. She had her child to consider. Her baby came first. From now on, Jackie's every decision was going to be weighed carefully to ensure that her choices were the best for her child.

Okay, she'd established that she wasn't interested in the man, or any man. But she was curious about the way he lived. And there was something mesmerizing about the strong, gentle hand he placed on the dog's head.

"What's your dog's name?"

"Bo."

"Really. I would have guessed Brutus or Sarge." Or Killer.

"My wife named him."

She did a double take. "Is she in the cabin?"

"Bo and I live alone."

He looked at her as if daring her to make something of it. He could have been divorced or separated. But she didn't think so. She didn't know his story, but she'd bet her eyeteeth that some woman hadn't simply thrown him away.

He was still looking at her, one hand on the dog's broad head. The only thing moving was the smoke curling from the stone chimney behind them. It would have made a wonderful picture. The definition was perfect. There was such contrast between the white of the patchy snow still on the ground here and there, and the bare earth, the logs waiting to be split, the brown of the man's wool jacket, the faded blue of his jeans, and the black of the dog's thick fur.

She snapped the picture, then hurried back to her car before he decided to sic his dog on her. Again.

She pointed the SUV in the direction he'd indicated. He could have been lying about that. Traverse City was exactly where he said it would be.

She felt better upon arriving home. Go figure. She'd been scratched by her own cat, nearly mangled by a fierce dog, and glared at by its owner.

Still, Jackie thought as she gave Tango fresh water and set out food for her supper, Clem was gone, the clouds were breaking up, and lo and behold, she wasn't feeling sorry for herself anymore.

CHAPTER
SEVENTEEN

"Wake up, Mama. Santa Claus was here."

Maggie squinted against the light shining from the hall. Grace and Allison stood near her bed, their hair askew, their long flannel nightgowns swaying in the girls' excitement. Maggie pushed her hair out of her face. Propping herself up on one elbow, she said, "Santa came? Are you sure?"

Allie hopped up and down. "You should see all the presents. Hurry."

Maggie threw the covers back and was reaching for her cane when Grace peered at Spence's side of the bed. "Where's Dad?"

Maggie's mind went blank. Luckily, Spence strolled out of the connecting bathroom. "I'm right here. It's only six-thirty. What are you girls doing up?"

"It's Christmas!"

"No kidding?"

"Dad." Grace, who knew about Santa this year, winked at her father before spinning around and following her little sister. Wool socks muffling their footsteps, the girls raced out to the hall and on down the stairs.

Maggie and Spence chanced a glance at each other. His side of the bed hadn't been slept in. Grace had been about to question it. That had been a close one. It was then that Maggie noticed the blanket and pillow on the overstuffed chair in the corner. "You slept there?"

Spence finished fastening his belt before answering. "I was on the couch until four. I was afraid the girls would be up early, and wonder . . ." His voice trailed away. "So I finished the night in here."

He was a good father, Maggie thought. He always had been. If only . . . She didn't allow herself to complete the thought. It was Christmas. This was no time for recriminations and futile wishing.

"Are you two coming?" Allie yelled from the bottom of the stairs.

Spence and Maggie almost smiled. "We're coming," Maggie called. She tied her robe, toed into her slippers. Cane in hand, she made her way from the room. Spence was waiting for her in the doorway. Together, they joined the girls in the family room.

Spence plugged in the lights on the tree, and sank to the floor between the girls. Maggie sat on the ottoman nearby. He chuckled at the way Allison tore into her first package, paper and ribbons flying.

Allison loved her doll, Grace her art supplies and books. They both were thrilled with their ice skates, and all the gifts Maggie had chosen. Spence hadn't been involved in the shopping much this year. It would have forced Maggie to spend time with him, and she hadn't allowed that. Spence understood to a point. He'd made a horrible mistake. Only someone who knew how it felt to be facing what he'd faced that dreadful night could understand how or why it had happened. He wasn't condoning it. But Maggie wasn't the only one suffering because of it. He accepted the suffering. He accepted the blame. But he couldn't accept letting his marriage crumble around him without trying to save it.

He'd stopped avoiding Maggie that night after the McKenzie party. He still honored her wishes that he find some other place to sleep, but he couldn't let her shut him out completely. He loved her too much, and there was too much at stake.

Christmas had always been a joyful, family time. Perhaps that was why she didn't stiffen when he sat next to her on the ottoman. Maybe it was only because she'd noticed Grace noticing things lately. Spence hoped it was more than that. He'd been searching for a way through the barbed wire of silence she'd strung around herself. Even if it was stilted, they talked. Sure, the conversations weren't about their feelings or the future. But it was a start.

These past few days, he'd noticed her watching him when she thought he didn't see. And she didn't flinch when her shoulder brushed his arm. Whether it was intentional or not, it was the best Christmas gift in the world.

The girls took turns opening presents. When every last one had been unwrapped, Grace gathered the gifts for Spence and Maggie, and presented them one at a time. Maggie exclaimed over the trivet Allie had made out of popsickle sticks, and the tiny picture frames to stick on the refrigerator from Grace.

"Open this one next," Grace told her mother. "It's from Dad."

Spence didn't think he was imagining the slight quaver in Maggie's fingers as she removed the foil paper. In their exuberance to see, the girls got between him and his view of the gift he'd lovingly chosen, so Spence couldn't see the unwrapped product. But he saw Maggie's eyes glaze over when she lifted the spring-hinged lid.

"Wow!" Allie said.

"It's beautiful," Grace exclaimed in a whisper. "Try it on, Mom."

There was no doubt that Maggie's hands shook as she lifted the bracelet fashioned of diamond chips and mother-of-pearl. He'd wanted to get her the earrings that matched, but she no longer wore the diamond earrings he'd given her for their second wedding anniversary, and he knew better than to give her another pair right now.

She fumbled with the clasp. Grace moved to help, but Spence beat her to it, gently pushing her hands aside. "Allow me."

Maggie's surprise showed in her wide blue eyes. She lowered her gaze to her wrist, where Spence's fingertips rested lightly. He turned her hand over, revealing the pale underside of her forearm and wrist. Her skin was slightly cooler than his fingers. It felt so damn good to be touching her, he was sorry when the tiny link slipped into the clasp on the first try.

She lifted her wrist and turned it so the bracelet caught the colorful lights on the tree. "It's lovely."

"It suits you."

Neither of them spoke, but their gazes held. Maggie couldn't look away. For once, she didn't want to. She felt warmed by Spence's look, flushed with heat at his smile, excited by something as simple as the brush of his fingertips on her skin. She could deal with those feelings. She'd gotten him a sweater. Not because it went with his eyes, although it did, but because Grace and Allison would think something was amiss if she got him nothing. Spence's gift to her was different. Early in their marriage, he'd told her it wasn't easy for a man to put his feelings for a woman into words. He'd always said that the only gift that came close was jewelry. His gifts had always made her go all soft in the head, not to mention everywhere else. The bracelet was beautiful. It made her feel cherished. And she had trouble dealing with that.

The way he was looking at her wasn't helping. It made her yearn. It made her think that perhaps . . .

"What about these gifts?" Allison asked, spying a sack of presents mostly hidden behind the couch. "Who are these from?"

"They're from your Aunt Jackie." Maggie cleared her throat. "Go ahead and open them."

"Where did they come from?" Grace asked.

She could feel Spence's eyes on her, but she didn't look at him again. She spoke to the girls. "Aunt Jackie's presents arrived in the mail earlier in the week."

"And you waited until now to tell us?" Grace seemed to be trying to figure something out. Allison tore into the packages.

If Maggie could have done so inconspicuously, she would have left the room. It was difficult to witness the girls exclaiming over these particular gifts. She hadn't told anyone about the box of gifts that had arrived from Traverse City because she'd had half a mind to send them back. But she couldn't do that to Grace and Allison.

"Do you think Aunt Jackie's alone on Christmas?" Grace asked.

It was Spence who finally answered. "You know your Aunt Jackie. She's probably made a lot of new friends."

Maggie didn't like feeling guilty. She had no reason to feel guilty. *She* hadn't done anything wrong. That felt so judgmental. She'd never been one of those people who thought going to church every Sunday automatically earned them a place in heaven. She'd gone to church to pray, and had always left the judging to God. She couldn't seem to do that now. She couldn't forgive, and she couldn't forget. What was she supposed to do, invite Jackie here, then pretend it wasn't Spence's baby growing in her belly? She couldn't pretend it didn't matter. It mattered. And because it did, they were all hurting. She wished she could be glad that Jackie and Spence were miserable. A little vindication might have gone a long way. All she felt was sadness. She ached with it.

The knowledge of what had happened had isolated her from the people she loved the most. She had no one to talk to. She missed Spence. She missed his smiles, his touch, the security that, no matter what happened, everything would be all right as long as they were together. She missed her faith in him most of all. She missed Jackie, too. She couldn't condone what had happened. She couldn't forget. She couldn't stare it in the face. And she couldn't tell anybody.

She'd never been so miserable, or so lonely.

Jackie lay on her side, petting Tango. He purred. And she sighed. For once, there was no smoke coming through the vent. Clem must have gone somewhere.

It was Christmas.

She looked at the clock. It was almost noon. Maggie and Spence and the girls were probably arriving at Yvonne and Gaylord's right about now. She wondered if Allie liked her new soccer ball and her oversized soccer jersey, and if Grace liked her camera. She hadn't sent anything for Spence and Maggie. That would have been pushing things. As it was, she'd half-expected to find the large parcel waiting on her stoop, *Return to Sender* scrawled across the top flap.

She should have known Saint Maggie wouldn't do that.

Jackie flopped onto her back so quickly Tango sprang to his feet in surprise. "Sorry." She sighed again. "I miss her. I miss all of them. How did my life become such a mess?"

Tango jumped off the bed and strode to his food dish in the corner. Propping her head on one hand, she said, "When it comes to listening to my problems, you leave a lot to be desired."

He crunched the first morsel.

"Maybe I should get a dog. What would you say about that?"

He ate on blissfully.

She got out of bed and padded over to the table where she'd placed the photographs she'd developed a few days ago. Most of them were of mediocre quality, but two weren't half-bad, if she did say so herself. She picked up her favorite. In it, the stranger in the lumberjack coat and his big black dog gazed into the camera. She wondered what they were doing for Christmas. Were they alone, too?

She held up the photograph. She had an idea. Where might she have a frame? After rummaging through several boxes, she came up with one that would work. Fifteen minutes later, the photo was framed and wrapped, and she was headed for the shower, a well-fed tabby cat on her heels.

She emerged from the shower feeling refreshed. Dressed in wool slacks and a warm sweater, she dried her hair and left it to hang loose and full around her shoulders. After lacing up a pair of ankle-high boots, she donned her warmest coat and grabbed the wrapped package and Tango's cat carrier. He balked at getting in. Jackie held firm. "Better to be safe than sorry."

They left the dreary apartment. After making only one stop at a convenience store, she drove back toward the cabin on the hill. "They probably won't even be there," she told Tango. "That's okay. We'll just leave the gifts by the door."

An inch of fresh snow had fallen overnight. More was predicted later. For now, the sun was trying to shine.

She cracked her window, smiling at the first scent of wood smoke in the air. She parked in the same place she had the other day. Carrying Tango in his cage in one hand, and her gifts in the other, she started up the hill.

To give Bo ample warning, she began to sing "Rudolph the Red-Nosed Reindeer," Allison's favorite Christmas song. The ploy worked. The dog didn't charge around any corners, teeth bared.

She was six feet from the cabin when the door opened, and the man and the dog stepped outside. Suddenly self-conscious, Jackie shoved the package at him. He had two choices. Let it fall to the ground or catch it before it did. He snagged it out of the air. She took a little more time presenting the dog with her peace offering, a rawhide bone wrapped in a red bow.

"Would you like to come in?"

An old line played through her mind. "Said the spider to the fly." She looked at him. His whisker stubble was less pronounced today. The intensity in his eyes wasn't. "That depends," she said.

"On?"

"You aren't an ax murderer, are you?"

It took about two seconds for the surprise in his eyes to turn into humor. "No. As a matter of fact, I'm not." Without further ado or hesitation, he turned on his heel and went inside, leaving the door open behind him. She was left with two options, too. Enter. Or leave.

She strode through the door and closed it behind her. The man was on the other side of the small cabin, placing the framed photograph on a shelf fashioned out of rough-sawn timber.

Jackie didn't know what she'd expected the cabin to look like, but it wasn't this. The room was square and clean and sparsely furnished. There was one door on either end, one window, one chair, one table, one narrow cot, a sofa that had seen better days, and a hand pump that probably had, too.

"You build this yourself?"

"How did you guess?"

There was a hurricane lamp on the table, a lantern near the cot. She didn't see a light switch anywhere. "There's no electricity?" she asked.

He unbuttoned his coat. Leaning down, he opened the door on the wood-burning stove and stoked the fire. "No electricity, no indoor plumbing."

"You mean?"

He straightened and put the poker away. Next, he stirred something in a pot on top of the stove. "This is it. One room and a path."

Then that shed out back wasn't a shed. Jackie pulled a face. "I'm real glad I didn't plan to stay." She sniffed the air. "What are you making?"

"Fudge."

Jackie was intrigued. "Fudge?"

"It's Christmas."

So it was.

"It won't set up. I must have done something wrong. It tastes good, though." He held up a spoon of the thin mixture. "Care to try it?"

He shrugged out of his coat. Jackie left hers on. She stayed long enough to eat two spoonfuls of the best-tasting fudge she'd ever had. They talked about the weather and the house she was going to be renting in Traverse City, and a few of Bo and Tango's more bizarre habits. She let Tango out of his cage. Although Bo watched him closely, the two animals stayed on opposite sides of the room.

"What do you do for a living?" Jackie motioned to

his hands. "You're not an ax murderer, and those aren't lumberjack hands."

"You're right. They're not." She noticed he didn't say what he did do, though. Instead, he shrugged, and asked, "What about you?"

"I don't even own an ax."

He cocked one eyebrow sardonically. "Glad to hear it. I know you're not a professional singer."

"A gentleman wouldn't bring that up."

"Maybe a gentleman didn't."

She studied him more closely. Was he flirting with her? She was so out of practice she couldn't tell. Still, it occurred to her that she liked him.

He seemed to feel the same way about her. There was something safe about not knowing, safe and a little exciting. "Right now," she said, keeping a close eye on Tango, who was inching toward the dog's side of the room. "I'm between jobs. Recently, I sold my vintage clothing store in Grand Haven. I think I'll try my hand at something else." She was silent, thoughtful for a moment.

He busted into her reverie. "You're not a half-bad amateur photographer."

That almost sounded like a compliment. Would wonders never cease? She'd thought about photography as a career. She liked taking pictures, but for a living? She didn't know. "One thing my ex-husband and I did very well together was invest. Therefore, I'm not destitute or desperate. The next order of business for me is finding a good doctor in this area."

"Are you sick?"

"What? Oh. No. Not that kind of doctor. I need to find an obstetrician." His gaze looked a little blank. So she said, "I'm expecting. A baby."

"Yes. I believe that is what most women expect."

She thought that was a strange reply. She also thought

she detected a slight change in him. Maybe she'd over-stayed her welcome. She scooped Tango up, took the cage, and headed for the door. "It's starting to snow outside. I think I should take my cat and go before the roads get bad."

He didn't argue.

"Bye, Bo. That's all right. Don't get up. No need to thank me for that bone. You just go on chewing on it and not on Tango. That'll be thanks enough."

She thought she detected a smile along the edges of the man's mouth. "Bo and I don't get much company out here," he said, as if trying to explain their lack of manners. "There's a reason for that."

"Nobody likes you?"

This time, a smile didn't simply lurk around one corner of his lips. It stretched from one end of his mouth to the other, revealing even white teeth and a crease in one cheek.

"I don't know your name," she said.

"It's Alex."

"I'm Jackie." She smiled, too, and held out her hand. He took it. His hand was warm, his grip firm. That didn't explain the buzz that went up her arm, radiating outward.

He didn't release her hand, as surprised as she was. She was the one who finally drew her hand away. She lifted the latch on the heavy door, just as a telephone rang, startling her.

Alex answered it after the second ring. "Yes?" A line of concentration formed between his eyebrows. His voice was low, his enunciation clear. "How long?" There was a pause. "I'll be right there."

He hung up. Suddenly, he looked at her as if he'd forgotten she was here. "If you're looking for a good group of obstetricians, four of the best in the area share a suite of offices on Boardman Avenue." He jotted the name of the practice and its address on a piece of paper.

She took the paper from him by rote. He must have read the question in her eyes, *And you would know this because . . .* because he said, "It's where my wife went."

Which only sent a dozen more questions to the front of her mind. He didn't offer any more information, though. He was too busy putting out the fire in the wood stove and readying the cabin for his departure.

"Merry Christmas," she called from the doorway.

Alex looked at her for several seconds. And then he smiled. "Merry Christmas to you, too."

She hurried out the door, along the lane, to her car. Cleaning the snow off the windshield with her mittened hand, she said, "Do you think he's strange, Tango?"

The cat purred.

"Me, too. But then, who isn't?" She started her car, thinking. Alex had had a wife who'd been pregnant once. Jackie hadn't seen any signs of a child in his life now. She wondered what had happened, and if it had anything to do with the reason he lived in a remote cabin without indoor plumbing or electricity. Even that didn't explain why he had a phone. Since she would probably never see him again, she doubted she would ever know.

"Do you have your insurance card?"

"Yes." Jackie handed the card to the stout, no-nonsense woman with the monotone voice.

"Name?"

"Pardon me?" Jackie had been nervous when she'd entered the suite of offices on Boardman Avenue. She'd been surprised when she'd called for an appointment this morning, and had been told there was an opening that very afternoon. She was here to check out the practice, the doctors, and the facilities. She wouldn't make any decisions until she'd done a thorough evaluation. At this point, she was having a little trouble getting past the receptionist.

"Your name?"

"Fletcher."

"First or last?"

"First or last what?" Jackie asked.

"First or last name."

Jackie leaned over the counter, looking down on the woman sitting behind it. "Do I look like someone with Fletcher as my first name?"

The woman finally looked up at Jackie. Obviously, she failed to see the humor. It was shortly after one. Jackie was the only patient in the lobby. Any second now, there was going to be none. Jackie started for the door.

"Is there a problem, Irene?"

Jackie stopped in her tracks. She recognized that voice. Turning slowly, she looked straight into a pair of brown eyes she'd seen before.

"Hello, Jackie."

"You know her?"

Alex nodded at the receptionist. "We've met, yes. You can go to lunch. I'll get Jackie signed in."

Suddenly, Irene didn't look all that hungry. "I don't mind staying."

He brushed her offer aside. "Work your magic with the phone system before you leave, would you?"

"Yes, Doctor." Irene punched a few buttons, forwarding any incoming calls to an answering service. With unveiled curiosity, she finally turned her computer on standby, and left.

Alex reached for the chart the other woman had been filling out. "Why don't we finish this in my office where it's more comfortable?"

He sauntered into an office at the end of the hall, and was sitting on the edge of his desk, one leg dangling, the other foot firmly on the floor when Jackie entered. He motioned to a nearby chair.

She shook her head. "I'd rather stand. You're Dr. Alexander Kincaid?"

"You sound surprised."

She gestured to the white lab coat, the stethoscope around his neck. He was clean-shaven, his sandy-blond hair neatly styled. His shoes were polished, for chrissake. "Let me get this straight. You're a doctor, and you live in a rustic, one-room cabin with no indoor plumbing or electricity."

"On weekends, yes."

At least that explained the phone. It certainly didn't explain why his gaze was making a slow climb down her body. It sure didn't explain why she was reacting in the most fundamentally female way.

"No wonder you recommended this practice."

He didn't seem to follow her line of thinking.

She had to work at refraining from rolling her eyes. "You must need patients pretty badly."

He strode to the other side of his desk and opened a cupboard door, revealing several dozen photographs of newborn babies. "I didn't recommend this practice because we need patients. It's the day after Christmas. I'm here because my partners have families. I don't. I have fourteen mothers due in the next three weeks. That phone call that cut my holiday short? Twin girls, both weighing in at just under five pounds, both healthy. I've delivered well over a hundred babies."

"But not your own?"

His face clouded.

She hadn't meant to cut him to the quick. "I'm sorry. I have a knack for saying what I'm thinking."

His gaze strayed to her mouth. "My wife used to do

that." He looked her in the eye, then. "Her name was Beth. We were married for five years. She died three years ago, five and a half months pregnant with our son."

"How . . ."

"A car accident. She sustained a closed head injury. She lived a matter of hours."

Jackie closed her eyes. Maybe someday she would tell him what she knew about closed head injuries. Opening her eyes, she said, "And your baby?"

He shook his head. "Beth died too soon. If it had been a few weeks later? Who knows? So no, his picture isn't with the others. The only picture I have of him is the ultrasound we took two weeks before the accident." He paused, as if to get his bearings. "Is there a father in your situation?"

Jackie took a deep breath. "It's interesting that you should ask." Lovingly, she placed her hand over her abdomen. "This is either my brother-in-law's child, or the result of another Immaculate Conception." She watched his expression closely, certain her candor would scare him off for good.

"Another Immaculate Conception, is it? I see at least two a year. Look, I've been numb for three years. And then, wham. This."

"What exactly, do you mean by *this*?"

His eyes delved hers. "I'm not your doctor. If I were, I wouldn't be able to say things like what I'm about to say."

"I'm afraid I'm not following you."

"If you'd let me finish, you might. Rest assured this isn't coming from your doctor, but from the man who watched you lick homemade fudge off an old wooden spoon. I've been fighting a serious attraction since you threw yourself between my dog and your treed cat."

Jackie's mouth fell open. She sat down after all. "Don't sugarcoat it on my account."

"That was the sugarcoated version. Just be thankful I didn't tell you what was happening while you were sampling that fudge. I think you should be aware of the facts. I would like to refer you to one of my colleagues, Dr. Jane Albertson."

"Are you telling me you don't want to be my doctor, yourself?"

"A man's anatomy is designed in such a manner that makes *this* impossible to ignore. But I'll deal with it in private. If you choose Dr. Albertson as your obstetrician, I'll confer if you'd like."

Jackie had half a mind to walk out the door and never return. Something held her back. It was the integrity in his eyes, and the sense that before her stood an honorable man.

All her life she'd been waiting for the kind of excitement she was feeling right now. For years she'd been wishing she had the courage to take the first step into that vast, unknown canyon that was her life. She had her child to consider now, first and foremost.

She raised her chin and looked Alex in the eye. "I'll need references. And I must meet Dr. Albertson before I decide."

"That's fair." He gestured for her to follow him from the room, talking about his colleague as he went.

Dr. Albertson sounded caring and qualified. If she turned out to be as good as he said she was, she was exactly the kind of doctor Jackie wanted to help her bring her child into the world.

When Alex was finished, he held out his hand. She shook it. It felt a little like taking that first step into a shadowy ravine. It wasn't without risks, but it wasn't a flying leap, either.

* * *

Maggie paced from one end of the house to the other, picking up wet mittens and socks and hats along the way. Earlier, Spence had taken the girls ice skating at the park. Because of the chasm between the two of them, Maggie had opted not to go. She'd missed out.

It was the day after Christmas. She'd never been so confused. She felt a lot of things. Anger, sadness. The confusion surprised her. She'd always thought she knew exactly what she would do if the unthinkable happened, and Spence strayed. Not that she'd ever believed it was possible.

She'd thought the marriage would be over. End of story.

That would hurt Grace and Allison. Placing a soggy purple boot on the register, Maggie knew it would hurt her and Spence, too. She didn't know what to do. She didn't know how to feel, or how to act. She felt lost in her own house, in her own body, in her own life.

She and Spence had tucked the girls in bed a while ago. Grace and Allison were asleep, safe and secure. A pipe rattled between floors. Spence was taking a shower.

She knew this house like the back of her hand, every sound, every nook and cranny. She strode to the window. The back light was on, the tree swing snow-covered and motionless. No matter what the season, she'd always thought of the backyard as her haven. How many nights had she stood, barefoot on the dew-dampened grass, looking up at the sky? It had always been so clear, the stars so bright. Everything in her world had made sense.

Nothing made sense anymore.

She wanted that life back. But she couldn't go back. Did she dare go forward?

She turned out the lights and made her way up the

stairs. Spence was coming out of their bedroom as she was going in. They met in the doorway.

"Maggie."

"I'm sad," she blurted. "I'm miserable."

"I know."

She lowered her voice to a whisper. "I want to hate you."

He nodded.

"I can't."

"I love you, Maggie." Spence proceeded with caution. He was afraid to read too much into the fact that Maggie wasn't backing away. He saw such yearning in her eyes it nearly buckled his knees. He raised a hand, placing it on her slender cheek. Her eyes closed, and she tipped her head slightly, resting her cheek in his hand, as if she was as lonely for his touch as he was for hers.

She opened her eyes, and he glimpsed sadness. He touched a finger to her lips. *"Sh.* I love you."

She whimpered, but she didn't draw away.

"For now, don't think. Just feel." He gathered her close and kissed her gently. His breathing hitched as she kissed him back. Her cane clattered to the floor. She bent over to retrieve it. Spence stopped her. "Lean on me, Maggie. I'll help you. I love you."

She straightened again, and grasped the arm he offered. The closer they came to the bed, the more her hand shook on his arm. He covered her lips with his. Her mouth opened hungrily. He kissed her again, and again, and he touched her, through her clothes, and under them.

"I love you, Maggie." He opened her blouse.

"I know." She whimpered when he rolled her nipple between his thumb and finger. She arched into him, until he couldn't help taking the hard nub in his mouth. She threaded her fingers through his hair, steadying him as he worked his way to her other breast, and then back up to her mouth, kissing every inch of warm flesh along the way.

He loved her so much. He hadn't lost her. She was here, with him, flesh to flesh, breast to chest, man to woman. They would work it out. He would spend the rest of his life . . . What? Making it up to her? He couldn't do that. He could only spend the rest of his life loving her.

"I need you to kiss me," she whispered.

He kissed her, with his mouth, his lips, his tongue, until kissing wasn't enough. She dragged in a ragged breath through her mouth, and inched her hand down his chest, along the taut muscles of his abdomen. She whimpered as she covered him with the flat of her hand.

She went perfectly still. And then she started to cry.

"Oh Maggie, don't cry."

She took her hand away. It didn't matter. Her tears unmanned him.

"I can't. I can't. When I touch you, I imagine you . . . and Jackie." Tears ran down her face.

He wrapped his arms around her, and held her, whispering words of comfort. "It's all right. *Sh.* I love you. It's going to be okay. This is a start, Maggie. We'll find our way back. We will."

Maggie wanted to believe him, but she didn't see how it was ever going to be okay again.

Maggie sipped her morning coffee, listening as the automatic garage door went down. Spence had an early meeting in Ferrysburg. The girls were still asleep. She'd had a hard time sleeping since she'd discovered the truth. Last night, she'd hardly slept at all. She'd spent most of the night thinking about her and Spence and their life and what he'd done. Mostly, she thought about their sex life. It had always been so special. Not only because of the passion, but because they'd been each other's one and only.

Maggie felt as if something had died. Something had. She wasn't his one and only. She never would be again.

She knew he loved her. God help her, but she was afraid she would always love him, too. What he'd done, even if what he said was true, and it was only once, had blown a gaping hole in their marriage. How could they fix it? How did people heal something like that?

It would never be the same. No matter what happened, this would always be between them. They wouldn't be equals. He would always be her one and only, but she wouldn't be his.

Maggie stopped suddenly. He would always be her one and only. What if he wasn't? Her face felt red-hot at the thought. She stood. With the help of her cane, she walked into the back room where the ice skates the girls had gotten for Christmas had been carefully stored in their boxes until the next outing. Grace's were figure skates. Allie's were hockey skates.

She thought of Ivan.

An idea came out of nowhere. It was preposterous. That didn't keep her from making her way to the shelves and lowering herself to her knees. Pushing Allie's boots aside, Maggie stared at the picture of the hockey player on the box. She wondered if Ivan still skated. She wondered if he ever thought about her. She wondered if she dared call him.

Her hands flew to her hot cheeks. She couldn't. Could she?

CHAPTER EIGHTEEN

"Here you go, ma'am." The taxi driver pulled to a curb in front of a brick apartment complex in Muskegon.

So this was where Ivan lived.

Maggie stared out the window from the back seat, wringing her hands. Her palms were sweaty and she was shivering at the same time. What was she doing?

"Hold on," the friendly driver said. "Someone's pulling out. I think I can get you closer to the door."

She opened her mouth to tell him to turn the cab around and take her back to Grand Haven. The words wouldn't form.

She'd almost backed out so many times she'd lost count. Whenever she was certain she couldn't do this, she'd thought about Spence and Jackie, and had proceeded to the next step. Aside from the fact that she'd questioned her sanity at every turn, the preparations leading to this moment had been a snap. It had taken but a few clicks of a button to order her new outfit over the Internet. Even when the package had arrived two days later, she'd assured herself the opportunity would never present itself. She didn't believe in fate anymore, so when Spence's brother Frank called to invite them to spend New Year's Eve with his family in a condo they'd rented at Caberfee Ski Resort, she'd had to call it a coincidence. She'd told Spence to take the girls and go without her. At first he'd refused. He couldn't understand why she would want them to go without her.

If she did this, she would do it without lying. Therefore, she didn't fabricate a reason why she wouldn't go. Even though she couldn't ski anymore, she didn't use that as an excuse, either. In the end, she'd calmly told him that maybe time apart was exactly what they needed. She couldn't say he'd looked convinced, but he'd agreed to take the girls and go. Maybe he needed a break from the ice that was at the heart of their marriage now as much as she did. Or maybe he was simply growing weary of feeling her stiffen when he touched her. She didn't react that way on purpose. An active love life had always been an important facet of their marriage. She missed it. She missed the ecstasy, the connection, the bond, the love. Whenever she came close to feeling any of those things, the image of Spence with Jackie pressed down on Maggie's chest with so much force she couldn't breathe.

She needed something to chase that image away. Spence couldn't do it. Perhaps only another man could.

Her entire body had been shaking when she'd called Ivan. Her voice shook most of all. Somehow, he'd known what she'd wanted. There had been a long pause over the phone line, and then his voice had deepened, and he'd told her he would be waiting.

"That'll be twenty dollars, ma'am."

That had been yesterday. And now, here she was.

"Ma'am?"

"What?" She blinked.

"I've got another fare. This is where you wanna go, right?"

She knew smiling was out of the question, but she nodded and pulled herself together. "Yes. Just daydreaming, I guess."

"If you can't daydream on New Year's Eve, when can you, huh?"

What a year it had been, Maggie thought. She could hardly wait for the old year to be over and a new one to begin.

She drew the fare and a tip from her coat pocket. Taking her cane, she got out of the cab and started up the sidewalk to Ivan's apartment. The heels of her shoes clicked with every step. They seemed to be asking, "What are you doing? What are you doing? What are you doing?"

She didn't remember reaching Ivan's door. Once she had, she couldn't bring herself to knock. It opened as if by magic, and there stood Ivan. Even when he was obviously happy to see her, he was all shoulders and sulk.

"I don't know what I'm doing here," she blurted out.

He reached for her hand and drew her inside. She was glad he didn't smile.

"Just throw your purse and coat over that chair." He pointed in the general vicinity of a shadowy corner in the tiny foyer then ambled into the next room.

She didn't know what she'd expected, but it wasn't this. "Now who's the bossy one?"

He waited to answer until she'd gotten rid of her purse and coat and had followed him. "We always were neck and neck in that department, weren't we?"

Perhaps this wasn't what she'd expected, but it was exactly what she needed. She rolled her eyes, shook her head, and ended up smiling. "Hello, Ivan."

He still didn't smile, but she could tell he was warming up to.

"I hope you didn't cancel . . . any important plans to . . . meet with me tonight."

He motioned to a sofa and a low table that held a tray containing a bottle of wine, two glasses, and a plate of cheese and fruit. "Here's a news flash for you, Maggie. I would have ditched an evening with Wayne Gretzky and every one of the *Sports Illustrated* swimsuit models for the chance to spend an hour alone with you."

Luckily Maggie was sitting down. That way she didn't have to fall down. "Wayne Gretzky. My, I do feel special."

He continued pouring the wine. "You are special." Bubbles popped. Maybe it was champagne. He handed a glass to her. "You look beautiful."

She swirled her drink, her eyes downcast. "I have a four-inch scar . . . on the side of my face. I limp. My speech is halting and my memory . . . isn't what it used to be. I'm a real beauty, all right."

Ivan reached over with one hand, lifting her chin with the tip of one finger. The look in Maggie's eyes was as naked as pride. He hated Spence McKenzie for allowing these kinds of doubts to fester in a woman like Maggie. The man didn't deserve her.

"You are beautiful. Your hair, your eyes, your lips." He touched her scar. "Marilyn Monroe had six toes."

Maggie's eyes showed her surprise. At least she wasn't thinking about any self-perceived flaws anymore.

He nodded. "It's true. And she was the most famous sex symbol of all times, Cleopatra not withstanding."

She laughed and relaxed and took a sip of wine. Ivan had a hard time taking his eyes off her. Her plum-colored mohair sweater looked soft and inviting, the straight knit skirt casual yet sexy. The clothes wouldn't have mattered to him. They mattered to her.

She crossed her legs. He was close enough to hear the swish of her nylons. His body heated at least ten degrees.

"I don't know . . . what I should tell you." She placed her glass on the table and clasped her hands in her lap. "About why . . . I'm here."

"You don't have to tell me anything."

She shrugged. "I appreciate that. Spence and I are . . ." She didn't seem to know how to finish.

"Having problems? I figured." He took a sip of his wine, then handed her glass back to her.

"Are you trying to get me drunk?"

"Would it help?"

She downed half the liquid in her glass, then sighed. "I don't want—"

"Sure you do."

Maggie could not believe the man's nerve. She'd forgotten how much she enjoyed it.

He placed a hand on her thigh, a few inches above her knee. He'd touched her there countless times before. Then, she hadn't been wearing a thin knit skirt with a slit to one knee, and lace-topped, thigh-high nylons and silk underwear. Then, she'd never given a thought to seducing him. "You don't mind that I'm here, using you . . . for sex?"

He had the audacity to grin. "Here's another news flash. Men don't mind. Hell, we're flattered. I'm pretty much a sure thing where you're concerned. In case you haven't noticed, I didn't bother with shoes. Underwear either, for that matter. Why don't you come here and kiss me and get it over with?"

"You want to get . . . this over with?"

He settled back comfortably. "Just the first kiss. I'll take it from there. Nice and slow."

Maggie felt a little like she had when she'd taken her first steps in rehab. Shaky and giddy and scared and, in some perverse way, incredibly appreciative. She leaned toward him, balancing with a hand placed gently in the center of his chest. She wet her lips with the tip of her tongue, then gently touched them to his. He deepened the kiss expertly, as if he'd imagined doing just that for a long time.

When the kiss ended, she drew away slightly, and looked into his eyes. "Oh, my."

He had her on her back before she could say it again. He kissed her again, hungrily, his hands gliding over her sweater. She'd felt his touch a hundred times. This was different. This wasn't the therapist touching his patient. This was a man touching a woman he wanted a great deal.

He covered her breast boldly. It felt different than when Spence did it. She didn't stiffen. She didn't flinch. She didn't melt, either.

She concentrated on touching him. His black cable-knit sweater bunched beneath her fingers. His chest was warm underneath, the muscles taut and well defined. His heart beat a steady rhythm beneath her palm.

His hand inched to her thigh, his fingers deftly drawing the hem up, up, his palm gliding over her nylon-clad thigh. She knew the moment he discovered the lace-topped nylons. An eyebrow went up; he was surprised, pleasantly so.

"I didn't want to have to deal with panty hose," she whispered.

"Nasty contraptions, undoubtedly designed by direct descendants of whoever invented chastity belts."

She smiled, grateful for the easy way he had of putting her at ease. "Ivan, I—"

"You can Ivan me later. Right now, I need to kiss you. Bad."

He did just that, and she let him. He smelled good. He felt good. There was more in his touch than desire, more in his kisses than the mating of mouths. He cared about her, deeply. She closed her eyes, willing herself to respond. And yet she felt little. She told herself it didn't matter.

She watched him through narrowed eyes. His eyes were closed, his lips parted slightly, his breathing deep, ragged. Shadows stretched across the planes and angles that made up his uniquely handsome face.

"Ivan." He opened his eyes, and she saw deep-seated emotions along with the rapture. She stopped his hand before it reached her most private flesh. Holding his hand still, she whispered, "I can't."

"Sure you can."

She pushed her skirt down. "I'm sorry."

"Don't be sorry." He took a deep breath. "I'm not done trying."

Joking aside, she saw in his eyes that his emotions ran deeper than he let on. "You know I can't do this. I think you know why." She didn't love him.

For a moment, she saw pain in his eyes. His face closed, as if guarding a secret. She knew his secret. Spence had seen it, too. Ivan loved her. And she couldn't use him. She couldn't hurt him, no matter how much he claimed men didn't mind.

"I don't think this was such a good idea."

"Anybody ever tell you that you think too much?"

She shook her head slowly, smiling in spite of herself. "What position?"

His eyes widened. "Um. Any position you want."

"I mean on the ice."

"I've never done it on the ice, honey. Cold and certain parts of a man's body don't mix well." He settled back on the couch.

Maggie felt his eyes on her as she straightened her skirt and sweater.

"Forward."

She glanced at him.

He indicated that she should make herself comfortable. "My position on the hockey team. I played forward."

"Were you good?"

He made a sound that clearly indicated that she hadn't needed to ask. She wished she could smile. Her dignity restored, she fumbled under the couch for her cane, then rose to her feet.

"Where are you going?"

"To call a cab. Do you ever play?" she asked.

"No. You're leaving already?"

She spied a telephone on a desk in the hall. After painstaking minutes spent dealing with alphabetical order, she located the telephone number she was looking for. Ivan broke the connection before she'd finished punching in the last number. She stared at him, and then at the telephone book she'd closed. She would have to start all over again searching for the number. "Why did you—"

"I'll drive you home."

"You don't . . . have to do that."

"I know."

She stared at him in disbelief. "Let me get this straight. I came here to seduce you . . . And even though I didn't, couldn't . . ."

"You got my hopes up." The lift of his eyebrows said, "That ain't all."

"I'm sorry."

He waved it aside. "You ended up rejecting me. And yes, now I'm going to drive you home. I must enjoy suffering." He took the phone from her hand, then placed it on the desk. "Come on. Let's get our coats." He made a disparaging sound universal to men. "Hockey was never this grueling."

They donned their coats and left the apartment.

While Ivan scraped ice off his car's windshield, Maggie got in. He looked young and virile and handsome. But he wasn't that young. At twenty-seven, he was an adult. She wished she could have loved him. But she didn't. Not that way. And she couldn't have an affair with him, not out of revenge. Sleeping with Ivan, morally wrong or not, wouldn't make her and Spence even. It would only hurt Ivan, and make her ashamed of herself. And right now, her pride was all she had.

Maggie didn't speak until they were well away from the city of Muskegon. "Ivan?"

"You're having second thoughts and want me to turn around?"

She glanced at him. He had a strong profile, even in the dark. "No."

"Rats. What then?"

The lights on the dash didn't reach his eyes, so Maggie had to rely on the tone of his voice and the subtle nuances and pauses to know what he was feeling. "You don't play hockey anymore. Do you still skate?"

"No."

"Why?"

"I told you. I messed up my knee pretty bad. Came close to never walking again."

"That's why you don't play professional hockey. Why don't you skate?"

He shifted uncomfortably in his seat. "What's the use?"

"I thought hockey was all . . . about skating."

"Hockey is all about hockey."

She rolled her eyes. "You're telling me you threw . . . away your skates?"

He didn't reply.

"You still have them, don't you?"

"So I'm a saver. So what?"

"I think," she said quietly, "that you're . . . a wonderful man, a wonderful physical therapist. And I think there's something missing . . . in your life. And that something is . . . collecting dust somewhere."

"You think I miss skating."

She nodded.

"I think you have a screw loose."

Maggie didn't have it in her to be offended. Traffic was intermittent on Highway 31. The next time they met a car, she studied Ivan's expression in the glare of headlights. He was scowling. "What's the matter? Am . . . I getting too close . . . to the truth?"

"Look. I got my first hockey skates when I was three. I wanted to play professional hockey before that. I would have made it, too. If I hadn't broken my knee cap, had surgery, gotten an infection, had more surgery."

"You know the game. You could . . . teach—"

He cut her off before she could finish. "Haven't you heard? Those who can, do. Those who can't, teach."

"You're living your life . . . according to a saying most certainly . . . coined by some little, little man or woman with . . . half a brain and no spirit, tunnel vision, and no ability to dream?"

"Do you always go around telling people how they should live? No wonder you and Spence are having problems."

All at once, the air inside the car was perfectly quiet.

"Maggie. I . . ."

"It's all right." She pointed to a sign. "Here's my exit."

He eased his car around the curve. "It is not all right. I'm sorry I said that. You don't deserve—"

"Go left here. I mean, please. See? I am bossy. Spence always used to say so, too."

"Used to?" Ivan asked.

She looked out the window at the familiar houses on

the outskirts of town. "We don't talk much . . . these days."

"That have anything to do with your sister?"

They were at a stop sign. Maggie was dumbfounded. "How? What? I mean . . ." And finally, "It's a long . . . story, but yes, it does." There was no sense wondering how he knew. "This is my street."

He turned onto her street. They drove slowly. The heater was blasting, the radio turned low. "Which house is yours?"

"There." She pointed. Snow clung to the boughs of the spruce trees on either side of the driveway. Moonlight spilled through the bare branches of the sugar maple tree closer to the house. A blanket of crusty snow reached right up to the front porch. There were lights on in the house. "Spence and the girls must have come home early."

"Where were they?"

"Skiing."

"Think everything's all right?"

They pulled into the driveway. She eyed the lamp shining in the bay window. Directly above it, Allison's night-light glowed a pale yellow. "It's almost midnight. Grace and Allison . . . are probably asleep. Spence is probably wondering where I've been."

"Will you tell him?"

"I'm going to tell him I was with a dear friend. That's . . . what you are. A sweet . . . kind man."

"Don't spread it around. I have a reputation to protect."

She almost laughed. "My lips are sealed."

"Don't I know it."

Now, she did laugh. And it felt good. "Goodbye, Ivan."

"Maggie?" She'd opened her door. They both

blinked beneath the sudden flash of the dome light overhead. "Good luck."

"Thanks. You, too."

"I might just dust off my old skates and see if they still fit. Don't let it go to your head."

She was smiling as she opened the door all the way and got out.

Spence was waiting for her in the kitchen. "Thank God. Where have you been?"

Her smile slid away.

He hurried toward her. "I've been calling everyone we know. Are you all right?"

"I'm fine."

"Are you sure?" His hand went to her shoulder, as if he had to touch her to make sure.

"What are you doing home?"

"It didn't seem right, being away from you." He helped her take off her coat. "Here. Let me help you to the chair. Are you sure you're okay?"

She turned to face him. "Stop."

He was holding her coat in both hands. He looked confused.

"Stop hovering over me. Stop . . . coddling me. Stop."

Spence's imagination had been running wild. He'd pictured several scenarios, each one worse than the last. Maggie had been hurt, harmed, and injured in all of them.

Now that she was here, he took a closer look at his wife. She wasn't injured. Her hair was mussed, her lipstick smeared. She was wearing an outfit he hadn't seen before. Something cold and nasty hit him out of the blue. "Where have you been?"

She sighed. "Where doesn't matter."

"It matters to me."

She retrieved her long, wool coat from him and started toward the closet. "Oh, you're mad ... at me now. That's priceless."

"It's a legitimate question. You are my wife. And you were home alone, conveniently, I might add. I haven't seen you this dressed up in a long time."

"I've been with a friend."

Spence could not believe what he was hearing. That was it? "Define 'been with.' "

"I don't want to talk about this."

Spence could feel the blood start to surge through him. "You've been with a man. A man who's kissed you, quite thoroughly from the look of things. And you don't want to talk about it. Well, by all means, we won't then. After all, you control what we talk about and what we don't, right?"

"I don't believe I'm hearing ... this."

"You just told me to stop coddling you." Anger roiled in the pit of his stomach. Along with it was panic. And dread. And God help him, jealousy. Maggie started to leave the room. He reached out with one hand on her shoulder, and held her back. "Are you having an affair, Maggie?"

She pulled her shoulder from his grasp. "No, I'm not. Where are the girls?"

"They're sleeping. You didn't buy that dress for me."

"You're right. I didn't. I wanted to get even. What do you think about that?"

He thought the top was going to blow off his head. He was having a stroke. Or a heart attack.

"But I couldn't. I couldn't ... go through with it. Isn't that ... priceless? You didn't ... have any trouble."

He didn't know what to say. He'd never witnessed this kind of anger in her. His mind was still stuck on the fact that she'd tried to have an affair, and failed. Thank God she'd failed.

"Maggie."

"Don't Maggie me, okay? I can tell you're relieved. Don't be too relieved . . . I'm not sure I'll . . . ever be able to forgive you. What will . . . we do then?" Her voice was getting louder, and shriller with every word. "What if I . . . never get over this? Maybe I'll flinch every time you touch . . . me. Maybe I'll always wonder if it would . . . have been better if I . . . would have died."

"Don't be stupid."

"Don't call me stupid. I'm . . . not the one . . . who's about . . . to have . . . a third child."

Maggie could see she'd stunned him. She should have stopped there. She couldn't. All her pain, all her sadness, all the anger and fear and disappointments she'd kept locked inside her broke free and came spilling out of her mouth. "Don't you wonder . . . what would have happened if I . . . had died?"

"Maggie, don't."

She shook his hand off. "What would you . . . have done then? Married her? Maybe that . . . would have been best. You could have been . . . one . . . big . . . happy . . . family."

Tears coursed down her face. The clock in the front foyer chimed twelve times. It was the beginning of a new year.

Spence didn't utter another word. Maggie tried, but she couldn't call back her words, either. They stared at each other in stunned silence. He went upstairs, and she found herself in the family room, miserable and alone. Sinking into a chair near the window, she drew a blanket around herself, and stared blankly at the blackness that was the backyard.

Upstairs, Grace lay listening to the heavy sound of footsteps on the stairs. Her dad was going to bed. Alone.

She heard a softer thud. And then Allie whispered, "Mama and Daddy were fighting."

Grace nodded. She hadn't heard the words, but she'd heard the anger in their voices.

Allie hopped onto her sister's four-poster bed. "Think they're gonna get a divorce?"

"Just because people fight doesn't mean they're gonna get a divorce."

"They never used to fight."

"I know."

"A couple'a nights ago?" Allison said, creeping closer on all fours. "I got up, and Daddy was sleeping downstairs."

Grace knew that, too. Something was wrong. Terribly wrong. She didn't know what. If Allie was noticing, too, it had to be bad.

"I'm scared in my room. Something bad's in there."

"Nothing bad is in your room."

"What if there is? Can I sleep with you tonight, Gracie? I'll try to be real still."

"I guess."

Allison scuttled under the covers. "Night, Gracie."

"Night, Al."

It took Allison about a minute to fall asleep, and another minute to roll over, dragging Grace's covers with her. Grace inched closer to the middle of the bed. Huddling under a corner of the quilt, she took comfort in her little sister's presence. Still, it took her a long time to fall asleep.

The atmosphere at the breakfast table the following morning was stilted. The only sounds coming from Grace and Allison were those they made cutting their pancakes and slurping their juice. Maggie felt horrible. Allison had been sleeping in Grace's bed when she'd checked on them last night. They must have overheard her and Spence arguing.

Poor babies.

Spence had noticed, too. He'd managed to get them talking, but even then, they hovered around the kitchen long after breakfast was finished. Neither of the girls cracked a smile when he suggested they go skating again that day. "Is Mama coming?" Allie asked.

Maggie answered, "I'll sit on the bench . . . and watch."

Only then did they relax enough to smile.

"Tell you what," Spence said. "I'll do the dishes while you girls get dressed."

They hurried upstairs. When Maggie was sure she and Spence were alone in the kitchen, she looked at him and quietly said, "I'm sorry. I shouldn't . . . have said the things I said. I'm hurting. I know . . . that's no excuse."

"It's all right, Maggie."

"That's just it. It's not all right. Don't . . . you see?" She bit her lip to keep it from quivering. "Maybe we should separate."

"No."

"Maybe . . ."

"We haven't even tried." He looked awful, haggard. "We can't just throw thirteen years away without trying."

"All right. I'll get dressed, too. And we'll try."

They tried. Maggie went to see a counselor. She went alone. The things she had to say, she couldn't say in front of Spence. She got a lot off her chest. But she and Spence were no closer to a reconciliation. She decided that perhaps what was lacking was sex. Maybe she just needed to get through it the first time. Maybe then, she'd reasoned, they could start over, rebuilding the intimacy they'd once taken for granted.

They began sharing a bed again. She didn't flinch when he touched her. And although having sex brought them both a release, it didn't bring them closer. Invariably, when it was over, she crept to her own side of the bed and fell asleep with her back to him. By the end of January, arguments were breaking out between her and Spence as easily as laughter used to. They argued over the stupidest things, things like bills and the television, and important things, such as what was the best way to deal with the increasing occurrence of Grace's sulks and Allie's unrealistic fear of the dark and sleeping alone.

Maggie had a few unrealistic fears of her own. She was undergoing therapy only twice a week now. That was a definite improvement. But she still wasn't driving. Every time she tried to get behind the wheel, she broke out in a cold sweat, and imagined that pickup truck heading right for her. She couldn't do it. She hated relying on Spence and her friends to drive her where she needed to go. But until she tamed her fear, she didn't see what else she could do.

Even worse, her marriage was spinning out of control. Other people were starting to notice. Nothing either of them tried seemed to help.

It was the dead of winter. The earth wasn't the only thing frozen. It was with an incredible feeling of sadness that Maggie went to check on the girls before going to bed one night in late January. Allison's room was empty. Again. Finding her younger daughter asleep in Grace's bed for perhaps the tenth time that month, Maggie whispered, "Allie, honey. Wake up." She jostled Allison's shoulder. The child slept on.

Grace rolled over, and in the light spilling from the

hall, Maggie saw tears on her precious daughter's face. "Are you and Dad getting a divorce?"

Maggie finally faced facts. The reason Grace sulked and Allie was afraid of the dark ... It was because of her and Spence. These precious children sensed the tension and the lack of harmony. "No one's talking about a divorce."

"Everything's changing." Grace sniffled.

Spence materialized in the doorway. Shouldering his way into the room, he hoisted Allison into his arms. "The way we feel about you girls will never change. Never. Got that?"

Maggie handed Grace a tissue. After restoring her dignity, Grace handed it back to her mother. Maggie tucked the covers under Grace's chin and kissed her smooth forehead. "I love you, Grace."

Maggie's heart felt heavy when she left Grace's room. Spence was waiting for her outside Allie's room across the hall. Together, they went into their bedroom. Spence closed the door.

For the first time in a long time, the eyes Maggie turned to him held no resentment or blame. "We can't go on like this."

"I know."

"We're hurting our most precious gifts."

Spence ran a hand through his hair, over his eyes, across his mouth. "*Do* you want a divorce, Maggie?"

"I don't know what I want anymore. But what we've been doing isn't working. I think we need to live apart awhile."

She could tell he wanted to object, but it was as if he knew that what she said was true. "I can probably bunk at Brian's for a while."

"Not tonight," she said. "Tomorrow's Saturday. We should tell the girls together." Maggie wanted to say she was sorry. Sorry that she couldn't forgive. That she couldn't get past what had happened. That he was hurting. That they were all hurting. She was sorry. She felt it all the way to her bones. Saying it wouldn't change anything.

Spence took a blanket and his pillow to some other part of the house. And Maggie thought, So this was it. She sank to her knees next to the bed and cried until her chest hurt. She lay on the floor, miserable. She was so tired of crying. Perhaps one day the tears would run out.

"What will you do without us?" Allison looked up at her mother, her eyes big and sincere.

The girls were spending the night with Spence over at their Uncle Brian's. Even though he'd dropped by three evenings, and called every day, they'd missed him terribly the week he'd been gone. Maggie could tell they didn't miss the tension, the discord, the words flung in anger.

Grace and Allison had both cried when Maggie and Spence had told them that morning a week ago. Now, they were both excited about this new adventure. Leave it to her daughters to be worried about her, too.

"I'm a big girl." She touched a finger to Allie's nose. "I'm not afraid of the dark."

"What will you do?" Grace asked.

"Whatever I want." Maggie wouldn't let her voice quiver. "Maybe I'll sleep in. Maybe . . . I'll read. Or have . . . lunch with Yvonne."

The truth was, she didn't know what she would do without Grace and Allison here. She'd never been alone for extended periods of time. She'd always had Jackie, and later Spence, and then Grace and Allison.

Perhaps it was time she found out what she was made of.

CHAPTER NINETEEN

Maggie still couldn't say she knew exactly what she was made of two weeks later. She had learned she was a woman of some strength. She could hold her head high, and meet the questions of the women of the Ladies Historic Society without flinching or revealing things she didn't want made public.

She wasn't faint of heart. It was a good thing, or she would have fainted when she opened the door to a loud knock in the second week of February.

Her mother and father stood on her porch, looking eager and tired and too tan for the middle of winter. "It's cold out here," the colonel said, his ruddy face a sight for sore eyes.

"Hello, sweetheart," her mother said. "You going to invite us in?"

Grace and Allison were thrilled. If possible, Maggie was even more so. Adelle Fletcher had examined Maggie's scar and fussed over her hair. Her father had simply hugged her as if he never planned to let her go.

Maggie had had no idea they were back in the States. And while she might have bought their insistence that they'd needed to see for themselves that their daughter was truly recovered, it wasn't until the second day of their visit that she discovered the other reason for their visit.

They'd attended church together. After Sunday dinner, the colonel announced that he was taking his granddaughters out for ice cream and a matinee. The moment the others were out the door, Adelle Fletcher turned to Maggie. "All right, dear. What's going on between you and Spence?"

Maggie had been tap dancing around the subject for two days, with excuses such as: People change, grow apart, want different things. Adelle had responded with an agreeable sort of hum. Translated, it meant she wasn't buying any of it.

"I told you," Maggie said, handing her mother the last dish to dry.

"Yes, I know what you told me."

Maggie didn't know why, but it was difficult to look into her mother's face. Once she had, she couldn't look away. Her mother's hair was gray now. She wore it in a short, feminine, but no-fuss style. There were lines beside her eyes, and innate intelligence in them.

"Your father and I are going to visit Jackie next."

She either caught Maggie's stricken look, or she suspected more than Maggie gave her credit for. "What is it, dear? You can tell me. I'm your mama, remember?"

Maggie took the dish towel from her mother and hung it over the peg near the sink. "I'm fine, Mom. It's been a difficult year, what with my accident—"

"Oh, horse pucky."

Maggie spun around in surprise. Adelle grinned. And Maggie started to laugh. "I haven't heard that saying in a long time."

"My mother used to say it." Adelle poured two cups of coffee and carried them to the table. Setting them next to a plate of cookies, she took a seat. "I may have been on the other side of the world, but I know when something is terribly wrong with my girls."

Maggie sat, too. She didn't have a clue what to say. "Have you talked to Jackie much?"

"She's been as tight-lipped as you. Which tells me a lot without saying a thing." She nibbled on a cookie. "Right from the beginning, you and Jackie were always so close. I never sensed an ounce of sibling rivalry. It was the two of you against the world. I often felt like a third wheel."

Adelle stirred sugar into her coffee. Maggie found herself staring at her mother's hands. They were delicate, the nails only slightly longer than the tips of her fingers. Only Adelle Fletcher could look stylish after spending nearly a year as a lay missionary in Africa. "But I thought," Maggie said. "I mean, you always seemed so content with your life, so, I don't know, busy and social."

"I was all those things. That didn't mean I didn't occasionally want more. We moved so much. You girls needed each other. And I needed you to be happy. And you were. We all were. We had a good life."

"Yes, we did."

"But?" Adelle asked.

Maggie looked up. Her mother was gazing out the window.

"Everyone's life has a few buts, dear. Don't get me wrong. Mine was a good life. It still is. But it hasn't been the life I dreamed of when I was a young girl."

Maggie hadn't known that, either. "What kind of life did you dream of?"

"Oh, a house with a big kitchen, a garden where I could plant vegetables and flowers every spring. Maybe enough land where a horse or two could graze and where I could watch my children grow."

"But that isn't anything like the life you got."

"I didn't *get* my life, Maggie. I lived it. I'm living it, still."

"Do you have many regrets?"

Adelle tidied her hair, and Maggie thought, She's pretty. "Everyone has regrets. They're part of life. We either adapt to them, or we don't."

Maggie was still trying to understand what it was her mother was trying to tell her. Adelle reached across the table and covered Maggie's hand with her own.

"Maybe we never lived in one place long enough to raise horses. But I've ridden horses through deserts, through mountains. I've seen more of this world than I ever dreamed I would. All because I met your father. After that, it was never a matter of choosing the life I wanted. I chose him."

Maggie smiled.

Adelle didn't. "I always thought you were more like the colonel, and Jackie was more like me. Now, the two of you don't speak, and she's going to have a baby, and you and Spence are separated. We cut our missionary work short because I needed to be here more than I needed to be there. You and Jackie didn't know it, but I always hovered around the edges of your closeness, just in case you ever needed me. You need me now. I just want you to know I'm your mother, and I'm here."

Maggie went into her mother's open arms. "Oh, Mom. It's such a mess."

"Why don't you tell me what's happened, and maybe we can begin to sort it out."

For perhaps the first time in her life, Maggie poured her heart out to her mother. She didn't start in any particular place, certainly not at the beginning. She jumped around, as she was apt to do these days since the accident. Her mother asked questions occasionally.

Once, she got up and brought a box of tissues back to the table. They both needed several.

When Maggie was finished talking, Adelle said, "Feel better?"

Maggie shook her head, nodded, and shrugged. She felt purged, and spent, but better? She didn't know how to feel better anymore.

"What do you want?" Adelle asked.

Now there was a question, Maggie thought. "I want what's best."

"Best for who?"

"For Grace and Allison. And for me."

"And for Spence?" her mother asked.

Maggie made an unbecoming sound in her throat. "I want him divided and quartered one minute, and the next . . ."

Her mother waited patiently in the ensuing silence.

Finally, Maggie finished the statement. "I don't want Spence to suffer. Not really. I don't want any of us to suffer."

"But you all are."

Maggie sighed. Her mother had always been painfully honest. "Yes."

"I'd like to give that man a piece of my mind for hurting you like this. It isn't easy not to judge. You don't know what Spence and Jackie went through." At Maggie's stricken look, her mother shook her head and continued. "I wasn't here, so I don't know either."

Moisture glistened in Maggie's eyes.

Adelle said, "You have a decision to make."

Maggie nodded. These days she hated making decisions as much as she hated trying to speak without pausing, or forcing her brain to do simple math.

"I'm glad you and the—Dad are here."

"So am I. Think your sister will be as happy to see us?"

"I'm sure she—"

"She has a new man in her life."

Maggie had had no idea.

Her mother shrugged. "Oh, she says they're just friends. But I know your sister, and I hear what's in her voice. Just as I hear what's in yours. Now, how about a game of Scrabble?"

Maggie looked at her mother dazedly. "That's it? You're not going to tell me what you think I should do? You want to play Scrabble?"

Adelle nodded earnestly. "I can't tell you what to do. I don't even know what I would do. I do know I've been dying to play for months. The natives in Africa didn't grasp the language enough to allow us to get very far."

Maggie grinned. "I'm not exactly as smart as I used to be."

After a pregnant pause, Adelle winked. "You thought I was going to say horse pucky again, didn't you? You see? You're smarter than you give yourself credit for. You've suffered a setback, that's all. I don't have a doubt in my mind that you'll figure it out. And when you do, you'll pick yourself up by the bootstraps, brush off the seat of your pants, and get on with this strange process we call life."

Unable to see how she could argue with that kind of blind faith or logic, Maggie went to the hall closet and dug out the old game of Scrabble.

Maggie's second visitor arrived the day after her parents left. Brian McKenzie ambled in with a masculine swagger and a boyish wink just like he always did.

"Look at you," he said. "Walking without a cane."

She gripped the doorknob tightly. "I'm a real ballerina. Haven't fallen on my head . . . since yesterday."

"Beats falling on your—let's just say I'd hate to think you'd bruised that cute little tush."

"But the thought of me bruising my head . . . doesn't bother you."

He grinned, and she was struck by how much he looked like Spence. Brian had always been the family rebel. Maybe it had something to do with the fact that he'd been eleven when his parents' plane went down. Maybe it was because he was the youngest. Or maybe he was just born to be wild. He'd gotten in some trouble as a kid, then up and joined the Navy. He'd surprised everyone when he became a Navy SEAL. A few years ago, he surprised them all again when he accepted his medals then got out. The only reason he'd given was that if and when he performed any more covert actions, he would be in charge of who and what and when. Maggie wasn't really surprised he was here today. As was the case with most family rebels, his feelings ran deep, his loyalties true.

"How are you, Maggie?"

"People keep asking me that question."

"That's because people are worried."

"About Spence?"

"About all of you."

She motioned him into the family room. Naturally, he dropped into Spence's favorite chair.

"We're all doing better, Brian." It was true. Seeing how much happier Grace and Allison were now that she and Spence weren't fighting all the time was such a relief. "I think the girls are adjusting. And you said yourself that I'm doing better."

"And Spence?"

"What about Spence?" she asked.

"Oh, the pressure. Badger, badger, badger me until I spill my guts. I'm worried about him, Maggie. He wants you back."

"Did he say that?"

"Hell no, he didn't say that. He isn't saying anything. Nobody knows a goddamn thing. What the hell happened? Nobody's more perfect for each other than you and Spence."

Maggie wasn't about to confide in Spence's brother the way she'd confided in her mother. Still, she was touched that Brian thought enough of her to want to help. "I'm glad Spence has you right now, Bri."

"God. You make me sound so responsible."

He sounded a little like Ivan. Maggie hadn't seen or heard from Ivan since New Year's Eve. But the other day when Crystal Douglas was waiting for Allison and Grace to buckle up for the drive to school, she'd mentioned some great new hockey coach, Ivan somebody or other who was taking students over in Muskegon. So. Ivan was skating again. She was glad.

She was concentrating on herself these days, on what was best for her family. That included Spence. He'd rented a house overlooking Lake Michigan. He'd moved two days ago. Maggie had divvied up some dishes and kitchen items and dozens of things he would need. Her friends said she was very generous. She wasn't being generous. She cared about him. Besides, half of everything was his. It felt odd to think in those terms. At least they weren't arguing all the time. Actually, she found herself looking forward to hearing his voice when he called to talk to the girls every night. She missed him. At the same time, she was no closer to getting over the rift between them. She was in limbo.

"Do you care if I help myself to a beer?" Brian asked.

Maggie started to get up. "Will a wine cooler do?"

He dropped his face into both hands. "Never mind." When he next met her gaze, his expression was serious. "Has Spence or Jackie or anyone talked about what it was like right after your accident?"

It was the first time in a long time she'd heard Spence and Jackie's names linked so closely. For a moment, Maggie wondered how much Brian knew. She shook her head.

He leaned forward, knees apart, forearms resting on his thighs, his fingers linked. "There are no words, Maggie. Spence was beside himself, out of his mind with worry. He refused to leave your side for days. The girls were basket cases. Only after he'd made arrangements for someone to be with you every minute, around the clock, did he agree to go home to Grace and Allison."

Maggie curled her feet underneath her on the end of the sofa closest to Brian. Other than a comment someone had made here or there, and what she'd read in Grace's journal, she had no real idea what it was like. Brian's words brought it to life.

"He wouldn't have a thing to do with negativity," Brian said. "You were going to come back to him, whole. And that was that. Days passed. Hell, weeks. It became apparent that you weren't going to get well overnight. The girls needed him. They loved Jackie, but you know how Spence is with them."

Yes. Maggie knew how he was with them.

"He talked to you. While you slept. He told me he used to have dreams about you. He wouldn't tell me what they were about. Knowing you guys, they were probably X-rated. I don't know how he did it all. Work, home, the girls, everything. But you were his focus. He kept up the vigil, day after day, week after week. His elbows bled where they were rubbed raw from leaning on your bed."

Maggie's heart ached imagining the scene Brian portrayed.

"Jackie pitched in every step of the way. I know Spence appreciated everything she did, but most of the time, I don't think he was aware of anything except you.

He ever tell you how close they came to taking your living will to the hospital board of whatever?''

Again, all Maggie could do was shake her head.

Brian leaned back in his chair. Bringing one ankle up to rest on the other knee, he continued. "I don't know why in hell he hasn't told you this. Maybe it isn't my place. I don't care. Something's gone wrong between you two. I don't know what the hell it is. But it's obvious to me he loves you, and it's killing him, and dammit, I've been quiet long enough." He jumped to his feet.

"Where are you going?"

"To get that wine cooler." He was back in seconds, pulling a face at the taste of the drink. This time he didn't sit in Spence's chair. He strode to the window and looked out over the backyard.

"They looked at facilities. Did you know that?"

"Who?" Maggie asked.

"Spence and Jackie. The hospital informed them they were kicking you out. Something to do with insurance forms and hospital policy and procedures and other mumbo jumbo. They told Spence you couldn't stay in the hospital indefinitely. So Spence and Jackie visited a couple'a facilities for people who were like you were. Pretty depressing places, I guess. Anyway, Spence couldn't do it. He said he couldn't put you in a place like that. Said you'd both put your wishes in writing years ago. He was going to honor yours. I don't know how, but he was going to let you go. I'm still not convinced he could have gone through with it. I mean, the man's strong, but that would have taken a strength I don't think even he was capable of."

He turned around, and even though the brightness behind him cast his face in shadow, Maggie saw the depth of emotion in Spence's youngest brother's eyes. "And then I tickled you, and out of the blue, as if by some cosmic force, you moved your toe, and here you are. And it looks like Spence is still going to have to let you go."

He'd barely touched his wine cooler, and obviously didn't plan to. He set it on the end stand. "I know it's none of my business. But you and Spence are my family. And I thought, maybe, I could help."

Maggie wiped the tears off her cheeks and rose shakily to her feet. Sniffling, she inched around the coffee table. Going up on tiptoe, she kissed Brian's lean cheek. "You're right. I think this was something . . . I needed to hear."

He left soon after. And Maggie was left wandering the floors of her house, waiting for Grace and Allison to get home from school, thinking about what Brian had told her. Out of everything he'd said, it was his reference about a cosmic force that seemed to have been indelibly inscribed in her mind.

Why had she started to come out of her coma precisely when she did? From the sounds of things, a day or two later would have been too late.

The conversation with Brian was still playing through Maggie's mind two weeks later, and two weeks after that. A few months ago, nothing had made sense. Although she understood more now, she still didn't know what the future held. Maggie was a planner and a doer. When there was a problem, she fixed it. She didn't know how to fix this.

All the thinking in the world brought her no closer to a resolution. She thought about Spence, and Brian's visit, and her parents' visit, too. She thought about everything. She thought so much, she feared she might go crazy thinking.

Grace and Allison were upstairs packing their bags in preparation to spend the night with their father. She heard the customary rap of Spence's knuckles on the back door. He never waited to be let in, but he always knocked twice to let Maggie know he was there. Every time it happened, her heart sped up and her breathing stopped.

He stood across the kitchen from her, tall and dark and rugged. She'd missed him. And yet every time she saw him, it hurt to look at him, just as it was hurting now. "The girls are almost ready," she said.

"I'm in no hurry." It was true. Spence was never in a hurry to leave. He was a little old to be homesick, but every time he walked through these doors, he ached because he couldn't stay. He knew it was better this way. For everyone except him. Allie was sleeping in her own bed again, and Grace hadn't sulked in weeks. There was more spring in Maggie's step, too. He was certain he wasn't imagining that she barely limped anymore. She was better. And he told himself that was enough.

He lied.

He tried not to let her see his deep-seated sadness. He was lonely. God help him, but he didn't see an end to it in this lifetime. He swallowed, hard. Upstairs, footsteps pattered and drawers squeaked. He smiled, if for no other reason than he would break a tooth, or crack his jaw, if he didn't stop clenching.

Having the girls with him in the house he was renting high on a hill overlooking Lake Michigan helped. Even so, the lake was cold and desolate, big and empty in February, much like his life. Brian claimed Spence was getting morose, and blamed it on the fact that he'd been spending time with Edgar Millerton. Spence happened to know that wasn't the half of it.

"Daddy!"

"Hey, short stuff. Hi, Lady Grace."

"You girls all ready?" Maggie asked.

Of course they said they were. To which Maggie replied, "Do you have your toothbrushes?"

That prompted Allison to trudge noisily back upstairs to get hers. Grace and Maggie talked until Allie returned. Spence put the sound of Maggie's voice to memory, so he could play it over in his mind in the middle of the night when he couldn't sleep.

He looked tired, Maggie thought as she hugged and kissed the girls. She touched the edge of his overcoat as he left. She doubted he felt it, but as she drew her hand away and watched them go, she felt as if he was taking a piece of her heart with him. And yet she couldn't call him back.

That scared her, and saddened her and angered her and perplexed her. It continued that way on into March. She kept the girls during the week, and Spence took them most weekends. Everyone was doing all right, but nobody was thriving. Instead, they all floated along. Sure, the sea was calm, but they weren't getting anywhere. Maggie knew this couldn't go on indefinitely.

Finally, on a cold, blustery Saturday in the middle of March, Maggie knew what she had to do. She watched Spence and the girls drive away. Lo and behold, she had to squint. The sun was shining! There had been no evidence of the sun six days in a row. Someone said it had been a record. It had been foggy every morning, growing thick enough each night to make driving a hazardous endeavor. The fog froze to the bare trees. Then, today, the sun appeared. It had been faint at first, barely visible through the white haze. But it was sunlight, no matter how wavering. By ten o'clock, the haze was thinner than it had been all week. By noon, the frozen fog was dropping out of the trees, hitting the ground like raindrops in a Disney cartoon.

If the sun insisted on shining, Maggie couldn't wait

any longer to do what she had to do. In exasperation and maybe even in defiance, she picked up the phone.

"Yvonne?" she said when her friend answered. "Would you mind doing me a huge favor?"

She had to hold the phone away from her ear slightly as Yvonne's voice boomed over the line. "Of course I don't mind. What would you like, dear?"

"I need a ride to the bus station."

"Are you taking a trip?"

"Yes, I guess you could say I am."

"That's nice. Where are you going?"

Maggie stared at the way the sunlight spilled into the house that had always been her haven, and quietly said, "I'm going to Traverse City."

"I could have Gaylord drive you."

"No." And then more gently, "Thanks, Yvonne, but this is something I need to do on my own."

She hung up the phone, then went to get ready.

CHAPTER
TWENTY

Maggie's knock on Jackie's front door was answered almost immediately. No matter how much she'd tried to prepare mentally, she wasn't prepared for the sight of Jackie, more than eight months pregnant. She was beautiful, maternally, eternally feminine.

Maggie had to close her eyes at the moisture gathering there. When she opened them, Jackie had stepped aside, awaiting her entry.

She did enter, eventually, although her legs felt stiff and her throat tight. She'd known Jackie was pregnant. She'd known she must be more than eight months along. But seeing her in a pale blue maternity jumper that looked soft and comfortable even as it clung to her pregnant belly was enough to buckle Maggie's knees.

"You look good," Jackie said.

Maggie simply didn't have it in her to return the compliment, even though it was true.

"How did you get here?" And then, almost as an afterthought, she added, "I didn't hear a car."

"I took a bus. And then I took a cab." It was easier to talk when she wasn't looking at Jackie, so she pretended a fascination in Jackie's house. It had wide, painted trim and old-fashioned charm. It suited Jackie. Maggie didn't say that, either. "I had the driver drop me off at the corner. I walked the rest of the way."

"Without a cane."

Maggie nodded. She knew their parents called both of them every week. Just as Maggie was kept apprised of some of the more impersonal aspects of Jackie's life, such as where she lived and worked, Jackie had undoubtedly been kept apprised of Maggie's physical progress.

If she'd hoped averting her eyes from Jackie would help stave off evidence of the baby, she was disappointed. Signs of the baby were everywhere. There was a box of disposable diapers in the corner, a ruffled bassinet in the next room, not far from the tabby cat asleep in the patch of sunshine spilling on the carpet. There was a childbirth magazine on the table, and pamphlets about pregnancy next to the phone.

Maggie wished she hadn't come.

Why had she? What had she been thinking? Being here, seeing all the evidence of why her marriage was crumbling, was rubbing salt in the wound. It only added insult to injury, and it just plain hurt too much.

Intuition told Jackie that Maggie was thinking about leaving. She knew Maggie backward and forward, inside and out. She was as lovely as always. Perhaps the layers in her hair were new, but the layers of blame and reproach, anger and resentment were still as impenetrable as a brick wall.

It was hard to stare Maggie's sadness in the face. Jackie had to clear her throat in order to speak. "Did you cut your hair?"

Maggie nodded. "Who would have thought I'd like it this length?"

"The wispy, tousled look suits you. But then, you looked good bald."

Jackie watched Maggie closely. She'd made the reference on purpose. When Maggie failed to take the bait, Jackie didn't even try to disguise her annoyance. "Ask, dammit."

Maggie turned in degrees, first her head, then her shoulders, and finally the rest of her. "I shouldn't have come."

"Come on, Maggie. You came here for a reason."

"You're right." Maggie's voice rose an octave. "I came because I can't stand all this thinking, all this useless tossing and turning and wondering." She blinked the tears out of her eyes and, in a voice with just a hint of a quaver, said, "Spence said it happened only once."

"Barely that." Jackie let that sink in before continuing. "There was no affair, if that's what you mean." She strode to the edge of the counter, and leaned against it for support. "I was always in your shadow. The funny thing was, I didn't mind. And then David left me and your accident happened. I helped with Grace and Allie. I stepped in. I was still in your shadow. Sometimes, I felt like I was becoming you. It wasn't until you woke up that I realized that I'd been sleeping, too. For years."

Jackie didn't allow herself to place a hand on her tired, lower back. She only allowed herself one deep breath, and then she said, "We went to look at centers. Places to put you. The thought of leaving you there, indefinitely, not really dead, not really alive, was so grotesque. And you had that living will. And we both knew what you would have wanted. To us, you were already dead. Your heart and soul were gone from us. We were mourning you."

Except for the tears running freely down Maggie's cheeks, she held utterly still. Jackie would have welcomed the opportunity to cry herself, but she had something to say, and by God, she was going to say it.

"Our grief felt as big and ominous as those tornadoes you see on news clips from Texas and Oklahoma. It swirled and churned until it sucked the breath out of everything in its path. It was late. The girls were asleep. And we both knew what we had to do the next morning. I went up to the spare room. Spence went to the den, where he put in a home video of you and Grace and Allison building sand castles at the beach a few summers ago. I heard his anguished sobs all the way from my room. I padded downstairs, and perched on the edge of the sofa, watching you, putting the sight of you to memory. We fell asleep. Spence was dreaming, of you. It was you he reached for."

"What about you?" Maggie asked. "Were you dreaming, too?"

Jackie took a shuddering breath. The tired muscles in her back were beginning to ache. She needed to sit down. But she wouldn't, not until she finished.

Maggie must have taken her silence as guilt, because she said, "You always had a crush on Spence. Now you have a piece of him. I hope you're happy."

Jackie lifted her chin. "Oh, that's priceless. I'm rolling in clover, can't you see? I'll take all the blame if it'll make you feel better. I'm not in love with your husband. I'm sorry you're hurting. I'm sorry we're all hurting."

"How very noble of you."

"How does it feel to be on the receiving end of everything sterling and pure and noble?"

Resentment washed over Maggie with so much force she didn't have time to think until after she heard the slap, and felt the sting in her hand, and saw the imprint her hand left on Jackie's cheek. Both froze, stunned.

Maggie was horrified. She'd never raised a hand to anyone or anything in her life. Ashamed, she turned to go.

"Maggie, wait." Jackie's voice shook with emotion.

"You came here for a reason. For God's sake, don't leave until you accomplish what you set out to do here."

"I slapped you."

"I'll live, and so will you. What is it you want?"

Maggie swiped the tears from her face. She was really getting tired of this weakness, this sickening penchant she had for crying. What did she want? Jackie had asked. God help her, she wanted to be the one pregnant with her husband's child. She couldn't admit that out loud.

It was as if Jackie knew. In a voice that had gone noticeably flat, Jackie said, "You've gone beyond your doctor's every expectation, but you haven't gotten all your brain back."

"You think I don't know . . ."

"Shut up and listen."

Maggie quit crying and turned around and did just that.

Jackie shoved her hair behind her ears then clasped her hands together in front of her. "You were always bright. That's why Spence fell in love with you in the first place. I never minded, because I was just so damn proud to be your sister, so damn proud of everything about you. Sure I was in your shadow, but I didn't mind. You never judged, never made rash decisions. You made a hundred friends in Grand Haven, but I was your only sister. And I loved you. Proud? Damn right I was proud. And that pride only grew those first months after you woke up, when you fought like a banshee to get your life back. I was proud of you right up until you threw your husband away."

Maggie's throat constricted, but she would choke before she would let another tear fall. "You don't know how it feels to be—"

"What? Cheated on? David had an affair, remember? But you're right. I didn't know how it felt to be you. Until I met Alex, I didn't know how it felt to have a man love me so much he lights up when I walk into the room. You're right. I don't know how it feels to have a man love me so much his elbows bled from the vigil he kept at my bedside. To have a man love me so much he doesn't care if I stay a fucking moron, just so long as I don't die. Sure you're smart, but you're not as smart as I gave you credit for. If you were, you'd be asking yourself why you're so hell bent on punishing a man who loves you like that.''

Maggie laughed, but there was no humor in it. "That was beautiful. But then, you always were the dramatic one. It might have been more compelling if the woman giving the speech wasn't pregnant with the child of the man who is supposed to love me like that.''

Jackie's lips thinned with annoyance and irritation. "Spence is a great guy. A helluva guy. Maybe when you stop feeling sorry for yourself, you'll take a look around. Maybe you'll notice he isn't with me. Maybe you'll ask yourself why you think that is.''

Jackie groaned.

At first, Maggie thought it was part of the speech. Until she did it again, this time with a hand placed shakily at the small of her back.

There was a splash on the floor between Jackie's shoes. "Uh-oh." She said something unbecoming but appropriate, then she doubled over in pain.

"Did your water just break?"

"How would I know? You're the one who's experienced at this.''

Maggie could not believe this. She simply could not believe this was happening. "Why me? Why now?" she sputtered as she yanked drawers open. Finding the towels, she shoved a few at Jackie. "Here. Put this between your legs in case there's more water." She dropped the other one over the puddle on the floor. "Why didn't you tell me you were in labor?"

"Who's in labor? I've had a backache, that's all."

"You idiot. My labor with Allison was entirely back labor."

Jackie doubled over again.

Maggie rushed to the phone. "Where's your doctor's number?" At the expression of pain on Jackie's face, she said, "Never mind. I'm calling 911."

"Maggie, wait. Please." When the pain subsided enough to continue, she said, "I don't want to have my baby at home. I want Alex to be there. The hospital is five minutes away. It'll take an ambulance longer than that to get here."

"You can't drive in your condition."

"I know."

While another pain tore through Jackie, realization dawned on Maggie. "You want me to drive you?" Her voice was shrill.

"I told you—Oh God—you were smart."

Maggie shoved a kitchen chair underneath Jackie. "Shit."

"Does that mean you'll drive me?"

"I only hope I don't stinking kill us both."

Taking advantage of the momentary reprieve from pain, Jackie grabbed her purse and coat and headed for the door. "Odelia would be pleased with our ability to express ourselves."

"Who?" Maggie closed the door behind them.

"Never mind."

Somehow Maggie managed to get Jackie to the car without either of them falling. Jackie breathed through the next pain, pointing the way to the hospital. Although Maggie's knuckles were white from gripping the steering wheel so tightly, she kept the car between the lines. Next to her, Jackie punched in a number on her cell phone.

"This is Jackie Fletcher. Tell Alex—Dr. Kincaid—

that I'm on my way to the hospital. The baby has decided not to wait until spring."

Jackie had been right about how long it would take to arrive at the hospital. It may have felt like an eternity, but in truth, a mere five minutes had passed.

Maggie pulled up to the sidewalk in front of the hospital. Jackie latched on to Maggie's hand and wouldn't let go. "I can't do this."

"Yes, you can."

"It hurts."

"I know."

"I hate hospitals."

Maggie smiled. She knew that, too.

Everything was a blur after that. A man Jackie called Alex came running through the sliding glass doors pushing a wheelchair. He had to pry Jackie's fingers loose from Maggie's hand in order to get Jackie out of the car. "Easy," he crooned. "I've got you."

"Don't leave me, Mags."

Maggie ran around the front of the car.

"Let's get you inside," Alex told Jackie. To Maggie, he said, "This is a restricted parking zone. There's a chance they'll tow the car."

Maggie pushed Jackie's wheelchair toward the door. "Let them. It isn't my car."

Jackie started to laugh. Until she groaned again.

Alex assumed the position behind Jackie's chair. After that, Maggie had to practically run to keep up. Surely, it was the fastest she'd moved in more than nine months.

They rode an elevator upstairs. In a room on the maternity floor, Jackie's clothes were peeled off her and exchanged for a hospital gown. Nurses bustled in and out of the room. A monitor was placed over Jackie's distended stomach.

There was no regard for modesty. Jackie had a job to do. An important one.

"She's dilated to nine," a nurse called, as if Jackie were deaf. "We have to get her to delivery. Where's Dr. Albertson?"

Alex appeared, wearing clean scrubs and gloves and a mask over his mouth.

"Oh, Alex."

"Dr. Albertson isn't here. Hang on, sweetheart." He spoke to the nurses next. "There's no time to move her."

"You mean?" Jackie said.

"He means," Maggie cut in, "that you're going to have your baby right here. Right now."

"But—"

It turned out there was no time for buts, no time for drugs, no time to move to a cozy, homelike birthing room, no time for a dress rehearsal. Jackie groaned again, the cords in her neck sticking out in her effort to keep the pain inside.

"There's no disgrace in yelling," Maggie said, her face close to Jackie's. "So yell if you want to, Jacks. Yell like a banshee."

Oh, boy did Jackie yell. Within minutes, the baby had crowned. Half a dozen fierce pushes later, and the baby was born into Alex's hands.

The room that had been bustling with noise and activity was suddenly strangely quiet. Out of the silence, a tiny cry wavered softly.

"Is that my baby? Is my baby all right?"

"Perfect in every way," Alex said. "Just a minute. You can hold him."

"Him?" Jackie whispered.

Maggie whispered, too. "It's a boy, Jackie. You have a son."

CHAPTER
TWENTY-ONE

Maggie listened to the phone ringing across the miles. When Spence answered on his end in Grand Haven, his voice was quiet, the timbre rich and deep. "McKenzie's."

"Hello, Spence."

He took an audible breath. He certainly had every reason to be surprised. She hadn't called him, not once, in all the weeks they'd been apart. Finally, he said, "Maggie."

She could hear the television in the background, and Grace and Allison talking over it. "You sound like you're in the next room."

"Why wouldn't I? Where are you?"

This time she was the one who had a hard time knowing what to say. "I'm calling from the hospital."

"Why? What happ—"

"It's not what you're thinking. I'm fine. Actually, I'm calling from outside the hospital, because cell phones aren't permitted inside."

"But that doesn't explain—"

"I'm in Traverse City, Spence."

The sky beyond the bright lights in the parking lot was black and clear. There was a slight chill in the air, but little wind. Maggie felt calm, too.

"I came to see Jackie. I ended up driving her to the hospital."

"You drove?"

"Yes." It was ironic, really. She hadn't driven in nearly a year. And when she finally did, it was to take Jackie to the hospital to give birth to the innocent baby whose very conception had inadvertently blown all their lives out of the water.

"Jackie had the baby." Her voice broke. "It's a boy, Spence."

The silence stretching over the phone lines was as thick as the fog had been earlier in the week. Maggie could only imagine what he was thinking. She knew he'd always wanted a son.

"Are you all right?" he asked.

For the life of her, she didn't know why she smiled. "I'm fine. Jackie and the baby are fine, too. They were both sleeping when I left them a few minutes ago. I'm tired, so tired, and I was wondering if you and the girls would come take me home."

"He looks funny."

"I think he's cute."

"You do?"

Grace and Allison were crowded close to their Aunt Jackie on the same side of her bed. "He looks just like you two once looked," Jackie said, her voice emotion-filled and deep.

"I looked like that?" Grace asked.

Jackie nodded.

And Allison said, "It seems funny to have a cousin who's so little."

Talk about blaring silences, Jackie thought as she looked at Alex, and then at Maggie, and finally at Spence. He and Maggie stood a foot apart, but there was more than air separating them. Jackie wished there was something she could do to help, but she knew there wasn't.

There had been a tense moment when Jackie introduced Alex to Spence. The two men had taken their time sizing the other up. Alex was the first to extend his hand. Jackie wondered what it cost Spence to accept the handshake of the man who would likely become the father to his only son. If there hadn't been enough symbolism in that handshake, Allison's comment about the size of her new cousin drove home the fact that, for all intents and purposes, Spence would, at best, be relegated to uncle.

"I can't wait to hold him," Grace said.

"I can't wait until he's big enough to play with," Allie insisted.

"I can't believe Mom drove to the hospital." Grace looked at her mother in total awe. "You're a hundred and ten percent!"

It was Grace's newest saying. The ensuing laughter it invoked helped ease the tension between the adults.

Jackie yawned, the baby squawked, and Spence turned to Maggie and said, "Are you ready to go?"

At her nod, Grace and Allison climbed up to give their Aunt Jackie a hug. Clinging tightly, Grace said, "Can you come visit us now that the baby's here?"

Jackie spoke to Grace, but looked at Maggie. "Maybe your mom will bring you here to visit, now that she's driving again and all."

Maggie was the first to look away.

The four McKenzies left soon after. Watching them walk out the door, the girls first, and then Maggie, and finally Spence, Jackie reminded herself that Maggie hadn't said she wouldn't come back for a visit. She hadn't said she would, either.

She found herself looking into Alex's brown eyes. He was standing at the foot of her bed, still wearing his scrubs. When she could no longer hear Grace and Allie chattering, he went to the door and closed it firmly before returning to his position at the foot of the bed.

She got lost in the way he was looking at her. "So that was your family."

"That's them, in all their tarnished glory." She turned serious. "You did great, Alex."

He strode around the bed. Sitting along the edge close to her, he said, "You did all the work."

"You're right. I did. Don't you forget it."

He chuckled, and Jackie knew she would never grow tired of the sound of his laughter, of his voice. He'd kept his word these past three months, being careful not to cross the line between consulting physician and patient. That didn't mean they didn't both occasionally walk up to the edge of that invisible line and lean over it. They hadn't made love, though. Instead, they'd gotten to know each other on every other level.

In the process, she'd discovered an exasperating, stubborn man, exactly the kind of man she needed. She'd discovered something even more important about herself. She could take care of herself. She could be alone if she had to be. Oh, she loved Alex, but her love for him exceeded her need for him.

Ever the doctor, he took her pulse then studied her chart. "Let's hurry up and date so I can marry you."

How romantic. "Your bedside manner leaves a lot to be desired."

She thought she saw a smile lurking along the edge of his mouth. "You just had a baby. As a doctor, I must advise you that it's too soon to be talking about desire."

"What about as a man?"

His eyes glinted with deviltry. "As a man, I can't wait to make you mine."

She blushed. And then she swatted his hand, which jostled the baby, which caused him to make a mewling sound in his sleep. "Tell me the truth," she said, gazing lovingly at her son. "I know you've delivered more than a hundred babies, but isn't he the most precious and perfect child you've ever helped into this world?"

Alex turned out one light. Leaving the dim light on over the bed, he adjusted Jackie's blanket carefully. As if in slow motion, he placed a gentle hand on the top of the baby's downy, fair head. "I could have delivered a million babies, and this one would still be the most precious of them all. Not because he possesses more beauty than the others." Alex quirked an eyebrow. "I hate to be the one to break this to you, but he's red and wrinkled, and has a pointed head. He's the most precious because he's yours. Do you know what you're going to name him?"

She'd known for a while. Adam, after the first man created by God, if it was a boy. April, for the month she was supposed to have been born if it was a girl. "Adam James Fletcher. For now."

"For now?"

Slowly, her gaze climbed from her son, to the man she loved. "If you still want us after the first date, we can change his name to Kincaid. I'll leave that entirely up to you."

"When have you ever left anything entirely up to me?" Alex stared at the sleeping child. It was uncanny how much he looked like Jackie. He weighed in at six pounds, one ounce, and was twenty inches long. He'd made his debut three weeks ahead of schedule. He was bound to be impatient, like his mother. There was no doubt in Alex's mind that he would want them after the first date, after the wedding, after the first hundred years. He was just giving Jackie a hard time because it was fun. She was an argumentative, contrary woman, no doubt about it. She'd refused to use the outhouse at the cabin. Already, he'd contracted a builder to design and construct an addition, complete with a full bathroom, a bedroom, running water, and electricity.

No one was as much fun to bait as Jackie was. No one dished it back with so much vigor. "Adam James Kincaid," he said quietly. "I would be proud to give him my name."

It wasn't like Jackie to be so quiet. Her silence drew his gaze. Her hair was mussed, her eyes closed, her lashes casting a shadow beneath her eyes. Even asleep, she was beautiful.

He eased the baby into his arms. Jackie stirred enough to let him. Already, the baby felt like his own. They were going to be a family. On second thought, they already were.

It was almost eleven o'clock by the time Spence passed the WELCOME TO GRAND HAVEN sign. The girls had been lively during the first leg of the two-and-a-half-hour trip. Seeing the newborn baby had prompted a hundred questions about their own births. They wanted to know how they looked, the time of day they were born, how they ended up with their names. About half an hour ago, they'd grown quiet. Allison was asleep, and Grace was looking out the window, thinking her thoughts.

Maggie was quiet, too. Spence knew she'd seen the way he'd looked at the baby. She probably even knew how much he wanted to hold him, to claim him, to raise him, the way they were raising Grace and Allison.

He'd never seen Jackie so happy. Finally, she had what she wanted. Not that she hadn't had her share of hard knocks along the way. He didn't begrudge her this happiness. Alex seemed like a decent enough man. He'd better be decent, or he would have Spence to answer to.

That left him and Maggie.

This wasn't any easier on her than it was on him. He'd seen the way she looked at the baby, too. She used to tell him he was like an open book to her. She'd loved delving the facets that made him who he was, had loved learning him by heart. That was what he missed the most.

He pulled the car into the driveway of the house he'd surprised her with years ago. Once upon a time, he would have driven right on into the garage. He couldn't do that now. Once upon a time, he would have bustled the girls into bed, then taken Maggie to theirs. And then he would have burned this restless emptiness off with passion, pouring into her until he felt whole. He couldn't do that now, either.

"Well." She seemed to come to her senses enough to remember that Grace and Allison were spending the weekend at his place. "I guess this is my stop."

She turned around in the seat, as if to say goodbye to the girls. Spence stilled her with a hand placed lightly on her shoulder. Perhaps he couldn't do those other things, but this, he could do.

"It's late," he said. "Grace and Allison would probably sleep better in their own beds."

Grace seemed relieved, which made Spence wonder how much she really enjoyed spending every weekend away from home.

"Are you sure, Spence?" Maggie whispered.

Their eyes met in the darkness, and he realized that she could still read him like an open book. She knew he was doing this so she wouldn't have to be alone tonight. She probably even knew what it was costing him. He turned the car off. "I'll carry Allison inside."

The wind had picked up, stinging their faces as they hurried into the house. He carried Allie straight upstairs. Maggie tugged off their daughter's coat and pulled off her shoes and socks. "It won't hurt her to sleep in her clothes tonight."

Spence covered her up, even though she would undoubtedly throw the blankets off in her sleep. Grace's light was out when they went into her room. Too tired even to write in her journal, she was already half-asleep when her father kissed her smooth forehead and whispered, "Good night, Lady Grace."

It was after eleven when Maggie walked Spence to the door. Maggie squeezed his hand before he left. For once, tears didn't course down her face. Perhaps she'd finally cried herself out. Or perhaps the time for crying had ended.

She stared out the window from her dark kitchen, watching Spence walk to his car, his overcoat flapping in the cold wind.

She stood there without moving, until his headlights disappeared down the street. Maggie didn't know why she strode to the den. Or maybe she did. She remembered thinking, when she'd first come home from St. Ann's, that it was odd that Spence had set up their bed in the family room, when the den would have awarded them more privacy. Now, she knew why he hadn't. Jackie had said this is where it had happened.

Brian had insinuated that some cosmic force had come out of the blue, zapping her out of her coma. She stared at the leather couch. For months, she'd been trying not to imagine what had taken place. For once, she tried to imagine it from Spence and Jackie's perspectives. It wasn't easy. It was like Jackie had said earlier today. Maggie had seen herself as sterling and pure and noble, while she viewed their souls as tarnished, and darkened by sin. She'd slapped her sister today. Who did she think she was?

She'd changed, and Maggie didn't much like the woman she had become.

She left the den, and meandered through the rest of the house. As so often happened when she was lost in thought, she found herself staring into the backyard. The wind moved the tire swing to and fro. Most of the snow was gone. It was the middle of March. It didn't require a lot of imagination to picture the yard as it would be in another month, trees budding, grass greening, birds singing.

She'd nearly come full circle. She'd almost died, but she hadn't. She'd survived a horrible accident. She still had a slight limp. She would never be a dancer, that was for sure. But then, she never was. Lately, she'd been thinking about going back to college to finish her degree and relearn what she'd forgotten about history. Deciding what to do about the people she loved was more difficult.

Casting blame hadn't exactly done a lot of good. She knew Spence loved her. Jackie did, too. Until lately, she'd believed she was worthy of their love. They'd made a mistake. As simple as that sounded, it had incredible ramifications. She, Maggie Fletcher McKenzie, could go on blaming them forever, and they could all continue to be miserable. Or she could find the strength to forgive and go on. And they could all start to heal.

The power was hers.

She didn't ask for it, or want it. What was, was.

It was two o'clock in the morning when she picked up the phone. She punched in Spence's number before she could talk herself out of it. It was time to stop thinking and start doing.

He answered on the first ring. "Hello?"

"Were you asleep?"

"Maggie?" And then, "No. I . . . No."

"Me neither. I've been thinking."

"What about?"

"Oh, this and that. And life." After a long pause, she added, "About what I should do with my life."

He was probably on pins and needles, waiting for her to continue. His voice held more than a hint of dread as he said, "What have you decided?"

"I'm going back to school. I never finished, remember? I was always going to, but then we got married, and Grace came along. I'm not sorry. It's what I wanted."

"I think going back to school is a wonderful plan, Maggie."

She hadn't been to his house, so she couldn't picture in her mind where he was sitting. She swallowed nervously. "I was wondering."

"Yes?"

"Would you like to have dinner? Tomorrow? About six?"

"At a restaurant?" His voice deepened, and although she couldn't picture his surroundings, she could picture his face. And it occurred to her that no matter what else she felt, he was still the first person she wanted to see every morning, his voice the last voice she wanted to hear every night. She loved him. Once upon a time, she'd thought they had a perfect life. Maybe perfection was an illusion.

"Actually," she said, slightly amazed at the humor in her own voice, "I was hoping you'd come here for dinner." And then, because she couldn't help herself, she said, "I'm twirling my hair."

"It isn't going to be easy to wait until six o'clock to see you."

"Maybe you shouldn't wait."

The line went dead. Five minutes later, headlights

flickered off the kitchen wall. Spence entered without knocking. Maggie met him at the door.

He looked her in the eye, and blurted, "I'm not going to ask you if you're sure."

That was good, because she wasn't sure of many things anymore. But she was sure she loved him. She was sure he loved her. She was sure that it wasn't going to be easy. Forgiveness never was.

He threaded his fingers through her hair. "I love you, Maggie."

She was accustomed to people touching her hair. The thickness, the texture had always drawn people's touch. But no one had ever touched her hair the way Spence did. She covered his hand with her own. Bringing it to her mouth, she pressed a kiss to his wrist. "And I love you."

He moved to swing her into his arms. She shook her head, then took his hand. With their fingers entwined, they walked upstairs side by side, as equals, starting over.

At the top of the stairs, he kissed her. And it felt like the first time. They had issues to deal with, problems to work through, questions that had gone unanswered for a long time. Tomorrow was soon enough to confront those. For now, Maggie concentrated on the love that had always been at the heart of who she and Spence were, where they'd come from, and where they were going. Maybe love truly did conquer all. Or maybe only a strong will could do that.

"Welcome home," she whispered.

The healing had begun.